EXIT PLAN

Dedication:

This book is dedicated to my wife, Jo

EXIT PLAN

A Novel by

Mike Sixsmith

Pen & Sword
MILITARY

First published in Great Britain in 2012 by
PEN & SWORD MILITARY
an imprint of
Pen and Sword Books Ltd
47 Church Street
Barnsley
South Yorkshire S70 2AS

Copyright © Mike Sixsmith, 2012

ISBN 978 1 78159 097 3

A CIP record for this book is available from the British Library

Printed and bound in England
by CPI Group (UK) Ltd, Croydon, CR0 4YY

Typeset in Times New Roman by
CHIC GRAPHICS

Pen & Sword Books Ltd incorporates the imprints of
Pen & Sword Aviation, Pen & Sword Family History, Pen & Sword Maritime,
Pen & Sword Military, Pen & Sword Discovery, Wharncliffe Local History,
Wharncliffe True Crime, Wharncliffe Transport, Pen & Sword Select,
Pen & Sword Military Classics, Leo Cooper, Remember When,
The Praetorian Press, Seaforth Publishing and Frontline Publishing

For a complete list of Pen and Sword titles please contact
Pen and Sword Books Limited
47 Church Street, Barnsley, South Yorkshire, S70 2AS, England
E-mail: enquiries@pen-and-sword.co.uk
Website: www.pen-and-sword.co.uk

Acknowledgements

There are many people that I have to thank for assisting with the birth of this novel. Some remain unknown to me, several would have been unaware hitherto of their contribution, but I am as indebted to them all as to those others who helped knowingly.

Firstly, there is the team at Pen & Sword who have had sufficient confidence in the story to publish: Sir Nick Hewitt, Charles Hewitt, Laura Hirst, Laura Lawton and Pamela Covey, and the rest of the team.

Prior to writing: Hugh Robertson MP, Helen and Charles Smart, Philip Grant, Robin Eccles, Richard Linforth, Arish Turle, Wilf Charlesworth, Edmund Sixsmith, Simon Collis, Mike Bell and many members of my local community.

During writing: Peter Duffy and Dame Antonia Byatt, Nicholas McMahon Turner, Jason Elliot, Sam Edenborough, Robin Wade and Ian Swingland.

Many thanks to Mr Akbar Ahmed, author of *Journey Into Islam*, for kindly giving permission to quote from his work in chapter three.

Throughout the time, my wife, and children Liv, Rob and Ed, have been a source of inspiration and pride, sharing in, and helping me through, some of the experiences which led to the conception of the book.

• • •

Although inspired in parts by the author's personal experiences, this is a work of fiction – it is not intended to portray real events.

Prologue

He issued a few staccato words in guttural Arabic. Immediately his people began a thorough search of the office. It did not take them long to discover the trunk in the storeroom. A couple of young Arabs opened it and whistled in astonishment. Immediately they called over the leader. Looks of surprise, then disgust, quickly turning to a gleam of triumph followed each other across his face.

'أبناء Sons of fuckers! Take these infidels and spies away!' said the leader. 'You know where to!'

1

The Boeing BBJ circled round Dubai, turning back over the Hajjar mountains and banking over The Persian Gulf in the direction of the city as the plane lost altitude on its automated flight path. The passengers could see the city's rooftops rushing towards them. On the starboard side the Creek was in view and further away the Dubai World Trade Centre stood proudly silhouetted against the setting sun. The plane passed over the Al Muraqqabat area, along Al Rigga Road and crossed the Sharjah Road before touching down. As soon as the pilot had depressed the flaps and put the throttle on full reverse thrust, the plane quickly slowed to taxiing speed. It began to cross the airfield. However, it did not head in the direction of the airport buildings, with their recently completed state-of-the-art new terminal. Instead it taxied to the far north-west corner of the airfield where it came to a halt near the perimeter fence. The pilot cut the engines.

At the same time a white 500 series Mercedes-Benz could be seen moving fast, away from the terminal buildings, in the direction of the parked aircraft. It was accompanied to front and rear by several other vehicles, black Mercedes, driving, as if in a naval convoy, in line astern. On approaching the plane the black vehicles moved to either side, turning at speed to face outwards, away from the plane and coming to an abrupt halt. Immediately their doors swung open and the occupants jumped out and, fanning out, adopted an on-guard position. It could be seen that each had a weapon, which they held at the high port with fingers along the trigger guards. Most had pistols, the Heckler & Koch HK Mark 23 .45 ACP, one of the most thoroughly tested handguns in history, with a match grade accuracy equal to that of the finest custom-made handgun, but exceeding the most stringent operational requirements ever demanded of a combat handgun. One person in each group held an Ingram MAC Model 10 point 0.45 sub-machine gun, with a cyclic rate of 1,145 rounds per minute. It would have been clear to any professional observer, had there been one in this remote area of the airfield, that these were highly trained professionals, acting in accordance with well-practised drills, using specially selected weapons.

The white Merc parked at the bottom of the plane's doorway, where some inboard steps had been lowered to await the visitors' arrival. The driver, and one guard from the back, dismounted promptly and assumed the same posture as their colleagues.

A tall Arab wearing a purple dishdasha got out of the back of the Mercedes accompanied by a larger, rotund Arab in a white dishdasha. There was no doubt that the man in purple was in charge. He had a haughty look with strong, aquiline features and the quintessential hooked nose of a Bedouin tribesman. At the same time, there was movement at the top of the aircraft steps. A squat, strongly-muscled Indian, with full, black, wavy hair and the look of a Bollywood buccaneer, wearing black trousers and black T-shirt with a flashing golden leather jewelled belt, emerged from inside the fuselage. He was followed by a retinue of similar ostentatiously dressed Indians. He came briskly down the steps so that he and the Arab met at the lowest step.

'Sala'am alaikum, Sheikh Abdul, kafh il hal?' said the Indian, beaming widely at the Arab.

'Alaikum sala'am, tama'am shokran, wa inta?' responded the Sheikh, with only a brief softening of his face in response to the Indian's effusiveness. The two embraced, kissing each other three times on the face from side to side.

The Indian beckoned to the new arrival and ushered him up the stairs past what looked like a guard of honour. The Indian retinue moved back on either side of the steps in order that the two principals could ascend, which they did arm-in-arm, until disappearing into the aircraft.

The inside of the Boeing was opulently furnished. There were a number of rows of seats up front, in what would normally be the first-class section. Passing through this, the group went into a compartmentalised area behind. This was laid out as an operations room with map displays and numerous computer terminals, CCTV and video screens, and a bank of twelve interlinked TV screens showing the latest Bollywood movie on six of them, and CNN and Al Jazeera, BBC 24, an Indian news programme and Sky

News on the others. The work stations were all manned by young Indians. Behind this section, they went through into a smaller, obviously more exclusive, meeting room. Leather-bound chairs surrounded the dark rosewood table.

'Please take a seat, Sheikh Abdul,' said the host.

'Yes, thank you, Sanjay,' replied the Sheikh. In addition to the Sheikh's companion, they were joined by only one other Indian.

The four men sat down. Two beautiful Indian girls, dressed in flowing, brightly-coloured Rajasthani saris, adorned with many trinkets and gleaming yellow Indian 22-carat gold jewellery, entered the compartment, made the slight bow of Namaste with hands pressed together, palms touching and fingers pointed upwards, and offered coffee, tea and dates. After the ritual, and once the girls had left, the two principals got down to business.

'You're welcome as always to Dubai, Sanjay. Thank you for coming in response to my request. I am only sorry that my cousin, the Ruler, does not share in my joy at your arrival,' said the Sheikh, archly.

'Your Highness knows that you can count on me at any time, Sheikh Abdul,' responded the other. 'But, beautiful as this airport is which your cousin, the Ruler, has built, I am always certain that I cannot leave my aeroplane in order to sample the delights of this Arabian pearl of yours!'

'Well, of course, it is not my Arabian pearl. At least not yet!'

'Let us pray that, with the Prophet's blessing, peace be upon Him, one day it will be restored to its rightful owner,' said Sanjay.

'Insha'Allah,' said Sheikh Abdul, longingly. 'That is why,' he continued, 'I asked you to come. We have some good business to transact. First, there is no danger that your visit will come to the attention of my beloved cousin?'

'Indeed, so,' said Sanjay confidently. 'Perhaps you saw the markings on the plane? The aircraft is registered in Uzbekistan, through a company set up there specifically to deter prying eyes and ears. It's called the Hindu Kush Airline and a flight plan shows it travelling from India to Kenya, with a re-fuelling stop here; and the manifest confirms that the cargo is 20 tons of re-conditioned IT equipment and electrical consumer goods destined for the East African market from Bangalore.'

'Excellent, excellent,' said Sheikh Abdul. 'As always, you have thought of everything, Sanjay. Now to the point. I have a large consignment of first-class cigarettes, which will arrive shortly from Port Said. They should be on their way any day now and indeed should be in Jebel Ali within the week.'

'But you always have cigarettes here, and, by far, many more than you could possibly need. The real question is, what is it that you want of me?' said Sanjay, challengingly. A flicker of a smile passed over the Sheikh's normally impassive face.

'Sanjay, my friend, you have enjoyed my protection extended to you as a brother here in Dubai for many years now. Despite the wishes of the Ruler. Without me you would be nothing. Now I need something from you. I need weapons, guns, and of course ammunition; rifles and machine guns and rocket-launchers. Enough for a special unit of forty-five men. And I need combat radios – the best you can find.'

Sanjay pondered for some moments and exchanged a glance with his colleague. He excused himself, and went out into the adjoining operations area with his companion for several minutes. He held a brief and animated discussion with his colleagues. He returned, his beaming smile displaying his white teeth against the dark-hued skin, and his confidence.

'Sheikh Abdul, I am not known as the Goldman without good cause! Yes – I can do this for you, but it will come at a price. Perhaps as much as …'

Sheikh Abdul interrupted. 'Sanjay, you know that, to me, money is no object. Just send all the bills to Mohammed Ali here,' he said, gesturing towards his companion, who had remained mute but ever watchful and attentive throughout the proceedings.

'May I be permitted to know the nature of this important task for which all this is required?' asked Sanjay.

'All in due course. I shall tell you all, my friend. When the time is right. But not now.'

'When do you need the equipment by? And also this group – all will have to be really well trained. Have you got the trainers which you need?'

'We're selecting the people even now,' responded Sheikh Abdul. 'They are being tested and purified at this very moment. They are, as our crusader brethren would say, the crème de la crème! Those who pass all the tests will be chosen personally by me and the Emir of Al Qaeda.' Silence fell on the group at the mention of Al Qaeda. The faces of all present became serious and expectant, and betokened an unspoken bond between them all.

The spell was broken by Sanjay. 'Insha'Allah, Alhamdulillah, God be with you and prosper you in all things, Sheikh Abdul.'

His mobile rang. 'We need you back. In Dubai. Tomorrow.'

'Who the devil are you?' he said exasperatedly, about to terminate the call.

'I'm a friend of Sandy's!' the disembodied voice said with finality. 'You have an invitation to the Queen's Birthday reception at the Embassy. It starts at six. Be there!'

It was inevitable that, eventually, payback time would arrive. Now, it had. When Bill had finally stopped running he found himself under the torrid desert sky in Saudi Arabia – one of those Middle Eastern powers seeking to control the region by exporting its extreme brand of Islam. Hot, sandy, no music and no drink, at least not legally; no women to be seen; at least not much to be seen of those few who you could see, all dressed, as they had to be in public, in the black abaya and niqab. An austere, sterile, inhospitable and inscrutable wilderness for most Westerners.

But the call brought him back to reality. He knew that if he did not obey, his whereabouts would be leaked to the Provisionals. The nightmare of the past was reawakened. But the information provided by way of verification was impossible to ignore. And so was the veiled but menacing threat. He left on a late afternoon flight the next day.

Out on the port side, the crescent moon lay on it's back, translucent and pure, providing a warm and enveloping ambience. It seemed to Bill to be welcoming him and enfolding him in its embrace. A harbinger of good things to come, he hoped.

Bill was sitting beside a British expat. They had exchanged pleasantries as the crew had prepared for departure. Comfortably ensconced in business-class, Bill had taken for granted the presence of many of his fellow passengers, both male and female, who were clearly Arabs. The standard Emirates in-flight meal was a choice between steak casserole and chicken biryani, the latter indicating the multi-cultural nature of Emirates passengers. The in-flight entertainment, with several Western music channels and also some of the latest films on general release, reinforced the theme of the global village; the global village as seen from a Western perspective. There was an Arabic language channel and a Bollywood film, the standard gushing romance, *Vaaranam Aayiram* with Surya Sivakumar and Sameera Reddy. Bill was watching *The Usual Suspects*: 'a boat has been destroyed, criminals are dead, and the key to this mystery lies with the only survivor and his twisted, convoluted story.'

Now something else caught his eye, however. Something which Bill had at first absorbed in a sub-conscious way: the constantly shifting pointer on the plane's map display. He suddenly realised that this was showing the direction of Mecca.

At that moment, the captain's voice on the intercom brought him abruptly out of his reverie. 'Ladies and gentlemen, we shall be landing at Dubai's Sheikh Mohammed International airport in thirty-five minutes. The time in Dubai is 18:40.'

The flight path was on a bearing of 92° and they were now crossing over Qatar on a heading for Dubai. When they had taken off the pointer had been almost due west. Now it was due east. He was in the very heart of Islam.

His neighbour leaned over towards him. 'The usual party mood.' He said enigmatically.

Jolted out of his reverie, Bill responded quizzically: 'Sorry, I'm not sure what you're getting at?'

Suddenly, one after another, the women on the flight began disappearing into the rest rooms of the plane. They filed past covered from head to toe in traditional black robes, some with black veils over their faces, only to emerge in fashionable European clothes. It was like a costume change in a play in which the actors slipped effortlessly into alternative roles. One minute they were reserved, whispering companions, sitting self-consciously in their seats with a subtle hint of deference, and the next they were transformed into Western-looking women chatting confidently with their husbands.

'Look at all these Arab passengers – especially the women. Back in the departure lounge, they were all severe and inanimate. Both sexes. Conservatively dressed in traditional clothes. No jewelry for the women; little make-up, and so on. Your probably didn't notice – you've been in Saudi for some time I guess?'

'Yes, I have.' Said Bill, not quite sure what his companion was driving at. "But this is my first trip to the Emirates.

'Well, I'm sure you know as well as I do, that Saudi's got to be one of the most soul destroying countries in the world to live in. Particularly if you're a woman.'

'No booze, you mean?' said Bill.

'Well …yes, but that's only the half of it! No music in public places; men and women can't touch each other, can't even hold hands in public…'

But men can!' interjected Bill.

'And do… ! But women can't drive; the penalty for adultery is death by stoning – for the woman that is. The men all get off scot-free. But look around.'

Bill looked around. Many of the passengers were now dressed in western clothes. There was an air of eager anticipation, with much chatter and laughter, as if they were school children released from the purgatory of lessons.

'They're getting ready to leave their own culture. Now they're in party mode. It may be not much more than 500 miles from Riyadh to Dubai, but they're worlds apart. The difference between Islam and the West is the 500 years between Christ and Allah.'

Bill nodded thoughtfully. 'But Dubai is hardly the West?'

'Don't you believe it. To the conservative Muslim, Dubai represents all that is wrong with the West. It's apostate. If it rains in Abu Dhabi, the people there blame Dubai.'

'But why do they have to pretend?' asked Bill. 'Why can't they just dress as they wish in Saudi too?'

'They've got too much to lose. In most cases, they have everything material they could possibly want. But if they were to challenge the conventions of their society they could lose it all. They could well be disowned by their families. Not many people have the stomach for such a fight. They know that the religious police will track them down and would treat them harshly, no matter what their connections.'

Bill realised that this costume change on the flight epitomised one of the modern world's great social dilemmas: how to maintain cultural traditions in the face of globalisation. In today's world, different societies overlap, are mixed, and juxtaposed – their people forced to walk a tightrope on which a slight slip could be disastrous.

His neighbour continued. 'These women would be completely at ease, sitting, on their own, in the latest Western clothes, fresh from one of Europe's catwalks, in a café in Regent's Park or the Champs Élysée. But back home they have to acquiesce in the segregation and modesty demanded there. It's like they're caught up in a global charade in which public appearance is locked in with tradition. Dubai's the only place in the Arab world where they can behave as they'd like.'

'If these women were to challenge their local customs by revealing another identity, they'd be gossiped about and slandered by their society. Their entire family might be ostracised. I analyse phenomenon like this for a living – I'm a professor of Islamic studies.'

He went on to explain to Bill that modern Muslim women, like those on their flight, who comfortably synthesize Western and Islamic cultures, are following the Aligarh style of Islam. On disembarking and submissively walking three paces behind their husbands, they switched to the Deoband model.

'Because of all the external pressure for change, the awareness of the outside world through travel, the internet and so on, women are both the embodiment of the values of traditional Arab society and its prime victims. The irony is that these values are divorced from the justice and compassion advocated by Islam. They're more in line with the vagaries of tribal custom and notions of honour. This phenomenon is outside the realm of theology. It has more to do with anthropology.'

Most expatriates would have had no clue about such analysis. The expatriates in the Gulf lived apart from the locals, often in gated compounds. They were kept apart from the locals by the locals. They were blissfully unaware of what went on beneath the surface of the countries where they lived an artificial western-style life.

But after his many years of travelling throughout the region none of this came as any surprise to Bill. Working and living cheek-by-jowl with Arabs, he had penetrated more deeply than most into Islamic culture.

'There's some sign of the tectonic plates moving, however. Because of all the external pressure for change, the awareness of the outside world through travel, the internet and so on. But I wouldn't count on anything much happening quickly. Not until all the ruling octogenarian oligarchy fall off their perches!'

They both lapsed into silence pondering the significance of what had been said, as the cabin staff prepared the plane for landing in Dubai.

14

4

A few hours later he was at the British Consul's residence inside the grounds of the Embassy. Much of the Embassy was modern but the Consul's house was redolent of an earlier era, from the time when Dubai was part of the Trucial States. Although the buildings were not something to excite the architectural connoisseur, the location was stunning. At this time of the year, Dubai had not reached the full heat of summer. The evening was warm and balmy. A faint breeze rustled the leaves of the oleanders and carried the scent of orange blossom across the spacious lawns of the Embassy. Over the Creek, the burgeoning skyscrapers and tower blocks of old Deira blazed with light reflecting over the ruffled waters and mixed with the headlights of cars on either side of the water and the fairy lights entwined around the guardsman-like rows of palm trees lining the dual carriageways which ran along both sides of the Creek. Even at this distance, the National Bank of Dubai building dominated the landscape, dwarfing the Commercial Department and the InterContinental Hotel, buildings of an earlier phase in Dubai's short, pell-mell development. Now, Bill knew, the next frenetic phase was rapidly taking shape along the Sheikh Zayed Highway, surpassing anything so far seen in the whole of the Middle East. Dubai's mantra now was 'world class'.

Signing in at the gatehouse, Bill wandered across the manicured lawns to the reception line. Although he had not met the Consul, James Williamson, Bill sensed that he was definitely an expected guest as James shot him a knowing and seemingly quizzical glance when he gave his name.

'Good to meet you,' said the Consul. A tall, precise, thin-boned man, he looked steadily at Bill as if to emphasise that he had been briefed and knew all about him. 'I'll catch up with you later,' he said, his eyes moving on to the next person in the queue with practised ease.

Bill was about to find out what had led to the issue of the invitation for tonight's event. Perhaps the Consul had a job for him? He could do with something comfortable working in the Embassy.

Dubai's oil reserves were said to be seriously depleted, but the same could never be said about its supply of alcohol, always available with a munificence starkly at variance with the emirate's Islamic underpinning. Clutching a substantial gin and tonic, Bill observed the other guests. The few representative locals were evident by their dress; several of these, Bill discovered, were attached to the Embassy and there was also a group associated with a senior sheikh, who was obviously there to represent the Emirate. Bill imagined that the Diwan, the Ruler's Office, published a Duty Sheikh roster for all such events.

At that moment, as if right on cue, James Williamson appeared at Bill's elbow. He was accompanied by a younger man, perhaps in his late thirties, Bill estimated, whose piercing brown eyes, set in a broad face topped by a generous head of wavy black hair, were studying Bill acutely.

'Bill, I want you to meet a colleague of mine, Andy Stringer. I think you'll find that you know someone in common,' he said, with emphasis. 'Ah, I see my wife needs some support dealing with Sheikh Rafa. I'll have to leave you but I'm sure you'll have no trouble looking after yourselves.' Whereupon, calling over a nearby waiter to fill their glasses, he left them together.

Bill had selected an apartment in the Al Muraqqabat Building near to the Al Ghusais shopping complex. This had the advantage of being relatively cheap, but more particularly it was an area in which few Western expatriates lived. They lived along the Corniche Road on the other side of the city; and, increasingly as the city's pace of development quickened exponentially, towards Jumeirah. It did not take long to move his few belongings in, and he was ready for business, whatever it might be.

After a few days there was still no contact from Andy. He was beginning to feel isolated and not a little foolish. What exactly was he doing here in the Gulf on his own? He had left behind all that he had, all that he knew, all that was real and was here in this Disneyworld called Dubai where everything seemed unreal, make-believe, the ultimate in bright lights, consumerism and irrelevance. Had it not been cowardly to run away from Ireland, to abandon all he believed in, to leave the centre of action for this place of inaction?

And he thought now, almost for the first time since leaving her, of Mary. He wondered what she was doing now. Had she married? Had she really wanted to break off the relationship? Had she done it to spare him, to protect him from the Provisionals? Generations of her family had been involved with the old IRA. And now, inevitably, the present one was inextricably enmeshed in the activities of PIRA, the Provisional IRA. Or was it because she had now completed her task for them? Whose side was she really on? Had she been the one running him, rather than the other way around as it was meant to be? He remembered planning it all with the Intelligence Group CO. He'd met her after the bomb at the Crossmaglen checkpoint. Two soldiers, boys they were, had been blown to smithereens. She'd been rounded up as a suspect by the local battalion. They had hit it off at once, despite being on opposite sides of the table. Somehow they had found common ground in the midst of division and hatred; and mutual desire.

'Recruit her: nothing better than a deep penetration source.' the CO had said, with heavy innuendo. 'One occasion where sleeping with the enemy is to be encouraged!' His emotions not yet engaged, Bill had sniggered complicitly.

He should have tried to contact her when he was in the UK. But everything had happened so fast, he had been in the thrall of events outside his control, a puppet in the schemes of others. And now here he was alone again, cut off from all that he knew and all that was familiar. Having been at the centre of events and master of his own destiny, he was suddenly transformed into an inactive suspension, totally dependent upon unknown forces to decide his fate.

Making a conscious effort to pull himself together, he remembered the axiom of Montrose by which he had always hoped to live: 'He either fears his fate too much, Or his deserts are small, That dares not put it to the touch, To gain or lose it all.'

Andy paused, took another mouthful of coffee, and continued, sotto voce, looking around as he did so. Bill had to crane forward to hear him. It was a couple of days later. Andy had called him earlier in the morning to say that he would like to meet. Now they were sitting outside on the Deck Bar of the Dubai Golf and Yacht Club, overlooking the Creek.

'The Commercial Department's headed by a Young Turk – Mahmoud Al Abdullah. He's the current blue-eyed boy of Sheikh Abdul. Al Abdullah is a pearl – a once-in-a-lifetime asset. Tells us everything that is going on behind the scenes at the top level in the Emirates. Not only in the Emirates – much of the Gulf and the Arab world as well.'

'So he's working for you guys,' interjected Bill. 'Why?'

'Fear!' said Andy. 'We caught him at it. He's frightened stiff that we'll tell all. That would ruin him. He'd end up in jail for life. And here life means life!'

'What did he do?'

'Well, you've heard of the Al Ghamdi Group?'

'Yes, someone mentioned them at the Embassy the other night,' said Bill, 'they have the Adventus Motors agency for Dubai, don't they? Is that the one?'

'Exactly – not just Dubai, but the whole Gulf – very lucrative. It enabled Mohammed Al Ghamdi to build up a massive business empire. Used to include a major bank before it all fell apart.'

'What happened?' asked Bill.

'Mohammed Al Ghamdi has a passion for the tables. Can't keep away from them. He racked up massive debts. Then, in the '91 downturn, the business ran out of cash. He was asset rich – and I mean mega rich – but cash poor. Couldn't sustain the pressure. Had to ask the government to bail him out. They stepped in, nationalised the bank and unwound the business, selling off many of the assets. Sheikh Abdul masterminded it all. Used Mahmoud Al Abdullah to do all the dirty work.'

'A good opportunity for him?'

'Absolutely – and believe me he took great advantage of it. The CIA picked up that he was buying a substantial property in California. Tipped us off. A little cursory check led us back to the source of funding. It was from the sale of the Al Hazzai Hotel in Jakarta, a swish five-star property in the city centre, which Al Ghamdi had developed. A major chain bought it. Al Abdullah's commission? Ten per cent – ten per cent of $10 million!'

'So from there,' said Bill, 'it was a no-brainer? Cough or lose your balls when we tell Sheikh Abdul!'

'Exactly,' said Andy, picking up his briefcase, obviously keen to be on his way. 'I'll catch you later. Normal procedure. Oh… by the way, we know our friend as the Rower!'

He sat down again heavily, parking his briefcase on the table, upsetting a coffee cup. The waitress appeared and wiped up the spilt coffee.

'Nearly forgot – you need to meet Red Larsen.' He paused until the waitress had taken their order and left. 'He's Mahmoud's special advisor.' He continued, 'American – and larger than life. I've told him to contact you – given him all your details and a mugshot! But ...' he bent low to whisper in Bill's ear, 'he has no idea that Mahmoud's working for us – or at least I hope he doesn't. He's a smart bastard and we don't want him to know. So be bloody careful!'

'RAKA's the jewel in Dubai's crown.' Andy began to brief Bill, 'That's Rub Al Khali Amalgamated Minerals. Like everything in Dubai, it's actually owned by the Government; and, of course, the ruling family, the Al Mansours, own everything belonging to the Government. But they've got a big problem. They're being ripped off by a number of the senior executives and management – that's some very heavy-hitting local people and some expats, who are creaming off enormous sums of money – have been doing so, it seems, for an extremely bloody long time! Not our problem, you might think? But it is! We think that these funds are not just being used to line people's pockets – God knows there's certainly plenty of that – but there are more sinister aspects, which we hope you can uncover. I'll tell you what we think after Red's briefed you.'

'We want you to to investigate the fraud. To get an inside track into what's really going on! The whole scam is absolutely massive. Not only the amount of money involved. But also because of its complexity, and the length of time it's been going on. Red's masterminding the judicial process. His official title is Commercial Department Legal Councillor.'

'Can we make it another hotel next time?' asked Bill, 'the coffee's crap here. And there are a lot of watchful eyes!'

Andy got up to leave but thought better of it and immediately sat down.

'Before you meet Red I'd better give you a bit of background. You've read Greenmantle, have you?'

'Yes, several times.' Said Bill, 'Real Boys Own stuff. Why?'

'Now they have a new Mahdi. Buchan's Mahdi was going to save the Germans' bacon – this Mahdi's going to destroy the Crusader west and restore the Caliphate.'

'It all sounds far-fetched to me. What the hell's this got to do with us sitting here in Dubai?' Bill interrupted, beginning to get exasperated with Andy's rambling circumlocution.

'I know what you're thinking. But I need to make it a bit of a history lesson. Need to put it all in context. Just hear me out please?'

'The First World War led to the demise of the Caliphate. Ataturk's "plunge into secular modernity" in 1924 was a wake up call for Islamic extremists. A guy called Sayyid Qtub was arguably the most significant modern Islamic thinker of times. He was an Egyptian who joined the Muslim Brotherhood in Egypt in the early '50s. He advocated a return to the Islam of the 7th Century, that of Mohammed and his Companions. It was a vision of totalitarianism no different from that of Stalin on the socialist left or Hitler on the fascist right. For Qtub, Islam was totality.'

"His doctrine has now spread throughout the Arab world – Algeria, Kashmir and Afghanistan; then Iran, Iraq and the Sudan. He high-water mark was the expulsion of the Soviets from Afghanistan. Its also spawned even more extreme proponents: the Islamist group of Sheikh Omar Abdel Rahman for one. They bombed the World Trade Centre in 1993 – put a car bomb in the underground garages – and Islamic Jihad led by Dr Ayman al-Zawahiri originlly.' Andy paused. 'I didn't mean to bore you with a lecture – but it's important that you understand what we're up against; what it's all about. Know your enemy and all that! Would you like another coffee?'

'Yes, thanks.' Bill said abstractedly, trying to absorb the enormity of what he was hearing. The sun was setting, its final rays slanting across the water in a rosy glow. The setting was magical and romantic; as the myriad lights of a power hungry Dubai came on to illuminate the balmy Arabian night. It seemed impossible to reconcile the beauty of the moment with the ugliness, which Andy was describing. He was brought back to earth by the evening prayer of the Muezzin. The spell was broken. The coffee arrived. Andy continued.

'Another Islamic thinker, Sheikh Abdulla Azzam, who was assassinated in 1989, said: 'No negotiation, no conferences, no dialogues.' His slogan was, 'Jihad and the rifle alone.'"

"Azzam knew Qutb. He became the organiser for the Afghan jihad - and the representative of the Saudi House of Al Saud in this regard. Perhaps it's no co-incidence that Pakistan, Saudi and, of course, this place, were the only countries which recognised the Taliban regime. Food for thought? But be careful who you discuss it with around here!"

Andy continued, "Azzam was echoed by Sheik Rahman in New Jersey, who was calling for random massacre of infidels. Azzam also said that 'history does not write its lines except with blood'. Nice lot aren't they? But this is the reality, its atavistic; it's back to the Dark Ages. Religion is irrelevant, other than as the rallying cry and the hook by which to radicalise impressionable youth. It's all about power!"

"An Islamic leader in Algeria, Ali Benhadi said this…' He paused, and pulled out a piece of paper from his pocket, saying: 'Just read this – I copied it from an email I received this morning. Bill picked up the small cutting. "If a faith, a belief, is not watered and irrigated by blood, it does not grow. It does not live. Principles are reinforced by sacrifices, suicide operations and martyrdom for Allah. Faith is propagated by counting up deaths every day, by adding up massacres and charnel houses." Bill handed it back and Andy stuffed the paper back in his pocket. He stared at Bill, as if challenging him to respond.

"That's pretty gruesome stuff!" ejaculated Bill. "The IRA became very effective, very professional; and they had their international dimension too – but nothing to compare with what you're talking about."

"Yes, indeed. But that's not all." Andy continued, "The really worrying aspect is the focus on suicide attacks. Hezbollah introduced this weapon into the armoury of the modern terrorist in Lebanon in 1983. Now the jihadists have turned in into a fine art. And they're going to use it against us, the Americans – all Crusader infidels!"

They were interrupted by the insistent buzz of Andy's mobile, indicating the arrival of a new text message. Glancing at the screen, he swore under his breath.

"Bugger – but I've got to go. Need to get onto London asap. I'll get in touch tomorrow and fix another meeting."

He left quickly, leaving Bill to pick up the tab.

Bill hired a car and drove around to familiarise himself. He drove down Al Wasl Road, parallel to the Corniche Road. Suddenly he was overtaken by a fast-moving small red car driven by a large florid man, flagging him down. They both pulled into the lay-by beside Al Wasl Park just before the Choitrams roundabout. The other driver got out and came across. From behind his twitching moustache, without introducing himself, he said brusquely, 'Come around to my office tomorrow morning. It's in the Commercial Department near the Corniche. Come about 09:30 and ask for me at reception.' He jumped back into his car, challenging it to get instantaneously to the rapid speed he required, and was quickly lost to sight. Bill was left to wonder at Red's ability to identify him with only the few details given to him by Audy.

By 09:15 the Commercial Department car park was full to overflowing. The reception hall with its numerous booths, each with its queue of petitioners, resembled a hive of drowsy bees moving as if in a formulaic ritual, each holding the required sheaf of papers, all duly stamped, with their requests for company licences, directors' registrations, payment of fees and a multitude of other bureaucratic transactions, each one a money-making opportunity for Dubai Limited. These 'fixers' or, more pompously, Protocol Officers, spent their lives moving from one government department to another.

The majority of supplicants wore the traditional robe-like dishdasha or thwab. Most were white but there were some purple, brown and black ones as well. There were Arabs of all hues, from the pale Circassians of the north to the coal-black Somali. A large proportion came from the subcontinent: Indians, Pakistanis, Bangladeshis and Sri Lankans and many who were clearly Filipinos. Apart from one other person, Bill was the only Westerner in the room.

The white-clad men's heads were covered by the white gutraj with its black band, the ogal. Bill was struck by the fact that this group appeared to be in uniform: crisp white headdress, freshly laundered white dishdasha, cut so that it did not touch the floor lest it become impure and unfit for prayer, and sandals. Designer sunglasses were much in evidence, accompanied by strikingly black designer stubble, short, neatly-trimmed beards and moustaches. Observing their air of aloofness and general attitude of superiority and disdain, it was clear to Bill that these were the locals.

Bill announced himself at the reception desk manned by a couple of young and pleasant Pakistani lads who were punctilious in directing him to Red's office on the third floor. At a further reception here, this time manned by a polite but serious, sallow-skinned young local, he waited for a few moments while a call was made. Bill had time to take in the surroundings. He was in a marbled anteroom, decorated in strict and very tasteful Islamic fashion. Soon a female in a black Abuya and burka, with heavy black-rimmed sunglasses, approached and announced herself as Ruth, Red's secretary. To Bill this seemed to be a surprising name for someone who was clearly Arabic, but on reflection, he appreciated that the Abrahamic origins of Islam would make the name completely normal. Bill judged that she was young and probably very attractive but it was difficult to be sure given her half-covered face. Her femininity and sweet nature were clearly evident, despite the barriers of cloth and glass. Her presence was in striking contrast to the more public areas of the Commercial Department through which he had come. There had been no women in evidence there.

Ruth, it turned out, handled all Red's papers and documents for the casework in which he was engaged, as the Department's Legal Counsellor.

'Best you familiarise yourself with all the background as a start,' said Red. 'Riad's going to meet us at the golf club tonight – you do play golf, don't you? I've just taken it up but it's a ponce's game if you ask me. I'm a rugger player myself. Anyway, we'll play nine holes; tee off at 7 pm.'

He saw the quizzical look which Bill gave him. 'Yes, 7 pm – it's floodlit, it's inside the racetrack – the Nad Al Sheba Club, you know, where they hold the Dubai World Cup race? And it's fully illuminated!'

The Councillor was a chunky, thickset individual, with a cauliflower nose. As soon as he spoke, it was clear that Red Bergman was a North American. His hometown was Reno, Nevada. He was an aggressive, pugnacious individual who took no prisoners.

'Let's go and have some lunch.' he said. 'I've asked Clive Worthington from Frederick & Stevens to join us. That's the law firm that advises the Government. They've just taken over the auditing of RAKA.'

The contrast between the two solicitors was stark: Clive, the urbane, somewhat unworldly looking, ex-public school Englishman and Red the North American redneck, a front row forward, who operated with all the delicacy of a miners' shop steward. Red held the floor.

'Sheikh Abdul has brought in Mahmoud Al Abdulla to clean out the Augean stables of RAKA. Made his name sorting out the Al Ghazi Bank fiasco in Singapore. And he'll certainly do that! He's very ambitious and ruthless to boot – like's to think of himself as the avenging sword of the Rulers. He's been made the Vice-Chairman of RAKA in order to take control. The Chairman's job is largely a sinecure; the real power lies with the Vice Chairman who reports directly to Sheikh Abdul! '

'Sheikh Abdul? Where does he fit in to all this?' Bill queried.

"He's the Chairman – I'll fill you in on the details as we go along. So far, Red continued, work had entailed reviewing a number of major contracts that had been entered into by RAKA with various parties for the supply of raw materials and the sale of the finished product. It was clear that there were many irregularities – and equally clear that Red was pretty sure that these irregularities were deliberate and indicated fraud on a massive scale.

Red told them that some years ago, the previous Vice Chairman, Talal Fahimi, had challenged the Chief Executive, an expat Brit, to explain the irregularities, which had been brought to his attention. But the CEO had had the arrogance to dismiss the issue out of hand, knowing that the hand that fed him protected him. The CEO – Luke Stanley's his name - told him to fuck off! He's an arrogant sod and he knew he could get away with this because Mohammed Al Turk was behind him.' Red went on, Mohammed Al Turk, reputedly the fourth richest man in the world.' Red paused, considering just how much of his suspicions to reveal at this stage. "He's known as Mr. Ten Per Cent in Dubai! He's from the older generation. He was the right-hand man of the previous Ruler of Dubai, the much revered and very astute, Sheikh Raheem. It was Sheikh Raheem who seized the opportunities provided by the disengagement of Britain from the region of Britain in the 1960s. He and was able to developed Dubai into what it is to-day.'

Red paused to order lunch; and beer. Then continued his potted history, enjoying the limelight enormously, his moustache, it seemed, permanently with foam as his beer disappeared at a prodigious rate.

'As a consequence of oil and gold smuggling; indeed, of smuggling any and everything; and a combination of British support and Sheikh Raheem's single-minded ruthlessness and charm, Dubai quickly overtook Sharjah as the most modern outward-looking emirate. In comparison, the other emirates, the small Northern Emirates of Ajman and Ras Al Khaimah and particularly Abu Dhabi, with its overwhelming oil wealth, were moribund. Al Turk was the chief functionary of Sheikh Raheem and as a consequence was able to amass a fabulous fortune. He's now the owner of several household name brands – like Kool Kola and the Granchester Hotel in London.' Red explained that, since the death of Sheikh Raheem, his sons had increasingly resented the power of Al Turk. 'Now they feel strong enough to take steps to cut him out.'

'It's rumoured,' Red continued, 'that all the Ruler really wants to do is to spend time in England during the racing season and in Pakistan during the hunting season, with his favourite wife. He only comes to Dubai in Ramadan for form's sake. His current wife's an ex-Gulf Air hostess. So was the last one; and no doubt so will the next one!' said Red with a wink.

'The real power behind the throne is the Ruler's cousin, Sheikh Abdul bin Nashiri. He's Minister of Commerce for Dubai.' As if by magic, another beer appeared as Red finished his third, or was it his fourth? 'The Nashiri tribe were formerly the rulers of Deira – that it was then a separate emirate on the southern side of the Creek - but Sheikh Raheem seized power from them in the 1950's and joined it to Dubai. They haven't forgiven him for this. They still consider themselves to be the proper rulers of Deira. The grandfather did a deal not to challenge the Ruler provided he was given a senior role in government and lots of lucrative agencies, drugs, cars, cigarettes particularly. There's a sort of *modus vivendi* but its only skin deep and there's still a lot of resentment beneath the surface. He continued, 'Anyway, it was Talal…'

'Who's Talal?' said Bill.

'Talal Fahimi was the Vice Chairman. He looked after RAKA for Sheikh Mansour. But he was as idle and ineffective as Mansour was disinterested. But not so Al Abdulla. It was Riad Abu Rahman - you'll meet him later - who uncovered the discrepancies when he was with the Parkinson & Peebles audit team. Bloody hell, that doesn't do it justice – it's a black hole! When Mahmoud Al Abdulla got to know of this, he got Sheikh Abdul's approval to move Riad in as Chief Financial Officer. Mahmoud's the one who's master-minding the investigation. I've been stuck in the Commercial Department in order to support him and take care of the litigation. We've already done some pretty good hits on people associated with other scandals in Dubai; and God knows, there's plenty of them all right. Financial fraud, I'm talking about. But there's plenty of even more juicy scandals around here too, as you'll quickly find out.'

"But back to Sheikh Abdul." Red went on to explain that Sheikh Abdul had been a playboy and rebel in his youth; he was always to be seen in the company of fast women and even faster cars – or was it the other way round? He was also a fearless horseman and renowned for his skill – particularly relishing long distance riding, at which he still excelled. 'In many ways, he's the de facto ruler; and Dubai is his personal fiefdom. But he has plenty of enemies; particularly the Ruler's brothers who don't want to lose their inheritance.'

Red continued, "It's Sheikh Abdul who calls the shots behind the scenes. He's decided that Mahdi Mohammed Al Turk will be cut off at the knees by public exposure of his fraudulent activities at RAKA. Not what these guys normally do – there're so paranoid that they usually sweep any bad news under the carpet.

'Its accepted practice in the Arab world,' explained Red, 'for those who are awarding contracts unofficially to exact a commission from the successful bidder or supplicant – you know, perhaps a ten per cent kickback. It's an open secret that Al Turk's enriched himself in this way. It's condoned and the ruler's trusted confidantes are allowed to help themselves to their boss's wealth – up to a point! But only up to a point - when they cross the line, woe betide them! That's when they get screwed.'

'What happens in this sort of situation then?' queried Bill.

'What happens? …. They're fucked….! I'll give you a recent example. Last year Sheikh Abdul went to the annual get-together of the powerful at Davos. You know, the World Commercial Forum. He had the Head of the Dubai Customs go with him to give a joint presentation on customs harmonisation – Dubai's pretty switched on to this sort of thing, e-Government and so on. The day after they arrived back, the poor sod was thrown in jail and charged with corruption. He got a mammoth prison sentence – 35 years! And … less than four months later, the Sheikh pardoned him! But his reputation is in shatters and he is in virtual house arrest. And so the point was made – and others were warned.'

'But that's outrageous!' exclaimed Bill, indignantly.

'Look chum, I know you Limeys like to think that you are whiter than white; and that the whole world should behave like your typical English gentleman. But that's bloody naïve. It just doesn't work like that here. Are you trying to tell me that there's no corruption in the western world? Get a life! I've seen your old boy network at work – what's the difference?' Red concluded pugnaciously.

Red then told them that that the Chief Executive of RAKA, an expatriate Scotsman called Luke Stanley, had been corrupted by Al Turk.

'I reckon what happened,' said Red, 'is that Al Turk took Stanley up to the highest point in Dubai – at that time that would have been the 29th floor of the World Trade Centre - and said: 'I own 15% of all you see – and, if you play your cards right, 5% is yours!' And Stanley managed to overcome any scruples he might have had – knowing the bastard, I don't imagine he put up much of a fight - and so the deal was done.'

'The scam was run through a group of companies registered in the British Virgin Islands….'

'A well-known tax haven; and a place where a company could be set up with no questions asked?' Bill commented.

'Got it in one. The main entity was Gulf Proprietary Development, which is still operating in Dubai.

26

'What I want to know', Red stabbed a finger menacingly in Bill's direction, 'is can you sort out this fucking mess? Can you find out where the money's gone? And, more importantly, can you get it back? I can handle the legal side and I know exactly what sort of evidence we need to put these people away where they belong? You get the evidence and I'll prosecute.'

Bill knew just the man to get him the sort of evidence he would need; someone who could get inside the most private bits of the most private of private banks – and do it in the most secretive of countries when it came to safe-guarding the financial affairs of its clients. The money was going to be well hidden but it had to be somewhere and there had to be an audit trail. And it would probably end in Switzerland.

'Give me the facts and I'll get you the evidence.' Said Bill confidently.

Red thought briefly and then said decisively, 'OK let's do it. Give me a couple of seconds." He left the room fingering his mobile as he did so. He was back within several minutes. "Right, here you go – we know that Stanley has a number of accounts with SBS in Zug in Switzerland. And he goes there probably from time-to-time. What I want to know is: how many accounts and what's in them?'

'Sweitzer Bank Switzerland?' queried Bill.

'Exactly.' Said Red as he scribbled a few notes on a piece of paper and passed it to Bill.

As soon as he had left Red and Clive, Bill immediately contacted Graham Booker to pass on the information given to him about Stanley. Graham was the classic Mr Fixit, able to do anything asked of him at the drop of a hat. His unrivalled repertoire of well-placed contacts was able to uncover the most carefully hidden of hidden assets. He called back that evening.

'What do you know?' he said, with the dispassionate air of a man who has seen it all before. 'That second account you gave me, the one in SBS in Zug, guess how much's in it.'

'I've no idea,' Bill had said, intrigued.

'US $18 million!'

'Christ Almighty, that's a serious amount – what do we do now?'

He had left Saudi only three days ago. Now, here he was in Dubai with Graham's full report, sitting in Red's office.

'Bloody hell, that's a fuck of a lot for someone who's only an expatriate manager!' said Red. 'I know he may be the chief executive but, even on a good screw and with a decent bonus from RAKA, there's no way he should have amassed that amount.'

'Got it. Look there's some more stuff as well. I've put it in the report but I thought you'd like to know this at once.'

'You bet your sweet ass I do,' said Red. 'This should cause a few raised eyebrows in the corridors of power! Leave it with me. I'll get back to you once I've spoken to Mahmoud.'

A few days later they were sitting in Red's office having a cup of coffee made with personal care and attention by Rasul, the Department's general factotum. Rasul had been working in the Department since he came to Dubai twenty-five years ago from Kolkata. He was devoted, loyal and undemanding; and underpaid and undervalued. Just like the large majority, Bill reflected, of the vast army of subcontinent, economic slaves that had helped to make Dubai what it was today.

Ruth, next door, picked up the jangling phone. Almost immediately the phone on Red's desk rang.

'The solicitors in London,' said Ruth, transferring the call to Red. He listened expectantly. Then a great grin spread radiantly across his broad, square face. Bill did not need to be told the content of the call as Red put the phone down and banged the desk exultantly.

'Excellent, bloody great! That'll settle that smug bastard's hash!' he said, adding needlessly, 'the High Court's granted the Mareva order. That's all our friend's assets frozen. He won't like that one little bit. Now though, he'll be forced to defend himself or lose all. He'll try to fight – he's so bloody arrogant he'll think that he's bound to win. But when he gets some sound legal advice, that there's not a cat in hell's chance that he can win, no point at all in even thinking about going to court, he'll soon change his mind. Better try to make a deal with us, the lawyers will say, rather than fighting it.'

'He'll be fucked,' rejoined Bill.

'Damn right, he will! He will not even be able to present any cheques without the Court's approval. And now that Mahmoud's got him by the balls, he'll grind them until his wallet's dry. They're pretty ruthless, these Arabs. Mahmoud certainly is; he'll want to cut him off at the knees.

'Right!' said Red, decisively, 'we definitely need to cover as many bases as possible here in Dubai to support the court case. What do you think?'

'Now that the shit's hit the fan, there's going to be a lot of running around in the hen coop. The more we can hear what they're up to, the better.'

'Bug them? That makes sense. Let me speak to the others.'

'We should get some good stuff from Al Fadl. I could do a collection every night. Then we should do something about this new office. Assuming that he doesn't come back, you'd expect him to phone Al Fadl a lot now – and presumably the office too, if we can find it,' said Bill. 'If we can bug these as well then we'll be covering the whole gang. That can be done easily enough – but only with cover from someone with serious wasta.'

'OK, I'll speak with Mahmoud,' Red continued in genial mood after his success in getting the injunction. 'This affair will certainly shake up the dovecot! Stanley's an arrogant bastard. Considered himself as the de facto British ambassador; held the most prestigious expat job in the emirate. Had the protection of Mr 110 per cent himself, Al Turk. He could do no wrong. Now he'll have to hang his head in shame – and with a bit of luck be forced to give the money back – and rat on the others.

'How much will it cost? When could you do it?' asked Red.

'I've already got the guy standing by to travel out at once. We could do it within twenty-four hours of getting instructions. As to cost, I'll work that out. I can let you have something this afternoon.'

'OK, do that. Mahmoud will want to do it. I'll call Riad straight away. If he agrees, he'll have to run it by Mahmoud whenever he's available. But don't hold your breath. You know what it's like trying to get hold of him. But I'm sure he'll be all for it. And spending money is no object when it comes to him stitching up a few local enemies. Might be different when you come to get paid – then it'll be like bargaining in the souk! I'll call you later though. Send me the figures in the meantime. Anyway, I've gotta go to the Diwan – call me later.'

He heaved his large frame out of the too-small desk chair. Grabbing his briefcase, he stuffed a sheaf of papers into it and headed for the door. As he left, he shouted over his shoulder: 'And find out where that motherfucker Al Turk's hiding out now. We need to bug his office asap.'

Bill winced as the name reverberated around the corridors. Who else might be listening who would warn off Al Turk? Mahmoud had made plenty of enemies in his short time in charge of the Department, Red had told him earlier.

9

He was in The Crown Plaza on the Sheikh Zayed Highway with Andy.

Surreptitiously, Andy slipped the small piece of paper across the table. The figures written on it meant something to Bill, + 971 50 6453463 was a mobile phone number registered in Dubai, well in the UAE to be more exact. But to whom did it belong? The piece of paper seemed almost to have been cut to size to accommodate the numbers – civil service economies, no doubt. The care with which Andy handled the paper, with his fingers on the edges only, was extreme. Wouldn't do to have his fingerprints on it and it would have seemed a bit out of place to be wearing gloves; the temperature had been nosing 40° Centigrade during the day, Bill thought irreverently.

'The Yanks say it was used by bin Laden. Got it from Mansoor Ijaz.'

'Mansoor Ijaz?' queried Bill.

'In the mid-1990s, when Osama bin Laden still lived in Sudan, Ijaz brokered a deal whereby the Sudanese would surrender bin Laden to the United States. But obviously he had contacts here from back then to get that number.'

'What, he was living here? Fuck me!' exclaimed Bill, thinking of the implications.

'Well, he obviously used it as a base. Let's bring it up to date.'

Andy paused, reflecting – again, Bill could sense him reviewing the intelligence, deciding what to disclose, what to withhold. He couldn't risk giving too much away, but on the other hand he had to tell Bill enough to capture his imagination, to make sure that he brought his skills into play.

'Now the whole world knows how bin Laden became involved with the Mujahedeen in Afghanistan during the Soviet occupation. That he was set up by the Americans to drive out the Sovs. The CIA trained him to fight the Russians. It provided the Mujahedeen with weapons. Stinger ground-to-air missiles and the like, much of it through Pakistan in conjunction with the ISI.'

'ISI – the Directorate for Inter-Services Intelligence?' queried Bill.

'Yes, Pakistani military intelligence. But it's a state within a state, answerable neither to the leadership of the army, nor to the President or Prime Minister.

'Bin Laden inherited the mantle of the Mahdi. He capitalised on the ferment of defeat, dispossession and alienation in the Arab world. The focal point of all these emotions is Palestine, of course, which for Arabs symbolises the oppression of the Crusaders. He grew to despise the Americans; particularly he resented their presence in the land of his birth, Saudi Arabia. Perhaps he was driven by an idealistic philosophy. Perhaps it was just basic human urges which motivated him: jealously, hate and a lust for power.' He took a sip of coffee. It was dark now and the all-enveloping evening induced an air of intrigue.

'Under bin Laden, Al Qaeda presented itself as the vanguard of the vanguard in the global struggle to reassert Islam. I'm quoting: "it defined itself as a broad movement, without an ethnic identity." Bin Laden,' he continued, 'wanted to kill as many of them as possible – Americans, that is.'

Andy cut to the chase: 'So, can you find out who the phone's registered to?'

'Shouldn't be too difficult,' Bill replied, 'I've recruited some great local contacts.'

Bill ignored the coffee now getting cold on the table in front of him. He was on familiar ground here. He knew about Marc Rich. Knew all about his involvement with RAKA from the briefing he had been given by Red. He'd seen the evidence of Rich's meeting in the Hotel Am Zee in Zug in Switzerland, where he lived in exile from the US tax authorities, with Mohammed Al Turk and RAKA's Chief Executive, Stanley. Who was that lawyer who had put all these birds of a feather together? He'd seen the photos in the office of a firm of local solicitors. Seen the 'guns' dressed in the deerstalkers and plus fours of respectable English gentlemen, counting the bag on a Scottish grouse moor. Only that several of these gentlemen were definitely not English. And it's a moot point whether they were respectable, Bill thought cynically. The pictures had been taken some years ago when Sheikh Raheem was still the Ruler. But the photograph of the current Crown Prince and de facto Ruler of Dubai was unmistakeable. Were these the same people who hunted a larger prey in Pakistan and Afghanistan today? It was uncanny how many plots, frauds and conspiracies seemed to have a link with Dubai, he thought. He brought his mind back to what Andy was saying.

'I was talking with my US counterpart last week. They're tearing their hair out at present because of all the hardware that's out there in the hands of the Mujahedeen. They know it's there because they gave it to the buggers!'

'To fight the Soviets?'

'Exactly! Now it's killing their own soldiers instead. The Americans call it "blowback".'

Across the Creek they could see the tailback of vehicle lights snaking over the Al Maktoum Bridge and into the distance. It was Thursday evening and the familiar Dubai shopping weekend was in full swing. Andy continued, 'Do you remember the bombing of that Al Khobbar compound in Saudi back in ninety-six? The one in which six US soldiers were killed?' Bill nodded. He had seen the carnage shortly afterwards when working with Aramco.

'Well, that was OBL's handiwork. He's bitten the hand that fed him.

'Bin Laden turned up in Afghanistan in the same year as the bombing. In effect he was on the run. The Clinton administration was tracking him, looking for ways of neutralising him. When he was in Sudan, the Sudanese government effectively offered to turn him over to the US.'

'That's when he was using that mobile?'

'Exactly,' said Andy. 'However, this would have been extremely awkward as they wouldn't have known what to do with him. They couldn't have dealt with him through due process – there was nothing that he had done for which he could have been prosecuted in a US court of law.'

'So why didn't they just bump him off?' asked Bill.

'Before 9/11 even the Americans quibbled about extra-judicial neutralisation, in other words, assassination! So they were stymied. And, when OBL turned up in Afghanistan, they were worried.'

'How did they know that he was in Afghanistan? If he was on the run, surely he'd have kept a low profile?'

'That's just it. He announced that he was there – challenged the Americans! He wrote a poem to the then US Secretary of Defense, William Perry. He sent it "from the Peaks of the Hindu Kush".'

'Go on!' said Bill, intrigued by the revelation, 'what did the poem say?'

'I know it off by heart,' said Andy. 'It was in the press, of course, but at that time, no-one outside of a few intelligence specialists appreciated its significance. But it certainly went the rounds of all the intelligence agencies with some wry comments, because in that community everyone knew who he was and had a good laugh at the Americans' expense. It went:

O William, tomorrow you will be informed
    As to which young man will face your swaggering brother
    A youngster enters the midst of battle smiling, and
    Retreats with his spearhead stained with blood.'

'Hardly wonderful poetry but pretty clear in its message,' commented Bill. 'I guess this worried the Yanks?'

'The understatement of the year. They were shit-scared because they knew the size of the inventory they'd given to the Mujahedeen – without any questions asked. Our assessment was that something like two to three thousand Stingers were unaccounted for! Not to mention all the other ordinance they poured in – none of it on inventory.'

'That many Stingers? They're the ideal weapon for what the Americans call asymmetrical warfare. It only weighs about 15 kilograms with a rocket loaded. I'm quoting from the pamphlet now – it has a range of about 5,000 metres; up to 4,000 altitude. The beauty of it for insurgents is that it can be operated by one man on his own, and it's automatic and heat-seeking, so they don't really need any training.'

'Yes,' said Andy, 'I've seen a host of reports of their effectiveness against the Soviets. Between '86 and '89 the rebels claimed to have downed hundreds of choppers and transport planes. In fact, the Sovs actually had to completely rethink their tactics.

'Anyway, the point of all this,' Andy went on, 'is that the CIA introduced a programme to recover the missing Stingers. The *Washington Post* editor, Steve McColl, described it as a "sort of post-Cold War cash rebate system for Afghan warlords". Supposedly the going rate paid by the CIA to buy them back was between $80,000 and $150,000 per missile!'

'Per missile! That's rich,' said Bill, 'a complete Stinger costs less than $40,000 new!'

Andy paused before replying, 'But here's the rub. The CIA was backing Ahmed Shah Massoud. He was nicknamed "The Lion of the Panjshir". The Americans saw him as "the man most likely to".'

'What's that?' interjected Bill.

'He was the best bet to counter the Taliban, who were just becoming a power in the land. That's why OBL teamed up with them. All the Yanks' funding and weapons and so on were supposed to have been funnelled through Massoud. Then when the Americans wanted to put the clock back, so to speak and ...'

'Put the genie back in the bottle would be more like it, as far as I can see,' said Bill.

'Yes, that's about the height of it. The CIA sent the station chief in Islamabad to meet with Massoud and sort out the recovery of the Stingers. When this guy, his name was Gary Schroen, eventually managed to track down Massoud, he got one hell of a shock. He discovered that Massoud had only received a fraction of the money which the CIA had sent him over the years, through supposedly trusted intermediaries. His brother, for instance. Even worse, when he brought up the issue of the several thousand Stingers, Massoud and his henchmen looked surprised and jabbered among themselves in the local dialect, Dari. Finally Massoud said that he had only received eight Stingers!'

'Do you believe that? Surely the Americans can't have been so indiscriminate in dishing out all this hardware?' said Bill.

'Well, it's easy to pontificate from the sidelines,' said Andy. 'The trouble with Afghanistan is that it's a free-for-all. The CIA had to trust someone but the reality is that you can't trust anyone because they don't trust each other and it's every man for himself. It's always been that way. The Persians knew that, the Russians did and so did we back in the nineteenth century. But we all had to try again because we were too arrogant to learn the lessons of history.'

'OK, so that's the history,' said Bill. 'Where does that leave us now? What's the deal with the number? You're surely not telling me that bin Laden was holed up here before?'

'There are a number of strands that we're trying to sort out – and we'd like to win a bit of credit with the Americans into the bargain.' He paused, ordering another cup of coffee for both of them, buying time to think. 'HMG's worried about proliferation. This puts the focus on Iran and Pakistan. That's my main job in the Embassy, although, as you know, I'm ostensibly the Protocol Officer in the Visa department!

'But it's a pot pourri. The Iranians are helping the Taliban but they are anything but natural allies. Quite the reverse. But anything to make life difficult for the Americans and the West. You know, "my friend's enemy is my enemy" sort of thing! Then there's the scenario of Islamic terrorists with a dirty bomb.'

'Doesn't bear thinking about,' said Bill, thinking about it.

Andy continued, 'It's a fucking nightmare! It's all to do with power politics. So the Iranians want to develop a nuclear capability.

But sure as God made little apples, the present nuclear club members aren't likely to help, not even the Russians. So who does that put in the frame? Developing states, who want to join the big boys at the top table, like India and Pakistan; rogue states who want to punch above their weight and make life difficult for everyone else, like Iraq and North Korea. No guesses which category Iran falls into! And so perhaps a rogue state decides that co-operation with terrorists might suit its book?

'I've got two problems. Iran, just over there so to speak – only a stone's throw from the Musandam peninsula. That's my proper patch. However, the bloody North Koreans seem to be trespassing on my patch too, by getting involved with Iran and doing their dirty work through Dubai. And both of them are also cosying up to Pakistan.

'You may be able to help us by getting details of a deal between the Iranians and the Koreans, which we think is being financed by Dubai Inc! But that's for another day. First I need you to deal with this mobile number.'

'Dubai helping the Iranians is a bit far-fetched, isn't it?' queried Bill. 'It would be suicidal, wouldn't it? I thought that Dubai and Iran were not the best of friends. Don't they have a territorial dispute over a border area or something?'

'Yes, over the Tumb Islands, which they both claim. They're miniscule little islands, but they control access in the north of the Gulf of Hormuz, which makes them of some strategic significance. But that's chicken-feed in comparison with everything else that's going on.' Andy paused instinctively as the waiter came up with the bill. He clearly worked on the principle that even walls have ears.

'But first things first. Let's see how you get on with this mobile number. What do you think you can do for me?'

'Well, I reckon that we'll get the subscriber's name, the address, as in a PO Box number but not where he actually lives, and some details about his sponsor. You can't get a number without being sponsored by one of the locals.'

'That would be a good start. What about copies of the itemised bills? That's what I really want – to see who's talking to whom!'

'Not sure about that,' said Bill pensively, 'I'll have to look into it.'

'Right-oh – see what you can do with the subscriber details and when you've got an answer, page me on this number.' Another piece of paper was slipped across the table; again, the caution to ensure no fingerprints, no forensic evidence. 'Ring and leave a voice message "Peter here" – I'll ring you back on another number as soon as possible and we can fix up a meeting. How long do you think it might take you?'

'Ummm, 'bout a week or so, I should think.' They left and went their separate ways.

Razak was constantly bullied in the playground at their primary school. Back then, there were few of them and the derisory 'Paki' had not entered the lexicon of racism. He had escaped from one ambush some months ago. Bill's father had been drawn to him from their meeting that first day at school when they had raced to bag a peg locker for their gutties and ended up having to share one. But it had not made him popular with his white peers.

Finally, now, they were trapped – Bill's father looked on as if solidified like Lot's wife; not wanting to watch, unable not to. Not able either to help or to flee.

Bill's father saw the darkening stain seeping through the front of Razak's short grey school trousers as he stood transfixed, awaiting the inevitable assault and beating. The three white boys slowly closed in upon him. He backed away. But the wall was behind him. Too tall to get over. The sickening thud of the first blow released Bill's father. He deserted his hidden vantage point without further thought. He took to his heels. He ran as one demented. Along the narrow streets. Past the mean houses of the immigrant community. He fell, picked himself up, fell again, scrambled up. And so it continued until he could no longer draw breath, could no longer see through his sweat-drowned eyes.

There were many reasons why Bill's father had never wanted to tell the truth about what he had been doing. Shahid's father had started crying. Bill's father could hear it echoing in the distance long after he had fled the scene. Later, he came to realise that the situation is wearingly familiar to parents everywhere. Across the world it is the same. It is human nature. But when race is involved it takes on an altogether more sinister hue.

11

Shahid completed his recitation. It had been good, he knew, very good. He could see the smile on his mother's face and the adoring love in her eyes. Even his father looked pleased, almost triumphant. There were only two more candidates after him, not long to wait for the results. It was the likely last night of fasting. The night before the Eid Al Fitr feast. The official Moon Sighting committee was expected to declare this night that the moon had been sighted. One of the eternal delights of Islam, Shahid mused, was the surprise generated every year over the precise timing of this very predictable event; one upon which so much in the Islamic world depended.

Some 200 boys aged between 7 and 13 had preceded Shahid through the period of Ramadan, each one attempting to recite the Koran from memory. All devout Muslims wished for their children to achieve this feat. It was the pinnacle of devotional attainment; a milestone on the way to heaven. On a par with doing the Haj pilgrimage to Mecca. But not sufficient to ensure martyrdom, as a suicide bombing would. Shahid was now in a trance-like state, carried away by the emotion of the event and the knowledge that he had, at last, pleased his father, Razak, a stiff and unbending man, quite a lot older than Shahid's mother, who was his fifth wife. Shahid had never been close to him, but he yearned for his father's approval.

After what seemed an eternity following the final two readings, the judges assembled on the school stage. The hall was packed with local dignitaries, Muslim community leaders, and teachers and parents. The boys who had read sat to left and right of the stage. The chairman rose. He was a well-respected elder Imam at the East London mosque. Shahid heard his name called. He had won. He was a true Muslim. His father would love him now. Barely aware of events, he somehow made it to the stage.

That had been ten years ago and his father had loved him. But not unconditionally – only so long as he followed the true path of Islam as his father perceived it to be. His father was an arch conservative. He had forced his three daughters, Shahid's beloved sisters, to go to Pakistan to be married to men of his father's choosing. Living in Britain, Shahid's father and mother, and all his father's other wives, remained remote and isolated from British society. Living bodily in the East End of London, they existed in their minds in the tribal lands of West Pakistan.

Throughout all his childhood, Shahid had remained a dutiful son and a fully observant Muslim. However, now that he was at university, Shahid began to see the world in a different light. He began to realise that, for all their protestations to the contrary, none of the Arab countries really wanted a Palestinian state. For them it was simply an inconvenient problem which made life difficult for them in controlling their burgeoning populations. Something like a third of their populations was now under 14 years of age. Their inheritance was most likely poverty and deprivation – ideal conditions for the Jihadi recruiters.

Now that he was at UCL, Shahid saw even more clearly the dichotomy between his family and the reality of himself as a second-generation Muslim growing up in the strident, multi-culturist, modern-day Britain.

'Sala'am alaikum, Brother. How are you? My name is Ahmed – Ahmed Al Farzi.'

'Alaikum sala'am – I'm Shahid,' responded Shahid instinctively. He had seen the other regularly in the Brick Lane Jamme Majid Mosque, the mosque where he had chosen to worship for several months now, since shortly after starting at UCL. He had not known the man's name or anything about him, but it had seemed evident that he had some function, some unstated role, acknowledged by the Imam. Shahid began to pray again.

'You're at UCL, aren't you?' Ahmed persisted.

'Yes – how did you know that?' said Shahid, defensively.

'The Imam told me. He said that you're a good Muslim. Someone who would want to serve the cause of the true Islam. Why don't we meet afterwards? I'd like to talk to you, to ask your help.'

There was a disturbing intensity about Ahmed. His piercing eyes seemed to cut into Shahid's inner being – into his very soul. He was the older of the two – mid-twenties, Shahid guessed. He had a maturity and calmness, and a magnetism too. Lean and muscular, he was taller than Shahid, perhaps 6'. His dishdasha was an immaculate freshly-laundered white. His blue eyes were set back in deep sockets above an aquiline nose.

Shahid had intended to go to the library to continue his research into Qtub, the founder of the Muslim Brotherhood. But, flattered by Ahmed's interest in him, not wishing to offend the older man, and with a mixture of curiosity and concern, he heard himself accepting the invitation.

Half an hour later they were seated in the coffee shop just across the road from the mosque. Both men had changed into jeans, T-shirts and trainers, for all the world like any other young people in the café. Shahid had placed his rucksack on the floor between them. It contained several textbooks from the library.

'What are you studying?' asked Ahmed.

'Philosophy and history, and classical Arabic as well,' responded Shahid enthusiastically.

'I did politics myself, at Leeds. That opened my eyes to a lot of things! What books have you got there?'

'These are my textbooks. I've got a couple of books on Qtub. I guess you know all about him? He was an incredible man. But I'm not sure that I really agree with his politics.'

Unnoticed by Shahid, at the mention of Qtub's name Ahmed's eyes had narrowed imperceptibly, gleaming with a brief intensity.

'What don't you agree with?'

'Well,' said Shahid, 'I've always believed that Islam is all about faith. Belief in the Prophet, peace be upon Him; observance; charity – those are the fundamentals which I was brought up to acknowledge and observe. Not in pursuing a political agenda, stirring up trouble and so on. But that's what Qtub advocated?'

'But surely Muslims have the right to be heard in the world? Just consider the facts! There are over one and a half billion Muslims on this planet; that's about a quarter of the world's population! Some Muslim countries, at least, are fabulously wealthy, with almost limitless oil reserves. But Muslims don't all live in the Middle East and aren't only Arabs – that's a completely wrong perception. Did you know that Germany has more Muslims than Lebanon? That China has more Muslims than Syria? And what about Russia? It has more Muslims than Jordan and Libya combined!

'Islamic money,' continued Ahmed, warming to his theme, 'has a significant stake in all those global financial markets we hear so much about. And yet, anywhere you look, it's America and its sycophants that call the shots! And it's Muslims, by which they mean Arabs, that are the unnamed enemy of these modern-day Crusaders!'

Ahmed was speaking passionately, but also in a didactic and hectoring manner that unsettled Shahid. Quickly perceiving Shahid's reticence to go along with his rhetoric, Ahmed backed off, adopting a bantering style.

'I can see we shall have much fun and a lot of coffee debating all this, my friend,' he said, putting his arm around Shahid's shoulders in a patronising way.

'I'll tell you what,' he said, 'why don't you come to hear a good friend of mine giving a lecture on all this sort of thing? He's very good to listen to. Makes sense of it all.'

Shahid demurred, 'Well, I'm not sure, I'm really busy. I have a couple of assignments to finish this week.'

'Look, you will really enjoy it, Brother. It'll open your eyes. And you can talk to him afterwards. He's coming across from Pakistan to do this. It's next Tuesday in the East London Mosque.'

'Well, I'll think about it,' said Shahid, by way of not having to make a decision.

'Good for you, Brother! Look – perhaps you could do me a favour? I've got a bundle of leaflets about the talk, gives all the details. Take one for yourself, of course, but could you also take these?' Ahmed thrust a large bundle of quarter-page flyers into Shahid's hand before he could refuse.

'Would you stick these up all around UCL? So we can get as many students as possible to attend. Do it with love for the Prophet.'

Unwilling to offend the forceful Ahmed, Shahid lamely took the leaflets and put them in his rucksack. On the bus on his way home he took one out and studied it. The meeting was being arranged by a group called the Young Muslim Organisation. The speaker was Omar Bakri Muhammad. He was going to lecture on 'The Islamic Dawn – Obligations of the Muslim in Western Society'. It all sounded innocuous enough, thought Shahid as he wondered why Ahmed had deliberately sought him out, as he obviously had, and was trying to befriend him.

As he entered the small two-storey house, 22 Klondike Avenue, where he lived with his parents and three sisters, the evening news was on the TV.

'The United Nations has protested to the Israeli government about the bombing of a school in Central Gaza which has been razed to the ground, killing six children and injuring at least twenty other students and teachers. An Israeli spokesman has said that this was a legitimate target as Hamas fighters were firing rockets from the school into southern Israel, where one civilian had received minor injuries in Siderot,' reported the ITV correspondent.

'I am at the Rafa border crossing-point from Egypt into Gaza, but am not being allowed by the Israeli Army to enter Gaza to see for myself what's going on. There is a large crowd here, several hundred Palestinians, who are also trying to enter Gaza. The majority either have family members there, or live in Gaza themselves.'

Shahid's parents were both watching the screen.

'We must pray to Muhammad, peace be upon Him,' said his father. He got out his prayer mat and placed it down in the corner of the room, in the usual place, facing the wall in the direction of Mecca. He began his ritualistic praying; his mother continued to watch the screen, keening silently to herself.

Shahid went upstairs to his room. Suddenly he was convulsed with anger and ashamed of his parents. His father was continually exhorting him to prayer and observance. He had always done this, as far back as Shahid could remember. His mother remained to this day what she had been when she arrived in England with her family from Pakistan some forty years ago. She had married Shahid's father when she was only 14, within months of arrival in England, at the diktat of her parents. She had had no say in the decision to marry this unknown cousin, sixteen years her senior, whose family came from the same place in Pakistan as her own. She barely spoke one word of English even now, seldom left the house, and then only in full purdah to go to the local shops, just around the corner, to buy spices, vegetables and naan bread. Shahid threw himself on his bed in frustration. Why did his parents not do anything about it?

Taking out his mobile, he stabbed the number that Ahmed had given him into a text with a brief message: 'What time is the next meeting?'

Almost immediately, as if Ahmed had known that Shahid would get back in contact, the phone jangled with its Islamic prayer call tune notifying the incoming text.

Ahmed responded quickly, 'Hi! So you're thinking of coming along? he said, calling him early the next morning. That's great. You won't regret it, Brother Shahid. It's on the 8th at eight o'clock, in the London Central Mosque. You know where that is?'

'Yes, in Regent's Park – I've been there several times with my Dad.'

'Good,' said Ahmed. 'I'll meet you outside at about a quarter to. You're doing the right thing, Brother, Ma'a sala'am.' The phone went dead.

'Perhaps this friend of Ahmed's will give me some ideas on how to right all these wrongs against our fellow Arabs in Palestine – against our fellow Muslims throughout the world?' thought Shahid. 'I just can't stand by and watch it all. Not like my parents, who don't do anything. Even though they constantly bemoan it all!'

On the other side of the country a young girl, not long out of university, handed the filled-in slip to her supervisor. It was the standard form which the 'listeners' had to complete when one of the 'on watch' targets contacted someone hitherto unknown. She explained as she passed the paper across: 'Ahmed Abu Yasir has just been in contact with someone called Shahid. His address has been given as 22 Klondike Avenue, SE 22 in London. Ahmed's taking him to a meeting at the Central London Mosque next Tuesday at 8 pm.'

Once she'd heard the call between Ahmed and Shahid, it had taken her only a brief moment to retrieve details from the GCHQ central database, which was linked to the subscriber list of all mobile phone providers' customers. The software had automatically flagged up Shahid's mobile as a hitherto unlisted number. Now the link between the two was inextricably saved in the memory of the giant database.

'Shahid who?'

'He's another Snu.'

'Thanks, Juliet. Well, at least he's not a Chimera-like suspect whose first name and surname are both unknown – another Fnu Snu! Get on to Research and have them try to dig out the surname.'

'Isn't the London Central Mosque associated with the Saudi government?' she queried.

'Yes, that's right – it's funded by the Kingdom and run by one of their diplomats, Ahmad Al-Dubayan,' said the supervisor. 'Another lamb to the slaughter?'

The supervisor already knew about the planned visit to the UK by Omar Bakri Muhammad, and the plans for his recruitment drive throughout the UK. The MYO was being very active at the moment, he mused.

'Pass the details on to the police in the usual format, please, Juliet.'

The supervisor moved on to another desk where the listeners to the world's radio traffic wanted his advice about other conversations plucked out of the ether.

But when he got back to his office, he made a call to Superintendant Jack Daniel at New Scotland Yard.

13

By the time Shahid reached the mosque in Regent's Park, there were already quite a lot of people outside. He saw at once that they all looked like clones: all wore the white dishdasha, with skullcaps and gutrah, had close-cropped hair with trimmed moustaches, goatee beards and designer stubble, and they were all young men in their late teens and early twenties. It was as if they were wearing a uniform. He felt uncomfortable. He went inside to try to find Ahmed. Eventually he saw him in one of the administrative areas, talking animatedly with several other men. From their actions, it was clear that they had an agenda. They were not having a casual conversation. Ahmed seemed to be reporting to the other men.

As soon as Ahmed saw Shahid, his eyes seemed to flash a warning to the others. They immediately stopped talking and looked interrogatively at Shahid, as if summing him up, running a slide rule over him.

'Hi, Brother, sala'am alaikum!' said Ahmed, his demeanour quickly changing to a welcoming smile. He beckoned Shahid across and introduced him to the other men, but did not tell him who they were.

'Right, the talk is just about to begin. But first, we will all pray,' he said and guided Shahid into the main hall which was by now almost completely full. The prayers were led by the Imam of the mosque, who then introduced the speaker. The Imam seemed subdued and uncertain. Shahid had been to the London Central Mosque quite frequently and knew the Imam. He was a most devout and placid person. He was a Sufi and revered in the Muslim community, but on this occasion he did not seem at ease.

'My brothers,' said the Imam. 'Our esteemed brother Omar Bakri Muhammad is going to talk to us on the subject of the "true Muslim's obligations to his brothers in Islam".'

As he began to speak, Shahid realised that it had been Omar Bakri to whom Ahmed seemed to be reporting earlier. Immediately, he seemed to cast a spell over the eagerly anticipating group of men.

'In the name of God, the merciful, the compassionate, may peace be upon Him, the cheerful one and undaunted fighter, Prophet Muhammad, God's peace be upon Him.

'The nation of Islam and the Arab nation: rejoice, for it is time to take revenge against the Crusader governments in retaliation for the massacres committed by them against Muslims across the world. The heroic Mujahedeen will carry out blessed raids in London. The world of the Crusader will be burning with fear, terror and panic in its northern, southern, eastern and western quarters.

'We have repeatedly warned the Crusader governments and people. We have fulfilled our promise and will carry out our blessed military raids. Our strong Mujahedeen exerted strenuous efforts over a long period of time to ensure the success of the raids. He who warns is excused. God says: "You who believe: if ye will aid the cause of Allah, He will aid you, and plant your feet firmly".'

There were frequent ejaculations from the crowd in acknowledgement of Bakri's rhetoric. 'Insha'Allah,' they chanted rhythmically, 'Allah Akbar!' Bakri was a mesmeric and powerful orator. He spoke fast, without pause, with no reference to notes or cribs, in a seemingly unending diatribe, punctuated by heavy emphasis and violent gesticulation. His whole tone and manner were strident and aggressive, his language atavistic, full of imagery and allusion. He fulminated against the 'Crusader' countries, exhorting Muslims to stand up and be counted; to exact retribution for the crimes being committed against their faith by apostates. Some of his most vitriolic threats were directed not at the US or British governments, but at those of Egypt, Saudi Arabia and Jordan; and, of course, throughout – underpinning all – was an extreme and paranoid hostility towards Israel and the Jews.

'Brothers, we don't make any distinction between civilians and non-civilians, innocents and non-innocents. Only between Muslims and unbelievers. And the life of an unbeliever has no value. It has no sanctity,' Bakri concluded.

He had finished, and sat down. The crowd began chanting in unison: 'Insha'Allah... Insha'Allah,' in an even louder voice. Some began flagellating themselves as if to expiate their sins, and to signal a commitment to take action to right the perceived wrongs inflicted on Islam.

Shahid was taken aback by the tone and language of Omar Bakri. But the television reports from Gaza the week before were imprinted, like fiery images, on his mind. Shahid was surprised and uncomfortable to realise that, as Omar Bakri continued to weave his spell, he began to find that he was more and more in agreement with the speaker's polemics. It was palpably evident that all in the audience thought the same way. Suddenly, Shahid felt that he was among brothers, that this was his natural constituency. Here was someone propounding with vigour and logic a path of action. He remembered his chagrin and how angry he had been with his parents, mouthing platitudes about how bad the Jews were and then just getting on with their comfortable lives, as if the thought had translated into action.

Shahid was simultaneously excited and afraid. He felt shivers of passion convulsing his bowels. This orgasmic feeling quickly passed. The spell was broken. Ahmed said, 'What do you think of that, Brother Shahid? He is a wonderful Muslim – an example to us all.'

Despite what he had just experienced, Shahid felt himself still wary of Ahmed. The other seemed cool and calculating. Everything he did was part of an agenda. Shahid had just experienced something to do with Islam and faith. He thought that it was the same for most of those with whom he had sat on the floor of the mosque. But Ahmed did not seem affected in any way, despite praising the cleric, by what Bakri had said. For him, it seemed to be a case of business as usual.

Shahid responded noncommittally. Although he had been fired up by Omar Bakri's fierce rhetoric, he was still unsure about Ahmed's motives; still uncertain whether he could trust him. Ahmed Abu Yasir's eyes were deep and impenetrable, the pupils like tiny dark grey pebbles.

'We had a great turnout tonight, Brother Shahid, you must have done a great job distributing those leaflets which I gave you.' Shahid had indeed done a good job, making sure that all notice boards and common rooms in the University had had a supply of copies. He had also given a lot to his friends and, together, they had distributed them around their estate, leaving them in shops and bus shelters and pushing them through letter boxes.

'I've got to get home now. Otherwise my parents will wonder where I am. I'm normally home by this time.' It was past ten o'clock.

'What will you tell them you've been doing?' asked Ahmed.

'I'll say that I was in a session with my tutor at UCL. We regularly have evening tutorials. That'll please my parents too.'

'Good, Brother,' said Ahmed. 'That's wise; no point in worrying your parents at this stage!'

'What do you mean?' Shahid was alarmed at the implication. Yet, he had instinctively thought that he should not actually tell his father, particularly, where he had been. That would result in an intense interrogation. His mother would dutifully take his father's side. He had seen his father strike his mother during previous confrontations between them. Both his parents wanted to control him, to dictate the path of his life, and his father wanted to dominate both him and his mother.

None the less, he was disconcerted that Ahmed had asked the question. What was it to him what he did or did not say to his parents? It suggested some subterfuge, a desire to conceal. Surely Ahmed should be encouraging him to spread the good news that Omar Bakri Muhammad had revealed to his ardent followers tonight? It was all very disturbing, coming on top of the overwhelming and conflicting emotions which Shahid had experienced listening to him.

Shahid had parted from Ahmed on the mosque steps and had caught the number 82 bus. As he left, Ahmed said, 'We meet again next week. I'll introduce you to the Brothers next time. I'll give you a call. Ma'a sala'am.'

To Shahid, it sounded like a command.

They met again a week later as agreed. It seemed that nothing Ahmed said was by chance. Everything was calculated and spoken with a purpose in mind. Even the chance meetings had been studiously arranged by Ahmed, Shahid had realised later. With Ahmed, Shahid had met more and more like-minded young Muslims, who had been born and brought up in the UK. Their parents had been subjects of the British Raj. But of a Raj which was in decline; which found itself no longer welcome in, and no longer able to maintain control of, those vast tracts of the world which had once been coloured red. The large maps, which from time to time had been unrolled by the history masters and geography teachers in those ancient public schools, showed the next generation of aspiring colonial administrators, tutored for their role in administering the Pax Britannica in all those far-off lands, their heritage. Then, in its declining years, the Empire had come to England, as the migratory flow was reversed.

Clutching their blue stiff-backed, gold-embossed promissory notes of safety and plenty, Shahid's friends' fathers had poured into the UK from all those red areas. From poverty-stricken Jamaica and the West Indies; from a fractured subcontinent on partition; from the apocalypse that was Idi Amin's Uganda.

They came in hope – but not willingly. They came in body – but not in spirit, leaving their souls on the other side of the world. Some of the new arrivals integrated quickly and easily into the life of their former colonial masters. Most, however, did not do so readily or easily – or at all. Unsurprisingly, therefore, their issue inherited a crisis of identity.

Unsurprisingly, too, the children of their former masters were touched by this. The lower down the social stratification, the more they were affected. These incomers were an inferior breed – surely science had proved this? They should have been the servants, worked for them for a pittance, been ever at the beck and call of their wives, or been in the chain gang which they supervised. Instead, their children went to the same schools, they travelled on the same buses, shopped at the same shops, and aspired to the same jobs – even lived next door!

It was against this backdrop that Shahid and his peers were moving towards adulthood. But another bond differentiated many from the island races of Britain. Irrespective of belief – or lack of it – and of an ever-declining faith among the indigenous population, Britain remained a country in the Judo-Christian tradition, and with an established church and Christian religion.

Not only were these new arrivals coloured, not white, but black or brown, not only were they over here instead of over there, they were in large measure adherents of Islam. They came from countries where Islam was all-embracing and all demanding; superseding, denying recognition of, any secular state or national borders.

Shahid and Ahmed had agreed to go together to meet with a group of Ahmed's friends at the Brick Lane mosque. The building that houses the Jamme Masjid, the Brick Lane mosque, may be said to represent the history of successive communities of immigrants into London; from this point of view it may be called one of the most remarkable and evocative buildings in the area and one of London's architectural and historic treasures. However, unlike any significant previous immigration into the United Kingdom over the centuries, the influx of Muslims posed a threat to the very existence of the state itself. The centuries-long struggle between Christian and Muslim had been generally quiescent since the high watermark of Arabic achievement and cultural and temporal control, at the time of Cordoba in Spain. Now a growing movement, led by Islamic scholars like Qtub, stimulated by increasing rage at the injustices of the Middle East, in particular, and the condition of Muslims in general throughout the world, sought to right these wrongs and re-establish Islamic supremacy.

'Come along Shahid, you will meet many good Muslim boys there. People you can work with,' Ahmed had said, enigmatically.

Shahid always felt ambivalent in Ahmed's company. He remained wary of him, suspecting some ulterior motive in the all-embracing friendship, but he could not put his finger on the reasons for it. It was not because Ahmed liked his company, Shahid knew. But the more he was in Ahmed's company, the more he began to see the world through Ahmed's eyes. Recent events in the Middle East had seemed to confirm the Qtub and Muslim Brotherhood view of the world. An Israeli-led, American-inspired conspiracy to crush and disinherit the Palestinians, and all Muslims. More and more, he wondered if he could continue to stand by and turn a blind eye to what was going on.

There were about two dozen young men gathered together in a room adjacent to the mosque when he arrived with Ahmed. They were arguing fiercely when the two of them got there. One of the men was speaking. He spoke reasonably and with great passion. His logic appeared unassailable. He held his audience spellbound, mesmerised by his utter assurance.

'Listen brothers, hear me! You don't have to look as far afield as Gaza to see the conspiracy of the Zionists and the Crusaders. What about those three brothers of ours who were arrested in Bolton last week? That was just a pretext by the police, harassing law-abiding Muslims. Just because they have long black beards, they are accused of being terrorists. Are all members of Al Muhajiroun terrorists, trying to destroy Britain? There is a growing trend in British society to eliminate us. Mark my words, brothers, these people are out to get us, to get rid of us! And I declare we should ourselves join the global Islamic fight against the blood-sucking Crusaders,' he said. He was slightly older than the others; it had been obvious that he was one of the leaders of the group when he acknowledged Ahmed, who was deferential towards him. 'Who is this you have brought to join us?' he asked.

Ahmed introduced Shahid: 'This is a friend of mine, a Brother, and now a brother-in-arms, I think!' he said pointedly. Shahid was uncomfortable with the introduction but still, he formally embraced all the other members who came up to him and welcomed him. They all seemed very focused, very fixated, with an intense and disturbing look in their eyes.

The man spoke again: 'Brothers, see for yourselves. Why don't you go to Israel and look and see what's up and talk to some people there. Go to Palestine too and see what's really happening. What torture your Muslim brothers have to endure daily. I'm arranging a trip to go to Egypt and then into Gaza for ten days. It's quite cheap, there's a student discount rate through a travel company. If anyone would like to go, then you can see with your own eyes the despair of our fellow Muslims under the Zionist yoke,' he said.

There was a general discussion; a number of people went forward, spoke to him. Shahid saw that their names were being taken and written down. It looked like they had agreed to go on the trip. It was to start in ten days' time. The cost was only £280 including board and lodging, and travel. 'How could it be so cheap?' wondered Shahid. He talked to a couple of the young men, people who had put their names down. One was called Omar, the other was Bakri. He discovered that they were both at university. They lived in Leeds. When he talked to them, he realised that they were just like him. They were intelligent and articulate, and were sincere Muslims. They had been born and brought up in Britain and considered themselves British. Each played football. They used to go the pub regularly, and have a few beers. They had played darts, just like many British people. Just like Shahid himself. The university term had just ended and the trip was scheduled for ten days' time. Eventually the meeting broke up. Shahid left with Ahmed.

They went down Brick Lane and turned left into Old Montague Street, heading for their houses. They were walking along talking to each other, oblivious to the world around them. Suddenly there was a noise behind them. A screech of brakes as a car slewed to a halt. Another came in front of them, pulling in diagonally towards the curb, mounting the pavement. Half a dozen men got out of the two cars. Shahid could see that they were all carrying sticks or clubs, pick-helves perhaps. Suddenly he realised they were rushing at him. At the same time, instantaneously, Ahmed also realised the threat: 'Run, brother!' he shouted. Shahid took to his heels. But he was not fast enough. Three of the gang soon caught up with him. Kicking and punching him viciously, they picked him up and threw him to the ground. One of them

49

stood on him and smashed his stave into Shahid's skull, with a sickening thump. The other two kicked him mercilessly in the ribs and kidneys. He felt blood running over his forehead. Bile rose in his gorge; he vomited. Suddenly, they stopped; then, laughing and joking with each other, they started to move back towards their cars. One of them shouted over his shoulder: 'Keep away from here, do you understand, you Paki bastard? Otherwise, next time we won't be so gentle!' They all laughed. They went back towards their cars. Shahid struggled groggily to his feet. He ran off down an alley on his left. He heard the cries of his attackers: 'Run, you Paki scum; go on, run back home to your own fucking country!'

His parents had been out when he got back home. They had gone to see the latest Hindi film at the local cinema. He went straight upstairs to his bedroom to clean himself up before his parents returned, so that they would not see the state he was in, would not see what had happened to him and how shaken he was. When he had cleaned himself up, he realised that he was not as badly hurt as he had thought. There was a lot of blood, but, thankfully, the injuries were superficial. It could have been much worse had he not been able to fend off some of the heaviest blows. They could have killed him; he knew that next time he might not be so lucky. But why should there be a next time? This was Britain, modern-day, considerate, caring Britain. And yet, here he was, in the middle of the capital, having been singled out simply because he had a black skin and had been wearing a dishdasha.

Shahid's mind flashed back. He remembered his father's story about that other beating to which he had been subjected all those years ago. 'Who was that English boy who had been with him, who his dad had been friends with? What had happened to him?' Shahid wondered. He had not stayed with his father when he had been attacked; he had run off immediately it became clear that the older white boys were after Shahid's father. One of them had clipped the white boy's ear as he passed him and said menacingly, 'Tell anybody about this and you'll be next!' Of course, they had seen each other again. After all, they were in the same form at school. But things between them had never been the same afterwards. It was a rite of passage for both of them, mused Shahid. His father had told him that it was the time when they noticed that they had different coloured skin and that this difference meant something – meant that they were altogether different. The difference was not just superficial. Now, they saw each other differently, and others, in turn, saw them differently. It had not made any difference when they were at the local primary school, sent by parents from different cultures who nevertheless

50

aspired to the same things for their children, who worked to give them a better start in life. Now the price of such friendships had suddenly become high; it was a price that they were not able to pay, perhaps should not have been expected to pay at that age. 'But why could their parents not have been friends?' thought Shahid. That would have made it all OK for them, too.

By the time his parents got back, he had sorted himself out and looked reasonably alright. He was able to pass off his black eyes and cut lip as the consequences of a clash of heads playing football. His parents did not know that he had gone to the Brick Lane mosque, or that he was regularly meeting with Ahmed and attending such meetings. Later that evening, after his parents had come in, he called Ahmed to see what had happened to him. Ahmed had managed to escape, running all the way home. He had appreciated sooner than Shahid what was happening and had taken to his heels in time to get away.

'What's the name of the person who's organising the trip to Gaza?' Shahid asked. The attack had stiffened his resolve. It was time he got involved. Now he *was* involved. He could no longer be a bystander.

Ten days later, Shahid was in Egypt. He flew along with another six people who had been at the mosque the night he and Ahmed had been attacked. He had decided on the spur of the moment. It was the attack which had caused him to do so. Ahmed had made all the arrangements.

'Why are you doing all this for me but not coming yourself?' Shahid asked Ahmed.

'Because I've done this already. I went over five years ago – that was the year I left university. What I saw, the things our brother Muslims in Gaza and Egypt told me... well, you'll see for yourself. We'll meet when you get back. It'll change your life, too. You wait and see!'

And it had. When he got back, Shahid immediately sought out Ahmed. He called him.

'When can we meet? I need to see you straight away.'

'Sala'am alaikum, welcome back, brother. Get to the mosque – Brick Lane – by nine this evening. I'll be there.'

Ahmed greeted him effusively: 'Welcome back, Shahid,' he said again, as they kissed and held hands in the habit of Islam. 'How was your trip?'

'It has opened my eyes, brother,' said Shahid. 'Before I went, I did feel sorry for the Palestinians. It was something remote, impersonal. Their pain was obvious, but it was symbolic, intangible – something I felt intellectually, but did not experience with my body!'

'And?' prompted Ahmed.

'Now I feel their wounds seared in my heart. Their pain is my pain. I cannot look at myself in the mirror because I stand by and do nothing to stop all this pain and suffering being inflicted on my people. And that's just it! I have realised that those people in Gaza and in Egypt are my real brothers and sisters.'

'Good!' said Ahmed, contentedly. He knew now that Shahid had been hooked. All his careful planning and well-disguised tutelage had borne fruit. Now, it was time to take Shahid into his full confidence; to take him to the next stage; to take him to the ultimate act.

'You have done well – very well. And now the Prophet Muhammad, peace be upon Him, has work for us. You must join Bakri and Omar and together go to Pakistan. You must prove yourself worthy of the Prophet by doing holy jihad!'

16

It was two days later when Shahid met Bakri and Omar with Ahmed. The other two clearly knew each other intimately. But they were wary of Shahid, as was he of them. His new brothers-in-arms seemed, to him, to be inhabiting a closed world of their own; a world from which all others were excluded. Shahid felt this exclusion acutely. He was not able to establish any rapport or contact with the couple. It boded ill for any meaningful relationship.

Ahmed explained all this away with a wave of the hand. 'Don't worry, Shahid,' he said, 'once you have been initiated, then you too, will be a soldier in Hizb ut Tahrir. You will join Bakri and Omar in Allah's all-conquering army. You will cast down the infidels, the Crusaders, in the heartland of their arrogance and treachery.'

As he spoke, Ahmed's voice rose higher and higher, eventually quivering with passion and resolve. He seemed almost in a trance-like state. Shahid, not yet caught up in the emotion of Ahmed's beliefs and standing back strangely disengaged from the rhetoric, detected a flash of artifice behind the words, saw the calculating look in Ahmed's eyes. It was as if he were an actor delivering a script learned by heart, by rote; a professional performance but none the less, first and foremost, a performance. Instantaneously, the moment passed. Despite himself, Shahid's anger was re-ignited by the words of Ahmed. He felt the pain of his co-religionists, of Muslims everywhere. The hurt, the ignominy, the despair. He felt it wrenching at his stomach, a physical response to his mental anguish. If this was hatred, then that was what he felt.

But this hatred needed an outlet. The pressure was overwhelming: mere words did not perform the function of a safety valve, rather they ratcheted up Shahid's urge to do something. Relief could only be achieved through action. He was like a cauldron of boiling water, heated so fast, to such a high temperature, that the escape valve was overwhelmed and the tank threatened to blow apart.

'Ahmed!' Shahid's sharp exclamation broke into Ahmed's increasingly ritualistic rant, bringing him to a sudden stop in mid-sentence. 'I must do something! Tell what me I must do, Ahmed. Tell me now, in the name of Allah!'

It was as if Shahid was a lover brought too quickly to a climax. Instantaneously, Ahmed realised what he had to do; realised that he had to capture Shahid's commitment and his passion at once, lest they evaporate and be lost. Beckoning to Omar, he whispered urgently in his ear. Omar appeared to remonstrate, to baulk at the instructions which Ahmed was giving him. But he was insistent.

Supported by Bakri, eventually Omar concurred. They were in a small two-up, two-down council house not far from where Shahid lived. Bakri left the front room where they had all been listening to Ahmed, putting an arm around Omar and taking him with him. Shahid could hear him whispering to Omar in a consoling manner as they left the room. Then their steps could be heard moving up the stairs to the room above.

Ahmed clasped Shahid's hands, 'Brother, you are ready?'

'Yes,' said Shahid. 'Tell me what I must do. Tell me now!'

'Are you ready to avenge your brothers? All those who have suffered at the hands of the Kaffirs? All those who are besieged in Gaza? All those who wallow in the squalor and humiliation of the camps, from which they can see the land of their birth? From which they can only watch their heritage, as it is systematically raped by the Zionists?'

53

'Yes! Yes, I am.'

'Are you ready to attain paradise? To grasp the just rewards of a martyr for Allah, as commanded by the Prophet, peace be upon Him?'

'Yes! Yes, let me go now!'

Ahmed ushered Shahid up the stairs. They went into a bedroom. It was sparsely furnished, devoid of any personal possessions. Omar and Bakri stood together in the middle of the room, side by side. They had been transformed. They both wore camouflaged commando-style combat uniform and black boots with heavy ridged soles. Outside their uniform jackets, each wore a heavy-duty black canvas belt with six pouches, three on either side of their body. Wires led from each pocket to the next. Both men had camouflaged bandannas. Across their chest each held an AK-47 Kalashnikov rifle. Their index fingers were held stiffly along the trigger guard. They stared fixedly ahead, at a point on the wall behind Shahid. Their eyes were glazed, as if they were watching some drama unfold a long way away. On the wall behind Omar and Bakri was a banner. Written on it in large black Arabic script were the words, 'Allah Akbar! Happy is the one who was chosen by God as a martyr.' By the opposite wall a video camera stood, mounted on a tripod, focused on the banner.

A man dressed in smart Western clothes, a dark suit with striped shirt and cuff links and a fashionable tie, stood behind the camera. Clearly Pakistani by descent, he spoke and looked for all the world like a modern-day businessman, such as could be found anywhere in the sphere of international commercial activity.

'Right, now!' this man said, authoritatively, to Omar and Bakri, 'you need to look happy, confident, uplifted. As if you haven't a care in the world. Until you start to speak. Then you need to look straight at the camera and be serious and focused when you read your statements. In fact, it'd be much better if you can both speak from memory – much more convincing. Provided you don't forget your lines, that is.' He laughed at his own joke. No-one else laughed.

'OK, so who's going to go first?' he continued.

Omar and Bakri looked uncertainly at each other. Both wore frowns and seemed strained and anxious, in sharp contrast to the exhortations of the camera-operator.

'Omar, you will go first. You are to be the leader of the operation.'

Ahmed took over in a commanding way. 'Do as Ravi says,' he said, motioning at the cameraman. 'This is not the time for doubts. Remember your commitment to Allah. Think of the brothers being persecuted in Palestine, their children dying in Gaza for the lack of ordinary medicine. The Zionist settlers are defiling our Muslim lands on the West Bank. Now is the time to act; to be grateful for the chance of action; to wreak havoc in Israel and sow fear in the heart of the Jew; to take revenge!' he concluded passionately.

His words seemed to have the desired effect; like Lady Macbeth to her wavering husband, or Henry V before Agincourt, thought Shahid, who, before his conversion, had considered himself a keen student of Shakespeare.

Omar and Bakri clasped each other firmly, their arms around each other's shoulders, like mates before the big game, each drawing sustenance from the other. At once their whole demeanour was transformed, their doubts dissipated, and their faces, previously clouded, now shone with a clarity of resolve and commitment. They stood in front of the banner, looking at each other as if they had been transfigured.

Ravi immediately started running the camera. Ahmed looked on appreciatively. The two Jihadis began to quote from the Koran.

Suddenly, after a few minutes, Ahmed held up his hand. Ravi stopped filming. Omar and Bakri snapped out of their trance-like state and looked expectantly at Ahmed. Shahid took it all in, his emotions in turmoil. A compulsive, inner urge thrust him forward.

'Let me go too, Ahmed!' he cried.

'You will, you will, Shahid, but after this. Just wait until we've finished, Brother, and we will discuss everything.

'Right,' he continued, transferring his attention back to the other two. 'You have your prepared statements?'

Both men nodded.

'I want you to read them now, just as Ravi said. You first, Omar. Bakri, sit in the chair over there. Off you go!'

Ravi started the camera again. Shahid could see the camera lens moving as it zoomed in on Omar, standing proudly in the centre of the banner.

Omar began to read his message in a strong and passionate voice; a voice solid with reasoned argument but devoid of polemics. He stumbled once or twice, searching for the words of his well-prepared statement, a statement crafted by Ahmed.

'I want to avenge the blood of the Palestinians,' he read, 'especially the blood of the women, of the elderly, and of the children, and in particular the blood of the baby girl Iman Hejjo, whose death shook me to the core... I devote my humble deed to the Islamic believers who admire the martyrs and who work for them. God's justice will prevail only in jihad and in blood and in corpses.'

'Again!' commanded Ahmed. After several attempts, Ahmed appeared satisfied. Then the procedure was repeated for Bakri. Finally, after about an hour's filming, Ahmed called a halt to the proceedings.

'OK?' he queried, looking at Ravi.

'Yes – that's good, very good. I've got plenty of material there. With editing it will be very powerful, very convincing.'

'How long?' asked Ahmed.

'Give me a day. I'll get it to you tomorrow evening.'

'That's good enough. We'll all meet here tomorrow evening at the same time. You as well, Shahid.'

Ravi had packed up his gear by now; quickly, he left the room.

Ahmed continued, 'Be ready to travel. Don't give anybody any idea that you are leaving. Don't say "goodbye", just act totally normally. You'll spend tomorrow night here with me. Then we'll be off early in the morning to the airport. I'll have all the arrangements made for you. I'll tell you tomorrow where you're going to. Put a few things that you think you'll need in a small bag. The sort of bag or whatever that you'd normally use, so that it won't look suspicious if you bump into anybody leaving the house, or on the way here.'

'We'll need our passports?' asked Bakri.

'No, you won't. Leave them at home. People will find them if they start looking through your belongings once they miss you. I'll have new passports for you, as well as tickets for your journey. But you'll need to present yourself at the airport as if you were going off for a period, as a student. So it looks as if you're going to be coming back. Which means you will all need to have a suitcase as well to be checked in at the airport. I'll let you have these as well. Don't worry, I'll make sure that they don't have anything that will attract attention when they go through the baggage X-ray at security.'

Omar and Bakri absorbed all this, listening intently to everything Ahmed was saying. Shahid realised with a mixture of excitement and apprehension that he too was committed, that he was about to make a fateful decision from which there would be no turning back.

Ahmed continued, 'Omar, Bakri, let me have that combat gear back. And the martyrs' vests. You'll get new uniforms when you arrive in the target area, and another vest each. This time, they'll be live!'

Quickly Omar and Bakri changed back into their own clothes; clothes which made them look like any other teenager on the streets outside, whether Pakistani or British, Christian or Muslim.

56

'Off you go now. Get ready – and pray,' Ahmed said to the pair, motioning to Shahid that he should remain behind.

'Shahid, my beloved Brother, Allah, peace be upon Him, has chosen you to strike a glorious blow against the Kaffir peoples. Your name will resound down the centuries as a beacon in the true path of righteousness, to be followed by all Muslims everywhere.'

'What… what exactly do you mean?' Shahid queried, taken aback by Ahmed's flowing rhetoric.

'The sword of Allah will smite the back of the unbelievers. They will be hit in the very heartland of their idolatry. The Emir has called for you. He has called from the high peaks of the Hindu Kush. I have told the Emir that I, Ahmed, know the man he needs. And that man is you, Shahid! One day I will bow down before you in honour of what you have done.'

Ahmed paused dramatically. Shahid was bemused and speechless. His mind was racing. He did not know how to respond. He did not know what Ahmed was getting at.

'Before the hour of destiny arrives,' Ahmed continued, 'I am your guide and mentor. The Emir has deemed it so in response to Allah's inspiration. There is other work to be done first. You will travel on Wednesday on the same plane as Omar and Bakri.'

Shahid's stomach churned. He was both afraid and exhilarated.

'But you will have no contact with them on the journey. And they will be told not to acknowledge you. You are to be the co-ordinator for their operation against the infidel. All the things that Omar and Bakri will need will be made available to them in the country to which they are going. You are to ensure that they get everything they need.'

'But Ahmed!' interjected Shahid, 'just exactly how am I supposed to help them? I don't even know which country they're supposed to be going to, let alone what the target is!'

'Patience, Shahid my Brother, patience. All will be revealed in due course. Tomorrow evening, when we meet here, I will explain all. But first I want you to do something else tomorrow. I want you to join the Air Force section of your university's OTC.'

'The Officer Training Corps? I don't want to have anything to do with that lot. They're a bunch of racist bastards!'

17

Early next morning, Shahid went to the University. He knew the name of the man who was in charge of the UOTC Air Wing, a retired Air Commodore, who was also the Bursar for the college. He talked through the application procedure with the Air Commodore.

'So why do you want to join the Air Wing, Mr Shahid?' asked the Air Commodore. His name was Ted Stokes and he had served in Iraq during the first Gulf War. He had got married since then and his wife had not wanted to see him go off time after time into danger.

'Because it's always been an ambition of mine to fly. I'd like to be a pilot.' Shahid had rehearsed his responses fully.

'Any particular type of plane?'

'Well, I'd really like to be a pilot in a commercial airline – BA or Pakistan International Airways probably – fly passengers around the world for a living. I'm fascinated by the idea of moving around from place to place. Perhaps it's something to do with my background. My parents moved around a lot. My father comes originally from Pakistan. But he went to work in Africa, to Kenya, where he met my mother. Her family went there from Bangladesh.'

'OK,' said the Air Commodore, 'let's get you to fill in this form then. You realise, of course, that not everyone who joins the Air Section gets the chance to fly?'

'What do I have to do to make sure that I get on a flying course then?'

'Well, first, you have to attend very regularly, every week without fail. Then, provided I recommend you, you will have to do some aptitude tests. You have to convince me and the other officers in the OTC, as well as the regular liaison officer from RAF Valley, that you really are committed, that you'll work hard to get the skills. You wouldn't consider joining the RAF perhaps? That's a very good career. They'd welcome a young man with your background – fits the current non-discriminatory profile.'

'I don't think they'd really accept someone with my background in the RAF, would they?' queried Shahid.

'Well, I guess there's always a chance of being one of the first. What an example you would be setting for your peers and young people in your community. I'm sure your parents would be very proud?' said the Air Commodore.

'Look, here you are. Here are the application forms. And here's some more information about the OTC, and the Air Wing in particular. We have a good time. I try to make it as much fun as possible for everyone. And there are several very pretty girls in it too!' he said, winking salaciously. Shahid had to struggle not to take offence at the man's blatant chauvinism and innuendo which offended his sensibilities and his faith. 'Shows the sort of things we do,' continued Stokes. 'Look, here's some information about the RAF, and other careers in aviation, which might come in useful?' He paused, 'You might even become a test pilot or fly cargo planes. That would get you to a lot of interesting places; more than just flying from A to B and back again in a passenger plane. I'll tell you what: why don't I introduce you to some of our members? Come along to the members' evening next week. It's always on a Wednesday here in the hall next-door at 7:30.'

Shahid took the proffered information. He immediately filled in the application form and gave it to the Air Commodore's secretary. He left and went back home, arriving early enough not to have to explain to his parents where he had been. He had never in his life expressed any interest in flying.

By 7 pm he was back at Ahmed's house. They both laughed when Shahid related the details of the session at the OTC; particularly at the Air Commodore's suggestion that Shahid should join the RAF.

Then Omar and Bakri arrived. The enormity of what he was now engaged in suddenly struck Shahid. His next experience of flying, the one which he had not disclosed to the Air Commodore, would be a flight of destiny. Shahid had tried to make sure that his departure from his home had been as normal as possible. He had told his parents that he was going to stay overnight with some friends. That it was Ziad's birthday party.

The sheikhs had their passions, centring on speed, the chase, and death. These passions were exemplified by their sports. Powerboat racing, horse and camel racing, the stone-like drop of the hawk to the kill, and the endurance of a long-distance horse race, all spoke of their origins as nomadic Bedouin hunters in the vast desert spaces of the Empty Quarter of the Rub Al Khali. Now the rich inheritance of gold – black gold – had allowed them to indulge their passions to excess, however and wherever they chose. It enabled them to mix business with pleasure. It facilitated the furtherance of their ambitions, whether purely personal or political – or both.

At this moment, Sheikh Abdul was engaged in doing all of this. He had flown earlier the previous day in his private jet to Kabul. He spent the night there in his private guest house. Already staying there were ten other members of his party, who had not travelled with him from Dubai. During the course of the afternoon and evening he had had a series of private meetings with some of the party.

Early on he met with Sanjay who had travelled directly from Mumbai. The two men greeted each other warmly and quickly got down to business.

'Sanjay, my friend, good to see you,' said the Sheikh. 'How are the plans for my special project developing?'

'Very well, Your Highness,' responded Sanjay. 'I have obtained virtually all the equipment. All I am now waiting for are some Stinger missiles – I think you need at least half a dozen to be on the safe side.'

'Good – where is it all coming from?'

'Most of the small-arms and ammunition and so on is Russian. I have many contacts in the republics of the former Soviet empire. When the Soviet Union split apart, a lot of military equipment and munitions was offloaded – to use the English phrase, liberated – onto the commercial market. Our Muslim friends in Chechnya, Uzbekistan and suchlike places were able to get their hands on a lot of it. Most of it was sold to the highest bidder without scruple and irrespective of national interest or any attempt being made to embargo its use.'

'Yes, of course,' said Sheikh Abdul. 'It is no surprise that so many Soviet apparatchiks suddenly became very rich selling off the state's family silver!'

'Exactly. And now we have the phenomenon of these new oligarchs controlling European oil and gas supplies, owning English football clubs, and so on!' Sanjay continued. 'And former members of the KGB running the state!'

'Ah yes, but that is not so strange. Before Putin, there was Andropov, and he had the whole of the Soviet Union to contend with, not just Russia. And Beria, of course, hoped to take over from Stalin but was beaten to the punch by Khrushchev.'

'You know your political history well, Sheikh Abdul,' said Sanjay appreciatively.

'I studied political science in the US, at Berkeley,' said Sheikh Abdul.

'But the biggest joke is that another ex-member of the KGB now owns England's *Evening Standard* newspaper.' They both laughed.

'Right, to business,' said the Sheikh. 'You said that you have not yet got the Stingers. Where will you get them from?'

Sanjay replied, 'Well, one benefit of all this is that our Islamic brethren have benefited from the demise of the Soviet empire, and many groups are well armed and able to support each other. They will be prepared to help us too. It's from these groups that I have been recruiting the men we need. So far, I have identified twenty good men, who got their experience fighting against the Soviets in Afghanistan. They were led by Osama bin Laden – trained by the CIA, of course!'

He paused, and then continued, 'But to come to the Stingers. The American CIA gave the Mujahedeen something over 2,000. They gave them to Ahmed Shah Massoud in 1989–91 because they had decided to invest in him as the main man through which to channel their support for attacking and undermining the Russian presence. At the height, they were funnelling over $200,000 to Massoud's Islamic organisation every month.'

'Yes,' said Sheikh Abdul, 'it was a good choice. I knew Massoud well. We used to hunt together. A very courageous and shrewd person.'

Sanjay went on: 'Since the Wall came down and the Soviets were forced to withdraw their armies, the Americans have been badgering Massoud to get the Stingers back. Apparently, only a small portion had been used, and the Americans thought that the stocks were still held by Massoud.'

'It is said that the CIA has been paying as much as $2,000 dollars per missile.' 'Have they got many back?'

'Most of them ended up in the hands of the various Mujahedeen groups. Al Qaeda and others, such as those I am trying to deal with now. In Chechnya and Uzbekistan, for example. All have a number of them, which we can buy. At a price! My men are in the region now, negotiating prices. I'm driving down the price. I don't want these tribesmen to think that we are a soft touch.'

'Well, Sanjay, remember that, although a good deal is always important, money is no object in this case. I must have those Stingers at all costs! I need to have them. I need them within the next six weeks. Can you do that for me?' asked the Sheikh, emphatically.

'Yes, I can certainly do that. I can conclude the negotiations at any time.'

'Excellent! Now, I have set up some very good hunting for us. I hope you will join us?'

'It would be my pleasure, Your Highness.'

'Tomorrow morning, then? But first, our other little bit of business. What is the decision with Osama?'

'I'm told that Osama is in Tora Bora at the moment. He spends a lot of time there now. That is where he is marshalling his forces; where he is developing with Ayman al-Zawahiri techniques for bringing a humbling to our mighty American friends. We are scheduled to meet him the day after tomorrow. The meeting will take place under the guise of our hunting expedition with Your Highness inviting various people, including Osama and al-Zawahiri, to join you. They are staying at a place in the Tora Bora area. I myself have not been told where it is. And we will not be told before we get there – those are his conditions.'

Sanjay paused to let the implications sink in. The Sheikh was not normally amenable to making blind dates. He was a man who needed to be in charge. 'The arrangements are being made by my people at present with Osama's. In order for us to make the meeting, we will be given instructions tomorrow evening. It will mean driving through the desert in convoy, following their people. They will meet us at the place where we are to land. We need to fly from here to Tora Bora; once in the air, the co-ordinates of the landing zone will be passed to the pilot.'

'Excellent, Sanjay,' said Sheikh Abdul. 'As you know, my plane is at our disposal…'

'Your Highness,' Sanjay interrupted, 'as I said, the arrangements are all in Osama's hands. He will provide the plane, with his own crew. Even they will not know where we are due to land until we are airborne. I am told that he never spends two nights in the same place. In any event, we will not be landing at a normal airstrip – not a strip that your Boeing would be able to use! Osama's people will also provide the vehicles to take us from where we land to the designated meeting-place. I am negotiating with one of his key men on all that. I will be seeing him here in Kabul later on this evening.'

'Good hunting then, tonight and tomorrow!' Sheikh Abdul stood, terminating the meeting.

The Hercules C130, the workhorse of Western air forces and commercial air operations, was on the apron at Kabul airport when Sheikh Abdul and his party arrived there at nine o'clock the next morning. The sheikhs each had their own fleet of aircraft. Hercules were normally used by them for their minions to ferry their gear around the world, and their horses. Sometimes, as now, it provided the best method of travel for themselves, so that they could land without an airstrip. Despite the best endeavours of the Sheikh's entourage, the cargo hold of the Herc could not equate to the premier service to which he was accustomed. However, this was no hardship to Sheikh Abdul. He was a hard and resolute man, who largely eschewed luxury. He kept himself in good physical shape. A half-hour physical fitness regime in his palace gym, after the first prayer call, taken by a British-trained Omani PT instructor, was obligatory for all his male staff.

This morning they dispensed with routine, leaving for the airport immediately after prayers. Sheikh Abdul declined the offer from the Captain to sit in the cockpit jump seat.

'Shokran, but no thank you. I can go up there later during the flight, Insha'Allah. For now I will sit in the cargo hold with Sanjay here. We have a lot to talk about.'

The jumpmaster checked that all the passengers were safely seated and that their seatbelts were securely fastened.

The pilot's voice came over the intercom. 'Your Highness, I am about to start the engines. I have not had the honour of flying you here before, but I know that Sanjay has explained the techniques. We do not want to have a case of mistaken identity.'

He spoke with a pronounced American inflection. He had been trained by the US Air Force Air Education and Training Command at Randolph Air Force Base, near San Antonio in Texas. Later he had been seconded to the ISI by the Pakistani Air Force in 1987, during the Soviet occupation. He had flown numerous clandestine missions in support of the Afghan Mujahedeen, attempting to destabilise the Soviet Army. Most had been jointly co-ordinated by the ISI and the CIA, but a number had been orchestrated solely by the ISI and unknown to the CIA. He was, therefore, well-practised in the latest techniques to protect his aircraft from ground attack, and was just about to put this experience to good use on this flight. But he was also an experienced intelligence officer. He had been employed by the ISI in the dual role of taxi driver for senior Mujahedeen commanders and intelligence liaison officer to the Al Qaeda leader. He was trusted by both parties. It was for this reason, more than for his flying skills, that he had been selected to fly Sheikh Abdul. Of those on board the aircraft, only he knew the Emperor of Al Qaeda, Osama bin Laden, and only he knew where the aircraft was destined to land. But even he did not know where the scheduled meeting between bin Laden and

Sheikh Abdul would take place or when. He continued his pre-flight briefing: 'So we'll take off just as quickly as we can when we have the revs. We'll climb up as fast as possible at 35 degrees. That's pretty steep for a bus like this. When we reach 32,000 feet, just about as high as it will fly, there we'll be safe from anything on the ground!'

He paused to let this sink in, to ensure that his passengers appreciated the realities of flying in Afghan airspace. He did not want to attract the attention of any freelance Mujahedeen who had managed to hold on to one of those US Stingers. A freedom-fighter who would presume that the Hercules represented authority – therefore, to him, it would be what was euphemistically called a legitimate target.

Captain Haq Azzar Huddin continued: 'The flight will take about one and three-quarter hours. Sheikh Abdul, you are welcome to come up to the cockpit. We can manage a reasonable cup of gahwa or some Arabic tea. And we have some delicious fresh dates. When I put the seatbelt sign on for the landing, everyone will please need to be back in the hold. We'll spiral down and then come in low and fast to land. Everyone who need be has been warned of our arrival and will do the needful in taking care of us all.'

As he finished talking, the automatic starter motor leapt into life. Within seconds, the plane itself was leaping down the runway.

Joining the pilots in the cockpit for the latter part of the trip, Sheikh Abdul and Sanjay saw the rugged countryside spread out below them. The terrain was tortured and near barren, with high passes winding through the jagged mountains. Occasionally a gleam of green could be seen outlined against the dark brown rock. Vegetation had sprung up somehow, managing to cling to the sheer-sided gorges through which tumbled the swollen rivers of the spring melt. Flowing westwards, much of this water would never find its way to the sea. Most of the rivers and streams end in shallow desert lakes or oases inside or outside the country's boundaries. Not long out from Kandahar they had crossed over the Helmand River.

'Over there on the left,' shouted the captain, 'that's Lashkar Gah. And that river's the Arghandab – it's a tributary of the Helmand. We should be seeing Tora Bora shortly. The Pashtuns call it Spin Ghar; it's a cave complex in the White Mountains. It's a most excellent place to live if you don't want any unwelcome visitors! We're only about 60 kilometres west of the Khyber Pass now. Over there on the right, that's the Federally Administered Tribal Areas in Pakistan.'

The wizened Afghan retainer, a member of the Hazara caste who was the nearest thing to a Gulf Air stewardess on this service, collected Sheikh Abdul's coffee cup when the Sheikh declined the Hazara's offer of more by the customery vigorous waggling of his cup.

'Yes, look over there, on the horizon, eleven o'clock. That's Tora Bora; only another fifteen minutes,' said the captain.

'Where can one land hereabouts?' asked Sheikh Abdul.

'Yes,' echoed Sanjay. 'There's hardly a flat piece of land the size of a polo field anywhere!'

'Well, we are flying in the mother of all aircraft,' said the pilot. 'This bird doesn't need a metal strip. It can land on ordinary ground just as long as it's flattish and firm. I've seen one being landed on an aircraft carrier!' said Capt Azzar. 'And we have a most fine place to go to. In a way, it is a polo field. This is the place where the Afghanis hold their annual game of what they call polo – the one where they kill a sheep, and then use the head as the ball. They all ride bareback, too. Perhaps our hosts will put on a demonstration for us.'

'I played polo in Delhi,' said Sanjay. 'In the shadow of the British Raj, the one good thing they did leave us!' They all laughed at Sanjay's derisory tone.

'Time to fasten seatbelts,' said the pilot. 'We'll be landing just to the right, to the north of Tora Bora itself – about thirty minutes' drive away. Your Highness, if you want to watch the descent, it will be all right to do so here, provided you both strap yourselves into the complete harness.' He indicated the equipment firmly bolted in three places to the metal frame which was at the back of the cockpit.

The co-pilot was flying the plane at this point. Abruptly he pushed the joystick down towards the floor, the nose dipped violently as the plane hurtled like a stone, it seemed, towards the approaching ground. Kicking the aileron full right he put the aircraft into an ever-decreasing spiral. The crescendo of the engines rose in tone as if in protest; the creaking and groaning of the aircraft intensified as the wings shook violently. To Sheikh Abdul and Sanjay it seemed that the plane would disintegrate at any moment. Perhaps it would have been better to have been in the back and not seen all this, thought Sheikh Abdul, as the plane suddenly levelled out, slewing from side to side, now only several hundred feet from the ground. Neither the Sheikh nor Sanjay could see anywhere that appeared to be a sensible place to land over 40 tons of metal and fuel – a flying bomb. Then after a few seconds, they could discern a group of vehicles and 4x4s and some horsemen and about a dozen people standing beside several tents. The plane hit the ground, bounced, and then bounced again; the co-pilot nonchalantly put the throttle on full reverse thrust. Clouds of dust rose on either side of the aircraft as it bumped erratically along the rough ground. After only a few seconds, the aircraft had been turned and was taxiing back towards the waiting group, the smooth mellow sound of the engines throttling down confirming their safe arrival.

As the plane drew to a halt, the Hazara and the jumpmaster quickly opened the doors and dropped down the inboard steps. By the time they had done that, a group of prancing ponies with their Afghan riders had reached the plane and excitedly began to circle around it. There were perhaps twenty of them. Over by the tents, about 100 yards away, another group of men in white dishdashas stood waiting expectantly by their 4x4 Land Cruisers. The Nissan open-back trucks held what appeared to be a cut-throat group of turbaned Afghanis armed with a miscellany of weapons, rocket-launchers and grenades. Sanjay noticed several RPG7s and, of more interest to him, at least one Stinger ground-to-air missile. The jumpmaster assisted the passengers to disembark. The plan was that the plane would remain there, while the principals went off to have their meeting. Captain Azzar Huddin would accompany Sheikh Abdul and Sanjay to the meeting. The three walked briskly across the rough ground from the plane to the vehicles and the waiting group of Arabs. As they approached, one man stepped forward from the group and moved towards the visitors, meeting them halfway from the plane.

'Sala'am alaikum, alaikum sala'am, God be with you,' he greeted them. 'I am Salim Ahmed Hamdan. I have been sent here by our Emir to meet you and to take you to him. He is waiting for you. Please come with me.' As Sheikh Abdul got near the group, he realised that they were indeed all in Arab clothing. From their accents when they greeted him, as they did one by one with due ceremony, Sheikh Abdul detected at least one Jordanian and one Egyptian as well as several Gulf Arabs, a couple from Saudi Arabia, one probably from the Yemen. And finally two whom he thought were probably Uzbekistanis. Sheikh Abdul was asked to get into one of the Land Cruisers, while Sanjay was directed to another. Each vehicle had two heavily-armed guards in the back. The visitors both sat in the front beside the driver. The man who had greeted them first on arrival, Salim, drove Sheikh Abdul. A third 4x4 moved off in front with several Arabs in it. And then, following on behind, several of the flatbed trucks bristling with weapons carried by the

Jihadis, careering along behind and on the flanks. 'Mechanicals', said Sanjay pointing them out to Sheikh Ahmed, 'invented in Somalia at the time of the Americans' humiliation there!' Salim drove fast, paying scant regard to the uneven terrain. Soon they joined an obvious but rough route. It wound along the twisting track in open country and then disappeared into a defile. They began to climb upwards. Eventually, after about half an hour, they drove past several rocky outcrops and then debouched onto a flat plateau.

There, ahead of them, was a large complex of buildings, all new and well maintained.

'Welcome to Tarnak Farm, Your Excellency,' said Salim, 'we are pleased to see you here, Alhamdulillah, God is great.'

He spoke on his radio; there was a brief exchange, a password given and received. As the leading vehicle drove up to the complex the massive gate opened inwards, allowing the vehicles with their visitors to pass inside, before it slammed quickly shut behind them. In the courtyard a tall bearded figure in a white turban and dishdasha waited for them. A beam of sunlight illuminated him, making it seem as if his clothes were incandescent.

Sheikh Abdul opened the conversation after extensive courtesies had been exchanged. Tea had been offered, accepted and consumed. Finally, when the cups did not waggle again, they were collected by the tea boy, a stooped and wizened tribal man of some fifty or sixty years who retired, leaving the small group together on the spacious veranda. There was a magnificent view of the towering peaks of the Hindu Kush. From the Hercules, they had looked quite benign and accessible. Now Sheikh Abdul was in awe of their grandeur. From this location there were views in all directions, as far as the eye could see. No chance of being surprised here, he realised, seeing the turbaned Arab sentries, with their AK47s and ammunition bandoliers slung over their shoulders, their keen eyes scanning the horizon, covering all quarters of the compass.

Across the valley northwards were steep-sided ravines, accessible only to donkey and mule. Here and there he could see caves, dark holes against the glinting sheen of the rocks, reflecting the sun.

'An easy place to hide, Sheikh, should the need arise?' he said to bin Laden, gesturing to the mountains as he did so.

Osama nodded reflectively, 'Indeed so, Sheikh, it is not by chance that we find ourselves here, is it Ayman?' He glanced over at the other man who had remained behind when the retinues of both men had left at a sign from bin Laden. The other, a small bespectacled man in his late 50s with a luxuriant and ill-kempt beard, nodded in agreement.

'Yes, indeed so. We are being well provided with security by our Afghan hosts, Alhamdulillah. Mullah Omar himself guided us here. He himself has used it – before, when other white Crusaders were looking for us! When the Americans were our friends!' Ayman al-Zawahiri looked like an absent-minded professor or the doctor that he had once been. He continued, 'I spent many long years in jail in my own country before escaping to join Osama. Since then we have had too many houses from which someone has always wanted to evict us. Now, we believe that finally we are at home here in Afghanistan.'

'We thought so in the Sudan,' said Osama. 'But the Americans were able to make it otherwise.'

'They will not be able to do that here, Sheikh. Unless they decide to mount a full campaign and send several hundred thousands of soldiers. The Soviets with 150,000 men could not subdue the heart of Islam. We have so many eyes and ears here that they cannot approach within miles of us without being detected. And when they do come, with their special forces, we move to another place. The people are with us. They will keep us safe, Insha'Allah.'

'America has no stomach for another Vietnam here,' Sheikh Abdul took up the other's train of thought. 'They're too interested in the pursuit of Mammon, of persisting in their idolatry.'

'All their banks and weapons of mass destruction will not protect them against the wrath of the Prophet, peace be upon Him,' said Osama. 'In all their actions, they continually offend against the holy Prophet, peace be upon Him. They neither know nor care how they offend against all true Muslims, as they ever more encroach into the world of Islam. We will have our revenge. Plans are even now in hand, which will strike a resounding blow against these Crusaders. The sound of the Crusader being smote will resound throughout our world of Islam, Alhamdulillah!'

Sheikh Abdul listened attentively. He was a cynical man, driven by self-interest, not by the observance of God's, any god's, precepts. But none the less, in his position and with his objectives, he knew that success depended upon harnessing the wrath of Muslims across the globe. It was essential that he appeared to all to be in strict observance of the Koran. Particularly at this moment, in the presence of one who seemed somehow to be the figurehead around whom all Islam might put aside its grievous schisms and coalesce into one furious whole, intent on righting the wrongs of the past, and of re-establishing Islam at the apogee of man's development.

'This is good news, indeed,' said Sheikh Abdul. 'If it pleases you, may I be permitted to learn more of your plans? I have plans of my own as a true Muslim. Perhaps we can work together?'

Al-Zawahiri and bin Laden exchanged glances. Bin Laden nodded imperceptibly.

Al-Zawahiri spoke forcibly. 'The Umma and its people, the youth, the elderly, men – and women!' he said, 'all must offer themselves, their expertise and all financial support, enough to raise jihad on battlefields across the globe. Jihad today is a duty of every Muslim.'

'We will take you to see our cohorts training for the task ahead of them. We have many men in training and some women also. Many are already experienced in the jihad – blooded with the Mujahedeen. The Taliban of Mullah Muhammad Omar's Quetta Shura have killed many Soviets alongside their rivals, Massoud and Hekmatyar. Now they will give their lives to throw out any other invader. They will also take the fight to the Crusader homelands. That is what we are doing now. I have shock troops ready to attack American ships in our ports, American embassies in our Arab world, American tourists in their decadent hotels. Across the world, the vanguard of our troops is targeting American interests.'

Osama broke in, 'We will demonstrate the reach of our power. At this very moment, plans are well advanced for an attack in the very heartland of Crusader idolatry. We will strike at the Towers of Mammon. We will knock them down. We will shake the foundations of their apostate lifestyle. They cannot escape the wrath of Allah!'

Sheikh Abdul responded appreciatively, 'Well Sheikh! You are indeed the leader of our world of Islam here on earth. You are blessed by the Prophet, peace be upon Him. You strike terror into the heart of all kaffirs, of all false Muslims and the apostate. But I can help you!'

'How so?' said bin Laden, reflectively.

'With your assistance, I can establish the law of the Islam of Qtub in my country and in the whole Persian Gulf. But I must become the Ruler to do this.'

'Go on.'

'My brother, the Ruler, is weak and feeble. He is apostate. He prefers to feel the bodies of Crusader air hostesses, of whores, rather than follow in the path of Allah's teaching. If I can replace him, then I can establish the true Sharia in my country. Then I can push back the bridgehead of the Crusaders. Together, we can take over the region and destroy the House of Saud for Allah and for ever!'

As they had talked, food had been prepared. Bin Laden beckoned to the visitors to join him around the rug where the food had been placed. The meal was appetising but simple and unembellished. It was the same as any tribesman in the local hills would eat daily with his family. So far, Sanjay had been silent. Now Sheikh Abdul invited him to tell their hosts about his preparations for the coup. Over the course of the meal, taken at a leisurely pace, the two pairs of men each powerful in their own way, bonded strongly. Each appreciated the advantages to their own cause of co-operating with the other. It was agreed that Sanjay and al-Zawahiri should brief each other fully on their current plans and intentions. That they should see how they could help each other. That they should maintain constant contact.

'We have a problem with passports,' said al-Zawahiri, 'the American immigration system is tight and well-policed.'

'We can help you with such things,' said Sanjay. 'For us to authenticate passports for any of the Gulf countries is not a problem. What I really need,' he continued, 'is some more Stingers, and several experienced Jihadis who have used them in anger to bring down the Hips and Hinds. They could form our attack team.'

'Please be sure that our friends have all the support they need, Ayman interjected Bin Laden.'

As they talked, the mutuality of interest became more and more apparent. Ideas were exchanged, techniques explained, aspirations aired.

The meeting broke up with exchanges of courtesies in an atmosphere of common interest and promise.

Al-Zawahiri himself took Sheikh Abdul and Sanjay in his Land Cruiser with the escort party to the waiting Hercules. On the way he detoured into a nearby valley. Here, a large tented encampment was sited, with several score of Arab men undergoing training in numerous military skills.

'We have trained over 6,000 Jihadists here, all now ready to give their lives in ecstasy for the Prophet, peace be upon Him!' al-Zawahiri boasted.

20

Bill was sitting at the Trade Centre Apartments poolside, under the shade of a beach umbrella. He watched idly as a large desert wasp delved into the pool's filtration system. He wondered why a wasp would be attracted to chlorine-impregnated water. Perhaps they were breeding a new strain of super-wasp? After all, chlorine is found in the skin of the Ecuadorian tree frog. Quickly his mind switched back to the matter in hand – the task which Andy had set him when they met at the Crown Plaza. 'Nearly a week ago,' he thought, 'got to speak to Malik.' He made a mental note, 'He must be having problems.'

Bill tried to analyse the implications of a recent research paper. It had been written by an ex-CIA operative from the Afghan war, who had helped train the Mujahedeen to fight against the Russians. He was also a psychiatrist and had tried to use his skills to provide an analysis of the global Salafi jihad; the global Islamic revivalist religious movement that was now sweeping across the Muslim world – and beyond. Andy had received a copy from London and passed it on to him: 'Here,' he had said, 'take a look at this. It makes fascinating reading, and its conclusions aren't by any means what one would have expected. It may be helpful in the job I want you to do.

'Like, for example, it suggests that initially Al Qaeda was responding to the global jihad, rather than orchestrating and directing it. And also, that the jihad itself has been remarkably haphazard, with no overall direction or organisation. It appears that essentially the whole thing relies on a very few intensely committed individuals who create nodes of jihad wherever they happen to be.' Andy had paused at this point, letting it sink in.

'Take Montreal, an unlikely place for Islamic fundamentalism, I suppose. Apparently it became a node just because Ahmed Ressam, the Millennium Bomber, ended up there, largely by chance.' Bill's thoughts were distracted by the sinuous movements of a delicious young blonde sitting at a nearby table, who was stripping off her clothes to reveal underneath a striking blue striped bikini, stretched over an even more striking body, nipples thrusting against the thin cloth. He thought how bizarre it all was, the contrast between this poolside beauty and the ugliness of the growing Jihadist threat. Did it all betoken Lewis's *Clash of Civilisations*', a mantra latched onto and made famous by Huntington? This whole experience was becoming more and more Byzantine. Behind the apparently civilised and normal appearance there lurked a burgeoning menace. He sensed that he was about to put himself in the way of this menace at Andy's behest. Would he become the immediate target of this threat as he penetrated behind the numerous veils of Dubai's carefully constructed façade, to expose the cruel, ruthless and self-serving opportunism of a dictatorial regime? Whereas the traditional dance of the veils led to something erotic and hedonistic, the dance which he now found himself part of was unlikely to prove so desirable.

Reluctantly, Bill forced his mind back to the matter in hand. 'Look,' Andy had continued, 'we want to find out who owns all the numbers that bin Laden called from this mobile – it's registered in his name. Perhaps he never used it; perhaps it was just a family phone? But there again, perhaps he did use it.'

'I can get the office to do the international numbers. But I can't afford to ask the intelligence people here to check the local ones. In fact, if I do ask them, it's a pound to a pinch of salt that the buggers will just take the bloody list and analyse it for themselves. Then they'll tell us it's not possible to help – not in so many words, simply by stonewalling, telling us that it's too difficult because of personal privacy and so on. Bloody hell – privacy indeed in a dictatorship such as this! Or perhaps they won't tell us anything, letting it just trickle away into the sand.'

'Meanwhile they'll contact all the people involved in Jihadist activities and warn them off.'

If bin Laden had had a presence here, Bill reflected, then it followed from the research that there had to be a Jihadi node here in Dubai. Too much of a coincidence to think that his presence here was only because of his family. Bin Laden is a Yemeni family which had made good in Saudi, where they still lived. It had become one of the largest construction companies in the Gulf with many massive projects throughout the region. This was the basis for Osama's wealth and influence. He was said to be the black sheep of the family, but it was also rumoured that some at least of his family members supported his activities. He professed himself to be a Salafist. And perhaps he was, thought Bill, and there again, perhaps like most other power-brokers, he was using the appearance of overwhelming devoutness to promote his real ambitions. Perhaps, as the scion of a leading Saudi family, his religious manifestations were simply a cloak behind which he sought the downfall of the House of Saud, with its overweening power and wealth. Perhaps, indeed, his objectives were temporal rather than spiritual.

Was this any different from the reality of Dubai where all appeared benign and normal to the undiscerning holiday visitor from any Western democracy? Bill tried to penetrate behind the veils, to see his quarry. According to this latest analysis, three-quarters of committed Salafi Jihadists came to the cause through ties of kinship and friendship. He saw now the thinking that lay behind this latest task Andy had given him. If it was possible to latch onto one active Jihadi terrorist, then, through research and surveillance, it should be relatively straightforward to identify the other members of the group. At least it would be if one could use someone who could meld into the milieu of these activists. Bill knew from experience that, even in somewhere like Ireland where hunter and hunted looked much the same on the surface, it was difficult to penetrate alien areas. Everyone knew each other in the hard areas of Belfast, whether Protestant or Catholic. An intruder would soon be identified through smell or body language, or by some sixth sense. How much more difficult for those with white skins to become part of the landscape in areas populated by those of a darker hue? And for the Salafi revivalists, the sanctuary of the mosque was the focal point for the propagation of ideas and the planning of active operations against the infidel Crusaders.

However, Dubai did present some advantages over somewhere like Saudi. In Saudi any social mixing between nationals and expatriates took place largely in the Western-occupied compounds, an artificial meeting place for those from such different cultures. In Dubai, socialising between expatriate and local was becoming increasingly less common, Bill had noted since his earlier experience in the mid-eighties. Then there had been fewer – far fewer – expatriates and the locals needed the active participation of their expatriate partners in order to establish their businesses along Western methods; and to acquire the licences, franchises and agencies which had enabled many of them to build up massive wealth and command monopolistic or dominating positions in their market place. Now the locals used the expatriates more as manager or functionary, while they had withdrawn back into their own culture, adopting in most cases an aloof, superior attitude to those upon whom they formerly depended. But Bill appreciated that, although expatriates and Emiratis did not socialise together, they did socialise often in the same places – restaurants, golf clubs and even pubs were, to some extent, the preserve of all. So there could be some possibility of carrying out effective surveillance, even if the mosque and the home, and all that took place there, would be off-limits to his enquiries.

Perhaps Malik could manage to get some indirect access to the mosque even, if they were very lucky.

One thing that struck Bill was that it was very clear Al Qaeda was not a top-down organisation. There appeared to be little effort by the leadership to recruit and set up a formal military-style organisation, as was the case for most terrorist groups in his experience.

He remembered how successful Harry's people had been in controlling the activities of the Provisional IRA in Belfast in the early 1970s before PIRA learned the game. They had maintained constant surveillance of the Belfast Brigade staff. They had watched them move out of the hard areas of the Falls Road and West Belfast into the comfortable middle-class university district. This avoided the constant scrutiny of the uniformed security forces and the local battalion seeking the current Top 10 so they could lock them up, only to meet them again after they had been released and the battalion returned some eighteen months later for its next tour.

It was a case of 'out of the frying pan into the fire' for the Brigade staff. They became prey to something altogether more devastating. By monitoring, literally and metaphorically, the activities of the planners and leaders, it became possible for the security forces to interdict and mitigate the activities of the terrorists.

Clearly, he reasoned, this would not work against this Salafi terrorist. These individuals, it seemed, came together largely out of religious conviction, following an intense experience of alienation from society and, in many cases, from family. They were not recruited so much as joining over a prolonged period of time through social and religious intercourse, discussion and meditation. When they progressed to undertaking operations, they did this largely on their own initiative, having themselves established the link to the global jihad and, perhaps, Al Qaeda. Bill had read that, surprisingly, there was little evidence of recruitment from the top, still less of any form of brainwashing, as widely portrayed or assumed in the Western media. He would have to take all this into account in whatever he was to do to help Andy. There would be no structured hierarchy to identity. No ASUs, the active service unit; no companies, battalions or brigades as in the case of the IRA, which aped the structure of the British Army. But there would be a group, or node, of several intense and closely-knit friends and family who faithfully observed all the rituals of the Salafists, who strove to live literally in the same way as the Prophet ('peace be upon Him'), despising even the Muslim clergy, 'the pulpit parrots', who they accused of being in the pay of the state. In all ways he could expect the adherents to proclaim their beliefs. They would have long beards and wear traditional Islamic clothing. In today's world they would not be able to achieve their objectives through mobilising vast Islamic armies in the style of Saladin. So they had to resort to terror, and adopt a political stance.

Most terrorist organisations emanate from nationalistic or ethnic and territorial wellsprings and have a more straightforward political agenda, with more realistically attainable objectives. It is clear to the national government with whom they should deal, when it comes to this, as it eventually must. But in the case of Political Islam or Al Qaeda, who should do the dealing and with whom?

The more Bill thought about life and the more he looked back at history, the more he became convinced that many, perhaps most, of the world's problems were caused by religion. To him all religions were the imperfect attempt by man to understand the divine creation. There could never have been nothing, he thought. Therefore, there must be an infinite creator. But why did man have to create God in his own image, while claiming that man was created in God's image, as in Christianity? In all the principal religions, God was seen as a man, never a woman. But why should God have need of a sexual identification? That was something for mankind, for the animal kingdom, for insects. All religions were only man's way of explaining the inexplicable, and inevitably he couched his interpretation from the perspective of man, not of God. And each religion claimed a monopoly on truth – on a truth that they could only imperfectly perceive. Why could they not see that their way was only one possible way, one of many possible scenarios of what the truth might actually be?

So every religion excluded all other religions as not having found the path to God; of being not kosher; of being unbelievers or sacrilegious; of being infidels and apostate and Kafir.

In reality, most of man's religious activity seems to have been a mantle to disguise one or another group's grab for power. A means by which one man or some group could exercise power over many other men. Indeed, as in most ancient societies, man, as opposed to woman, had been the defining force. Men had written the rules, which were biased in favour of men over women. This had been carried on throughout the ages. In Western society women were increasingly making their voices heard and asserting their rights – their right to be equal. But here in the Middle East? And elsewhere in the Islamic world? Men were not going to allow that. This was another tectonic

75

plate defining the progress of humankind. This story was only just beginning, at a time when the struggle between Islam and Christendom was heading to a climax.

Historically, the exercise of power had, more often than not, been in a local and limited context. But Hitler, and before him, the empires of Greece and Rome – and perhaps even Great Britain – had had the aspiration to rule the whole world. Now it seemed that it was the turn of Islam to have the same aspiration. The concept of the Umma encouraged, indeed, obliged, Muslims to strive to create a universal state with no national borders, at the service of Allah and under the rule of Sharia law.

The Salafists are Old Testament: an eye for an eye, and so on. The 500 years between Christ and Muhammad is exemplified in the different stages at which both Christian and Islamic civilisations have reached.

In the Old Testament, Christian and medieval tradition there were genuine martyrs – Cranmer and others. 'Where is this in Islam?' he wondered. In Islam, it seemed to Bill that martyrdom meant killing as many innocent people as possible when you take your own life. To what end? To reach paradise? To be rewarded with seventy-two virgins, in the vernacular. Bill laughed dryly, remembering the joke that had done the rounds after the Islamic terrorist attack on Glasgow airport: 'Seventy-two virgins? In Glasgow?' Surely this was essentially selfish, and against any rational concept of the worship of a true God?

How 'believing' are the insurgents and suicide bombers, the martyrs? Is there a difference between the IRA or ETA operative and the Islamic terrorist? Is the latter more 'believing', therefore more justified in his or her actions? Or are their actions simply pragmatic and focused on the attainment of power? As Mao stated so starkly, 'power grows out of the barrel of a gun'. How much is straightforward criminality – the Ordinary Decent Crime of Northern Ireland? And to what extent is it a case of psychopaths becoming involved, conferred with a certain degree of legitimacy by virtue of the fact that they are associated with a supposedly just cause? So many questions but few answers, thought Bill resignedly.

Surely Islam does not 'allow' let alone 'promote' the idea that suicide killings are acceptable or should be aspired to? This is the corruption of men, using this as a means to exert power over their fellow men. Christianity is based on sacrifice: the self-sacrifice of one man, Jesus Christ, for the redemption of the whole world. Christ did not take people with him to his death. However, countless numbers of people have since been led to their deaths at the hands of 'Christians' supposedly acting under God's commands in holy war – the Crusades, and so on.

In Western society, man 'hath no greater love than to lay down his life for another'. To die in battle is seen as glorious. Not even the wholesale slaughter of two world wars has changed this perception.

Islam is atavistic in comparison with 'Christianity', or Western secular civilisation. Is Islam trying to recapture its lost glory, its lost empire, starting with Spain?

Christianity has never countenanced the idea of the deliberate killing of oneself to take as many of the enemy with you as possible. This is outside the mental comprehension of Western civilisation, but not of the Oriental mind, as demonstrated by the Kamikaze pilots.

The peremptory ring of his mobile dragged him out of his reverie.

'Malik here, Boss, I've got it!'

'Got what?' asked Bill. Malik had a long shopping list of things which Bill's clients wanted to know. Anodyne information, like the registration details of a company which would be readily available in any normal transparent commercial environment, was hard to get here. But here, as Bill was beginning to see more and more clearly, all was not normal.

'That mobile phone number, you remember, the one you gave me last week? It is – was – registered to bin Laden. Do you want all the details now?'

'No!' said Bill hastily, mindful of the ease with which phones could be listened to, either by mistake or deliberately. He felt a spasm of fear, as he remembered Andy's warning. 'I'll meet you in the office after lunch, in about an hour. Don't tell anyone else about this, Malik.'

'Right-oh, Boss.' Malik rang off.

When he reached the office Malik was already there. He looked particularly smug. He always did when he reckoned he had a coup. Although Bill was pretty sure Malik had no idea what this was all about, he would know the name bin Laden, as did everyone in Dubai. But he was pleased, just because he'd managed to achieve a result.

'Look!' he said. 'Here are the details: the registered user was Osama bin

Laden. I reckon I could get some itemised billing, perhaps for the last six months. It would cost, though.'

'Here, let me have a look,' Bill said, trying not to make his excitement evident. Sure enough, the print-out from the Etisalat records gave bin Laden's name, another number as well – a land-line – and the post box number. Andy would be pleased with this, thought Bill. He hadn't really believed that the number actually was connected to Osama, as Andy had thought when he had briefed him. But here was proof. He wondered what he should do next.

'Malik!' he said, suddenly. 'What about your contact in the post office? Could she find out who the post box is registered to?'

'It'll either be an individual, perhaps a local or, more likely, a company. If it is an individual, he will have to be linked to a company, unless he's a local, that is. He'll have to be sponsored by a local. Either way, we should get a lead!'

'OK,' said Bill, purposefully. 'How long?' He grinned at Malik.

'Give me a couple of days, Boss. I'm not sure if this lady is around.'

'Well, anyway, can you try straight away please?'

Malik left the office, dialling as he went.

Next day, Malik was again looking very pleased with himself when he came into the office. Immediately he buttonholed Bill and thrust a crumpled piece of paper into his hand. Peering at it, Bill saw that was the registration details for a post box. It was in the name of the Al Quoz Ceramics Company. The names of several directors of the company were listed. The details gave the plot number in the Al Quoz industrial area. This meant that it was not far from Bill's own office, just a bit further along the Sheikh Zayed Highway and off into the desert area, adjacent to the main road.

On his way back to his apartment near Al Rigga Road, Bill detoured across the Sheikh Zayed Highway into the Al Quoz industrial area. He was quickly able to find the plot belonging to Al Quoz Ceramics. A large sign with peeling black and white paint hung over the doorway of the property, which was an old corrugated iron warehouse, typical of so many in this less salubrious bit of Dubai. This place must have been one of the first to have been built in the area. It must be about twenty years old, thought Bill. It was definitely showing signs of age; a lot of the corrugated iron sheeting was beginning to rust. The whole site was nondescript, observed Bill. At first glance it seemed pretty ordinary, just like all the others in the area, and in numerous other similar sites which blighted the environs of Dubai city.

Something did not seem right to Bill but he could not put his finger on it. At this time in the evening there were only a few people around, mainly Indians or Pakistanis, who probably slept in a compound in the desert which encroached on the industrial site.

About to get into his car, he decided to have another look. This time as he approached, a security guard, an Indian, wearing an old Hard Rock café T-shirt, denim trousers and a baseball cap with the logo First Security, appeared from behind the warehouse. Bill had noticed the little guard box beside the main gate before. Now, however, he suddenly realised what he had also subconsciously registered before: the fence surrounding the facility was new, much newer, than any of the other fences in the vicinity. And it was a very high specification fence: it must have been 3 metres high, with a double overhang topped with barbed wire coils. Also, on both front corners there were small CCTV cameras. Clearly something of value was stored there; something that someone didn't want anyone else to see or get their hands on.

Once alone in his office, Bill called the number that Andy had given him: 'Peter here. I've got a present for you!' he said, and rang off. About an hour later the mobile rang. It was Andy but on a different number from the one which Bill had called. He was taking no chances.

'It's me. You've got something for me, I gather. Look, I'm tied up for the rest of the day – wall-to-wall meetings – and then a reception at the Consul's this evening. Meet me about ten tomorrow, can you? In the Crown Hotel on Bank Street, that's not far from my office, how is it for you?'

'Should be possible,' said Bill, looking at his diary. 'Yes, that's OK for me. Is that the one on the Creek side just past the Citibank tower heading towards Computer Street?'

'Yes, that's the one. I'll be in the downstairs lobby. See you there – take care.'

The Crown Hotel on Khalid bin Al Walid Street, known colloquially to the expatriate community as Bank Street, was a small three-star hotel frequented mainly by Asian businessmen and expat sports fans watching the latest sporting drama on the big screen in the upstairs bar. Like most hotels in Dubai, which focused on satisfying the demands of the flesh in an un-Islamic way, it was possible to spend a whole evening of pleasure there, starting in the bar on the first floor, having dinner in the ground-floor Italian restaurant or the second-floor Persian restaurant or in the luxurious penthouse fish restaurant, where you speared your own fish in the vast aquarium, then finishing up in the night club and the cellar bar. Bill was going to watch the England versus South Africa World Cup rugby match there later that evening.

Andy was already there when Bill arrived, sitting at one of the small round tables near the little courtesy bar in the foyer just inside the hotel entrance. Bill ordered two coffees and pleasantries were exchanged.

'What have you got for me this time?'

'Aha, right,' said Bill, 'look here, this is the information.' He pushed his notebook across the table a bit so that Andy could squint at it – the documents were inside. There were only a few people in the foyer other than the staff. They all seemed to be ignoring him and Andy but he did not want to take any chances.

'That mobile number you gave me, it is registered to OBL. The post office box address...'

'My God!' Andy interjected excitedly. 'Is it really registered to bin Laden? Let me have a look at that.' Bill could see that Andy was taken aback, surprised even. Rather smug-looking too, Bill thought. Perhaps there was more to all of this than he had thought?

'So it's true! Phew... that was a long shot – more of a guess, in fact. I didn't really believe that it would be connected. The office will be really happy with this; it gives us a good start, a chance to show the Americans that they can't do without us.'

'Hang on a minute!' said Bill, 'just let me explain it all first.' He pointed out the other details on the registration form. 'See here, this is the PO Box to which the phone is tied. You can't get one unless you are an Emirati national. Bin Laden could have been given citizenship but it doesn't look like it. You must be sponsored by a local, by a national, or have a contract of employment with a locally registered company. So, bin Laden must be sponsored by this company – here,' Bill showed Andy.

'It's the Al Quoz Ceramic Company and that's the P O Box number there – 34823,' Bill pointed to the numbers on the form. 'It also shows the plot number – from this it's possible to locate the actual place on the ground. I took a look around there after we spoke yesterday evening. It's a very nondescript area, like most of the wasteland behind the Sheikh Zayed Highway that's quickly being reclaimed from the desert. Strange thing I noticed, though. The fence on this place is virtually brand new and quite a high spec – must be 3 metres high with an overhang. It's got a guard and a couple of cameras at least, probably more round the back. That's a lot more protection than anything else in the vicinity. Whatever's in there they must think someone would like to know what it is and they don't want anyone to know! Also …'

'What's that?' exclaimed Andy, the tension showing in his voice. As Bill talked, he had been scanning the registration document from the Chamber of Commerce.

'Those are the directors of the company. This one's obviously the local…'

'I don't believe it! Hugh Davies! So he's here too – and tied up with bin Laden. This is beginning to ring a lot of alarm bells. We've been after this bastard for many years. He's been a thorn in our flesh since the Berlin Wall came down! He's usually managed to keep one step ahead of us. He's even been prosecuted a couple of times but got off scot-free. This time the office has the knives out for him. We thought that he was in Jordan. Lo and behold, the bugger's here right under our noses! Must be involved in something big to risk being here, particularly if he's tied up with bin Laden.'

'You've lost me,' said Bill, interrupting Andy's diatribe. 'What's it all about? Who is this guy?'

'He's a serial proliferator. Has a track record as long as your arm. British – a renegade. Doesn't have an ounce of morality in him. Simply after the money. He helps countries who are trying to develop a nuclear capability. He supplies the bits and pieces needed to enrich uranium, like spent fuel rods and so on. In the past he's helped Gaddafi and the Pakistanis. Not hard to guess who he's working with here, I'm sure. Can I have this?' Andy gestured to the registration document.

'Yes, sure, that copy's for you.'

'Thanks. If he's turned up here,' Andy continued, musing to himself, 'and is associating with the likes of bin Laden, that's a turn-up for the books. It really does have a very bad smell about it. I'll have to report this to the office pretty damn quick. Look's like a full day in the comms centre exchanging telegrams with London. We'll have to decide what to do about all this. Don't do anything more at the moment, please Bill… on second thoughts, would you be able to get a list of the calls that have been made from this phone, do you think?'

'I don't know. Always very difficult, this sort of thing,' Bill prevaricated. He did not want to hand it over on a plate. 'I can give it a go. You never know. Yes, leave that with me.' They left separately in different directions.

Bill got directly onto Malik. Within a couple of minutes, Malik was on the job.

Later that evening Bill headed out to the Nad Al Sheba golf course. He went along the back road past the Al Ahli football club ground. The oleander-lined road skirted the edge of the Creek where the waterway turned into a wide salt pan. It was a paradise for bird-life. Pink-hued flamingos strutted their stuff there throughout the summer months. Eventually the water drained away entirely and the desert took over. Looking back in his rear-view mirror, Bill could see the red setting sun reflected off the burgeoning skyscrapers of Deira to the left and the Sheikh Zayed Highway away to the right. He drew into the side of the road and stopped. He got out of the car and gazed at the scene. Not far off to the right in the desert he could see the camel-racing track with its iconic sail-like grandstand. A few trainers were still having some late practice with their strings of camels. Astride each beast, just discernible through the gathering dusk, the diminutive boy jockeys perched precariously on their single hump, hanging on grimly as their ships of the desert, in Lawrence of Arabia fashion, galloped past their trainers in their galumphing splay-footed charge. The camel boys were only nine or ten years old; indentured servants, indeed slaves of their rich Emirati masters, sold to them by penurious parents from the subcontinent.

An explosion of light drew Bill's eyes to the icon of that Dubai of the previous recent but now, with the headlong pace of development, seemingly long ago era. The floodlights transformed the majestic Dubai World Trade Centre tower. Built by a British architect for the former Ruler, Sheikh Raheem, with its stylish, dramatic, lattice-ornamented four-square forty-two floors, this building was the acme of an earlier, less brazen, era. The new buildings on the skyline being built by the descendants of Sheikh Raheem, which dwarfed the earlier building, did not outclass it. Rather, in their grandiose and self-promotional pretension, they seemed to illustrate an increasing secularism and a deviation and departure from the purity of faith of the true Islam. This small Bedouin tribe had been seduced by the acquisition of vast amounts of black gold.

Bill's reverie was shattered by the discordant ring of his mobile.

'Is that Bill Sloan?' a voice asked. 'My name's Arun Chandra. I work for Globalsoft. My job's to stop software piracy in the region. I've been told that you might be able to help me?'

No beating about the bush here. Globalsoft! What a great client to be able to get, Bill thought excitedly. He responded positively.

'Hi,' Bill said. 'Yes, this is Bill Sloan. I hope that I'd be able to help you. When can we meet, so you can tell me what you want?'

'Right!' said Arun purposefully. 'Any chance we could meet later this evening? I've got several urgent problems to deal with now, and I'm travelling to Mumbai first thing tomorrow morning.'

'OK,' replied Bill. 'I'm out at Nad Al Sheba right now and for a couple of hours. But if you don't mind doing it later, I could certainly do that.'

'Do you know the Biggles Bar near the airport, part of the Airport Hotel? That would suit me fine. Say, after nine o'clock?'

'Fine by me too,' said Bill, 'I've got your mobile number now in case I need to call you. See you then.'

Now getting late for his game, Bill quickly moved off to the clubhouse.

Soon after 9.30 he was in Biggles Bar. This was one of the original British expatriate-instigated pubs in Dubai. Part of the Airport Hotel, it served good beer and reasonable food, surrounded by a plethora of Biggles-era memorabilia. Arun was short, sparse and wiry, with a friendly face. An Indian, but American through schooling and culture, he headed up the Globalsoft piracy control operation in the Gulf and India. He explained that in many developed countries it was common practice for people to share proprietary software with one another as a matter of course. For most people, this was something that was taken for granted: there was no thought that this was illegal; that it was, in effect, theft.

'So, we're trying to educate the general public,' Arun said. 'That's one of my main tasks. Globalsoft loses a lot of revenue on account of this. But,' he continued, his puckish face now becoming more serious, 'it's one thing for individuals to do this. But it is altogether more serious when it's done systematically by the retail industry! It's a lot easier to shift all other boxes, if they come pre-loaded with all the latest Globalsoft software for free!'

'Yes, I can see that it is,' said Bill.

'Well, Dubai is a major culprit as far as all this is concerned; we're making the authorities aware of the problem and it takes time to get the message through. The best way – and the one that has an immediate effect – is for offenders to be fined or, better still, shut down by the Commercial Department. That way, everyone in the market gets the message.'

'I can see what you're driving at,' said Bill, 'but to do this you need proof, of course.'

'Exactly,' said Arun, 'and that's where you come in, I hope? All the retailers know me and I can't be everywhere at once anyway. So I need help.'

'What specifically would this entail?'

'What I need is to get proof of purchase of PCs which are pre-loaded with our software at the point of delivery to the customer, but where there is no charge for the software on the invoice. Then Globalsoft can take this to the Commercial Department and pressure them into taking action. They don't like it, but Globalsoft is big and has enough clout to make them sit up and take notice! They can't afford to piss off Bill Jones as they're trying to present themselves as a great place for foreign companies to do business! And, anyway, Sheikh Abdul and Bill probably know each other. They'd have met at Davos.'

'OK,' said Bill, 'this is just up my street. I have got a number of people who can do these things. Where and when do we start?'

'Tomorrow, if you can! Here, take this. It's a list of suspected offenders. Work your way through that. Send me your fees and your quotation and then send all your invoices personally to me. But be careful! These guys are all very streetwise. They know they are breaking the rules. They're as wary and clever as a bag of monkeys. Many of them are very well-protected. The biggest ones have high-rolling sponsors, with access to Sheikh Abdul's ear!'

'We'll try the first ones tomorrow,' said Bill, glancing at the list, which included the names of several significant, well-known local traders. All these companies would have a senior Emirati sponsor, who'd use his clout to keep them out of trouble and to minimise any threats or competition.

Leaving Arun, he called Rory, one of his staff. 'I've an interesting job for you! Meet me at the office at eight tomorrow, and I'll let you know what it's all about.'

24

They both got to the office in good time the following day. Rory was there first. Malik, too, was already ensconced there, poring over a pile of documents.

'Hi there! Just had a call for you,' said Rory, 'a guy called Peter Gilroy. He's the boss of the Gulf Tobacco anti-counterfeit set-up. Apparently they've got a massive problem with counterfeit cigarettes in the region, they're haemorrhaging out of China like there's no tomorrow! Wants to know what we can do to help.'

'It's already proving to be a busy day! Seems that all of a sudden everyone wants our help. Not sure how we can manage all this, but it's a great problem to have!'

'Hi, Malik, couldn't you sleep? You've never been in as early as this!' said Bill.

'But Boss,' said Malik in mock horror, 'you know I am always working round the clock for you! I have already spent over one hour at the Commercial Department.'

'What have you got there?'

'These are all the registration documents for those companies on that list from Globalsoft, the one you texted me last night,' said Malik. 'I've been checking up on them. I've got most of them but I think some are not properly registered.'

'Ehhhh… quick work!' exclaimed Bill. 'Well done. I'd like to have a look at them myself. Bring them into my office when you're finished analysing them.'

'So that's fixed then?' Bill continued. 'You get a team together and blitz the retail market. Once the word gets around that the authorities are intent on sorting out this piracy, there will be few companies that will want to continue behaving as blatantly as they're doing at the moment. There'll be some hard nuts – some will go to any lengths to continue making an illegal buck. Between us and Globalsoft's clout, the Commercial Department will be very focused on clamping down on the rogue traders.'

'When they put their minds to it, the Department's ruthlessly effective,' said Rory. 'Anyway, I've got the message. I'll head off now and get things under way. I'm just going to work my way alphabetically through the list.'

'Yes, that's as good an approach as any, given that we don't have any other basis for categorising these offenders. I'll let Arun know it's all been set up to begin immediately. Brief me at once as soon as anything interesting happens.'

Rory left. A few moments later Malik appeared in his office with the list.

'I've kept back the ones that Rory is dealing with today, Boss. There's another twenty or thirty over and above that lot.' He left the list, with all the Commercial Department's registration documents, on the desk.

After a few phone calls, and having looked at some other stuff that had come in, Bill decided to look through the list of registration documents. There were details of six companies that Bill knew well. These were all names of companies which Bill knew were all fairly large. There was another one as well, which caught his eye: Octagon Computers. He glanced at the details as he had done for the others. He was just about to put it aside and pick up the next one, when something caught his eye. His attention was attracted by the list of directors. One of them was listed as Hugh Davies. The name took him back immediately to the last conversation he had had with Andy. So what was the link between these two companies, Octagon Computers and Al Quoz Ceramics? Intrigued, he quickly looked up the details of Al Quoz and compared them with these other ones. Yes, it certainly looked like the same person. In this case there was a mobile number – that would be very helpful as he would be able to get that checked out to see what the phone records threw up. The P O Box number was the same as well. So it seemed to be more than just coincidence; more than just two separate ventures that have the same post office box but are otherwise entirely separate, such as two companies sponsored by the same local. It definitely looked like there was some closer link between them. He compared the other names of the directors of both companies. Sheikh Abdul bin Nashiri was listed as a director of both companies, and there were a couple of other names which tallied as well, one which looked Iranian and one which Bill reckoned would be Pakistani. It all seemed pretty rum, he thought.

He called Malik in: 'Here, take a look at this, Malik. See this company which we're looking at for Globalsoft? Well, I've got an interest in it for another reason – I'll tell you about it later. Something else I need urgently – and I mean urgently Malik – that phone that is registered to bin Laden, what about getting me the calls itemisation of the last three months?'

Malik nodded in his normal Confucian way. 'I can do anything around here, Boss. You know that,' he said jauntily as he went out of the office. Malik always said that, but from experience, Bill knew that the gap between expectation and achievement with Malik was frustratingly great. It was always 'Bukra, Insha'Allah', but tomorrow never came.

He frequently came up against a brick wall when it came to getting apparently very straightforward things; the sort of things that would have been in public domain documents in Britain or the US or Europe. Other things, which it would be the devil's own job to get anywhere else, were bizarrely quite easy to get here. It certainly is a topsy-turvy world, he reflected.

He rang the number he had been given for Peter Gilroy. A voice answered: 'Ah, hullo! It's Bill Sloan here. I gather that you were talking to my colleague Rory earlier on today about a problem with counterfeit cigarettes? How can I help you?'

'Good, I'm glad you called,' said a voice, in a soft American drawl. 'I'm looking at the size of the problem in this neck of the woods. Non-original we call it, non-original. We all know, everyone has known for a long time, that Dubai is at the centre of the parallel trading market for cigarettes. But now it's rapidly becoming a major centre of non-original product too. It's a hub for the whole of the Middle East and Gulf region and is causing severe damage to our main brand. A lot of people are benefiting from it at our expense.'

'I'd like to meet with you. When can we do that? You're not free now, are you?'

He had been going to fix up something quick at home. He was looking forward to an early night. He had a backlog of tapes to listen to. But hell, business was business.

'Just about to go for a run. But I guess I could make it. In about twenty minutes?'

'OK, that's good for me as I need to do something quickly and I'm only here for a couple of days. What about we have dinner? Drop by the Intercontinental about nine o'clock. There's a fine place on the top deck here – in the penthouse. Has a very fine fish restaurant, if you're into fish?'

'Sounds good to me.'

'Great! See you then. Goodbye.'

A shaven pate appeared out of the water a few seconds after Bill had settled at a nearby table. It was followed by the bronzed figure of Rory as he pulled himself effortlessly, it seemed, out of the apartment's pool. At 5' 11", slim and muscular, the obligatory six-pack rippling in the late evening sun, Rory looked the picture of health, an advertisement for the expat life in Dubai, as he sauntered casually across the marble tiles. On the way he ordered a couple of Margarita cocktails from the bar.

'Give me a couple of minutes, Boss. I'll just quickly go and change,' he said, and disappeared into the changing rooms behind them.

It was still only early February but even at this time, with the sun beginning to drop behind the Trade Centre Apartment buildings, the temperature was a comfortable 21° Centigrade. Back home in the UK everyone would be dealing with this year's unexpected snowfall, which would bring the country's transport system to a grinding halt as ever. Here, even at this time of the evening, quite a number of people were catching the sun's last rays.

Rory reappeared, their drinks arrived and they talked.

'Well, we had a pretty good day! Checked out half a dozen places on the list. Several were really cagey about software, but the majority are blatantly offering one or more Globalsoft products – in addition to the operating system – that can be bundled with the sale of the desktop. And all seem to be indicating that this extra software would be provided free, already installed on the machines and would not feature on the invoice. One company, Maghreb Software, says it can do a deal straight away. I've stood up Ahmed Al Tamsin at the Commercial Department for ten o'clock tomorrow.'

'Excellent!' said Bill. 'That seems to be a good start. If it works OK we'll go and see Arun at Globalsoft afterwards and talk through the whole thing with him.'

'One of the cagey ones I mentioned is called Octagon Computers. It's more than cagey, in fact. I went into this one myself after one of the guys mentioned it. Completely different from any of the other outlets, which are the normal Arab street-trader type. You know, a lot of noisy activity, haggling about the price, sales chat, trying hard to hassle customers into a quick sale, lots of special offers but all done in a bantering good-humoured way!'

'Yep, I know what you mean,' said Bill. 'Go on.'

'Well, this place is very different – sort of spooky, not much obvious activity, suspicious and unsmiling staff and no real attempt being made to sell anything. Looks like they're simply going through the motions. Quite a lot of fairly heavy security as well – CCTV cameras and so on! Anyway, I need to go now to meet one of the guys down at Spinney's supermarket.'

'OK, we'd better mention this to Arun. Thanks for all that. See you tomorrow then?'

Rory left – leaving also the bill. 'Fair enough,' thought Bill. If Rory had paid he would then claim it back from the company anyway.

Moving away from the pool towards the adjacent gardens, amid the heavily-scented oleanders, Bill made a brief call to Malik.

'Busy, Malik?'

'You know me, Boss, always busy!'

'Malik, I know you only too well. Who are you trying to stitch up now with one of your fancy deals? Look, another urgent thing for you. Can you get all the data on a company called Octagon Computers? It's on Computer Street, Rory was there earlier. Hey… fast, top priority, Malik!' He rang off.

Pausing at his apartment on the way past for a quick change, Bill was soon back in his car and crossing the Al Maktoum Bridge. At this time of the night everyone and his dog was out and about in Dubai. It was possible to move only at a snail's pace across the bridge but eventually Bill was able to peel off to the right, circle round beneath the flyover and head along the Creek-side road. Parking near the Intercon Hotel was never easy at the best of times but he was finally able to squeeze the small BMW into a slot between two large 4x4s. Like most of their type in the Emirates, neither vehicle looked as if the 4-wheel drive capability was ever required.

Riding the lift to the seventh floor, Bill entered the elegant foyer. At this level in the hotel, as in all Dubai hotels, there were several restaurants offering competing national cuisines. People in the foyer were already clearly waiting for dinner partners. They were all male. After a quiet analysis, Bill selected a short, stocky individual of about mid-fifties, balding, with short grey hair as his most likely companion. Instinctively their eyes locked and a look of recognition seemed to pass quickly over the other man's face. They moved towards each other and introductions were effected. They found a table in the seafood restaurant.

With their fish selected from the giant illuminated tank, cooked and on the table, and a crisp Sancerre well broached, they turned to business.

Bill liked Peter Gilroy's no-nonsense approach. He was based in Cyprus in Gulf Tobacco's regional office. Bill was surprised at how much he knew about what was going on in Dubai.

'I've been dealing with this area for about fifteen years now for my company. The last six have been in our compliance set-up dealing with parallel trading and non-original product – that's the term for counterfeit,' said Peter, obviously enjoying holding the floor.

No sooner had they put down their knives and forks than the hovering waiter swooped down and removed them. Sometimes there was too much service in Dubai, Bill thought. No time to savour the first course before one was being pressured to select the next. Like London buses, there were often too many waiters and sometimes none.

'As I was saying,' Peter continued, 'the non-original product is my real problem at the moment.'

An interesting terminology, Bill thought to himself as the waiter, again in evidence, promptly removed more plates and cutlery. To Bill, the term non-original sounded like a euphemism – a cop-out. It gave an impression of ambiguity, of not being prepared to call a spade a spade.

'Parallel trading's when an agent sells genuine product into another market for which he has no agency deal.'

'Perhaps, if it's original product and not counterfeit, it's fair game for some agents?' queried Bill.

'Well, you can see how it all works,' said Peter. 'Here in Dubai the agencies for tobacco products are invariably held by sheikhs. Sheikhs who are both immensely rich and powerful. They're certainly aware that it's good business to trade in counterfeit – or should we say, non-original – if you're one of those with sufficient political clout to protect your business from interfering foreigners.'

Gilroy continued: 'This region is awash with non-original product. The size of the problem has increased exponentially over the last four or five years. Ever since the Communist Party of China started to take on a distinctly capitalist hue!

'China has the largest per capita consumption of cigarettes of almost any country in the world. There are about 350 million smokers. That's more than the total population of the US. There are legions of cigarette-manufacturing factories throughout the country. Making cigarettes is a bog-standard, low-tech activity, and there are plenty of good forgers able to produce cigarette paper, wrappers and boxes to a very high standard. Even the brand owners can't always tell them apart.'

'And China is a kind of Wild West market at present, isn't it? No central control on this sort of thing and a sophisticated and energetic people thrusting to break out of the Communist strait jacket?' said Bill.

'Exactly,' said Peter. 'What would you say if I told you that we estimate there are twenty containers – that's 40-foot containers – of non-original product in Port Said at any one moment?'

'My God! That sounds like one hell of a lot of cigarettes,' said Bill.

'Some 200 million, to be precise. There's a whole series of people to be paid off along the way – police, customs, managers and so on – but they still can make a hundred thousand dollars trading a container of genuine product into a parallel market, so just imagine what you can make on a container of counterfeit. Unit costs are insignificant and the mark-up's massive!'

Their table overlooked the Creek. At this time of night, the whole of Dubai stretched out before them, with the magnificent Trade Centre Building on the horizon, illuminated like a fairytale world. Everything seemed so pure, so perfect and without threat. It was an Islamic wonder-world – a magic kingdom. But Bill was being rudely exposed to the true Dubai in all that he was now becoming involved with. Underneath the idyllic surface was a ruthless and grasping reality.

Peter said, 'I've been coming to Dubai now for several years, but only on brief trips. I always stay in this hotel and I usually eat in this restaurant. I meet with our agents, and, perhaps, talk to the Customs out at Jebel Ali, but I don't really get to know any of these places that I visit.

'Take Egypt, for example. I despair of being able to achieve anything there, ever. It's all so venal. Everyone, it seems, is on the take. But it's all accepted as perfectly normal! In order to get any official to even start to do what you think he's paid to do, you have to bribe him. It's completely blatant. There's no shame at all.'

'How much is he paid – the ordinary official, I mean? How much?' interjected Bill.

'That's the operative point. Most officials in places like Egypt are paid only a pittance, and even then they are probably only paid months in arrears. It's every man for himself from the President down. But I guess Dubai's different?'

'I haven't been here very long, Peter, but as far as I can see it's a case of "yes and no"! Certain officials appear to be straight and official – very upright and proper. And everything is very well administered, the bureaucracy is very efficient. The legal framework is good and generally well administered too.'

Bill continued, 'But… but – and there is a "but" – I can't put my finger on it but the more I get asked to do things by clients like yourself, the more I get the feeling that "there's something rotten in the state of Denmark", to coin a phrase.

'However, what they have done here is amazing. It's this blaze of light in the middle of an otherwise barren desert, the thrusting clutch of skyscrapers, a host of taxis and 4x4s and the ubiquitous white Mercs with their fabulously wealthy locals at the wheel in their immaculate dishdashas!'

'I could look at this view for hours,' said Peter.

'Yes,' said Bill, 'I agree, it does seem like paradise. Look down there, to the right along the side of the creek. You see all those large piles of boxes? That is all stuff about to be loaded onto the dhows and shipped to Iran. Bandar Abbas is only about six hours' sailing from here.'

'Right-oh,' said Peter, 'this brings us nicely to the reason we're meeting here. Are all those items – the TVs, fridges, air-conditioners, whatever – going to be traded legally? Are the WTO rules going to be observed?'

'I wouldn't know,' said Bill.

'Well, I wouldn't bet my bottom dollar that they would be. It's a pound to a pinch of shit, as you limeys say, that most will be smuggled into Iran or somewhere else. Perhaps the east coast of Africa as well. Most of that stuff is the genuine article, but I bet you that there is also a significant proportion that's counterfeit,' Peter said emphatically.

'It's the same for our business, as I mentioned earlier. This region is awash with counterfeit oscillating from port to port waiting for a buyer: Limassol, Piraeus, Port Said, Jebel Ali, Mersin. And Dubai is certainly one of the principal hubs. If all cigarettes imported into Dubai were smoked by the population here, then each citizen would be smoking a couple of million a week!

'What I need,' he continued, 'is support on the ground. The customs, the Commercial Department, the police and so on, are ambivalent. They know that in order to prosper and become a significant player on the world stage, to attract tourism and to build up income streams to replace the oil when it runs out in the not too distant future, they have to be seen to be playing by the rules. So they have the legal framework to ensure protection of intellectual property rights, and so on. They've even joined the World Trade Organisation.'

'I know,' said Bill. 'The Head of Dubai Customs was last year's President. He's the one who went to Davos with the boss and was then locked up for corruption!'

'Right on, that's the ambivalence. They've done all the right things as it were, so, on the surface, they're kosher. But... '

Bill interjected: 'They want to have their cake and eat it?'

'That's just it; you've put your finger on it. While they want to attract the world to their doors, there are a lot of people, some very senior and close to the Ruler, who benefit from being able to trade illegally – not that they would consider it illegal. To them anything that makes a dime is legal. These people have too much political power to be ignored.'

'I'm beginning to get the picture,' said Bill.

'Good! The only way in which a company like mine can move the situation forward to get a level playing field is to keep the pressure on through the WTO, diplomacy and so on the one hand, and by providing specific incontrovertible proof on the other hand in specific cases of fraud.'

'So if I can help you get the evidence?' said Bill.

'Exactly! Then perhaps, with our collective muscle, the cigarette companies can bring pressure to bear on the government. The same way as the pharma companies are trying to do.'

'Not with much success, however, so I've been told,' said Bill. 'There's a conflict of interest as the Emiratis very much want to support their home-grown industry. To help you then, I've got to get my people out and into the market to insinuate themselves into the gangs who are running these counterfeit operations?'

'Can you do that?' said Peter.

'I'm sure I can,' said Bill, cautiously. 'But, of course, it won't be easy and it could be very risky. Particularly because Dubai is such a fishbowl and the whole region's very incestuous. Just like the fact that, sitting over there in Cyprus, you still manage to know a lot about what's going here.'

After some further discussion, Peter evidently thought that Bill might be worth trusting. He gave him a large wad of documents, including some reports. As Bill took them, they left the restaurant and, descending in the lift, strolled across to the main hotel's main entrance.

'Have a look at these and see what you can make of them,' Peter said. 'This is some research which I had my people in Limassol do with head office in London. They have a large intelligence section there. It's got some names of people and companies in Dubai who they think are involved. Let me know if you think you can do anything with it and whatever it'll cost. I don't have a very big budget. Some board members would just as soon take the cost of counterfeit on the nose. As far as they're concerned, it's simply a cost of production!'

'Or else they have another agenda of their own?' suggested Bill as he said goodbye and strode off to his car, saying over his shoulder, 'I'll call you in a couple of days, no more.'

'The question is,' said Rory, 'do we have enough resources to do the thing properly? It'd be pretty risky at the best of times, but we really need more people, more cars and so on.'

They were in the office having a brainstorming session to decide how to handle all the new work. If only they had the resources, they could do so many things. But the wholehearted co-operation of the authorities was also necessary.

'It's hard to believe the level of inertia in the Commercial Department. There's a lot of bullshit and superficial posturing, but not a lot of positive reaction to anything we've ever reported to them involving cases of counterfeiting and so on,' Rory commented.

Was this just plain laziness, Bill wondered, or did it indicate that there was something altogether more sinister driving this attitude? 'It's not as if they have to do any work. We hand it to them on a plate. They simply have to turn up and nab all the villains, after we've set them up for an arrest,' he said.

'Money talks!' said Rory. 'We have to get hold of some people in the business, and pay them more than they'll get from the official deal.'

'Yes,' said Bill, 'but more than that we've either got to pay them sufficient to make it worth their while to take the risk of ending up in jail, or we do a deal with the police to ensure that such peoples will be given immunity from prosecution.'

'Easier said than done, Boss,' said Malik, who had been following the conversation with interest.

'Look Rory, you and Malik! How about if you get out in the market, contact those people Peter Gilroy gave us, and try to insinuate yourselves into the business? Could you do that, Malik? You're the obvious person to do it as you have Arabic and Hindi. Rory can act as your wing man. Nose around and try to get alongside someone who's involved in a deal and then try to get yourself involved too. Outbid the other buyers if necessary.'

'Well, I know everyone in the market, Boss. Some are involved in tobacco deals, but also I know some people in the port police and customs. I'll keep my ear to the ground and put it around that I represent a large Mumbai distributor. I have a cousin in Mumbai who would be able to back that up.'

'What do you think, Rory?'

'Sounds OK to me but our cover will be pretty thin; unless, that is, Peter Gilroy's prepared to stump up the wherewithal to set up some front companies through which we can transact sufficient proper business to set up a track record and establish our cover!'

'Yep,' said Bill, 'I'm with you on that. We'll need to bring in more firepower or we'd be blown out of the water as soon as we make a move. Did you know,' he continued, 'that HMG is so concerned about syndicated crime – that's Mafia business to you and me – that they've actually had the police, MI5 and MI6 sit down together with the customs to see what they can do to sort out the problem?!'

Rory's eyebrows shot up, 'That'll be a first!' he said. They laughed.

'Apparently,' Bill continued, as the possibilities this offered began to develop in his brain, 'the UK Exchequer is being done out of about four billion pounds a year through the loss of tax revenue. That's on genuine fags which don't have duty paid on them!'

'How does that do anything for us?' Rory interjected. 'Our clients are the cigarette companies – they couldn't give a stuff who buys it. It's the purchaser who has to pay the tax, so they're sitting pretty.'

'Yes, but there's a wider agenda,' said Bill. 'Drugs! For the Mafia gangs there's no such thing as illegal and legal business. It's all either just good business or bad business, depending upon the size of the profit. The only other factor which concerns them is risk. Dealing in parallel-traded cigarettes is less risky than trading in counterfeit, which in turn is less risky than dealing in drugs.

'The British Government's pissed off at losing tax revenue. And no reputable government wants counterfeit on the patch. But the real threat to the government is from the drugs. So it's more, much more than just a financial issue. The drug money is used to fund terrorism and the Mafia are the best at building the businesses: supply chains, distribution networks, and so on. And where do the bulk of the drugs come from in this region?'

'Afghanistan!' exclaimed Rory. 'So the Mafia gangs peddling genuine cigarettes into the UK and other European countries are linked in an un-virtuous circle with the Taliban, Al Qaeda, the Iranians and all stations east!'

'Exactly. So Kipling was wrong – East is East and West is West, but, in this unholy alliance, the twain do meet,' said Bill.

'If we're to do anything worthwhile to help Gulf Tobacco, we need to widen the net. We all know how incestuous this place is – if we're only working in the local market, using local people as sources and making seizures, we'll be dead in the water before we start. I reckon we need to look at all this on a regional basis. So if, say, we get a hot tip here but we can arrange it so that the seizure takes place in Cyprus or Mersin, then it'll be much more difficult for the gangs to work out where the info's coming from. Source protection's all important in this game!

'So, you guys look after the local market. If you develop sources and so on, I'll concentrate on the wider aspects. Then with luck we can join it all together. I have a couple of chums in Cyprus and also some contacts in Egypt,' he concluded.

'I've been looking at this dossier that you dumped on my desk! There are several companies that seem to be up to no good, particularly Disney Trading,' said Rory. 'I vote that you and I sit down together, Malik, and work out a plan to penetrate this company.'

All agreed, and the meeting finished with Bill making arrangements to go to Cyprus. He called Peter Gilroy.

'Is that you, Bill? Good to hear from you. I've just got off a plane in Bogata`. What's the gen?'

'We're working on a plan to penetrate several local companies, and also to look outside Dubai as well. I won't go into details on the phone, but we'll need some decent funding if we're to make this work. Unless we set this up professionally, we won't get anywhere at all. Particularly here – and I know it's the same in Egypt – these gangs have a lot of powerful top cover. And I mean top!'

'Right,' said Peter, 'I hear what you say. I don't have any resources at my disposal other than money. So, if I provide the funds, you'll provide the other resources on the ground, is that what you're saying?'

'You've got it in one, Peter. These gangs are very switched-on. Apart from having protection, they're completely ruthless, as you know as well as I do. Particularly where you are just now, I'd say!'

'OK, I must go now, send me a costed proposal. I'll be back in Cyprus the day after tomorrow and will try to get a quick decision.'

'Excellent,' said Bill. 'Look, I'm planning to get over to Cyprus anyway. So we can meet up then and I'll talk through with you how I see it all going.'

'Call my secretary, Maria. Set up a time to meet on Friday. Goodbye.'

The setting sun dappled through the vine leaves in the overhead trellising. It was a beautiful balmy evening and the fragrant scent of orange blossom enslaved Bill's senses. It took him back to his first trip to Aphrodite's island all those years ago on his way back from Aden, the beauty here contrasting vividly with the mean streets there. The bride, in her white lace-covered dress and train, and the bridegroom emerging from Bellapais Abbey to the sounds of the bouzouki. Then the same delicious scent had hung heavy in the air. The dark-jowled groom had led his bride joyously up through the village above Cyrenia, up the steep time-rounded stones of the narrow streets, past the Bitter Lemons house of Lawrence Durrell into the mountainside. As they sat at the Harbour Club bar, looking across the Mediterranean to the clearly discernible mainland of Turkey, the haunting strains of the bouzouki had traced the path of the happy couple.

Dick materialised with a couple of cool beers in tall iced glasses. In the dappled light under the olive tree, the sun shafted off the glasses, changing direction with the gently swaying leaves. They chatted for some time with the easy familiarity of those who trust and respect each other on the basis of a friendship and comradeship born in the shared experience of adversity. Although it was several years since they had last met, they might well have been together only the day before.

Eventually Dick said, 'It's great to see you after all this time, but I get the feeling that you haven't turned up on my doorstep entirely by chance?'

'You're absolutely right, as ever,' Bill responded with a laugh. 'However,

I didn't want to say too much on the phone. I could do with your help, that's providing you're not completely retired?'

It was Dick's turn to laugh. 'I'm all ears!'

'Well, I'm investigating counterfeit cigarette scams in the region.' He explained the background to Dick.

'Sounds like old times,' mused Dick, ordering another couple of beers from the waitress. 'So where do I come in? Mind you, I don't think I really need to answer that question!'

'No, I'm sure you know the answer better than I do!'

They laughed, relaxed but energised as the prospect of another campaign quickened their pulses in the idyllic surroundings of the Grapevine. To the casual observer it would have seemed incomprehensible that they could be discussing getting entangled in such a seedy underworld. Indeed, it was hard to imagine that this underworld existed here in Cyprus, any more than it appeared to in Dubai.

'I have some very good contacts in the police,' Dick began. 'That's the Sovereign Base Area police, and the Cypriot police as well. I also know some people at the Embassy in Nicosia, including the local resident, a guy called Paul Ambrose. When I was detached from the SAS to the Firm, he and I did an op together. Long time ago now in a different era. I remember that we had some lectures from an old and overweight gentleman who cheerfully instructed us in how to blow up trains. Sadly I never had the chance to put this into practice, although many's the time I thought of doing it standing on a dilapidated station platform on a freezing January morning, and the 07:48 late again!

'Anyway,' he resumed, 'I've seen Paul a couple of times since he arrived just before Christmas. He's got several people working with him, including a customs guy.'

'I knew I could count on you, Dick!' Bill exclaimed. 'That's exactly what I was hoping to hear. The customs bloke will be the Drugs Liaison Officer – there's one in Dubai too. They're at the heart of the government's inter-agency push on drugs.'

During the next couple of days Bill and Dick developed a plan of action, roping in a friend and former colleague with whom they had both worked over the years. Terry McBride was a veteran of the IRA campaign. He had worked with them both in Belfast, when he was an undercover police officer. 'Left when I got the warning from the boyos; wasn't fair on my family.'

'Do you remember Terry McBride?' Dick had asked that first evening at the Grapevine. 'He lives here in Cyprus. Been here about ten years now. Definitely the person to get inside the local gangs, to sniff out what's going on.'

Terry had jumped at the idea of getting into action again; he had been missing the excitement. The adrenaline-fuelled kick, as an inside source passed him a crucial nugget of information. He had missed living on the edge.

Bill and Dick then had lunch with Paul Ambrose at the Embassy. He also agreed to work with them. It was all in line with HMG policy. They put together a bid, with some costings. Bill e-mailed it to Peter Gilroy. His secretary, Maria, called him a couple of hours later. They went to his office in Limassol immediately. Over a cup of coffee, they elaborated their ideas.

'OK, gentlemen,' said Peter, 'I like your ideas – they seem to stack up. You've done well to move so fast. So we'll give it a try. I've spoken with my colleagues. We've agreed to let you run this programme for a three-month trial. I'll wire the initial fee payment – 10 per cent up front – to you tomorrow. Then I'll expect monthly invoices.'

Bill and Dick stood up to go.

'One final point,' said Peter. 'This is a straightforward commercial deal as far as you and I are concerned. However, as far as Gulf Tobacco is concerned, this is all off the record. In other words, it's deniable, so don't screw up!'

Bill drove up the Al Wasl Road. It was after midnight. He turned back on himself at the Choitrams roundabout and then took the second left turning into the desert near the mosque. The mosque was brightly lit. The area here was desert, but the municipality format had been imposed so that roads had been built. Yet, there was nothing other than a few scattered houses, which had been there before the planners' plan was made. There were some large compounds closed off to the outside world, behind high walls and gates. There was a short row of five or six large smart new villas. Across the road from them stood another large new property. Bill's target lived here. Hamid Al Fadl was the sales manager of RAKA.

A few days earlier, Bill had met with Riad and Red to discuss the latest information from Graham Booker.

'We've had some expert analysis done on the historic price of aluminium,' Riad began. 'This has concluded categorically what I instinctively knew, namely that RAKA has been selling its product at a price substantially below the median world market price assessed against any meaningful criteria. It's easy to check this. The market is essentially controlled by the LME. That's the London Metal Exchange,' Riad explained for Bill's benefit. 'This has been going on for at least ten years.'

'Bloody hell!' said Bill, 'what sort of amount below the LME price?'

'Give or take 10 per cent,' interjected Red. 'That's at least $150 million at a conservative estimate!' There was a pause while they each reflected on the enormity of the loss of revenue implied by what Riad had said.

'But that's not all,' continued Riad. 'By the same token, RAKA seems to have been paying about 10 per cent more for all the raw products, material, and so on, which it requires. That would mean they spent an extra $100 million or so to make the aluminium.'

'Which means,' said Red, taking up the account, 'that we're talking about a total loss to RAKA – to Dubai, in effect – of something like a quarter of a billion US dollars! The evidence leaves absolutely no doubt. This was all one fucking big fraud! And we can prove that on the basis of the expert witness testimony.'

'OK then, if you can prove it all already, what do you need from me?' asked Bill.

'Well, we can prove that RAKA lost out because of the contracts which its officers negotiated on its behalf. But they'll obviously say that they did everything in good faith, and if they can convince their Lordships in the High Court that this was the case, or more to the point, if we can't prove otherwise, the buggers will get away scot-free.'

'Yes, I can see that,' said Bill. 'What you need is some evidence that specific people in the RAKA hierarchy enriched themselves at the expense of the company; that, between them all, they pocketed the $250 million?'

'Exactly,' said Red, 'so we need you to check out the ownership of all the various entities involved. And to follow the money trail – to see what funds changed hands between RAKA and these companies and were then siphoned off to the key individuals.'

'Got that,' said Bill. 'Let's agree where we're starting from: we're already looking at Luke Stanley; you've told me about Mohammed Al Turk. Obviously, we need to look at other Dubai and RAKA people who might be involved. Anybody else, any other companies?'

'Hamid Al Fadl, for a start,' said Riad. 'He's the sales manager. If Stanley was up to something, then Al Fadl must have been aware of it. So he would have to be in cahoots, or been paid off to turn a blind eye.'

'There are several other entities involved too,' said Red, taking up the running. 'Gulf Resources Company handles all Dubai's sales and purchasing.'

'I'm sure I've heard that name before,' said Bill, trying to place it. 'I remember,' he said, 'I saw their logo on a sign at the golf club, when we were playing there last week. Aren't they sponsoring one of the races at the World Cup horse race that Dubai's hosting next month at Nad Al Sheba? Lots of hype building up on this event; it's going to have a pretty global reach, some well-known celebrities due to attend as well.'

'That could be a little more than embarrassing,' said Riad, 'if it transpires that GRC was effectively defrauding the Dubai government!'

'You're fucking right it would!' Red fulminated. 'There's also a guy called Hani Mubarak behind it,' he continued, 'he's a Lebanese, but he's been in the Gulf for a long time. He's a cohort of Mohammed Al Turk.'

'We'll certainly check him out too,' said Bill.

'And we shouldn't forget about RAKA International,' said Riad. 'That company was set up by Stanley about five years ago – has some links to Iran, apart from anything else. But it took over the sales and purchase contracts for RAKA because of earlier suspicions about what was going on. Stanley and Al Turk were able to brush this aside – they were powerful enough then, as the old man was still alive. We don't know much about who is behind the company or about some of the parties it's buying from and selling to.'

'What about bugging their phones?' said Red. 'Could you do that?'

'Certainly,' said Bill. 'If you give me the authority. You work for Mahmoud, he represents the government. Technically, it's easy – just a case of joining a couple of wires together really. The difficult part's not letting anyone know, unless it can be done officially through Gulf Communications?'

'Can't do that,' said Red. 'Dubai's not a democracy with a homogeneous government and bureaucracy. Everyone's out to shaft everyone else, to get the Ruler's ear and gain influence. And,' he continued, 'Mahmoud doesn't get on well with the bosses of Etisalat and CID.'

'What exactly are you saying?'

'If you get caught by the police, they'll bang you up if you say you work for Mahmoud. The local cop will immediately call his boss, and he'll rub his hands with glee. He won't, of course, call Mahmoud. But he will call the Ruler!'

'But what we would be doing would be done for the Ruler at the end of the day,' said Bill. 'Dubai's an oligarchy. The government and the royal family are one and the same thing and it's simply run as a family business,' he protested.

'That doesn't matter a shit,' said Red, 'the Ruler would be embarrassed. Wouldn't be prepared to admit that he knew what you were doing. He'd just hang Mahmoud out to dry.'

'And in turn,' Riad took up the warning, 'Mahmoud would hang you out to dry, and then the police would throw the book at you!'

'There's gratitude for you!' said Bill disconcertedly. 'Doing it clandestinely would pose all sorts of problems.'

'Such as?' challenged Red.

'Well, for starters, it would be one hell of a job to identify the right two wires without the official records. Then there's the little issue of actually listening to the calls. Do you do it in real-time? But that means someone listening twenty-four hours a day – clearly impracticable. So you record everything. But someone's still got to trawl through all the tapes and make sense of it all, and then select any material of interest. Then it's got to be transcribed and annotated so that someone – probably you, Riad – can read or listen to what's important and not waste time listening to the dross: the target's daughter chatting interminably to the current love of her life, or to her friend about how great the sex was last night – even more boring – or some other trivial crap. And then, of course, there's the language problem. I know Dubai's lingua franca is English but, apart from Arabic, in this polyglot society lots of people speak Hindi, Urdu and Farsi. The way people flip from one language to another, you'll need interpreters for every language.'

None the less, it had been decided to go ahead with monitoring Hamid Al Fadl's home phone.

Finally they came back to the information from Graham. Bill began: 'Those telephone bills you gave us. Graham's done some digging about in Switzerland, around the time in May last year when Stanley made several calls from there to Dubai. It transpires that he stayed in the Grand Hotel in

Zug for a couple of nights. Mohammed Al Turk and his lawyer, a Brit called Owens, were also there at the same time!'

'Zug – that's where Stanley has that UBS account!' said Red.

'Exactly,' said Bill. 'It all seems to fit together. And that's not all. It may be more than coincidence that another guest in the hotel at the same time was Marc Rich.'

'The Metal Man!' exclaimed Riad. 'Is he tied up in all this too?'

'Graham's already onto it. He'll check all Marc Rich's companies and so on.'

That had been two days ago. Bill had since been joined by Yigal Shomek and they were together now. Yigal was an ex-Mossad operative. He didn't discuss his past, but rumour had it that he managed to find and bug the house of one of the Black September leaders, Abu Daoud, so everything that was said in the house was fed back live to Tel Aviv, where the Israeli Cabinet was able to listen to it.

Al Fadl's house was in an exposed area. Just across and down the road to the side of this house was a narrow track. This ran past it and a couple of adjacent houses, to an open space behind Choitrams supermarket. The other side of the track had a high chain fence, behind which was a DEWA water purification plant. The path was a short cut for pedestrians. It could be negotiated by 4x4s but there were plenty of better alternatives. Provided all the houses did not have their side rooms lit up, the track was secluded and dimly lit.

The previous night Yigal and Bill had reconnoitred the area. The telephone cable from Al Fadl's house ran along the line of the fence to the junction box in the open space beyond.

Stopping the car a quarter of a mile away, Bill and Yigal slipped into the white dishdashas, fastened with an ogal, which they had bought that afternoon in the Deira souq. There was no-one about as they crossed the wasteland towards Al Fadl's house. Crouching down midway along the fence, Bill carefully shielded the torch. Yigal's fingers quickly located the telephone cable. In the still darkness, the snap of the pliers clipping the cable seemed to Bill like a rifle shot. Yigal bared the wires. It was the work of only a couple of minutes for him to connect the wires of the recording device to the line. Then they put it in a plywood box to keep out the sand. While Yigal duck-taped the bare wires, Bill quickly scooped out a hole under the large dollop of cement supporting a fence post a few feet away, put the box in the hole and covered it all with sand. Moving leisurely in order to avoid suspicion, they took a roundabout way back to the car. They saw nobody, and felt pretty sure that no-one had seen them. Their pulse rates dropping to normal, they drove back into Dubai.

30

They had decided that Bill should change the tapes nightly. Bill was reluctant to do this so frequently. He did not want to run the risk of setting up a pattern and getting caught. But it was important not to lose anything significant or – even more frustrating – get some piece of dynamite too late, now that they had taken such a risk to set up the operation in the first place.

The next evening, he approached the area warily. Yigal had gone back to the UK that morning. Bill had warned him that he might be needed again very soon. There was no shortage of potential targets whose phone conversations would prove very helpful in investigating fraud at RAKA. There was no doubt that it was massive and had been going on for years. But there was much doubt about exactly who was involved. The more he looked into it, the more apparent it became to Bill that its tentacles spread deeply into the fabric of Dubai, like a cancerous growth striking at the very body politic itself.

It was Thursday evening and the area around the Choitrams roundabout was busy with the expatriate community shopping in advance of the weekend. Turning into the desert area behind the supermarket, Bill found a suitable parking spot adjacent to an unlit wall behind the local school. Again, he changed into the Arabic clothing. 'What would happen to me,' he wondered, 'if I got caught by the police looking like this?' Was he breaking the law? Perhaps Sharia had some prescription against non-Muslims wearing Islamic clothing? Would it be considered an affront to the Prophet? As he pulled the dishdasha over his head, having first had a cautious look around to see that the coast was clear, Bill wondered nervously about whether Mahmoud Al Abdullah would in fact be able to bail him out, would in actual fact even try to bail him out, should the shit hit the fan. He was not at all sure; he certainly did not have any 'get out of jail free' card from Sheikh Mansour. Red's warning that Mahmoud and the chief of police, General Mohammed din Al Dawley, did not get on with each other rang in his ears.

'Like all apparatchiks, they are always competing with each other for the Ruler's ear and a larger share of Dubai's largesse,' Red had said. 'Many of them hate each other's guts.'

'Just like in the UK with New Labour,' replied Bill. 'Blair and Brown needed the Third Man to keep them from each other's throats. With his Svengali-like scheming he had them dancing to his tune. They both hated him.'

'But not as much as they hate each other!' said Red.

Only a couple of weeks ago Bill had shared a lift alone with Mahmoud down from Level 33 in the Trade Centre. At Mahmoud's request, he had given him a brief resume of how the investigation was going. That was the day before Yigal had arrived.

'Be very careful,' said Mahmoud, his open, boyish features clouding over. 'Whatever you do, don't let the CID catch you.'

However, the die had been cast. The equipment was in position. Now was not the time to let cold feet deflect him from his task. He could not back out now.

Getting out of the car, he walked circumspectly across the desert towards Al Fadl's house. Although he was worried about the consequences of getting discovered as an expatriate wearing Arabic clothes, equally they afforded him a sense of protection. To some extent, he felt invisible. Al Fadl's house was in an area of expensive, modern villas. However, this was not an area where Western expatriates tended to live. They were all further down towards the beach road and the sea. Here the occupants were well-off Arabs and Indians, not local Arabs but foreign Arabs: Iranians, Egyptians, Palestinians, Yemenis. At this time of night, most of these people were behind the high walls of their compounds. It was well after eleven o'clock, so there was not a lot of movement. But Bill was sure that wandering around in the area at this hour he would attract less attention as an Arab than as a Westerner.

He passed by Al Fadl's house on his left and went along the pathway where the device was hidden, along the chain-link fence, and out into the open ground beyond. The fluorescent lights in the municipality workshop compound cast an eerie light over the surrounding area, leaving alternating patches of darkness and bright light. The light just by the main gates was only 10 metres from the device. The houses across the street here had no lights on this side; their main entrances were all on the other side. All seemed clear.

It was the work of only a few minutes to retrieve the buried recorder, dust off the sand which had penetrated the shoebox in which it was wrapped, take out the cassette, put in a new one, wrap the machine up again, replace it in the custom-made wooden harness, and bury it as before. Carefully levelling off the sand and using the palm leaf which he had taken care to collect, Bill quickly smoothed out the area around the hide, taking particular care to get rid of any tell-tale footprints leading off the main path which might attract the attention of anyone, perhaps the guards in the municipality facility. He had no reason to suppose that anyone would be taking any notice of such things, let alone actually looking for a buried device. But in this game, thought Bill, you could not be too careful.

It was essential to practise tradecraft; not to take anything for granted, not to relax. By the time he got back to his car and was on his way back to Dubai, only some ten minutes had passed since he had parked there. But to Bill, it had seemed interminable: his nerves on edge, expecting at any moment to be interrupted and to have to explain himself to an inquisitive local.

Back in his apartment and despite the lateness of the hour, Bill immediately started listening at random to the tape. The clarity of the recording was excellent; he could clearly hear everything which was said between Al Fadl or someone else using his phone and the callers at the other end. Mostly it was just chat, routine domestic stuff: had the driver been to pick up the laundry from Satwa? What time was he to collect the children from the cinema? Al Fadl's wife ordering a carry-out meal from the Indian curry stall on the corner by the chemists in Rashidiya. Bill knew that all he would get would be a snapshot of Al Fadl's contact with other people, not all the picture by any means. Not what he said in face-to-face conversations at home or in the office. Not what he said, nor to whom he said it, when using his mobile – everyone in Dubai was wedded to their mobiles. But it was always like this in the intelligence game. One saw through a glass darkly. The blanks had to be filled in by other sources or by assumption. Bill remembered Sandy's warning all those years ago: 'assumption is the mother of all fuck-ups!' It was all too easy to draw the wrong conclusions – to try to make the facts fit into one's preconceptions – and end up barking up the wrong tree. Suddenly Bill felt ineffably tired; the nervous tension of the evening's activities had caught up with him. He took the dishdasha out of the small bag from his car and quickly put it in the washing machine. After switching it on, he lay down on his bed, not even bothering to take off his clothes.

He was awake at six o'clock. At once, he started to listen to the complete tape, transcribing as he went. Fortunately Al Fadl, a Bahraini Arab, spoke in English for most of the calls. Quickly, it became clear that he had two businesses. Some of the calls were to colleagues in Dubai. Al Fadl seemed to spend a lot of time not in his office in RAKA, despite having a full-time job there. More than that, though, it became apparent that much of Al Fadl's business activities involved a separate business, which was based in London. This company was in metal trading. But it was not easy for Bill to work out exactly what was going on. He did not at first recognise any of the other voices; working out who was who would require time.

It had been a call made yesterday morning, about eight o'clock, which had first attracted his attention: 'Hi there, Hamid, it's me. Sorry to call you so early.'

'I'm just getting my first coffee. What's on your mind? When are you planning to come back to Dubai?'

'Early next week – I want to be back in the office for the meeting on Monday with the contractors of the new pot line. ABB has a team coming over from Switzerland. There could be quite a lot in it for you and me if we play our cards right.'

'OK, OK, don't go into too much detail on this,' said Al Fadl, guardedly. 'As you English say, the walls have ears!' He paused, 'I don't want to say too much. The Rower's back in town from Singapore. And, since he did such a great job there, he's been told to sort things out here too. You know where!' he said, with special emphasis.

'I think you lost me there,' said the other. 'Who's back in town?'

'Get out your Arabic dictionary. You'll recognise the name – used to work in the Central Bank. Sheikh Abdul sent him out to Singapore to sort out all the Al Ghamdi shit.'

'Mohammed Al Turk was over here last week,' said the London voice. 'We had lunch together. There's a lot I need to tell you about. But not on this; it'll have to wait until we meet. Anyway, he told me about the Ghamdi scandal months ago. I gather they're going to nationalise his bank and pay off all that toxic debt.'

'You mean his gambling debts!' said Al Fadl. 'Look, what I really want to tell you is that with our friend the Rower on the job, the shit will really hit the fan, as you're so fond of saying.'

He continued: 'Apparently he's taken over from your friend. He's brought a high-powered team in on the job. Put one of the auditors in full-time to investigate everything. He's already in the office. Using one a couple of doors away from yours – Ramadan's old one.'

'Bloody hell,' said the man in London. 'Nothing has been said to me about all this, or to Mohammed, otherwise he would have told me last week. Shit, the bastards! Mohammed said he was off to his estate in Scotland for about ten days. They've done this deliberately, knowing he couldn't do anything to pre-empt it, couldn't appeal to the Ruler before it's a fait accompli.'

'It's bad news,' said Al Fadl, 'and this accountant's already sniffing around my office, asking all sorts of pointed questions, and collaring loads of files!'

'That's disgraceful. How dare he do that? Mohammed will be spitting blood when he hears this! What sort of questions has he been asking?'

'Well, he seems to be focusing on pricing. He's taken all the contracts and files which relate to purchasing and sales. He's asking about the LME historical prices, and so on.'

'This could be very serious for me, and for you – I don't need to tell you that.'

'For you maybe, but not for me! I'm just telling you, so you know what's going on.'

'Oh yes? You think I don't know about your grubby little deals? If I'd spoken to Mohammed about it all you'd have been out on your ear long ago, Hamid! Back to that barren piece of desert in Palestine. Where your family came from originally, before you went to Bahrain. Don't bite the hand that feeds you, otherwise it'll get chopped off.'

This clearly struck home. Bill detected a distinct change of tone in Al Fadl's reply.

'OK, OK, take it easy! Look, if you take my advice, you'll not come back. I'm certain that the Rower will be gunning for you. He'll have you hung up by the balls to get what he wants out of you,' said Al Fadl, in an ingratiating tone of voice. 'I'll cover for your visit at this end.'

'Right, and make sure you do, otherwise I'll cut your balls off. You attend that meeting on Saturday on my behalf; make sure you buttonhole the Sales Director, Wolf Schmitt. Remind him that we have a deal and he needs to stand by it. The pot lines programme is going to go ahead whatever. They can sell as much aluminium as they can make in the present market and Dubai needs the extra electricity generation capacity. That comes as an added benefit. You look after me and I'll make sure you get your cut. Tell them to charge the US 22 million dirhams as a contingency.'

After Al Fadl had acknowledged his instructions, the person at the other end concluded: 'I'll book a flight straight away to Edinburgh. I'll warn Mohammed and see what can be done to retrieve the situation. Keep in touch!'

The same person came back on-line, a few minutes later. 'It's me again. Whenever you do, for God's sake make sure it's booked through the company in the pink tower!'

31

General Mohammed Ali Makbool was a large and powerfully-built man in his mid-50s. He had lived his career in the shadows. His title was honorific. He was not a member of the ruling coterie of sheikhs. He was not a regular policeman – had never been on the beat – and he had no military experience or training. But he had a significant distinction. He had more information about the inhabitants of Dubai than any other person. The more senior the personage, the more he knew.

For that reason, he was one of the most hated men in Dubai and was feared by all. At this particular moment, his power was about to be significantly increased.

Sitting in front of him in his office in the Diwan was one of his most trusted subordinates; someone who might aspire to take his job one day, thought the General. Perhaps that would be no bad thing, he mused, provided he'd finished paying for his estate in Kentucky by then. Provided it was on his terms. Provided he decided when the time was right. But could he really give up his power, he wondered? Would watching his string of thoroughbreds really give him the same sense of exhilaration, the same adrenaline rush, that he got from closing in inexorably as his latest victim grew larger and larger in his sights? Now he sensed that Colonel Tamimi was about to help bring the present object of interest into much closer focus. It was time to get rid of his only serious contender for the position of Sheikh Abdul's right-hand man.

'Sala'am alaikum, General Mohammed,' began the younger man. The Colonel was some twenty-five years younger than his boss. His meteoric rise in the secret police had been due to the General's patronage. Now he hoped to reward that belief in him, and also to repay the debt so that in future he would not be under any obligation to his former patron.

'You asked me to have a look at Mahmoud Al Abdullah, General. I have made this my main priority for some weeks now. Did you know that Al Abdullah has a large property in America, in Miami?' said Tamimi.

'Yes, I did know that,' replied the General. 'What about it?'

Tamimi knew very well that General Makbool knew this. He also knew that Makbool himself owned a large property in the US, and he was pretty certain that both men had acquired their properties in a similar fashion. It would do no harm to let the General know that some of his secrets were not as secret as he thought.

'I've checked the ownership, purchase details and so on of this property through an agent in the States. To cut a long story short, the property was paid for in two tranches: an initial deposit of US $250,000 and the second of $1,750,000 on completion.'

'Go on!' said the General, not sure where all this was leading. Clearly, he would need to keep a close eye on this protégé of his. He brought his mind back to the immediate subject. He could think later about whether Tamimi was dispensable at this stage. There was no way that Al Abdullah should have access to those amounts of funds in his own right. Neither his father nor his mother came from wealthy families. His father's family owned a reasonably successful glazing business, and it was doing well in today's building boom, but not that well! His father had only a small share, and Al Abdullah did not work in the business but was a government servant. Quite a lowly one at that. Before he was sent to Singapore.

Tamimi continued: 'It was difficult to trace the audit trail for these payments. However, one of the largest settlements to creditors of Al Ghamdi's bank was to the Bluegrass Casino in London. Al Ghamdi owed them about US $20 million. Well, something struck me about this credit. Of all the claims from Al Ghamdi's creditors, it was the only one that received 100 per cent payment. In the case of all the other creditors, Al Abdullah negotiated deals. Typically, he paid them between 70 per cent and 85 per cent – never 100. So I had someone follow the payments from the Al Ghamdi Foundation account in Singapore into the casino's offshore account in Jersey.'

'That's the account for restructuring the Al Ghamdi assets?' queried the General.

'Exactly – controlled, of course, by Mahmoud Al Abdullah. We then looked at the account in Jersey. We found that, within two days of the final payment being made, the sum of US $2,500,000 was paid to a bank in the Virgin Islands. And both payments for the Miami property came from this account!' he finished triumphantly.

Mohammed Ali was careful not to show his satisfaction. He, too, felt triumphant, but he did not want Colonel Tamimi to know just how he felt about it all. His hunch had paid off; Al Abdullah had betrayed the Sheikh's trust in him. He had ripped him off behind his back. Even though the Ruler had rewarded him generously, by putting him in charge of the majority of day-to-day business affairs. Now, Mohammed Ali knew he had him by the balls.

'You have done well, Colonel Tamimi, very well indeed. I shall personally inform His Highness of your excellent service to Dubai. Now,' he continued, 'I think we should keep a very close eye on our friend Mahmoud Al Abdullah. I want you to put him under intensive surveillance. Follow him wherever he goes for the next month. Put your best team on the job.'

Bill was in the office studying the lists which Malik had given him earlier that morning.

'Boss, you need to give me another 5,000 dirhams,' said Malik. 'My contact had to take a lot of risks to get these. If she had been caught she'd be dismissed from her job. She has a family of three small children and her husband's only a municipality workman and gets paid very little.'

'But Malik, we agreed to 15,000 – altogether. A deal's a deal.'

'I know Boss, but she's gold dust. See how quickly she got this stuff?'

Bill relented. He realised that Malik's contact had done extremely well to get the itemised telephone bills, and that she had done so very quickly, in only three days. Sometimes, he was pestering Malik for months to obtain something much more straightforward. After all, information was just a commodity. The suppliers knew that. And sometimes greed was not far away and outrageous prices were often asked by ex-patriot Indian and local nationals alike.

'OK, Malik. Here's the money with the extra 5,000, but be sure to tell her to be realistic in future. Otherwise it will be the end of a good relationship,' said Bill, wondering just how much of the money Malik's contact would actually get from Malik. Bill paid Malik well. Everyone had a living to make. But one never could tell; every time he raised the issue with Malik he had vehemently denied extracting his own cut. And perhaps it was true. Malik was an ardent and observant Christian. But on the other hand, he lived within the realities of Indian society in the Emirates.

Checking the numbers was a laborious job. Bill did not have any sophisticated computer technology. It would be much easier just to call Andy immediately and hand it all over to him. It would go back in the diplomatic bag the same day. Probably be with GCHQ in Cheltenham in less than forty-eight hours. There, the analysis would take no time at all, depending on what priority it was accorded in the intelligence world. 'Knowledge is power,' Bill concluded. He decided to spend some time using a rudimentary Excel programme, which he had set up. After all, it wasn't as if he was dealing with a particularly large number of transactions. Over the three months, up to the end of last month, for which Malik had obtained the records – it was now the 10th – there were perhaps 400 calls to and from Davies' mobile number. Quite a few of them were to the office. He also had the list of calls made from the office. So all those between Davies and the office could be identified and discounted. They would only be of interest if he could have heard what had been said. But he could not do that, not retrospectively anyway. However, he could always set up an operation to do so in the future, if it was considered worthwhile. For the moment he had to be content with simply making connections between numbers and working out to whom Davies was talking. Was it merely his wife – or girlfriend – or someone more interesting? He decided to concentrate on the mobile numbers first.

Bill wanted to identify any numbers which were on both of the lists which he had obtained for Andy. In total, there were about 100 mobile numbers for Al Quoz Ceramics and Octagon Computers. It quickly became apparent, however, that there was a significant correlation. The mobiles registered to each of the companies were ringing a lot of the same numbers. Bill prepared a list of correlations, and listed some other frequently occurring numbers. Once he had worked his way through the whole batch, he printed off a copy. He would need to set up another meeting in order to pass the list across to Andy.

He made himself a cup of coffee. Looking at the data which he now had, it confirmed that there was a link between Al Quoz Ceramics and Octagon Computers. There was a very high level of calls, both between the two mobiles and by both of the main mobiles and some other common numbers. The next logical move would be to work out to whom all common numbers were registered, particularly those frequently called and those to and from the two main mobiles registered to the companies. Most would undoubtedly be of no interest to him: calls to suppliers and clients, and social calls. Then he reconsidered: if there was something dubious about Davies, and therefore, by extension, either or both of the two companies with which he was now involved, it could be very interesting to know who the clients and suppliers were. It might throw up some leads. He finished copying. He would give Andy a call after lunch. He got up to put the paper in his file. One of the numbers triggered something in his mind.

Quickly, excitement mounting, he delved into the filing cabinet behind his desk. Finding what he was looking for, he drew out the red folder, thumbing furiously through it. He put his finger on a number. Yes, it was the same. 'Jesus Christ!' he exclaimed to himself, 'what a turn-up for the books.' Grabbing his mobile, he quickly dialled Andy's 'Call Peter' number. The message record system activated.

'Peter here – ASAP!' he said. Immediately he closed the line.

Their next meeting was at the French Connection café along the Sheikh Zayed Highway. 'Almond croissants to die for!' Andy had said, the anticipation evident in his voice. Bill needed to get all the stuff about Octagon Computers off his chest. It was all moving into deeper waters and he knew he did not have a life-jacket.

Andy came in just after him. Clearly, he was in a hurry. It was difficult to work out whether he was pleased Bill had called earlier to set up the meeting, or would rather not be there. But any doubts in Bill's mind were immediately dissipated.

'Thank God you called!' said Andy breathlessly. 'I've got something very hot for you! Another job,' he continued, seemingly forgetting that it was Bill who had requested the meeting because he had something to pass on to Andy.

'Hang on a minute!' Bill responded. 'Before we move on to something new, can I just brief you on what I've come up with so far?'

He quickly told Andy of his meeting with Arun and what he had found out.

'So it looks like there's a close connection between bin Laden, Sheikh Abdul and the two companies Octagon Computers and Al Quoz Ceramics?'

queried Andy. 'Exactly,' said Bill, 'It's too much of a coincidence that so many details tie up. Do you want me to do anything else on this? We're still following up on Octagon Computers for Globalsoft, so I can probably do other things for you under cover of this.'

'Right-oh!' said Andy. 'What would be really good would be to hear what all these buggers are saying! Any chance you could bug their phones?'

'The thought had already crossed my mind. Technically it would be a piece of cake. But it would be the risk of being caught that we would need to think about. Is it worth it? Let me have a look at that and see what's what. I can let you know tomorrow.'

'OK,' said Andy. 'Now there's another thing for you. How are you on getting bank account details?'

'Such as?' Bill responded.

'We've developed a really good source in Iran. He's telling us the Iranians are getting technical information on nuclear technology from the North Koreans. Obviously, it's no great surprise that the Iranians and North Koreans are associating – both are fanatically committed to acquiring nuclear weapons. We've been aware of that for a long time. It's not exactly secret. But what's really significant in this new material is a report that some of the parts are being procured through Dubai! Just think of the implications.'

Andy paused to let the enormity of his remarks sink in.

'We're getting reports that someone here in Dubai is facilitating the procurement of WMD by North Korean and Iranian agents. We're trying desperately to get some hard int.'

'There'll have to be a money trail!' said Bill.

'Exactly! And that's where you come in – to get some proof. Pound to a pinch of salt it's going to be through a Pakistani bank. How are you on them?'

'I'll do some homework.'

'It's not what one would expect,' continued Andy. 'Iran and Dubai are hardly natural bedfellows. So it would be more than a little surprising if the government here were helping Shia Iran. In reality, all the Gulf States, including Saudi, are predominately Sunni – I should imagine that all of them would be shit-scared at the thought of a nuclear-armed Iran. But Iran is a fascinating county with a long history and a fabulous cultural heritage. And a lot of pride. They're not going to lie down and put their feet in the air!'

'Yes,' said Bill. 'The situation there's a knock-on effect of the US habit of installing its own puppet leaders in such countries and then wondering why the local population are not too favourably inclined. Just think of the names of some of the strong men they propped up long after their sell-by date. Mobuto, Noriega, Suharto and the Pahlavi regime in Iran, to mention only a few!'

'I agree with you there,' said Andy. 'The US has been reaping the whirlwind ever since the Iranian revolution. Anyway, I'd better be on my way now. Here are the details, they're in the middle page.' Andy surreptitiously moved the copy of the *Gulf News* closer to Bill. 'Let me know how it looks on the bank account, and keep checking on Octagon Computers.'

It was a few minutes later when Bill called Graham Booker. 'Hi there Graham, what're you up to?'

'I'm in Zug, so you can imagine what I might be doing! But no names, no pack drill!'

'Well, don't ruffle any feathers there! I was going to ask you to do something for me. Seeing as where you are, I won't say anything! I'll send you an e-mail. When're you due back in the UK?'

'Should be tomorrow; I'll call you when I get back. Let me have those details.' Graham rang off.

Rory was in the office. He looked up as Bill came in, and then followed him into his office, shutting the door behind him. 'I had one of the lads make another attempt to get a deal organised with Octagon Computers,' he said. 'Same reaction – not a dickey bird. They offered him a PC, but not at a very competitive price and the guy he dealt with – a Pakistani – didn't seem at all bothered about making a sale. A take it or leave it attitude. And they'd only provide legitimate software; whether they were suspicious or not, I can't work out.'

'Doesn't sound like your normal Dubai trader, biting your arm off to make a deal!' said Bill, musingly. 'But look – there's a guy who's involved with Octagon Computers and also with Al Quoz Ceramics – he's a director of both. Name's Hugh Davies.'

'What's so strange about that?' asked Rory. 'There's a lot of people here are directors of more than one company. In fact a lot of locals make a tidy income just acting as sponsors for foreign entities without having any involvement in the business. Don't have to lift a finger – until, that is, it comes to time to collect the annual sponsorship fees!'

'Yep, I realise that,' said Bill, 'but this looks different. From the name it's obvious that this guy's not a local – British, probably. I met the Drugs Liaison Officer at the Embassy this morning; he mentioned Davies to me, said HMG had a serious interest in him; they reckon he's big into drugs. They have been trying to nab him for some time – to catch him in flagrante delicto so that they can get him put away. He asked me to do anything we can to get a bead on Davies. So could you see if you can get behind him, house him, find his offices, and so on? Particularly see if you can get a good close-up photograph of him?'

'OK,' said Rory. 'Sounds like an interesting little job.'

Bill had been somewhat economical with the truth. It had been Andy who had asked him about Davies. But better, Bill considered, that Rory didn't know everything, for his own sake. Bill had actually been to the Embassy earlier in the day to meet the DLO. Patrick Timms was a bluff northerner and had been a customs officer all his working life. Approaching retirement, he had been given the chance to see a bit more of the world than hitherto. Jebel Ali had sounded more glamorous than Liverpool or Hull. However, a port was always a port, no matter where it was. That Patrick was obviously thoroughly enjoying his new posting was obvious. He and his petite wife Moira with her close-cropped blonde hair, who joined them briefly when they were having coffee as she worked in the Visa Department, were obviously having the time of their lives.

Patrick said that he knew his opposite number in Cairo. 'He and I worked together on a large parallel trading scam in the UK several years ago. It involved a number of cigarette manufacturing plants in Bulgaria. The government was involved in the racket that sent hundreds of containers full of product into the UK. They used Bulgarian and Romanian immigrant workers living in the UK to feed the product into the market. Quite a diplomatic hot potato, it was. Eventually, the Bulgarian government got the message and closed it all down. A couple of factories went out of business as a consequence.'

Bill told Patrick about his trip to Egypt. 'I know your job here's about drugs, but I'd like to think that you could help me on the cigarettes as well?' said Bill. 'From what you've just been telling me, you obviously know a lot about the cigarette business.'

'Yep, that's true,' said Patrick, 'one hell of a lot more than I do about drugs – I've never had any direct involvement with them before. However, what I'm finding out is that there are numerous parallels, links and

116

common names. I was in Pakistan for ten days before I came here, with my colleague in Karachi. That sure was an eye-opener. I'm on a fast learning curve! Anyway, I would be pleased to help as much as possible, as it's definitely on HMG's agenda... and I'm sure I can count on you to help me in return?'

Bill showed the documents to Andy. There was no doubt about it. Davies was a director of both companies. And both companies were owned by Sheikh Abdul. They were back in the coffee lounge of the Crown Plaza Hotel again.

'Take a look at this list of phone calls made on that bin Laden number last month,' said Bill. 'Look, see here, highlighted in green, those are all calls to or from Octagon Computers, and the ones in red are to Sheikh Abdul's private office. Five of one and three of the other.'

'Go on,' said Andy, the tension rising in his voice.

'Right – well, we've also found your Mr Davies! Lives in some smart apartments in Al Rashidiya. We have managed to get his mobile number too.'

'How did you do that?'

'Quite easily really, simply called the Al Majoroun Apartments management office – that's the company that manages the building he's living in – and spoke to someone there. Very kindly gave us the number.'

'They won't normally do that,' said Andy. 'They're generally pretty cagey. Very secretive about many things, more so than in the UK.'

'Well, over here, it all comes down to nationality. One of my guys made a visit to the office, supposedly checking on rental availability. He noticed that the secretarial staff are mainly from Sri Lanka. That's the way it goes here, you know. An Indian is only likely to hire another Indian, and so on. Anyway, I have a Sri Lankan secretary – a real gem she is, too – she simply calls the office, they get talking about home. And so we have the number!'

'Great stuff, so where does that take us?' asked Andy.

'We've checked out his phone – got the calls list for last month as well. Comparison with the other mobile number is extremely interesting. Davies is calling both offices regularly and also bin Laden, and vice versa. Here,

117

this is bin Laden's bill again. Those ten calls are either to or from Davies!'

'Let's just recap,' said Andy. 'There is a strong link between both companies then; there are two common directors, who regularly talk to each other. This could, of course, just be what it purports to be: normal, legit business?'

'Yes, but it's not only that,' interjected Bill. 'First, there are, in fact, four common directors: two others who are probably Indian, we haven't looked at them yet.'

'OK,' Andy said. 'So you'd better check them. See if there's anything that comes out of the woodwork.'

'OK, I'll see what we can find.'

'So let's continue then. It could just be legitimate business, the link between these two. On the other hand, we know that bin Laden's linked to the Mujahedeen. He was involved with them fighting the Soviets. Provided a lot of the funds. He was set up and run by the CIA, with the connivance of the ISI in Pakistan! And now I'm not sure what's going on, but the Mujahedeen are a law unto themselves, not controllable by the CIA. Or anybody else for that matter, now.'

'What about the Pakistanis and the ISI intelligence services? Aren't they running them?' interjected Bill.

'More like the other way round, as far as our assessment goes. They are probably in cahoots with them. But as far as the Pakistanis go, it's like they've got a tiger by the tail. The ISI undoubtedly still has links to various groups, but it's all pretty murky. They are paranoid about getting control over Kashmir and the threat from India. They see the Taliban – and other groups like them – as a bulwark against Indian aggression. There are legions of different Islamist splinter groups, with differing and overlapping objectives that coalesce and move apart again. And if the Pakistani government does take action against them, they merely change their name and reappear somewhere else as something else. But now the Taliban poses as much of a threat to Pakistan itself as it does to us, the Yanks or anyone else. The Paks have just begun to wake up to it all, to appreciate the threat.'

'Just like Ireland,' said Bill. 'At the beginning, romantic sentiment and self-interest led the Irish government to provide tacit support to the IRA. Rather late in the day, they realised that the IRA was just as much of a threat to them as it was to the British in Northern Ireland. The Pakistanis know that they will probably have the Taliban in charge before too long now that the Russians have gone.'

'It's real politick,' Andy continued. 'We know only too well that Davies is a dangerous piece of work. I don't think he has a moral fibre in his body. Anything he does is strictly done to make money. He's got a record as long as your arm, as I've said before, trying to help countries such as Libya and North Korea get WMD. Certainly in the past he's been in touch with the Pakistanis. In fact, A.Q. Khan, the "Father" of the Pakistani bomb, a national hero, worked at CERN Geneva, and nicked all the information which he then took to his own country. He's been lying low recently, but there's good reason to believe that he is somewhere in the offing. And now we have Davies and bin Laden talking together as well!'

'That just leaves Sheikh Abdul as the other common denominator,' said Bill.

'He's always been considered a dark horse, and I'm sure he hasn't forgotten that his family was kicked out of Deira all those years ago by Sheikh Raheem.'

'He's very involved in the cigarette business,' said Bill. 'He's the sponsor of a company, a trading company based in Jebel Ali, which deals in tobacco products. In fact, it so happens that we're looking at it at the moment. For one of the major tobacco companies.'

'Which one?'

'No names, no pack-drill!' Bill responded discreetly. It wouldn't do to let Andy in on all his trade secrets. 'All the big companies are so worried that they're having a blitz on it. But, of course, they're all working independently, which is not the most effective way. The smugglers don't just target one brand; they deal in whatever's in demand in the market. But there's no way the companies will co-operate.

'Anyway, we've come up with several companies which are particularly active in the counterfeit business. I guess you're familiar with all this and you must have been talking to the DLO about it?'

'Yes,' said Andy, 'I'm more than au fait with all that. There's a well-established link between Mafia gangs dealing in drugs, prostitution and cigarettes, and, of course, terrorism. It all ties in together. Anything for profit is the name of the game. So you reckon Sheikh Abdul's tied up with it?'

'No doubt about it! This company I mentioned – the one sponsored by Sheikh Abdul – we've been trying to set up a deal with them to catch them at it for some time. We're working with the CID on this.'

119

'Aaaah! What's that saying about "birds of a feather"? Looks like we've uncovered a nasty nest of vipers here in our midst,' said Andy, unashamedly mixing his metaphors. 'What the neocons would call a nexus of evil. Because I've got something else for you!

'We've got some really great sources covering proliferation. I got this the other day from London. It's inside the sports page this time.' Andy motioned to the copy of the *Kaleej Times* on the table beside him. Bill, having caught Andy's eye in acknowledgement, placed the folder that he had been holding in his hand on top of the paper, looking around discreetly so as to ensure that he was not going to attract anyone else's attention. The hotel was quite busy, and there was a constant stream of visitors coming and going through the hotel reception at the other side, beyond the escalator.

Several pairs of businessmen were at nearby tables, trying to tie up the latest deal in this or that. The family of an Arab man, with three wives and two small children, probably Saudi judging by the man's red and white chequered shemagh, was visible to Bill over Andy's right shoulder. The maid – a Filipina, like so many – was struggling valiantly to stop the children smearing their very large chocolate sundae ice creams all over the table and over each other. Oblivious, the three women were joking among themselves. The man sat apart, aloofly superior.

Behind Bill, a couple of Indians were animatedly discussing India's recent defeat at cricket by Pakistan. 'Whatever they're doing,' thought Bill, 'they're not interested in me.' Neither could he see anybody else who might be. And why should this not be so, he reflected; after all, Dubai was a place where many came to lose their identity. Anything went here, as long as it brought in money to tumble into the pockets of the sheikhs. Then he thought about what was at stake, and was jolted back to reality.

Andy was speaking: 'You'll see all the details when you look at the paper later. It's documentation on two substantial financial transactions which I need you to look at. They're bank transactions from a company in Tehran. You don't need me to tell you about Iran's position on nuclear weapons acquisition!' Bill nodded.

'These payments went to the Rub Al Khali Commercial Bank – they're both quite recent. We reckon we know what they were for. We need you to find out to whom they were paid, and where the money went next.'

'I'll speak to Mahmoud Al Abdullah about this... No! On second thoughts, why don't you go and brief him? I told you he's working for us? He doesn't know that you're working for us – not yet; I'll brief him later. Why don't you go and tell him everything that you're up to at the moment and see if you can get his help? If he doesn't report this to me, then I'll know that he's playing both sides off against the middle!'

'He already knows much of what I'm doing,' said Bill. 'He's the one who's tasking me on the RAKA job.'

'He should be able to help, then. He can give you the lowdown on Sheikh Abdul to help with the other work you're doing. Given that he's in charge of the Commercial Department, he should at least be able to make sure that you have easy access to the company records and so on.'

'That'd be a help indeed,' said Bill. 'Sometimes it's the devil's own job to get hold of perfectly ordinary information – it's not secret stuff, or shouldn't be anyway. Wouldn't be in any normal society. These buggers are inordinately secretive. Perhaps it's a throwback to the tribal culture and nomadic days, when presumably everyone knew everyone else's business? I'll go and see him as soon as possible,' he concluded as Andy paid the bill and they left together, but in different directions.

It was several days before Bill managed to meet up with Mahmoud Al Abdullah. He had just returned from a spell in his house in Miami. They met in the elegant Commercial Department in Mahmoud's spacious and well-appointed office, looking across the road to the Maybury Hotel. As ever with Mahmoud, the meeting had had to be delayed. Scheduled for the very early morning, it eventually took place late that day.

'I was summoned to go and brief Their Excellencies. Mohamed Al-Fayed and the Trade Centre are causing problems again,' said Mahmoud, matter-of-factly. Bill knew that Mahmoud regularly had to jump like this at the drop of a hat.

Mahmoud was in high spirits. He had just signed a deal with the offshore power-boating organisation to sponsor powerboat racing in the Emirates at Mina Al Seyahi. He was much more interested in telling Bill about this than discussing the boring matter of looking through Commercial Department records.

'Yes, yes, fix it up with Leila. She'll arrange it all for you,' he responded distractedly to Bill's request. Leila was his very attractive and sassy Jordanian personal assistant. 'Bernie's in town next week. Next stop, F1!' he confided to Bill after they had exchanged a few brief pleasantries.

This would bring a lot of tourists and money into Dubai. And, of course, more kudos for Mahmoud. And an even higher public persona. Already, it was being rumoured that the Ruler was getting concerned about this. Almost every day in the *Gulf News* or the *Kaleej Times* there would be a photograph of Mahmoud, opening this or that exhibition or showroom, speaking at this or that conference, or giving his opinion to the world press about some current topic. On the face of it, he was very good news for Dubai. He was very Western-orientated, very personable, highly articulate, spoke perfect English, albeit with the inevitable American accent, and on his feet he thought like a Westerner. But he could behave conservatively when necessary. He was ultimately an Arab: young, dashing, devastatingly good-looking, and highly photogenic. But all this was not popular with his peers, who increasingly resented his success and, especially, his ready access to the Ruler. It was clear that the Ruler had begun to feel quite put out by all this. He had given instructions, so the rumour went, to the local press that, whatever else happened, his face was to appear more frequently than Mahmoud's. Thinking about this before meeting with Mahmoud, Bill had wondered if Mahmoud was aware of the risk that he was becoming too big for his own boots; that hubris was getting the better of him. Bill remembered Red's comments about Al Abdullah when they first met. Like Icarus, were his wings about to be melted in the searing heat of his master's retribution?

As they had done for the last four weeks, Colonel Tamimi's men followed the usual routine. So far it had all been mind-numbingly boring. The target left the house at about 7:20 each morning, bumped over the stretch of desert to the new Spinney's supermarket at the end of Al Wasl Road and turned left heading towards the centre of town and the Creek. Usually, the 4x4 Land Rover Discovery turned right at the next major roundabout, headed away from the seafront, and joined the other increasingly frustrated commuters on the Sheikh Zayed Highway via the Al Quoz intersection. From there it was a slow but easy journey into town, and then a left off the highway by the Law Courts just before the Al Maktoum Bridge which went over the Creek into Deira. Staying on the north side of the Creek, the target vehicle would quickly arrive at the Gatehouse with its barriers, behind which lay the large plot of land encircled by a high fence contained within which were the small buildings dotted among spacious lawns and immaculately tended flower beds with a profusion of oleander, hibiscus and bougainvillea, and clumps of date palms. At this time of year, the orange blossom was almost overpowering with its sensual fragrance.

Occasionally, for no reason that was immediately apparent to the watchers, their quarry would elect not to turn right at the roundabout for Al Quoz, but instead would carry on straight down the Al Wasl Road, go past the Dubai museum, along the perimeter of the Ruler's Majlis, and then turn right, along the Creek, finally entering his destination from the other direction. During the third week, on the Thursday, there had been a deviation, an alteration to the routine. The target, instead of going along the highway, had turned off at Defence Roundabout, headed down towards the Dubai Hilton, as the main prison was referred to sardonically by expatriates, and then doubled back towards the traffic lights, made a couple of further turns and parked up behind the buildings adjacent to the highway. The driver had got out and, walking quickly, gone round to the front of the buildings. At that point, the surveillance team had been slow to get someone out of the vehicle and on foot, so that the target had been unsighted for several minutes.

Then one of the team had seen their man emerge from the French Connection Café carrying a white paper bag. The target had gone back to his vehicle, retraced his steps to the Defence Roundabout, joined the thickening traffic and carried on in his normal routine.

'Wa' Allah!' exclaimed Tariq to his driver. 'Since when did our friend acquire a passion for French croissants on his way to work? And why here, when there's another French Connection Café more or less on his direct route to work?'

He jabbed the radio transmission switch: 'Zero One, Ibrahim, get into the café and take as much photography as you can. Try to get good mug shots of all the customers particularly, but also the staff.'

Tariq knew that Ibrahim was dressed in smart Western clothes. He looked for all the world like a switched-on Indian executive, just over from Bangalore to transact a major computer services contract. Parking up,

Ibrahim quickly got out of the car. The camera was in a briefcase with a shoulder strap. Fortunately for Ibrahim, there was a lengthy queue at the counter in the French Connection. This enabled him to gaze in apparent disinterest around the room, shifting the camera with its carefully-concealed Canon EF-S 18-55mm lens as he did so. It was always a bit hit-and-miss, but he trusted that the wide-angle fisheye lens would capture most of those seated at tables. Now at the head of the queue, he ordered a takeaway latte.

The Secret Police surveillance team were no slouches. They had been well trained – ironically, by the British. They had done the long course run by A4 at Bursford Manor, hidden discreetly in the small Kent town, with the final two-week phase taking place in the Emirates so that local characteristics could be taken into account. In Dubai with its modern dual-carriageway system, compared to most Western cities, the speed of traffic resulted in hair-raisingly fast urban surveillance.

After each phase they had debriefed. What was the reason for the two different routes taken by their target? Was there some sinister reason why he went this way or that? Was the target practising counter-surveillance? Did he, therefore, have something to hide? Each surveillance operator had his own theory. The problem was that they had no collateral intelligence on which to base an assessment. With surveillance alone, all they could do was literally to record what they saw and try to make some sense of it. On the evening of this loss at the café there was a heated debate as to the meaning of it. Had the target had enough time to meet up with someone? Or was he just caught in a long queue for the delectable croissants for which it was renowned? Did he pass someone a quick verbal message? Or was it a quick drop, a sort of dead-letter box?

That was last week. Now it was for real again. It was Thursday, a half-day for most government offices. A week since the trip to the café. The target came out of his house at the normal time, and took the more frequent route along the highway. No detour to the café – too much to expect a second bite of the cherry for the eager watchers. As on most days, the target drove to the British Embassy. The only thing that was untoward was that Andy was wheeling a travel bag. One larger than would be allowed in any airline's business-class cabin. Quickly a message was passed to Colonel Tamimi by the surveillance commander, Captain Tariq, on the secure in-car phone.

'Sala'am Colonel, it looks like our friend is getting ready to travel somewhere to-day.'

Without pausing for thought, Tamimi replied, 'Stay with him, wherever he goes!… Make sure you have enough people with you, and that they all have passports, money and so on.'

Managing not to show his irritation at this affront to his professionalism, Captain Tariq responded, 'Yes, that's all in the crash-out bags in the cars. We have whatever we may need, wherever he chooses to go. I've already got Research and Analysis trying to confirm any outgoing flight bookings in Ratcatcher's name.' Tamimi made a mental note to find out when he got back to the office who was responsible for concocting these bizarre code names which they were obliged to use.

'Good! Keep me posted. Let me know any confirmed flight details as soon as possible,' said Tamimi emphatically. 'Ratcatcher indeed!' he murmured to himself. 'It's me who's the ratcatcher around here. And Al Abdullah who's the traitorous rat that I'm about to catch, Alhamdulillah.'

Quickly, Tariq briefed all the team: 'Wherever he goes – wherever – is that clear?'

It was a normal midsummer's day in Dubai. A sweltering 41° Centigrade, barely relieved by a scorching onshore breeze. At 3 pm most people were either in their unnaturally cold air-conditioned offices, in their swimming pools or enjoying the peaceful slumber of their siesta. And still the watchers watched. There was no respite for Tariq and his team. Fortunately, it needed only one car positioned along the road on either side of the Embassy gate to maintain control of the target. The cars rotated every fifteen minutes to combat the monotony; those on sentry duty struggled not to let their attention wander from the entrance to the Embassy, not to succumb to the temptation to close their eyes, their eyelids ever heavier with the urge to sleep.

Suddenly the radio net squawked into life: 'Stand by!' Instantaneously the whole team was ready for action, each man tense and expectant, the urge to sleep banished as the adrenaline flowed through their veins.

'Zero Four!' – that was Khalid who had the long view from the Creek-side car park across the road to the left of the Embassy – 'Target moving now, at barrier… Turning right, right.'

Quickly the barrier at the main gate had risen, the Gurkha guards saluting the occupant as the Discovery left the compound, the barrier closing rapidly behind it.

'Shit! Son of a pig!' said Khalid, as the driver stalled the vehicle in his excitement. By the time the vehicle had re-started, negotiated the car park and joined the Creek-side road, the Discovery was nowhere to be seen.

'What's happening, Zero Four?' called Tariq. 'Have you got control?'

'Negative, negative! Lost going right towards Zero Three.'

'Satan's teeth!' exclaimed Tariq, in exasperation. 'We sit here all day doing nothing and just when we have to do something, these donkeys mess up.'

'I have Zero Three, left at Bur Juman heading for Al Maktoum Bridge.' Allah be praised, thought Tariq.

Two minutes later: 'Zero Three, over bridge, looks like he's going off right, towards the airport.'

Ninety minutes later, Tariq was sitting in seat 14B of British Airways flight BA1008, Dubai London. From where he sat, he could see Andy three rows in front on the starboard side. Andy appeared to be alone. Tariq was not alone, however. Four other members of his team were scattered throughout the aircraft. Another four operators were already booked to travel on the next London flight, an Emirates flight three-quarters of an hour later.

Their contact in the London Embassy had been briefed and would be at Heathrow when the flight landed, with three vehicles from the Embassy. A photocopy of Andy's passport had been e-mailed to him. If Tariq and his people did not get through customs and immigration alongside Andy, then he and his colleague would have to take over the job and ensure that Andy was kept under surveillance at all times.

They knew that Andy's parents lived at Kingston-upon-Thames. And that he and his wife owned a house at Farnham, to the west of London. It would probably be too late for Andy to get into Century House by the time he got to central London, unless he was on an extremely urgent task. He might meet up with someone from the office during the evening, of course; see someone else, go to a good movie, or simply book into a hotel and have a good meal there; or he might just go off somewhere for the night, and then report to the office in the morning. There were numerous options. Perhaps he was on leave and wouldn't even go to the office at all. But this was unlikely, Tariq thought, as he had left his wife back in Dubai. It would be a long night for Tariq and his team. Fortunately, they had all spent time in either the UK or America, so they would have little trouble blending in with the diverse ethnicity of modern-day Britain.

Tariq watched a couple of videos during the flight. He particularly appreciated Will Smith in 'Enemy of the State'. He could identify with Will Smith's character. Both felt themselves oppressed within their culture. In the film, Smith was fighting the modern-day bully-boy Ku Klux Klan-like thugs of white Anglo-Saxon Protestantism, and the anonymous state. For Tariq, the enemy was the colonial Crusader, the aloof superior British administrator, who promised the same thing in the same place at the same time to two different peoples wishing to establish their nationhood, and who drew arbitrary lines across the desert kingdom of his forebears. Now, for him and his kind, their time had come.

He dozed fitfully on occasions, waking each time with a start, feeling that somehow Andy would have escaped his clutches. And each time he was there in front, completely unsuspecting.

'If only,' Tariq thought, 'if only I can catch him at it!'

Andy left the business-class section quickly. There was several minutes' delay before his luggage arrived. But soon he was on his way out of the terminal building. He hailed the next taxi in the queue and headed towards central London. It was just 6 pm now and traffic was slow all the way into the city. Reclining comfortably in the back of the cab, Andy deliberated whether to call June, who lived in a flat on Pont Street. She had been his secretary several years ago. As well as working very well together, they had also spent a lot of extramural time together, and a lot of time within the walls of her flat where they had seen everything of each other in a steamy affair that had extinguished as quickly as it had begun when he moved to Dubai. Perhaps her flat would be more comfortable than the Holiday Inn on Berkeley Street, where his secretary had booked a room for him earlier that day at his request? However, June was probably married now, Andy thought, so perhaps better leave well alone. Besides, he would have a very heavy itinerary the next morning, followed in mid-afternoon by a promotion board interview panel. He was not at all sure what his chances were. Competition was fierce and he could not afford to screw up, otherwise he might as well start looking for a new job – outside the service.

His thoughts elsewhere, with darkened windows and without the benefit of any rear-view mirrors, Andy was not thinking about the following traffic. Had he been, he might just have noticed that several of his fellow passengers on the BA flight had teamed up with their colleagues who had been waiting in several vehicles for their arrival. Had he looked hard at them, Andy might

127

indeed have recognised them; Tariq, for example, who had been only a few seats away. But Tariq had been at pains not to let Andy become aware of his presence. He had made sure that their eyes had not met, denying Andy even a brief impact on his senses, which might just have been triggered by seeing the same face again so shortly afterwards, albeit in a different context. But action and context were not in Andy's favour. Tariq remained firmly in control of his target; although in full view in the taxi driver's mirrors, he remained completely undetected, and Andy remained completely oblivious to the tail.

At the hotel, Andy paid off the taxi, grateful that the hefty charge would be recoverable from the office. He had arranged dinner for 8 pm, so he would just have time to take a shower and get into a change of clothing.

'Zero One,' called Tariq, 'Green Park Station going left, left on Berkeley Street.' Tariq was grateful that their new quantum teleportation secure communication system gave them full protection from eavesdropping, allowing them to speak in clear. He had been assured by the Chinese makers that even the CIA could not break it. No chance, then, that the Brits would pick them up here in London.

'Zero One, stop! Stop! Stop!' Tariq gave the peremptory call to the other vehicles. He reacted urgently, having seen the taxi turning right and into the covered area leading through to Dover Street. 'Let me out here,' he said to the driver, and the untrained Embassy driver of his vehicle screeched to a halt in the middle of the road. A cacophony of indignant horns erupted: several drivers, who had narrowly avoided collision with each other, wound down electric windows and vented their spleen on Tariq as he leapt out of the car and dashed to the side of the street. Had Andy seen him? Had he realised that Tariq was the cause of the commotion? Had he clocked Tariq's face for future reference?

The aggrieved driver of the following vehicle put his hand firmly on his horn for several seconds, winding down his window to shout at Tariq as he ran across the front of his vehicle.

'Shit!' thought Tariq, 'I'd sack any of my team if I saw them drawing attention to themselves like this!'

By the time he came round the corner off Piccadilly into the area where he had last seen Andy, the taxi had gone and Andy was nowhere to be seen. He moved quickly up Berkeley Street. There was no sign of Andy, although Tariq had an unimpeded view along the pavement. On the right was the cut-through to Dover Street, underneath some buildings. He must have gone down there! Tariq went through as fast as he could without attracting undue attention. No sign! Suddenly Tariq realised where he was. He dashed back to the hotel entrance which he had just passed.

'Zero One, looks like he's gone into the Holiday Inn on Berkeley Street – I'm going in to have a look. Box the area; get several of the team out.' Tariq issued his instructions quickly. 'Be prepared to send someone into the hotel.'

Within seconds, Tariq was in the hotel. Trying not to look as if he was searching for someone, he checked out the reception area.

'There's no sign in the reception area. He may have gone... No, wait, possible… yes, confirmed in lift with porter and bag. He must have checked in for the night.'

When he had turned around from reception Tariq had caught a brief glimpse of Andy as the lift doors closed. There were several other guests in the lift too. Watching the progress of the lift, he saw it stop at several floors. Andy could be on any one of them.

An hour later, Tariq saw Andy again. Tariq had reserved a room for the night, and another operator, Said, had also booked in too.

Tariq had made a call to reception as well: 'Hello!' he had said, 'I'm just calling to see if my friend – Mr Stringer – has booked a table for us this evening? And what time for, as I shall be joining him?' The hunch paid off.

'Good evening, sir. You'll be Mr Al Abdullah then, I guess? Yes, Mr Stringer has booked a table for 8 pm in the Nightingales lounge; just the two of you, I believe.' Tariq put the phone down, his hand shaking. Al Abdullah meeting Andy – in London? Perhaps there was some innocuous reason for this. But why would they need to meet in London?

Once safely ensconced in his room, Tariq got out the largest item in his small amount of luggage. Quickly he fitted the scrambler device to the phone in the room, and dialled 020 7581 1284.

At the other end, the phone was answered by another Arab voice. Major Saeed Qasari was the Embassy duty officer that night. He was just settling down for the normal uneventful evening. This was the only occasion on which it was possible to get a beer in the Embassy. There for the benefit of foreign guests, duty officers knew where the key was kept and that no-one was going to see them having an illicit drink. Major Saeed had prepared himself with a Stella Artois six-pack, some McCoys crisps, and a couple of juicy pornographic DVDs.

He placed a CD of Mohammad Salem singing *Galeb Galeb* in the machine and was about to play the first track when the call came through.

'Sala'am alaikum, Masa'a al-khier,' said Tariq.

Major Saeed had been briefed to be prepared to assist Tariq's operation. He had not been told the nature of the operation, but had a pretty shrewd idea that it was a surveillance of an Emirati. The number on his screen authenticated the caller. He had been given it earlier when he came on duty.

'Patch me through to State Security,' said Tariq, authoritatively and without preamble. Major Saeed complied without question. Almost instantaneously the phone rang and was answered.

'It's me, Tariq,' said Tariq, recognising the voice at the other end.

'How're things going?' said Jamil in Dubai, the envy evident in his voice.

'Well, great, but I can't talk now. Put me through to the boss, will you?'

There was a pause, and then he heard the clear tones of Colonel Tamimi's voice asking the same question as Jamil.

'They are well, Colonel – can we go secure?'

'Yes – now!'

There was a brief hiatus on the line, some crackling interference. After a few seconds Tamimi's voice came back, now sounding further away, deeper, hollow.

'Can you hear me, Tariq?'

'Yes, Colonel, I can. It's going very well so far.' The Colonel picked up the constraint in his voice, the pent-up excitement. 'Saturn 1 has booked into the Holiday Inn, near Green Park underground station – it's just off Piccadilly.'

'Yes, I know that area well,' said Tamimi, 'from my time in the Embassy there.'

'He's booked into a room here, number 7001. I'm in a room on the same floor. It's just across the corridor and I can see his door through my keyhole. The new gadget's excellent. Magnifies the view – and stops me getting a draught in my eyes! And it takes a video too. If I go out before the target, I'll get one of the others to keep watch.

'Said is three floors below, and there are two men in the lobby. The whole place has been staked out thoroughly with several vehicles. It's difficult, though, with all the parking restrictions and so on. But that's not all!' said Tariq, meaningfully.

'Tell me,' said Tamimi forcefully, irritated with Tariq who was obviously keeping the best bit till last, keeping him in the dark, in suspense.

'Checked with Reception, and guess what?'

'Don't string me along, Tariq,' said Tamimi, his displeasure evident. 'I am the one who asks the questions around here!'

'He's reserved a table for dinner for two. Can you guess who's joining him?' Tariq continued instinctively, blanching at the realisation that he'd just asked his boss another question. 'Mahmoud Al Abdullah!'

'I see,' said the Colonel, trying not to show his surprise and excitement, trying to let Tariq think that he, Tamimi, had known all along that this was what would happen. So, Al Abdullah was in London. Why had he not known this? He'd have to sharpen up his surveillance of him in the future – keep tabs on him all the time. His mind racing, he said, 'Tariq, have you got your plan for covering this meeting sorted out?'

'Yes, Colonel, I certainly have. You can rely on me. The table's booked already. Said will be at one as near as possible to the target with one of the girls. I'll be outside in the foyer.'

'Good. Let me know the minute anything happens,' said Tamimi peremptorily, before ringing off.

In Dubai, General Ali picked up the call immediately.

'Yes, Colonel? Masa'a al-khier.'

'General, it looks like Mahmoud Al Abdullah is about to meet with the British Embassy spy Andy Stringer in London!'

'Come and see me,' ordered the General.

Colonel Tamimi went immediately to the Diwan. General Mohammed Ali Makbool was a large, lugubrious bear of a man in his mid-50s. Heavy, drooping eyelids and a fleshy face gave a misleading impression of somnolence, lethargy and inattention. But this facade belied the reality. General Ali had a sharp and incisive brain. A brain which allowed him to process information instantaneously and calculate the best course of action; the best course of action for himself. He was also adept at ensuring that his superiors would believe that this was also the best course for Dubai – and, therefore, for themselves too.

He listened impassively, as his protégé briefed him on the events in London. But he could not stop his eyebrows rising at the mention of the forthcoming dinner engagement that night, betraying his surprise at this development. Had he been a Westerner, he might have sworn volubly at the news. As it was, as a devout Muslim he restricted his utterance to a restrained, 'Wa'Allah! – My God!'

He fixed Tamimi with an impassioned stare, his eyes seeming to bore, gimlet-like, into the Colonel's very being. The Colonel could almost feel the activity in General Ali's brain as he computed all the possible permutations that this new piece of information implied. What did it mean? What were the implications? How could he use it to best advantage – to his best advantage? The Colonel knew very well the depth of enmity between his boss and Al Abdullah.

'Colonel, make sure this works. I'm depending upon you. We need to find out exactly what Al Abdullah is doing meeting a member of MI6, and in London, too! I won't tell anyone yet. I need to be certain. We need the evidence. Get me that. Then I'll tell Sheikh Abdul!'

'And Colonel,' said the General decisively as Tamimi got up to go, 'put all the resources you need on this. Let me know if you need any further support.'

'Thank you General, I have already presumed that this is what you would want me to do. I have another four men about to board the evening's Emirates flight to London. This will give me two teams on the ground. I can follow both subjects tomorrow.'

'Smart bastard!' thought the General to himself. 'He definitely needs watching! Still, better on my side than against me.' Aloud he said, 'Excellent, Colonel, I shall mention all this to Sheikh Abdul at his Majlis this evening. Anything else?'

'Yes, General, can you try to find out what their offices think they're doing, where they think they are? Difficult for me to do it as it might raise a red flag, but not at your level, General. You could do it without raising any suspicions, perhaps?'

'Yes, indeed. I'll ask Sheikh Abdul about Al Abdullah. He'll know what he's supposed to be up to. The British Consul is sure to be at the Majlis tonight. He'll be paying his respects – it's Sheikh Rashid's anniversary today, as you know. I'll tell him to have his man meet with you first thing tomorrow morning to discuss the co-operation on drug smuggling that they're always asking us about. You should be able to see what he's up to that way. Good hunting, Colonel, and goodnight, Ma'a sala'am.'

Half an hour after he had contacted him, Tariq was back on the phone to Colonel Tamimi.

'Colonel, they have met – at the hotel. They're having a drink in the bar now. Sloan's booked a table. We've got one nearby. Not perfect but it should be possible to get some sound.' The tension was evident in his voice. 'When they finish and split up, who do you want me to stay with?'

'Tariq, you're to cover both targets. House Al Abdullah – knowing him, he'll be at the Dorchester. You can easily check that out. See if you can get a room number and book an adjacent room. Let me know at once if there are any developments. And be careful, Tariq. Don't try to push too hard! We can't afford to alert Al Abdullah.' 'Faud and his team will be with you tomorrow, so it should be easy to cover both of them.'

'I'll be careful. I've got a very good girl from the Embassy here, a natural for the job. So I'll see if I can get her at a table beside theirs, Ma'a sala'am.'

It was past 3 am. They still had not found what they were looking for. Bill and Rory had spent the whole evening poring over the Trade Centre companies' directory. The flagship building of the Sheikh Raheem era had attracted many household name companies. One complete floor was occupied by the US Consulate. Another, the prestigious Trade Centre Club on the penthouse floor, offered indulgent luxury and panoramic views of the burgeoning new Dubai on one side, and the old Dubai on the other, to a select fraternity of local Arab businessmen and highly remunerated expatriate chief executives.

They were in Bill's apartment in Deira. Outside, the streets, which had earlier been thronged with eager visitors, had become quieter. Lights still blazed everywhere. And, considering the lateness of the hour, there was still a substantial amount of traffic, mainly taxis carrying late-night partygoers from or perhaps to their latest tryst.

'Bit like Ibiza,' said Rory, 'there must be more nightclubs and bars here than in San Antonio. Only difference is that here they're all inside the hotels!'

They were standing on the small balcony, looking across to the Al Ghurair Centre. At one time the only shopping centre in Dubai, now it was only one of many.

Both men had a whisky in their hands. They had broached the bottle earlier, when they thought they would finish quickly. Now, it was less than half full. They had been able to obtain a considerable amount of information with the connivance of Mahmoud Al Abdullah. He had arranged for Leila to give them the master key to the record office. Bill was well-known to the Pakistani guards at the Commercial Department, and frequently worked there in the office which Red had made available to him. None the less, Bill knew that he could not afford to be seen in the record section late at night. So they had had to move fast, selecting the records of the companies from the list which Mahmoud had given them. They had taken them in batches to the little alcove at the back of Leila's office and photocopied the whole lot.

Bill and Rory had arrived at the front desk of the department about 7 pm, each with a large suitcase. Both were packed full of clothes; mainly sweaty sports gear, selected just to fill the space. Security at the Commercial Department was relaxed, Bill knew; however, it did not do to take unnecessary chances.

'Masa'a al-khier,' Bill said genially to the guards on arrival. 'I'm just going up to the office for an hour or so before going to the airport,' he added, glancing by way of explanation at the suitcases. 'My colleague Mr Rory is travelling with me.'

'Masa'a al-noor,' responded the guard, fingering Bill's suitcase as if to carry out an inspection. A flurry of activity on the 6-inch TV screen behind the security desk, accompanied by Hindi music, attracted his attention. His fellow guards stared fixedly at the screen. They had barely registered the presence of Bill and Rory. The other guard smiled obsequiously and motioned Bill to carry on, his eyes quickly reverting back to the screen.

Now Bill and Rory had finished photocopying this mass of documents. The original files had been returned to their usual homes. The guards continued to be distracted by the latest Bollywood film, and so they had been undisturbed. Bill was relieved.

'Thank God we've got that out of the way!' he said.

'Yes, so far so good,' responded Rory.

'Quick, let's get all this in the suitcases. I'll put all these clothes in these

134

bags and leave them in the office, which I use. I can get them back out another time.' Bill was breathing more easily now that the documents had disappeared into the suitcases.

'You never know who might be paying off the guards to let them know what happens: who works late?... comes in out of hours?... and so on. Mahmoud has made plenty of waves in the Department. He has lots of enemies, with strong connections. Sacked the head of compliance, only last week; scion of a big-hitting tribe.'

Back in the apartment, they had been through all the documents.

'Let's listen to that tape again,' said Rory. Bill quickly wound the tape back to the marker points and pressed the start button. The by now familiar voice of Hamid Al Fadl said: 'The Mahdi people will be over next week. They want to conclude the project deal, sign heads of agreement. They had hoped to meet with you in the office – next Thursday?'

'You deal with it for me Hamid,' said the equally well-known London voice. They played the tape again several times, listening also to the sections before and after.

'We've looked at all the rented offices and accounted for all the companies. Most are household names, aren't they? Like Johnson & Johnson, not by any means what we're looking for, I reckon,' said Bill.

'Yes, I agree with you there. Let's run through again, one more time,' suggested Rory.

'Right-oh – we'll need to refill these first!' Bill poured another two generous tots. The smooth, fiery liquid stimulated them into action.

They began, floor by floor, starting at the top. By the time they got to the eighth floor, Bill had become extremely frustrated. 'There's the Swiss and Italian Embassies on one side and on the other side is that large local law firm, Al Dawli Al Shaab. Below this we get into the conference halls and function rooms, surely? None of this is what we're looking for.'

'We'd best go through it all, just to be sure that we have accounted for everyone,' said Rory. 'What happens on Level 7? That's where the restaurant is, isn't it?'

'Yes, that's right,' confirmed Bill slowly. Something triggered in his mind. 'Wait a minute. The restaurant – it's just a café really – only takes up the left side of the floor, as you come out of the lift.'

'Who's on the other side?' asked Rory.

'That's what I'm asking myself,' said Bill. 'Hold on a minute, I remember now. There's a batch of managed offices. It's a collection of small units. One person on their own sort of thing, managed by the Trade Centre Management Company for the tenants. All the facilities provided centrally, and so on. We overlooked it because we assumed that it was part of the Trade Centre's own operation. But that's all on the floor below.'

They went quickly back to the pile of documents, taking out the Trade Centre Management company files. They immediately found the documents in a separate category, which related to other companies renting space there. There were about fourteen of these altogether. One by one, they went through the registration documents of all of them. Some were obviously not of interest, like the representative offices for a major brand of chocolates.

Suddenly, Bill caught his breath. He was looking at a section of the files categorised as terminated tenancies.

'Look at this,' he shouted excitedly, 'it was right under our noses all the time!'

'What's that?' asked Rory, looking at the piece of paper which Bill had thrust at him.

'Mahdi bloody Consolidated Enterprises International, would you believe! Look at the list of shareholders – Mohammed Al Turk and Luke Stanley! Last year its assets were taken over by another company called Fountain Trading! It's got to be something to do with the Al Mahdi Project – they claim it's an aluminium smelter. But the CIA reckon it's a nuclear facility. Part of the Bushehr Nuclear Power Plant.'

'Wait a minute,' said Rory. 'Do you remember in that section of the recording when Al Fadl was referring to the visitors coming over next week?'

'Yes,' said Bill, reflectively.

'Well, he also said something that was a bit garbled – some interference on the line. I thought he had said Rakesh, or something like that – that it was a person's name – one of the visiting party.'

'Go on,' said Bill, intrigued.

'Right! I reckon what he actually said was via Kish!'

'Via Kish? Kish Island, you mean?'

'Exactly,' said Rory. 'The party's coming from Iran!'

'My God! I reckon you're right. Let's listen to it again.'

This time there was no doubt about it. Al Fadl had said that the visitors due to meet with the London voice would be coming in via Kish Island. That could only mean that they were coming from Iran.

'Hang about,' said Bill, 'these people are coming to see London voice, are they not? Look at that list of directors of Mahdi Enterprises, it has only

136

one Anglo-Saxon name – the others are Arab – and that one there,' he jabbed his finger on the paper. 'Pound to a pinch of salt he's Iranian.'

'So what's linking all these people together?' said Rory.

'Given the people we're dealing with here at the Dubai end, it's got to be money. The only thing they're interested in is feathering their own nests!'

'What about the Iranians?' asked Rory.

'Can't say without knowing who's involved. Iran's a central economy under the Ayatollahs; not much room for free enterprise there, I don't suppose. It's got to be driven by politics; by a power game! It would be bloody surprising if it wasn't for money too, somewhere along the line. We need to cover that meeting on Saturday. That way, we find out what it's all about.'

'But we don't know where this company is, now that it's moved from the Trade Centre,' said Rory.

'I know, but we can check.'

'Yes, but that means going back to the records in the Department. Somebody's going to get suspicious if we keep turning up there.'

'Right,' said Bill, 'we'll have to get Malik to work on it urgently this morning and go through his usual contact. But wait a minute. Let's just check the documents which we have here again,' he said, a sudden thought occurring to him. 'Where are they?'

Rory was already thumbing through the Trade Centre ledger. 'Here we are!' he said, after a feverish search.

'Here, let me have a look!' said Bill. After a few minutes, he held up a document with an exclamation of triumph. 'Got it! This is their lease termination pro-forma – gives some forwarding details. A PO Box number – that won't help much, except to give us a general area. However, we also have a couple of numbers, a landline and mobile.'

'We can call them later when the office is open and use the old "courier package for you…" routine. "Where do you want it delivered?"' said Rory. 'I can do that.'

'No, best if Malik does it. Not many deliveries are organised by well-spoken Brits!'

'I can use my best Indian accent, "Please to let me be having your beloved address?"' said Rory, with a grin.

'No bugger will understand that! Actually, best get Salami, rather than Malik, to do it from the office. Can you fix that?'

Rory nodded.

'Right, I need to get onto Riad and Red at a more civilised time and jack up arrangements to bug Al Turk's new offices, wherever they turn out to be. I'll send Yigal a text now as well – we only have three days altogether before the meeting to get something sorted out.'

40

Without pausing to put the phone down, Colonel Tamimi immediately made another call.

'State security, Jamil speaking.'

'Jamil, it's me. I need something done urgently. You're to get all the photographs that have been taken on this job so far, video, stills, whatever. Get them all together and review them. We need documentary proof that Al Abdullah is working for the British.'

'Yes sir, but... '

'Jamil, no buts! Just get it done. If he's meeting in London with the MI6 man based here in Dubai, it can't be a coincidence. There's no way he should have any non-official contact with Stringer; at least, not without our agreement.'

'But they could just be friends, Colonel. Al Abdullah is very big in the Gulf, remember. Perhaps they play golf together?'

'Possibly... possibly, but it stinks to me. I'd be surprised if it wasn't another game which they're playing together. So get all the photographic coverage and sit down with your guys. What we're looking for is either any regular contact between Al Abdullah and Stringer or, more likely, we're really looking for a go-between. Stringer wouldn't take the risk of meeting Al Abdullah regularly himself if he was trying to recruit him or if he had already recruited him and had to meet to debrief him. He'd do it through someone else, another of his agents. It's the Third Man we're really looking for!'

'Yes, I understand,' said Jamil apprehensively, 'but the problem is the guys in London, they have most of the coverage with them there. There wasn't time to get it all downloaded before they got on the plane.'

'Use your initiative, Jamil! Get on to Tariq. Tell him to sort out some arrangement with the Embassy staff to get all the material, stills and video, downloaded, consolidated and into the diplomatic luggage on the overnight flight. I don't want it sent over the internet. We can't take the risk of GCHQ picking up on it!'

'Right, sir, I am onto it. I'll let you know how it goes.'

A couple of minutes later, Jamil was speaking with Tariq.

'Doesn't he realise we're on the job at the moment? I don't want anyone distracted. That's just the moment when things will kick off. Then we'll miss the key event!'

'Look, Tariq, the boss is adamant. If we don't do this now he'll chop me off at the knees. And if I were you, I wouldn't bother coming back to Dubai!'

'OK, OK,' said Tariq. The pressure was beginning to tell. 'Serves him right,' thought Jamil.

'Look, all you have to do is find someone to get everyone with any shots to download them onto a memory stick, collect them all together.' Whereas a few minutes ago Jamil had seemingly been at a loss as to what to do, now he heard himself lecturing Tariq in just the same way, and sounding very superior. 'And then get one of those donkey's assholes from the Embassy to collect them and stick them in tonight's bag.'

'And we will probably be back in Dubai on the same flight, man!'

'No way – you'll make sure that you fix another couple of days living it up in London, lucky bastard, yla'an haramak!'

First thing next morning, Jamil gathered those team members still in Dubai together. He explained what they were trying to do. It took some time to get everything collated. It was just about half-seven in the morning by now. The courier arrived from the airport off the overnight flight. Despite his grandstanding, it had proved very easy for Tariq to get all the coverage from London on the overnight flight, EK010, which arrived in Dubai at 07:05. Shortly after that, everything had been collated and they all got together. For the next couple of hours they looked intently at the material, constantly reviewing and re-reviewing all of it in the hope of discerning some tell-tale pattern.

'There's nothing very conclusive here,' said Jamil eventually. 'I know it's not very satisfactory without the guys in London. But let's at least try to draw up some sort of a shortlist – a starting point. Then we can review everything again, along with any new stuff, when they get back. And then we'll debrief all that's happened in the last few days.'

Eventually, they settled on a short list of six people: four white, and two from the subcontinent, probably Indian.

Jamil despatched several of his colleagues with the short list to visit other agencies, immigration, CID and so on, while others in the team reviewed recent press articles, TV current affairs programmes, business directories, the membership books of foreign business groups – anything which might provide a clue. All of it a long shot, he knew, but it had to be done. This business wasn't all the glamour of high-speed chases and sleeping with luscious white chicks in fabulous foreign capitals. Most of it was repetitious drudgery, confined to a small, windowless box-like office, looking at the most minute details and hoping to connect them to other equally small details, hoping gradually to put the whole together into some sort of coherent picture. Later, given hindsight, all would seem blindingly clear; but at the time, everything was unclear, uncertain, misleading, impervious to the rays of light. Usually information was illusory, like a mirage shimmering in the white-hot heat of the desert; promising everything but, all too often, failing to deliver on that promise.

The waiter brought their desserts: crème caramel for Mahmoud Al Abdullah and for Andy, the chef's speciality, chocolate slice. The restaurant was busy but not full. Given its prime location just off Piccadilly, the Holiday Inn hotel was surprisingly downmarket, not to say depressingly dull. But its low-key style was ideal. The two diners wanted to be able to discuss their current association with an anonymity which they would not have had in the incestuous, febrile society of Dubai. But they were not to be granted the privacy which they sought. It had been relatively easy for Tariq to get his couple at a table adjacent to the one at which Andy and Al Abdullah were sitting. Said had graduated from Leeds University. His father had spent several years as an under-secretary in the UAE Embassy in London, when Said was a teenager. Moving back to Dubai after university, he had been a natural choice for State Security training. Although it was evident that he was an Arab, his English accent did not betray his Gulf origins. Laura Stubbings' father had, conversely, been First Secretary at the British Embassy in Dubai. His career had been cut short by an adverse report from his Ambassador. He had been scapegoated over a security breach and had been forced to leave the service. He had become embittered, and now lived in Amman.

Laura was working temporarily at the UAE Embassy in London. She and Said blended in well as a couple. Certainly they did not attract the attention of Andy, the professional intelligence operative, off-guard in his home base. Andy and Al Abdullah had been relaxed and conversing casually during the meal. Then, unobserved by all but Laura, the tenor of their conversation changed.

'Mahmoud, it's essential that no-one realises we know each other. We might perhaps meet briefly and informally at an Embassy cocktail party in Dubai. But you mustn't do other than exchange ordinary greetings with me. No discussion about anything, even the development of UAE golf! Otherwise, someone will notice and bring it to General Ali Makbool's attention! So we can only meet outside Dubai, like now, to talk business.'

From the now earnest, serious demeanour of the two diners, it was clear to Laura, straining to hear every word from the next table without appearing to do so, that Andy was giving instructions to Al Abdullah.

She could hear snatches of their conversation, but it was difficult against the general hubbub of conversation in the restaurant to decipher it all. The recorder in her handbag might help, she thought, discreetly pushing her bag further along the floor towards the other table. 'Not too far!' she said to herself, 'otherwise, one of the waiters will trip over it!'

Now Andy was giving further instructions to Al Abdullah.

'Don't worry, Mahmoud, we have a way to sort this out. You know Bill Sloan, who is working with your people on the RAKA investigation?' Mahmoud nodded his head.

'Well, he's one of our agents too.' Al Abdullah's face registered his surprise.

'You are to report to him. He'll debrief you and give you your instructions from us as we go along. It's easy for you to meet under cover of the RAKA project, I think?' Al Abdullah nodded his assent.

'Sloan reports to me, I report to London. You'll meet my boss tomorrow.'

Andy paused, summoned the waiter and ordered coffee.

Laura had picked up the name 'Bill' but it did not mean anything to her. She was dying to let Said know, but knew it might compromise everything if the subjects became suspicious. She wondered what Said had heard as well, but he was sitting on the other side of the table, less well positioned than her. She bit her tongue, hoping that her memory and the recorder, together with whatever Said had heard, would be sufficient for them both to end up with an accurate report of the conversation. Clearly, it was dynamite.

Andy was giving further instructions to Al Abdullah. But the noise level had increased as the diners' tongues were loosened by conviviality and wine. It was impossible to work out what he was saying.

Presently, Andy paid the bill and he and Al Abdullah left the restaurant. Outside in the foyer Tariq received a double bleep from Said, indicating that the subjects were on the move. At Andy's behest, the doorman hailed a taxi for Al Abdullah; when he had seen him off, he returned to the bar and ordered an Edradour malt. He added half as much water again but no ice, which would have turned the un-chill-filtered whisky cloudy. He made several telephone calls and read his texts. And then, finishing the malt, left the bar and went up in the lift to his room, observed by Tariq and one of his team. Five minutes later, the other team reported back: Al Abdullah had gone to the Dorchester, where he too had gone straight to his room.

Both Tariq's teams stood by all night and were covering their respective targets from early the next morning. At the Holiday Inn, Andy had a leisurely breakfast, went back up to his room and then reappeared about five minutes later. He was in a dark grey business suit with a charcoal stripe and wearing a blue shirt and a quiet patterned tie. Carrying a briefcase, he looked every inch the civil servant.

Quickly, a description of his dress was flashed across the team's radio net. Tariq was monitoring this. He immediately passed the information to Fuad, leading the second team covering Al Abdullah.

'Zero One, looks like this one's on the move. How's your friend?'

'Zero Two, haven't seen him yet. He had some fruit juice, coffee and a bowl of cereal taken up to his room about half an hour ago,' replied Said.

'Zero Five, stand by, stand by!' This was Said leading the team at the Holiday Inn. 'Getting into a taxi.'

Almost simultaneously, Fuad was back on the other net, also being monitored by Tariq: 'Zero Two, Ratcatcher in foyer. Wearing blue blazer and smart khaki flannels. He's hanging around – looks like he's waiting for somebody.'

Twenty minutes later, Tariq heard the conclusive report from Said's team. Both their targets, travelling together, had been given access to a large government building at 85 Albert Embankment. Andy had collected Mahmoud Al Abdullah from the Dorchester and then gone down Park Lane, along Grosvenor Place past Victoria Station, down Vauxhall Bridge Road and across Vauxhall Bridge to the futuristic castellated new building on Albert Embankment, which was Britain's new spies' centre.

This was proof positive that Al Abdullah was working for British intelligence. That he was betraying his country. 'General Ali will cut him off at the knees when he hears this!' thought Tariq irreverently.

The teams saw the two subjects emerge from the building later, after lunch. Not just a brief meeting then, Tariq observed to himself. There must have been a very comprehensive briefing for Al Abdullah, probably some training too. As well as that there would doubtless have been the chef's menu lunch in the plush executive penthouse suite occupied by 'C' and his cronies. They would have pushed the boat out for their latest recruit.

Not a Cold War triumph like Penskovsky or Gordievsky perhaps but, none the less, in this most unstable new world which had emerged from the perverse security of mutually assured destruction after the collapse of the Berlin Wall, it would be seen by MI6 as a notable catch! Al Abdullah was a rising star, destined to attain ministerial rank in the UAE government. With its fabulous oil wealth and independent stance, the UAE was an important player in the Middle East and punched well above its weight in the international circles of the UN. The emerging threats of international terrorism, political Islam and Al Qaeda were all centred in the Middle East. At the heart of these complex, interrelated problems lay Israel and the Palestinians. The UAE was the obvious broker. It would be invaluable for Britain to have someone at the top table, able to tell them what was going on behind the scenes. Most importantly, it would be a powerful bargaining chip for the UK, something to help redress the balance of the special relationship with the US. All this Colonel Tamimi appreciated in a flash as Tariq reported to him later that morning, using the secure communication facilities at the UAE Embassy in Princes Gate.

Andy had dropped Al Abdullah back at the Dorchester and then gone on to Knightsbridge where he had done some shopping, buying a smart ladies' blouse in Harvey Nichols and a pair of deck shoes in Harrods. He had then gone back to the Holiday Inn, collected his bags, checked out, and got a taxi to Heathrow. He caught the early evening flight back to Dubai.

Al Abdullah had paid a visit to Frederick & Stevens' smart offices in Savile Row. Then he too had checked out of his hotel and, at Gatwick, had caught the overnight flight to Miami.

143

42

Tariq and Colonel Tamimi were huddled together in a corner of the Colonel's office. Between them, the mini-cassette recorder was playing. Tariq turned up the volume.

'There's a lot of interference, scraping of plates and clinking of cutlery. Fortunately, the tables are very close together, so it was possible to get something.'

Tamimi nodded, as the tape began playing. Against the background noises, he heard two people talking. One spoke English with an obvious Arabic inflection – and in an American accent – while the other spoke in his native tongue with an accent which might have been centred on Oxford. Tamimi would have recognised the Arab speaker's voice, had he not already known who it was. Tariq had previously told him the gist of the conversation between Al Abdullah and Andy in the Holiday Inn restaurant. But Tamimi had wanted to hear it for himself. It would bring him closer to his quarry; help him to worm his way into his brain; help him to understand his motives and predict his reactions.

Most of the talking was being done by Andy: 'It's vital, Mahmoud, that you help Bill as much as... '

'Stop the tape!' said the Colonel peremptorily. 'Who is this man Bill?'

'Not sure at the moment, Colonel,' replied Tariq. 'We're rechecking all our recent surveillance of Al Abdullah and Andy Stringer. We have a few possibles. Now that Stringer is back in Dubai, we've redoubled our efforts. I hope to have something tomorrow.'

'Very good! It is now your most important task. We need to identify Al Abdullah's contact urgently!'

'All we have is this reference to someone called Bill. Let me play some more of the tape, Colonel.' He pressed the start button.

Andy was still speaking: 'As he is working for you on the RAKA investigation, it's very easy for you to meet each other without arousing suspicion. I'll need to get your office swept to make sure no-one is listening with you on the phone! I can get Bill to arrange that when you return.'

'I'm worried about surveillance from the Sheraton just across the street,' said Al Abdullah. 'I read that people can pick up vibrations on windowpanes with high sensitivity long-range microphones?'

'It's possible; some agencies do have this capability. Easy to protect against, however. I'll look into it and get Bill to deal with the problem for you.'

Tamimi picked up the note of disinterest in Andy's voice. Clearly, he considered Al Abdullah to be paranoid. But had Andy been aware that he, Tamimi, was even now listening to this conversation, two days after it had taken place, he would have found his own complacency misplaced.

'The most important thing for you and Bill is to find out where the RAKA funds are going to. What Sheikh Abdul's playing at!'

'I can keep you informed on what's happening with RAKA, of course.' Al Abdullah had taken over the conversation: 'Bill's already looking into the accounts. I have access to most of the financial information but there is one account which the Sheikh controls himself. That's the one we're working on now.'

'Why is that?' said Andy.

'What do you mean?'

'Why doesn't he let you deal with that account as well?'

'RAKA's a business like any other… '

'You must be joking!' interjected Andy. 'Have you forgotten that this is Dubai? You of all people should know that!'

'Look, I am running the business for him – I'm running all his public businesses. But I'm not in his confidence when it comes to some other things. That's the way we Arabs operate. Anyway, I don't really know what he's up to. But whatever it is, I don't like it. I can't put my finger on it yet. I think that the Prosecutor General, Talat Fuad Khadr, is involved. And Sheikh Abdul also meets frequently with Sanjay Dal.'

'Who's he?' asked Andy.

'He's a well-known hood. Used to live here in Dubai until he fell foul of the Ruler. He's an Indian, a famous Bollywood actor. He's idolised by the women of India. But he's also a Mafia godfather, and he's a passionate Muslim. He's known as the Goldman..'

'Sounds like a contradiction in terms?' said Andy quizzically. 'This is what we need to focus on. What links these people together?'

At this point, several new voices were heard on the tape.

'This is when the two couples sat down at the next table to ours,' said Tariq, 'it's not possible to make out anything else. There was too much noise.' He switched off the tape.

'OK, what have we got from all that?' said Colonel Tamimi rhetorically.

'It's certainly proof that our friend Al Abdullah is in the pocket of the British.'

'Enough to charge him, Colonel. He's betraying our country! We should pick him up tonight,' said Tariq indignantly. 'Throw him into jail. The Secret Police court in Abu Dhabi would make mincemeat of him. He'd be sentenced to death, but... '

Tariq was just getting into his stride, it seemed, fulminating against the traitor, but Colonel Tamimi interrupted him.

'Hold back, Tariq. I tell you, we have to think in the long term. If we rush in and arrest him now we'll lose the chance to get any of his accomplices, like this British businessman. We'll miss the opportunity to embarrass the British government. When the time is right,we'll declare the Protocol Officer in the Embassy persona non grata. That way we'll create a major diplomatic row. It'll make them realise that they now can't do what they like. They can't just treat us like any other colony to be exploited any more to suit their best interests whenever they feel like it. I'll teach them to try to fuck with us! Now let's continue.'

'Well yes,' said Tariq, 'we know that British intelligence is behind the involvement with RAKA. The main task given to Al Abdullah and Bill is to discover details of Sheikh Abdul's private account in RAKA. What does that mean?'

'I don't know, Tariq. I'll have to ask General Ali when I get to see him later. Leave that to me. Find this man Bill. It's your main task now.'

Tariq headed back to the operational centre, where he would give the teams their orders for the evening's work.

'It's in the Al Khobar Building, not far from the Trade Centre on the other side of the Sheikh Zayed Highway. That rather fine pink tower standing on its own. There, in the penthouse suite on the 18th floor. I've had a look around already. There's a couple of people working there permanently: a Pakistani gofer; then a guy who must be an Iranian – he's obviously the manager – smart, intelligent, looked pretty switched-on.'

'What's his name?' asked Red, who had been listening intently and had made a few brief notes.

'Sajjad Shirazi. I was wondering if there was any significance in him being Iranian. Sort of expect him to be Indian, or perhaps even a Brit,' continued Bill. 'There's space in the office for two or three other people.'

'Probably Al Fadl and our friend Luke. But I don't think we're likely to see him back here now!'

'Putting his head in the noose to come back, I guess,' said Bill.

'Exactly. Do you know that Brit involved in the golf club scandal? Arrogant sod came back to take photographs and so on to try to prove that he had not been involved. Hardly surprising that they picked him up coming in, and threw him into jail. Still there five years later,' explained Red.

'There was a time when they'd never have dared to do that – to stick a Brit in jail, I mean.'

'It's a wake-up call for you Limeys, eh!'

'And it was you bloody Yanks who started it all with the Boston Tea Party!' retorted Bill.

'The biggest headache's going to be dealing with the entire product. There are five lines into the office. They might all be busy at times. To make it worthwhile, someone has to listen to everything that's said.'

Malik had been quickly able to locate the building to which Fountain Trading had moved. They had rented the plush penthouse suite at the top of the Al Khobar Building. This was one of the first office blocks to have been built along what was becoming the teeming Sheikh Zayed Highway. It was a prominent futuristic pink building, midway along the highway. After a brief reconnaissance, it did not take Bill long to get the proposal with the costs off to Red. A few hours later, Red called to confirm that the job was on – in time for Yigal to catch the overnight flight from Heathrow.

Abdul Raheem had appeared in many Hollywood films, perhaps even with Bogie in *Casablanca*. Or, at least, he looked like someone caricaturing an Arab who had done so. He had a large lugubrious face, hooked nose, stooped shoulders and a large gut, evident even under the forgiving folds of the dishdasha. Bill already knew that he was Mahmoud Al Abdullah's Mr Fixit. He had been put at Bill's disposal. Abdul Raheem obtained the key to the telephone switch room at the rear of the building; no-one took any notice as all three of them went inside. It took Yigal only a couple of minutes to find the terminal numbers which he needed to look for within the building. Earlier in the morning, Bill had rented one of the managed offices in the Al Khobar Building, which was similar to those which he had come across at the Trade Centre with Rory. This office suite was on the eighth floor. Bill had told the office manager that he was setting up an office for a South African company which he represented, dealing in mining products, which had just won a major contract in the region and would be using Dubai as its hub to support their operations.

'I'll be on my own to start with. And then here from time to time only, until my colleagues begin to arrive in a few months' time,' he told the manager, 'but I'm anxious to move in at once, if that's OK?'

'Yes, certainly. I can let you have the keys this afternoon. I need the deposit first, of course.'

So far, so good, Bill had thought. Now he also needed to get hold of his friend Asif at Al Wasl Keys. Abdul Raheem had introduced him to Bill. His skills had come in useful already in the Commercial Department – using him had proved safer and easier on a couple of occasions than taking the risk of alerting targets by doing things officially. Yigal determined that the best approach was to tap into the lines to Fountain Trading in the roof space above the office that Bill had rented that morning. Now that he knew which lines belonged to it, it would be a very simple matter just to tie in the extra wires on the cable frame.

'That's fine,' said Yigal. 'If you can get me into the roof space, that's all I need. It'll only take a couple of minutes for me to do the job.'

'Right,' said Bill. 'I'll get the locksmith working on the keys; he should be able to give us sets of master keys so that we can go anywhere in the building.'

'That's great! In the meantime then, I'll go down to the souk and buy some voice-activated cassette recorders. I'll get a taxi to save having to bother you.'

'What time would you like to do the job tonight?'

'About eight or nine o'clock,' said Yigal.

'Well then, I'll pick you up at the hotel about 7.30 pm. By the time we get to work, the offices should be pretty empty – not much chance of being interrupted, unless one of the guards is going round on patrol.'

Yigal left to get a taxi. Bill went to the office to wait for Asif. When he arrived, Bill briefed him on the job and explained what he wanted him to do.

'I need you to ensure that we have master keys which will let me get into the offices on the eighteenth floor. And also, very important, so that I can get into the roof space on this floor. Have a look around and see what you think. Then come back and tell me what you need and when you can do the job. I need access into the roof space later this evening,' said Bill. 'I'll be in the office here. OK, have you got that, Asif?' Asif nodded enthusiastically.

'There's just one little problem I need to tell you about! The access hatch into the roof space is in the ladies toilet just outside the office door.'

He indicated the door to his newly-acquired office. Already, he had brought over some spare working files from his proper office and spread them around to make it look as if he meant business.

Asif smiled benignly. It was sometimes difficult, Bill thought, to be sure if the message had gone in. Asif was convinced that he understood English perfectly, but Bill realised this was very far from the reality. And he did not speak any Urdu.

It seemed to be taking Asif a long time, thought Bill. It should only have taken him a couple of minutes to have a look around and sort out in his mind what he needed to do. Then he would be able to go back to his shop and do the work there, so that he could come back in the evening and make the adjustments, enabling Bill and Yigal to get access. Suddenly there was a loud commotion in the corridor outside. Then the door was flung open. The Centre manager, a small, thin Canadian woman, came in peremptorily. In Dubai, as in much of the Middle East, policemen dress like soldiers. Behind the manager were a couple of large men, dressed like soldiers. There was no doubt. They were policemen. In their khaki drill uniform with smart shorts and shiny silver numbers on their epaulettes, they stood ominously in the doorway, holding the hapless Asif between them. Asif's hands were forced behind his back. The two policemen had him firmly by the shoulders. His heels were raised off the floor. Bill saw the silent plea in Asif's eyes. The policemen forced Asif around in order to face the manager of the rented offices, the Canadian woman that Bill had negotiated the lease with that very morning. Bill saw that Asif's wrists were manacled. The manager stepped forward.

'This man!' she said, pointing at Asif with a look of disgust. 'He say's he's working for you?'

'Yes,' said Bill, lamely.

'Well, he has just been found skulking around in the ladies toilet – one of my colleagues found him there. She thought that he was going to rape her. She's hysterical!'

'Oh hell!' thought Bill. This was going to be an ignominious end to everything before it had even started. One of the policemen drew out another set of handcuffs and moved menacingly towards Bill. Bill stood firm. The blow struck him at the same time that Bill realised it was on the way. Time froze as the policeman's arm rose, and chopped down in an arcing back-hander. The blow caught him on the side of the temple. He fell like a stone. He ended up in a crumpled heap on the tiled floor.

44

They met this time in the café at the top of the escalator in the Crown Plaza on Sheikh Zayed Highway. Just as soon as coffee had been placed in front of them, Andy's demeanour changed. He looked concerned. He usually looked concerned, but this time it was more pronounced. For once, he dispensed with his usual pedantic and elliptical manner. He got straight to the point. 'Look, there's something I have to tell you, something serious. I need to warn you!'

He leaned forward, his voice dropping, 'We've got good reason to believe that General Mohammed Ali Makbool, he's the Secret Police boss, is on the warpath – against us! He's been tasked by Sheikh Abdul to provide as much covert assistance to the Taliban as he possibly can!' He paused, took a sip of coffee. Bill's blood ran cold; a shiver of fear coursed up his back, he felt his mouth go dry, his hands became clammy. The implications were obvious and grim. Andy proceeded to confirm this with chilling detail.

'Look,' his favourite introduction again. 'Look,' he said, 'we've known, or at least suspected, for some time now that Dubai Limited has stepped out of line. We thought we were working with them. And in fact, we were working with them on investigating RAKA and the Trade Centre Arbitration against Mohammed Al-Fayed, not to mention the Al Ghazi saga. But only up to a point, it seems. A point selected by them in their own interests. But not bloody well in our interest! They were just using us while it was convenient. But now the stakes have gone up. Sheikh Abdul and his henchmen have gone up too – up to their necks with the Taliban. I'm bloody sure they're hatching something but I just can't get on to whatever it is.'

The pretty waitress, probably a Sri Lankan, Bill noticed, cleared their coffee cups. Andy called her back and ordered two more – a sign of further talking to come. His government service budget didn't normally allow such liberality.

'The other thing we've found out is that the Prosecutor General is the interlocutor between Dubai and the Taliban,' he said.

'That's why the bugger is always in Afghanistan or in Pakistan's western border region,' exclaimed Bill. 'The bastard! What a hypocrite; he's supposedly managing Sheikh Abdul's Islamic charities there!'

'Well, he probably is,' said Andy. 'But charity is a loosely-defined concept here; most of the charities are linked to the Jihadist groups and their Madrassas.'

'It's just the same as the Americans and bloody NORAID. The naivety of the Americans in being conned into supporting the IRA!' Bill said, with feeling.

'Not quite the same. As you say, the American public was generally naive and many who gave money genuinely thought that their donations were going to help oppressed Catholics in the North, not IRA gangsters.' Andy continued: 'In this case, the money comes from senior Gulf Arabs and they know exactly where it's going!' He paused, then went on, 'But what I really wanted to say was that General Mohammed Ali will now be hell-bent on finding out exactly what we know – and who's telling us what we do know!' Again Bill felt that shiver up his back.

'It's really got to the stage where we're not even pretending to co-operate with the Secret Police. The situation has become extremely bloody uncomfortable! We know we're under constant surveillance: in our homes, at the office, on our mobiles, when we're out and about.'

'Where the hell does that leave me?' exclaimed Bill.

It was a bumpy landing. But his progress through Gatwick had been uneventful. Or so it had seemed to Shahid. He was unaware that his departure had generated a number of communications between GCHQ in Cheltenham and Thames House in London.

Tel Aviv airport was in darkness when they arrived. Shahid's papers showed him to be returning home for a brief visit to his parents in the West Bank after the university term. 'You are Nadir al-Hourani, one of the more than 3 million Arab citizens of Israel. Your father was a policeman,' Ahmed had said. Nearly true, reflected Shahid.

At the exit from the baggage terminal, his proxy father met him. Each had been shown good photographs of the other. They were able instantly to recognise each other and embrace like father and son.

Shahid knew that Omar and Bakri were also meeting the new relatives of theirs that had been arranged for them through Ahmed's administrative support network. He had caught a brief glimpse of Omar standing at the baggage carousel waiting for his luggage. Once during the flight he had passed Bakri as he made his way to the toilet at the rear of the aircraft. They had studiously avoided making eye contact. Now he was in his new father's car, an elderly Honda Civic, heading along the north-west side of the airport. He had been told that his father's name was Yasir.

'Come with me, my dear Wahab,' he had said, after their welcoming embrace. 'We'll soon have you home to Mother. She's cooking your favourite mezze. It's wonderful to see you! What a shame that you cannot stay. But by Allah, we'll enjoy the little time we have.'

In the car, Yasir became alert and businesslike. Shahid could see that he was paying particular attention to his rear-view mirror. They left the airport. Yasir was clearly satisfied that no-one was following them. He began to give Shahid his instructions. He did not notice the helicopter flying at a height of 500 metres, a quarter of a mile behind them.

'I have all the equipment in the car. We'll be there in about fifteen minutes. I'll drop you on the main road. It is only about 100 metres up the rough track and into a disused quarry on the left. It's surrounded by trees and bushes – good cover. Your two Brother soldiers in Islam will be following shortly. They're being taken by roundabout routes. My people will ensure that they are not followed. No reason why they should be. None of us are known to the Jews. They'll also be dropped off by their drivers and make their way to the car to join you. The keys are in a plastic bag buried under a large piece of slate, just by the exhaust pipe. Your job is to drive them to the target. They'll know the way and what the target is. All you have to do is drop them off when and where they tell you and then drive to the airport and get the afternoon flight to Kabul. Park the car at the main airport. When you get back, tell your controller in London where the car is parked. Then we can pick it up later, if it's clean. We have separate keys, so just lock the keys you have in the car under the driver's mat.' He paused, 'Any questions?'

'What's the target?' asked after a few minutes.

'You'll find out – your colleagues will tell you. Right, get ready to get out now.'

A few minutes later, the car pulled across to the side of the road, at the start of a narrow track.

'Out you get! God be with you, Brother. May he bless your endeavours, Ma'a Sala'am.'

Shahid barely had time to get his small bag out of the back before the car pulled out, back onto the main road. Its lights were soon lost in the darkness.

The bag bumped along the uneven stony ground. There was a three-quarter moon, which provided just enough light by which Shahid could follow the track. He cursed constantly as the bag continually tipped over on the large stone-strewn path.

Up above, the pilots noticed the car stopping.

'Hang on a minute,' said the co-pilot, observing with the binoculars. The pilot circled the chopper. But, almost immediately, it was on its way again.

'Must've been having a piss,' said the pilot, the senior of the two.

'A bloody quick piss!' said his colleague. 'I guess you're right. Should we go down and check the area just in case?'

'Better stay with the car – it's a new one on us. This way we'll find out if our friend from London is up to anything, and we also have an ident on his contact.' He reported back to Control. There the Duty Intel officer called his contact in Thames House to update him.

Shahid proceeded with his task, without the company of the Israeli watchers.

He was watching Al Jazeera's latest breaking news, which interrupted the travel programme on Jordan. An attractive place, he thought, somewhere he ought to go. It seemed that it had a softer edge than much of the Middle East.

'Israeli sources are reporting that a suicide bomber has just blown himself up in Tel Aviv. At the moment we have no details of any casualties. We'll have an update from Hamid, who's on the ground, in a few minutes.'

The announcer, a pretty young Arab woman in hijab, with heavy make-up, kohl-blackened eyes and long, purple manicured nails, engaged the camera earnestly. It was clear that she was trying not to look distracted. She passed on to the viewers the message which had been received in her earphone thirty seconds previously:

'We are also getting reports of a shooting incident in the vicinity of the bombing. It seems that there was a second attacker who fled the scene after throwing away his belt. He was wounded by police but managed to escape.'

By this time, video pictures were being screened from the site of the bombing. The scene was all too familiar. Distraught women and children were milling about, crying and wailing. Men ran in different directions, as if fulfilling an urgent personal mission, in reality being in the same state of shock as their women. There were several badly wounded young children, including a 10-year-old girl whose stomach had been torn open by a piece of shrapnel. Her intestines were strewn over the rough hardness of the brick paving, not far from the entrance to the shopping centre. An old man, keening and weeping as he did so, tried to scoop up the bloody mess and put it back inside the child. Probably the girl's grandfather, his instinctive but unsuccessful efforts were mercifully interrupted by an efficient Israeli doctor, accompanied by two paramedics. The camera panned away reluctantly to show pictures of the debris-strewn entrance to the shopping arcade. Smoke was pouring out of several shops which, until a few minutes ago, had been modern-styled glass-fronted buildings and were now a twisted, shattered framework. Stones and bricks were piled up in crazy unstable piles, the jagged shards of broken glass sticking out at random angles like some piece of futuristic modern art. Now the announcer, her beauty a sharp contrast to the ugly scene which Shahid was witnessing, was back on with more breaking news:

'This is some footage which we have just received from our reporter at the scene, Hamid.' The reporter was seen outside the area where the bomb had detonated, beside the police cordon. 'It is understood that several people may have been killed and there are many injured. The target was a bar, Mike's Place in central Tel Aviv... '

The announcer interrupted: 'A taped message has just been received by our Doha offices from Hizb ut Tahrir, claiming responsibility.'

'Alaikum, Allah Akbar!' A familiar voice rang out. Shahid recognised it at once, even before Bakri's stern and unforgiving face appeared on the screen. With a shocking jolt he was transported back to East London, to Ahmed and the suicide tape.

He did not need to listen to know what Bakri would say next. Just then his flight to Kabul was called. Reluctantly, he started to move towards Gate 5A.

Glancing over his shoulder as he left the holding area, he saw that Al Jazeera had reverted to its normal programme. There had been no mention of Omar.

It was a night flight. Shahid was unable to sleep. In his mind's eye, he saw the pictures from Tel Aviv. It was as if he was watching a loop of film, endlessly repeating itself, on playback. His mind transposed the face of the beautiful Arab announcer and the scarred and torn body of the pretty Jewish girl. That was someone's daughter, someone's sister; the thought bored into Shahid's brain like a weevil.

He tried to pull himself together. This was jihad. He had known that it would not be easy, would be difficult. He had played a part, a small part, in the overall plan. The operation had been a success. Bakri had achieved his objective. He, Shahid, had done his bit. He was a blooded Jihadist. But in the cold darkness of the blacked-out plane, he could not escape the image of a little Jewish girl. This was his war, but was she his enemy?

He had been told to go and check in at a small, nondescript boarding-house. Shahid had been given his instructions by Ahmed, before leaving London. He was to go to the Golden Light Hotel on Muslim Street, just across from the Delhi Darbar Indian restaurant, one of the most popular eateries with Afghanis. The formalities at the airport on arrival were brief and cursory. Picking up his luggage, he had hailed a taxi. He gave the hotel name to the driver. The driver's eyes narrowed; immediately, he began an animated conversation. 'By Allah, brave Jihadis strike a massive blow against the Zionists, Allah Akbar.'

It was at once evident where his sentiments lay. Shahid was surprised. Surprised that this taxi driver should already be aware of, and interested in, a bombing in far-off Tel Aviv. He was surprised by the willingness of the driver to express his sentiments so unequivocally to a complete stranger at first meeting.

Then he remembered a conversation with Ahmed when he was being tutored for his new life.

'As a Jihadi, you will find that you are always among friends in the Muslim world. When you are in Pakistan, you will immediately realise that you are at home, back where you belong, back where your heart is. And you will see that, as a Jihadi, you are not one among few, but rather one among many. You will not need to hide your views, because those that you meet will think as you do. Not many will have the courage to act, as you have. Many will be jealous of you, that you have done so.'

At the time, Shahid had been sceptical. He thought it was just Ahmed's sales talk. Now he began to take it seriously. Thinking of the taxi driver's reaction when he named the hotel, Shahid wondered whether or not it was an open secret that the hotel was a Mujahedeen safe house. Nevertheless, he knew that he must remain cautious and not wear his sentiments on his sleeve for all the world to see.

Probing gently, he asked the taxi driver to tell him more about the events in Israel, telling him that he was unaware of anything as he had been travelling.

The driver needed little prompting.

'It was some Jihadis from England. They carry out attack in Israel. In the name of the Prophet, peace be upon Him. There were two men, both from London. Imagine it! Our Muslim brothers in England are with us. The infidels cannot stop us.' He slammed his brakes on hard to avoid a careening motorcycle appearing suddenly from nowhere. 'Everywhere up in arms. The world will be ours and we all have rightful place in new Islamic order!'

Again, Shahid was taken aback by the openness of the man and his passionate support of the jihad.

'But tell me, brother,' he said, 'what happened? What did they do, these Muslim men from England?'

'One blew up at a bar in Israel. Killed over twenty Jews, God is merciful, Alhamdulillah! He in heaven now and will get the reward of the Prophet, peace be upon Him.'

'You said that there were two men. What happened to the other?'

'He shot and wounded by police. CNN say that he run away. He drop his suicide vest by supermarket. Then bomb go off.'

Omar had lost his nerve, thought Shahid. He'd always thought that Omar was the stronger of the two. But Bakri had gone through with it, and Omar had not. Now he faced spending the rest of his life in an Israeli jail thinking about it, trying to work out why he had chickened out. Deep down, Shahid realised that Omar would not be able to live with himself because he would know that he had not done the right thing. And all the world would know it, too.

The taxi ride was not long, and soon Shahid was checking into the run-down hotel on the outskirts of the city. The receptionist eyed him sharply. Shahid used the name he had been given by Ahmed. The receptionist checked his list.

'Yes, I have a booking for you, Mr Wahab. Room 34 – it's on the second floor at the front. A nice room!'

He handed the keys to Shahid, took a deposit of $20, and directed him to the room.

Early next morning Shahid was awakened by an urgent knocking on his door. He had eventually slept long and heavily after the journey and the dramatic events of the previous few days. At first when trying to sleep, his mind had been full of a kaleidoscope of flashing lights accompanied by the sound of guns and nearby explosions. Then the contorted faces of Bakri and Omar appeared as if begging him to join them on some idyllic journey. But no matter what he did to follow them, he was thwarted by some unseen hand.

Bleary-eyed and with a towel around his body, he opened the door.

'Sala'am alaikum, brother Shahid,' exclaimed the visitor, 'come quickly! You need to come with me now. Hurry, or we'll be late! Alhamdulillah!' Shahid was alarmed.

'Sala'am, but who are you? I was told that someone would meet me here this morning at breakfast time.' He glanced at his watch. 'But it's only 5.30 am, and it seems that you have not come to meet me, only to take me away somewhere else.'

'I have orders to take you to meet someone. So quickly, get a move on!'

Taken aback by the man's abruptness and apparent hostility, Shahid had no idea what was going on. He realised that he did not even know the other's name.

'Never mind my name,' said the visitor, 'you do not need to know it!' With that, he turned and went to the doorway. Pausing briefly, he looked round and said, 'I will be in the car. Be there in five minutes; otherwise go back to the airport whence you came!' He added as an afterthought: 'And you must try to forget my face as well.'

After the door slammed shut, Shahid made a quick decision. The man clearly knew who Shahid was. That he would find him here. If this person was not who he claimed to be, an emissary of Shahid's contacts, then he would have taken Shahid hostage or killed him, not given him the opportunity to escape.

Quickly but conscientiously, he performed his morning ablutions in full observance of Sharia. Then he discarded the clothes in which he had travelled the previous day, and also slept in. As soon as he dressed in a black dishdasha and skullcap, he threw everything into the rucksack and went swiftly down the stairs, bypassing the slow and unstable lift; a lift which in most other parts of the world would have long since been consigned to the local museum.

His new companion was sitting at the wheel of a battered Russian UAZ69 Jeep. Signalling Shahid to get in, the driver gunned the engine and drove fast and recklessly along the cobbled, potholed streets of the city.

Quickly they left the built-up area and were soon in the open countryside. It was a beautiful summer's morning. There were some patches of billowing white clouds but the sky was mostly blue, azure with a sharp clarity. Occasionally they saw small groups of people, probably families, labouring in the fields. The main crop – almost the only crop – was unknown to Shahid. In answer to his enquiry, the monosyllabic driver uttered the single word 'Poppy!'

'Of course, of course!' exclaimed Shahid. 'How did I not realise that?'

After several hours they were driving along a flat valley bottom. The ground was stony and the soil thin. Shahid wondered how anyone could eke out a living in such harsh conditions. On either side the valley rose steeply to the foothills, leading to much higher mountains behind. Many of these retained some winter snow and some, Shahid realised, had permanent icecaps. This was the fabled Hindu Kush, familiar to all students and practitioners of the Great Game. He could see from the sun's position, just appearing over the flanks of the mountains in front of them on the right side of the valley, that they were headed in a north-easterly direction.

At a late hour in the day, as the sun sank behind the hills, they arrived at Pir Zadeh. They had stopped at a small village where they were able to buy some local unleavened bread and some dates. Shahid filled up his water bottle from the village well and urinated in the communal toilets, under a tree accompanied by a myriad of flies. Again they stopped by the roadside and Shahid helped the driver fill up the petrol tank from a couple of jerry cans. Shahid noted the Cyrillic script. He was able to decipher the date of manufacture – 1971. He wondered what sights these metal containers might have witnessed, had they been able to do so. Now here they were still in use, fighting for a different cause. They set off again. And still his companion maintained a stony, almost unbroken silence.

Finally they stopped by a goatherd's rustic shack at a point where the road divided, one branch deviating to the left from the valley bottom, heading upwards towards the beckoning mountains now rose-tinted from the glow of the rapidly disappearing sun.

Suddenly he heard behind him his companion speaking volubly in an Urdu dialect which Shahid did not understand. It was as if the floodgates had suddenly been opened. A torrent of pent-up words tumbled out. Turning, Shahid saw that the man was speaking animatedly into a mobile phone. Finishing the call the man, now almost friendly, said, indicating the phone: 'My friend, my blood brother! We do jihad together against the Ruskies and now the Amerikis. We will send them home, dead or alive! I leave you here. I must not know where you are going. Someone will pick you up.'

Whereupon he leapt into the Jeep, gunned the engine and drove away, back in the direction from which they had come. It quickly disappeared from Shahid's view, concealed by the deepening gloaming and the dust cloud which hung heavily in the dense atmosphere.

After an early morning shower and breakfast, Bill drove to the Bur Juman Centre and went to the ATM on the Trade Centre Road side. He printed a mini-statement. It showed the 75,000 dirhams deposit he had been expecting. It had been sent by the swift interbank transfer system from the National Bank of Cyprus the day before. Just as Peter had promised. He withdrew 50,000 dirhams. Carefully putting the money in the prepared envelope and then the envelope in his small briefcase, he went inside the centre through the car park, coming out at the end facing the Creek. He went into the Orchestra Café and ordered a large latte. He did not have to wait very long before Rory appeared, drew up a chair opposite him and sat down. 'Hi there,' said Rory. 'Have you got the cash?'

'Yes, it's here,' said Bill, reaching into the briefcase. He handed the envelope across the table to Rory who took out the wad of notes, counted them and nodded. He put them all back in the envelope and put the envelope in his own briefcase.

'Right, so it's all go?' asked Rory. 'I had a call from the contact about ten minutes ago. The truck that's collecting the consignment is on the way at present.

Last night the stuff was taken out of Jebel Ali. They just nodded it through. There were no customs formalities. The guards glanced in the back, but they looked with a Nelsonian eye. So the big boss, whoever he was, had clearly done his stuff and everyone had been taken care of. They took it to a warehouse just near the Sheikh Zayed Highway. You know, you turn off the highway as if you're going to Nad Al Sheba.' Bill nodded.

'Well, just down from the roundabout and over the main highway there's a petrol station, Emirates Petrol. You turn across to the left just before the petrol station. Go along about a quarter of a mile. Take the third right-hand road and then the second left and Bob's your uncle. The warehouse is just along on the left-hand side. It has a large sign – Star Batteries.'

'What time?' asked Bill.

'They're due to be there at half-eleven. According to our source, there are five or six containers in there, in addition to the two we're interested in.'

'What brand?'

'A mixture of brands of all the big three. The two we've been offered are Sherburne Light,' said Rory. 'Do they know?'

'Yes! I've warned off Peter Gilroy and he's looking forward to scoring a hit. So make sure it goes off well, Rory. Peter did say that there's a lot of chatter in the market. People know that we're out there. There are more and more indications that the people behind it – the big hitters – are getting their corns trodden on. They've got the political clout to safeguard their position. It's not going to be possible to do it this way for long. We'll have to re-think our tactics, otherwise it'll be too dangerous.'

'Where did you get all that from?' said Rory.

'Do you remember I told you a week or so ago that Peter told me he knew what happened in Dubai? He's obviously got good sources over there in Cyprus who, in turn, are linked into the local market here. The whole region's like a goldfish bowl. Dubai's particularly incestuous, as we all know!'

'Certainly there's been a change in the market. Anybody offering counterfeit now is demanding a substantial up-front deposit and obviously doing a lot of checking before they agree to do the deal. A year ago, you could do it no questions asked,' said Rory. 'Anyway, it's time I got on the road or I'll miss the RV.'

'Fine,' said Bill. 'I'll be right behind you. I'll wait in the area of the petrol station. Give me the call-in when it's all set up. I'll tell the CID to get their man there at a quarter-past eleven. It'll probably be Sergeant Mohammed Akbar again.'

160

'Well if it is, see if you can get our video camera back from him. Bugger's had it for about two months now and we could do with it ourselves.'

Bill looked hard at Rory. 'Right-oh. Good luck, see you later,' he said. They both headed off to their cars. Bill called the CID office. He wasn't able to speak directly with the Anti-Counterfeit Department. He left a message. A few minutes later Sergeant Mohammed called him back.

'Yes Mr Bill, I will be there in time – I know the place well.'

He took a call from Rory, 'There's going to be a half-hour delay.'

'Are they getting cold feet?' wondered Bill.

'I don't know,' said Rory, 'but they're definitely pretty jumpy at present. I've never seen them like this. Anyway, I've got the truck the shipment's to be loaded onto in position – it's all ready just a few blocks away from the depot. I'll be in the front with the driver. You come along as back-up just as soon as we make contact. I'll send you a text to let you know when to break cover.'

Bill relayed the message to Sergeant Mohammed.

The industrial estate was like any other in Dubai, or any other of the Emirates for that matter: serried ranks of warehouses with corrugated iron roofs, stretching along the metalled road on both sides as far as the eye could see, apparently plonked at random in the desert. Few exhibited any signs of life. It was like many aspects of the phenomenon that was Dubai. One moment there would be nothing. Then there would be a perception that they should do something, but what? Then the theme would be selected. Today, it might be finance; tomorrow, information technology. The word would go out from on high – a royal command. Dutifully, with the expectation of gaining both kudos and profit, and in the hope of catching the Ruler's eye – or, more to the point, the eye of Sheikh Abdul – high net worth individuals would invest their otherwise idle petro-dollars in the new idea. Innumerable cranes would sprout out of the desert; facilities and infrastructure would be developed; miles of road built and telephone cables laid in what had been the day before a barren desert. And suddenly a new area of this fascinating experiment in city development would emerge. And then there would be a pregnant pause, while they waited for the hoped-for business to materialise, to fill the vacuum and repay the investment.

How long could this cycle continue? Could the ruling family sustain the constant reiteration; would the bubble never burst? Down the road in Abu Dhabi jealous eyes were casting covetous glances in the direction of the apostate neighbour. But while the current conservative regime remained, those who were more farseeing – and were inclined to worship Mammon before God – would have to bide their time. Sooner or later, they knew, Dubai would have to come, cap in hand, to petition them to bail it out of its excesses.

Bill parked at the petrol station as planned. While waiting for Sergeant Mohammed, he called Malik.

'Morning Malik, can you check out something for me? I need to find out who owns a particular warehouse. Do you think you can do that?'

'Not sure, Boss. I know you'll be talking about the one Rory is working on today.'

'Yes, that's right. There's got to be some chain going upwards to whoever is behind it all. Whether he knows it or not.'

'What do you mean, Boss?' asked Malik.

'It's a question of whether the local who is sponsoring the company hiring the warehouses actually knows what's being done in his name. Perhaps he has absolutely no idea.'

'As your famous Mad Hatter said,' Malik responded philosophically, 'pigs might fly! But I'll see what I can do – I have some church friends in the garment industry who use large warehouses everywhere. I know the place. I went there with Rory on a look-see yesterday. The site details are in the file. I can start by looking up Star Batteries.'

'Alice, Malik, it was Alice, but I'm glad you know your Lewis Carroll. Most British people would have no idea where that expression came from!' Bill rang off. He never ceased to be amazed by the unexpected associations between Britain and India. He checked his watch. Only ten minutes to go, and still no sign of the police back-up. He called Sergeant Mohammed. The phone was on voicemail.

His voicemail was urgent: 'Mohammed, what's happened? Where are you? The deal will be going down in a few minutes and we need you here.'

A few minutes later, Rory called and rang off and then immediately repeated the procedure. It was on! That was the signal that all was going ahead. They had shaken hands on the deal and were about to take delivery of the goods. Where were Sergeant Mohammed and his people? At this moment, there should have been several police vehicles approaching the warehouse from each direction, ready to spring out and arrest everybody in sight, Rory included. 'If they don't come now, it will be too late,' thought Bill. Rory would be in deep shit. Unless he blew his cover and did a runner from the warehouse, he would end up with two containers of cigarettes and no money with which to pay for them; and some pissed off sellers.

The containers they were buying were 45-foot, high-cube containers with no cover-load used. This was so that they were able to stuff them with the maximum number of cigarettes — one they had helped the police seize a few months ago had contained more than 6 million cigarettes. Only the other day, Patrick Timms had told Bill that the Irish Customs Service had just seized four containers, moving on one bill of lading, which were found to contain 25.8m cigarettes in total.

The money which Rory had collected from Bill earlier that morning was only a sample, a pretence, and nothing more. If Rory could not pay and did not run, he would be likely to get a severe beating at best. At worst, he could end up dead. Bill knew that the reach of the Indian Mafia was long, unremitting and merciless. It would not be the first time that someone had reached out from the Indian subcontinent to take revenge on someone here in Dubai.

Bill tried again to get hold of Sergeant Mohammed, but the phone just rang and rang. In desperation, he called the police joint headquarters, hoping to speak to General Saeed Sadhanah. There was a long pause after he got through to the General's private secretary's office and was then put on hold. Eventually a voice – unknown to Bill, and not the secretary with whom he normally dealt – advised him that the General was travelling; would he like to leave a message? It had taken a suspiciously long time for someone in the General's office to realise that he could not speak to Bill because he was out of the country, thought Bill, suspicion growing in his mind. He could not let Rory deal with the crisis on his own. His mind was racing. He was on the edge of panic. Everything would unravel and, worse, he might have a dead employee.

As they watched the display by the Mujahedeen fighters of bin Laden, Sanjay and Sheikh Abdul heard, high overhead, the drone of an aircraft. At first the Jihadists were oblivious, each consumed, trance-like, by their desire to outdo each other in impressing the visitors with their warlike virtues. It seemed as if each would take on overwhelming odds for the chance to strike a blow against the enemy. But who was their enemy, Sheikh Abdul wondered to himself? Was it the spiritual enemy that they all proclaimed to the outside world to be fighting on behalf of, God's holy kingdom? Was it for Allah's kingdom on earth that they were prepared to lay down their lives in dutiful and self-sacrificing observance of the precepts of his disciple the Prophet Muhammad, peace be upon Him? Or was it all for a more prosaic and human cause: to right the presumed wrongs inflicted on them by the hated Crusaders; to establish a kingdom of man, to be imposed upon all others on Earth, led by the mercurial and charismatic man that he and Sanjay had just met? When it came to the actions of men, Sheikh Abdul was a cynic. Glancing over at Sanjay, Sheikh Abdul sensed that he too was of the same mind; that he too saw these men simply as tools that he could use to achieve the objectives given to him by Sheikh Abdul, which coincided with his own. Neither of them, it seemed to the Sheikh, harboured any illusions about the task on which they were now irrevocably embarked. It had nothing to do with any god; only with their personal craving for power and the control of others. And the bloodlust of the desire for revenge.

Overhead, the engine pitch of the circling aircraft changed suddenly to the straining, high-pitched whine that he remembered from the previous day. He could sense each rivet in the wings and fuselage vibrating furiously; the wings buffeted and flexed in such a way that it would seem impossible that they would not blow apart; could sense the unbearable g-force pressing down remorselessly on all those on board.

Immediately al-Zawahiri and his visitors realised that this was the returning C-130 coming to pick them up. Not so the Jihadis into whose consciousness the searing sounds now forced themselves. Shouting furiously at each other, as one, they scrambled towards the nearest piece of cover, no matter how small, that they could find. Briefly, the plane's engines were drowned out by the sound of weapons being made ready, magazines slotted noisily into position, 100 breach blocks being pulled rapidly back and recoiling instantaneously as the rider on the slide caught on the rims of the waiting bullets, slamming them along the guide plates and into the welcoming breaches.

Simultaneously, al-Zawahiri's voice rang out powerfully, calling the Jihadist commander, informing him of the nature of the plane's task.

Slowly, sceptically, the Jihadis absorbed the message and reluctantly accepted it, the chance of glory gone. Weapons were unloaded. The fighters started to jabber excitedly at each other. The tension relaxed. Sanjay and Sheikh Abdul climbed into the 4x4, al-Zawahiri gunned the engine and shot off at breakneck speed, bouncing over the rocky terrain like Jeremy

Clarkson on a road test of the vehicle's suspension. 'Showing off to his men!' thought Sheikh Abdul sardonically to himself, saying aloud: 'Very impressive, Ayman – you have built an army of virtue and faith, you and Osama! I look forward to fulfilling the Prophet's injunctions to all Muslims Insha'Allah!'

Within minutes they were in the Hercules, taking off on the flight back to Kabul.

It had been a successful meeting in Kuwait. They were near Qatar when the call came through. His assistant, a young man from the Al Ahli tribe and a cousin of his fourth wife's, passed him the phone.

'Sheikh Abdul, General Mohammed din Al Dawley would like to speak to you. Says it's very urgent!'

'One moment please, General Mohammed,' he said politely, '... here is His Highness Sheikh Abdul, Ma'a sala'am.' The phone changed hands.

'Sala'am alaikum, General Mohammed. How may I help you?'

'It is I who can help you, Sheikh Abdul,' said the head of the Police Department. 'I understand that you have an interest in Universal Trading?'

'Really General, I am sure you know that I own it! So why do you ask me?'

'Your Excellency, it has come to my attention that the company's warehouse in Al Quoz is about to be raided by some of my people. In about half an hour! Apparently, a complaint has been made to the Commercial Department by Genuine Tobacco Limited. They claim that the cigarettes – or at least several containers of them – in the warehouse contain counterfeits of their brand "Smoke Me!"'

'But my dear General, how can this be? Who is running this country of ours? Are our police no longer applying the principles of Sharia as given to us by our beloved Prophet Muhammad, peace be upon Him?' said the Sheikh angrily. 'Perhaps I need to talk to His Highness the Ruler? Sheikh Abdullah bin Al Mansour does not like foreigners interfering in our country,' he continued menacingly.

'Please, Sheikh Abdul, Your Excellency. It is only because I agree with you that I have called you. There is a company run by some British people and a British legal firm both working together for all the major cigarette manufacturers. You will know that the Ruler is intent on making Dubai a place where all Western – all foreign – companies feel comfortable to work. He has given these instructions to Mahmoud Al Abdullah ...'

'Al Abdullah is a lickspittle, a lackey of the Americans and the British!'

'I share your view on this entirely, Your Excellency,' said the General ingratiatingly. 'But you know that I too have my orders to follow. If a complaint is made to the Commercial Department about any alleged trading irregularities and the Department calls for my assistance, I am duty bound to follow up on this. To demonstrate the transparency of the market, as our British and American friends would say! But this is exactly why I have called you – to warn you. To give you time to warn your people. But please, be quick – we have only a few minutes in which to act.'

'Go on,' said the Sheikh.

'My man has called me for instructions. He is in the area near to the warehouse. Speak to your people. See that they clear everything up – get rid of the evidence – before my people arrive. I can give you fifteen minutes, but no more, Your Excellency.'

'Shokran, thank you. I shall remember this, and now I must move quickly, Ma'a sala'am.'

Clearing the line, Sheikh Abdul told the pilot to patch him through to Sanjay. He knew Sanjay was in Mumbai at this time. It took only a couple of minutes for the call to go through and for Sheikh Abdul to issue a few brief instructions.

'Make sure it's sorted out properly, Sanjay. We can't afford any mishaps, particularly at this stage!'

It needed only a further two brief calls from Sanjay: one to his man running the counterfeit deal and the other to Colonel Faisal in the Police JHQ. Colonel Faisal immediately called Sergeant Mohammed. All the necessary arrangements had been made.

At the petrol station in Al Quoz, Bill was beside himself with anxiety. If this went wrong it could unravel all that he had been working for all these months. Finally he could wait no longer. He would have to go it alone, without Sergeant Mohammed. 'What's the bastard up to?' he thought.

Bill found out all too soon. Just as he revved the engine to move out of the petrol station, his mobile rang: 'I can see Sergeant Mohammed and the other police approaching now,' Rory said. The voice was low, an intense whisper.

The line went dead before Bill could respond.

Bill parked the BMW up again in its original position. He was not supposed to be part of the action. His presence on the scene would give the game away – would immediately make the gang aware who had been responsible for interdicting their transaction. His company would be exposed and the technique would be compromised. Bill swore profusely in frustration, hitting the steering column violently with his fists. There was nothing for it but for him to remain an impotent bystander.

Ten minutes passed like an eternity. Why hadn't Rory called? He knew Bill would want to know at once how it had all gone. Surely it couldn't take this long?

The phone did ring. And it was Rory: 'What the fuck's happening? The bastards are arresting us all – Sergeant Mohammed and his people!' Bill could hear the sounds of fighting in the background, accompanied by hysterical shouting in guttural Arabic and aggrieved swearing in English. 'They're beating everyone with their batons. We need medical attention quick – Jimbo's bleeding like a stuck pig. And it looks like Fred's had his nose broken!' Rory continued: 'They're claiming the goods are genuine. We're being taken to the Bur Dubai police station. We're… ' The click of the abruptly terminated call echoed in Bill's ear. He stared blankly ahead, seeing nothing, panic suffusing his whole body. What now? What was he to do? What could he do?

51

It was later that evening before Colonel Tamimi managed to get some time with General Ali. They were at Sheikh Abdul's Majlis. Sheikh Abdul had a sumptuous palace out in the desert area behind the airport, towards Sharjah. It was on a raised pedestal of artificial rock and was brightly illuminated with powerful lights every five metres along the high wall which surrounded the property. Those who approached the Sheikh's lair were left in no doubt about his power and position. The whole edifice was a statement of aspiration. Security was discreet but tight. It was the first time that Colonel Tamimi had been admitted to the august presence of Sheikh Abdul. It was the Arab custom that anybody, no matter how lowly, could approach a sheikh and petition him on an urgent need. But the Colonel knew that this was largely a romantic idyll in today's fast-paced world. Had his name not been on the sheet of paper meticulously checked by the guards at each of the three checkpoints through which he had to pass, he knew that he would not have reached the tent where the Sheikh and his cronies idly passed the evening, scheming in their perpetual quest for self-aggrandisement and power.

General Ali and the Prosecutor General Talat Fuad Khadr were the principal lieutenants of Sheikh Abdul. Both were by his side when Tamimi entered the tent. On seeing him, General Ali at once beckoned him over, speaking quietly into Sheikh Abdul's ear as he did so.

'This is the young man I told you about, Excellency. I'd like you to meet him. He's doing some very fine work for your cause.'

As Tamimi approached, he could see the Sheikh eyeing him with a penetrating stare. It was September and the overblown heat of the summer had given way to less burnishing days and pleasant, cool and refreshing evenings. The high-columned marble-floored construction was spacious and cool. Designed to look like a tent, it was in reality a very modern permanent building. The many bright lanterns were supplemented by fairy lights, coiled around each of the many palm trees. Incense was burning in several places around the tent. The refreshing night air wafting in was heavily scented with bougainvillea and frangipani blossom. The whole atmosphere was redolent with exotic sensuality and intrigue.

Sheikh Abdul greeted Colonel Tamimi with extreme courtesy, inviting him to join him on one of the large carpet-covered cushions spread over the lavish Afghan Khal Mohammadi carpet on the dais at the top end of the tent.

'Masa'a al-khier, Colonel, General Ali has told me of your good work in support of our projects. We will all go on to achieve great things together. There is a princely future for you in the Prophet's name, peace be upon Him!' he said, appreciatively.

Colonel Tamimi responded carefully, not knowing exactly what it was that the Sheikh was driving at. Glancing at General Ali, he got no help there; the former's face remained inscrutable and benign. But Tamimi knew that his boss was anything but benign, and was disconcerted to see him appearing so. Courtly niceties ensued and then, after a few minutes, the General glanced meaningfully at Sheikh Abdul, stood up, exchanged farewell greetings with all the others in the group on the dais and left, indicating that Colonel Tamimi should follow him. They went into the palace, to a room which was obviously the General's office. Colonel Tamimi was surprised, as he had always assumed that the General's only office was the large one on the first floor of the Diwan in town, where they had always met before. General Ali dispensed with the niceties.

'What's the latest then, Colonel?'

'We now have positive evidence that Al Abdullah is working for British intelligence, and we know the identity of his case officer in the British Embassy. Also there is a go-between, a British man called Bill, who works with him on the RAKA project. We will establish shortly exactly who he is.'

'Very good, Colonel, I was right to introduce you to His Excellency indeed. There are many things I need to tell you. But not now, not tonight. Come to my office tomorrow morning.'

The General dismissed Colonel Tamimi and returned to the Sheikh's tent. Now the party was in full swing. Hitherto, demure girls had been serving non-alcoholic fruit drinks, coffee and Arabic tea, accompanied by delicious sweetmeats. All, previously dressed in black hijab or burka and fully covered by the abaya, had now undergone a metamorphosis. The single Arab piper had been joined by another six musicians. All, men and women, were suddenly revealed not as Arabs but as dark-skinned Indians. They were dressed in the colourful, vibrant hues of Rajasthan, with swirling, diaphanous yellow, red, purple and green scarves. The men wore large red and green turbans coiled over their heads, silk shirts, multi-coloured waistcoats and white and red pantaloons. The pulsing, erotic beat of the drums, the screeching wail of the pipes and the ringing of the tambourines assailed General Ali's senses as he approached the tent. As he entered, he saw one of the guests make a lunge at a girl carrying a tray of drinks. Teasingly, the girl deftly evaded her would-be seducer. She managed to avoid spilling any of the drinks, which were now whisky, gin and beer. The girls were now only scantily clad, in flimsy bikinis with flowing diaphanous silk scarves attached to their waists and little fingers on each hand. Several of them were dancing in an increasingly frenzied manner as the tempo of the music increased. Faster and faster they gyrated, entwining their bodies with each other, but sometimes breaking out of their partner's embrace to slide effortlessly and enticingly around the men lounging on the cushions on the floor. Still the pace of the music increased, the girls now entering a trance-like state. General Ali knew that these girls were emulating the dervishes, the assassins of a former era. As the music reached

169

a crescendo, several of the girls threw off their clothes to reveal oiled breasts and thighs the colour of polished mahogany. Suddenly the climax was reached and the girls threw themselves down on the rug between the men, who by now were fully aroused. The lights were dimmed, the band departed and the only sounds heard were the murmurs of desire and the stroking of smooth firm flesh, as the paired-off couples moved towards their ultimate climax.

Only three people were unaffected by the hysteria of communal arousal. Sheikh Abdul had beckoned General Ali over to him as the music played. He was observing the passions of his men with complete disinterest, his thoughts clearly elsewhere. General Ali was similarly disengaged.

'Let them have their moment,' said Sheikh Abdul. 'It is not for us to interfere with their pleasures. It is better that they should release their frustrations in this manner than that we risk them going off the rails at a critical moment. Or risk losing their loyalty altogether.'

This statement, the General realised, was made for the benefit of the only other non-participant in the orgy, Talat Fuad Khadr, who had been standing beside Sheikh Abdul when the General rejoined him. An arch conservative and strict Muslim, the Prosecutor General's distaste for the proceedings was evident. Truth to tell, both Sheikh Abdul and General Ali enjoyed the pleasures of the flesh as much as any man. However, they had ample opportunity to indulge their desires at a whim, and both did. But they were more cerebral individuals than Sheikh Abdul's foot soldiers. And they had an agenda. The three men moved away from the tent into the Sheikh's palace. All three remained observant, taking only water or Arabic coffee together.

'What did the Colonel tell you, General? I liked him. I can see why you value him so highly,' said Sheikh Abdul.

Quickly, the General summed up his meeting with Colonel Tamimi. He concluded by saying, 'It's clear that British intelligence is aware that there is a special account into which you pay the funds for Osama and Mullah Omar. Does Al Abdullah have any way of finding out about this? That's what they've asked him to do,' responded General Ali.

'You must stop him getting access!' ordered Sheikh Abdul, concern causing his eyes to narrow, creases appearing in the flesh around his eyes, his anxiety uncharacteristically evident.

'I'm not sure, I'll need to check it out,' said General Ali, lamely. 'It's important at this stage not to alert him, not to let British intelligence know that we're onto him. He's too valuable as an agent in-place to compromise.

170

Where he is now we can control what he passes back to the British – and what he doesn't!' The General's inflexion was uncharacteristically taut, his eyes lowered as if he were seeking to avoid the Sheikh's opprobrium and afraid to challenge him.

The General was then peremptorily dismissed from the august presence. Sheikh Abdul did not want him to waste any time.

Bill drove like Jehu from the petrol station. Jumping the lights, he turned left into the industrial area. It took him less than two minutes to reach the Star Batteries warehouse. The place was deserted. He tried yet again to raise Sergeant Mohammed; yet again the phone rang unanswered. A cold dread gripped his bowels; he ejaculated involuntarily, the warm semen dripping down his leg. He remembered a phrase in a colleague's letter to a friend when he had been under fire in Aden during a revolt by the police: 'now I know what it really means when someone says they've shit themselves!' Bill could feel the panic rising through his stomach and into his gullet; a physical feeling which threatened to engulf him. His mobile rang, an unknown number. The strident ring-tone broke through the paralysis that had transfixed him. He got a hold on his nerves and pressed the receive button. An Arab voice came on the line.

'Sala'am alaikum, Mr Bill. Your people are at the Bur Dubai police station. They are there now. I am here. Meet me, I can help you.'

'Who's this? Who are you?' asked Bill, his suspicions aroused, his nerves jangling, not recognising the voice.

'I am Karim, you will know me when you see me!'

The phone went dead. Automatically, Bill saved the number. He couldn't afford to lose the number; couldn't afford not to take the line which had been thrown to him.

It took Bill about fifteen minutes to reach the police station, which was in the middle of the warren of streets in the trading district of Bur Dubai. Bill drove unseeingly, his mind a blur. The only Karim he could think of, who might have been the mystery caller, was someone who had offered to help him some years before by providing some information at an exorbitant price. That Karim had claimed to be a government official of some sort or other

171

from one of the small northern emirates. Bill had never discovered whether he was genuine.

Parking was difficult here. It always was, the streets being too small for the volume of bustling traffic, because of all the parked vehicles, and the merchants carrying exotic spices and bales of fabric on large trolleys on one side of the street while in the other direction came trolleys with the latest electronic gadgets: the one from Iran; the other bound for Iran. Eventually, Bill managed to squeeze his car into a slot between two white transit vans. Leaping out of the car, he dashed up the road to the police station on the corner. How would he be received? He wondered whether he would be arrested as soon as he said who he was.

The General's instructions had been crystal clear.

'There are foreigners – British – undertaking investigation business here. Anything they get finds its way back to MI6 sooner or later. That could be very dangerous for us all. You find out who they all are, what they're up to, where their offices are – everything, absolutely everything. Then I'll decide how to deal with them.'

'But there is no law against this surely, General? Sharia doesn't prohibit it either, unless you're an arch conservative like the Prosecutor General. Everyone knows he would ban everything if he got half a chance! Aren't we trying to get business going here as they do in the West – and this is what they do, isn't it?'

General Ali paused reflectively, considering whether to make Colonel Tamimi aware of his real concerns. Then, decisively, his eyes crinkling slightly at his subordinate's irreverent reference to the senior law officer in Dubai's government, he said, 'There may be no law against it Colonel, but we can't let it happen. Someone is passing information to the British – to MI6. We need to know who it is.'

Colonel Tamimi's instructions to Karim had been equally clear. Karim had needed no second bidding. He had been brought up in abject poverty in Palestine. He had lived in Balata camp, the largest on the West Bank, with his family and over 21,000 other refugees, since it had been set up in 1950.

Every day, he had lived with the humiliation of his father. A wealthy landowner, he had been dispossessed of everything he owned by the creation of Israel. Karim had been then a richly-endowed and indulged, carefree five years old. Too young to remember the events of 1948, he remembered all too vividly the consequences of the Six Day War, when Israeli tanks had smashed through their camp, just because it was on the most direct route from the start line to their objective on the Golan Heights. He remembered the keening and wailing of his mother and two sisters; saw daily in his mind's eye the mangled, bloody bundle of what had been until then, his little baby brother with whom Karim had done everything since he had arrived in the world a year after Karim himself. He remembered the history his father had taught them. That was the day too, that he had lost his other friend, his adored father, whose mind had been dislocated by grief; who overnight became a tremulous, withdrawn old man.

He knew that the British, who had promised the land to the Jews, were the authors of his family's misfortune. Now he had the chance to exact revenge. It was Ali who had called him.

'Karim, you'd better get down here. We've just arrested a bunch of Englishmen. One of Sheikh Abdul's companies made a complaint against them. I'll tell you all the details when you're here.'

Sergeant Ali was the desk officer of Bur Dubai police station. He was responsible for processing all arrested personnel. Today his normally tedious job had just been enlivened by the arrival of eight angry, indignant and frightened young British men.

It took Karim about twenty minutes to negotiate the traffic in the twisting, tortuous, narrow streets crammed with slow-moving cars, loading and unloading trucks, and sandal-footed Arab and Indian men in grey dishdashas labouring under the weight of huge boxes of refrigerators or the latest TV sets on large trolleys, ready to be loaded onto a Creek-side dhow bound for Bandar Abbas less than 200 miles across the Straits of Hormuz. Here, in what had been a rustic Bedouin nomadic settlement only a couple of decades earlier, could be found any consumer product that was available in any shopping mall anywhere in America. Here was the Gold Souk with its plethora of shops all selling the same wares, gaudy 22 carat gold rings, brooches, necklaces and, to the Western eye, vulgarly large ornamental jewellery. The next street was favoured by tailors and interior designers, with sumptuous Indian silks, vividly coloured shawls and the finest of pashmina scarves. In another area were numerous perfume shops selling the heavy, strong, exotically heady scents favoured by those who lived in extremely hot climates. And over there, in yet another area, all the hardware shops were clustered together. Sights he had seen all his life barely registered with Karim. He was intent on getting to the police station just as quickly as possible. Sergeant Ali's news had set his mind racing with numerous possibilities. Following his remit from Colonel Tamimi, through a CID contact, he had already managed to get quite a lot of information about these Englishmen. These people would be completely at sea in the treacherous waters of the Dubai judicial system. They would need help. They would be prepared to pay well for any help. So he could kill two birds with one stone. He would find out what they were up to for his boss, and get some baksheesh for himself. He would not really help them; merely look as though he was doing so. Meanwhile, in response to Colonel Tamimi's instructions, he would be able to manipulate them in conjunction with his friends in the Prosecutor's office.

Driving along the same tortuous route ten minutes later, Bill had not noticed his surroundings either, as he had done on previous occasions. Then he had been struck every time by just how like a little piece of India the souk was. It could be the Darabi market in Mumbai. The shopkeepers and storeowners came from all parts of the Muslim diaspora, mixed with a blend of Hindus from India; Christians from Syria and Lebanon; Afghanis from the Khyber Pass and North-West Territories; Uzbeks and Chechens; and tourists from all parts of the world, increasingly from Russia with their solid, blousy fair-skinned women. Not the classy, sophisticated and beautiful young women which Bill had seen in St Petersburg on a business trip there last year.

But whereas Karim had barely noticed his surroundings when driving through due to familiarity, Bill did not notice because of his anxiety and fear. It seemed as if a mailed fist had gripped his throat; his mouth was dry; his stomach churned.

At the police station a large number of people, the men in dishdashas and casual T-shirts but the women all veiled, some in full purdah, were coming and going. There was an atmosphere of uncertainty, which transmitted itself to Bill. He went to the reception desk manned by a uniformed policewoman, her head covered by a scarf underneath a police side hat, and explained that he wanted to see his colleagues. She was not hostile, but she was unaccommodating and dismissive. With complete indifference, she lifted the beige-coloured Etisalat phone on her desk and spoke briefly to someone. Bill did not even know if she was speaking about him. She gave no hint that she was. And Bill's rudimentary Arabic provided no clue. Cursorily, she indicated that Bill should sit on one of the benches near the desk. There were several of these, all nearly full. On them sat a rainbow mix of people. There was one other male Caucasian. Bill thought that he looked like a prize fighter who had badly mishandled several of his most recent bouts. Evidence of the latest was a heavily swollen right eye. He also had a series of nasty-looking cuts on his forehead. The crude bandaging had failed to staunch completely the flow of blood, which had dripped down over his shirt collar. At the other end of the bench was a woman in a sari with two small children, both in ragged clothing; the older child was trying to run around. The severe policewoman watched her disapprovingly. And still the stream of people came and went; some nonchalant, some bowed down with worry. The minutes dragged by, and with each one that passed, Bill's anxiety increased exponentially, it seemed.

Eventually, he got up and went back to the desk. The policewoman still ignored him, dealing with several other people who came after him. Bill tried to make eye contact but she continued to ignore him. His anger and exasperation increased to boiling point. A feeling of intense foreboding enveloped him. Here he was a non-person; he had no status with the administrators. He was an exile, a foreigner. The hitherto benign holiday paradise became suddenly an alien place. Bill knew that he could not throw his weight around. He could not afford to explode. He had to stand his ground and be humiliated for the sake of Rory and his colleagues. He knew that the policemen standing at the door would take great delight in chucking him in jail if he remonstrated with their colleague.

Bill felt trapped. What could he do? He could not get access to his colleagues, locked away somewhere in the station. The policewoman was ignoring him. He had not been able to raise Sergeant Mohammed all day. He had left frantic messages and sent a text as well. He could not make any attempt to contact Andy; that would incriminate them both.

On the edge of despair, he felt a tug on his shirt sleeve. Turning round wildly in his pent-up state, he nearly knocked over the Arab figure standing behind him. He had not been aware of Karim's approach. Someone he recognised was like a lifeline splashing into the water alongside a drowning man. He had always considered Karim as the worst kind of Arab; an ingratiating, bloodsucking vulture; a man without scruples who would sell his own grandmother for a handful of dollars. But now he was as a friend;

the saviour, a local, someone who would have the key to solving this problem, thought Bill.

'Sala'am alaikum,' said Karim, 'you have a problem, Mr Bill?' Karim had appeared as if by magic, his shifty eyes peering out of a lugubrious face, not looking into Bill's. He wore a well-used dishdasha, which rode up around his protruding stomach. His sallow skin had a yellowish tinge.

'My God,' exclaimed Bill. 'It was you? On the phone just now? I thought I recognised the voice.' In fact he had been so knotted up with fear that his mind had gone blank and he had not taken in the fact that he did know the voice. Karim's ingratiating whine, like some groucho Mexican out of a bad spaghetti western, was unmistakable. 'Yes, oh yes! I really do, Karim – can you help?' he said, barely keeping the panic out of his voice.

'Tell me what the problem is. I have friends here. I can help you.'

Quickly, Bill outlined his predicament.

'My people have been arrested – six of them. They were working with the CID, trying to catch some cigarette counterfeiters. It was all set up with Sergeant Mohammed. But he didn't show up. Instead, the other police attacked my people. They looked at the cigarettes and said that they were genuine product, and they let the gang go. They attacked my people with batons. Several of the lads were badly beaten and had to have medical attention; one had several teeth knocked out and then Sergeant Mohammed turned up – but he didn't help us!'

Karim appeared surprised by all this, as Bill explained the situation.

'Now I can't get to see them. I've been here at least an hour. They're ignoring me. The policewoman at the information desk won't even talk to me.'

Again, Karim appeared surprised and solicitous.

'I'm sure that there is some mistake, Mr Bill. Let me see what I can do.'

There was no reason why Karim should have been surprised at what Bill said. His friend Sergeant Ali had already told him everything that had happened to Bill's people.

After a quick conversation with the policewoman at reception, Karim came back.

'Don't worry, Mr Bill, everything will be alright. I have spoken with the lady. It's obviously a big mistake. They're just embarrassed. They don't know how to get out of the embarrassment. They don't want to lose face. I'll go and talk with my friends. Wait here!'

Karim disappeared from Bill's sight, into the depths of the police station.

After getting Sergeant Ali's call, he had immediately contacted the Secret Police, sensing a commercial opportunity. Karim prostituted himself for anyone and anything and the Secret Police were one of his main clients. Initially, the person taking the call had been dismissive: 'What's new about some foreigners being arrested, even if they are British? This happens all the time these days! The jail is full of foreigners; we're having to build more prisons.'

'These people are secret investigators. They've been looking at some of Sheikh Abdul's companies!'

Instantaneously the listener's tone changed.

'Sala'am – hold on a moment.' Almost at once Karim was transferred to Issa. Major Issa was his normal contact in the organisation. Years ago, they had both worked together in the Ruler's office in Ajman. Issa had gone on to greater things with the Secret Police; Karim had been sacked for passing secret information to the Diwan in Dubai.

'Sala'am alaikum, Karim,' he said. 'Good to hear from you; how are you?'

After the usual pleasantries had been exchanged, Issa said: 'Well, you've got something for me then?'

Karim explained what had happened to Bill's people – told him all that he knew.

'I'll only be a few minutes, Karim,' said Issa. The phone went dead.

'Karim,' said Issa, back on the phone after several minutes, 'my boss will speak to the Station Commander. You're to get alongside these people, become their friend, put their minds at rest. Make it look as if you're on their side; like it's all a big mistake. And report anything back to me at once. Call in at the Diwan tomorrow – the normal office – and collect your money, the usual rate. Who'd you say was running all this?'

'A British man called Bill Sloan. Came here from Saudi about six months ago.'

'Bill Sloan?' said Issa, ruminatively. 'Does it ring a bell. Keep close tabs on him, Karim. I want to know where he's living, where his offices are, what he's doing all the time, all about him. I'm relying on you. We'll make it look as if you fixed their release. That should make them grateful to you alright! Ma'a sala'am.'

Karim went over to the Station Sergeant's office.

'Ali, my friend, the Secret Police are going to speak with your boss. We need you to give them a hard time. Rough them up a bit more. Threaten them;

accuse them of spying. Tell them they'll be transferred to the Secret Police prison in Abu Dhabi and tried in the special court as spies. Minimum sentence fifteen years! Manacle them and throw them into the cells overnight. Then I'll come along early tomorrow morning with their manager who's out there – Bill Sloan. We'll go with you to your boss's office, I'll speak on their behalf to your boss, who will reluctantly agree to release them provided I vouch for them. That way, you avoid the shit hitting the fan, because your people beat the fuck out of them when they were working with the police. That would look just fine in the international press!'

Sergeant Ali never had been sure how much wasta Karim had; whether he really did have a connection with the Secret Police or was just a bullshitter. 'Better be on the safe side,' he thought, 'in case it all falls in on top of me.'

Karim was continuing: 'I'll have a hold on these Brits now, particularly Sloan. Now I'll be able to find out for the Secret Police what they're really up to. And they'll think that they're out of the woods. Little do they realise! You'll have the last laugh, Ali.'

Karim left Sergeant Ali's office and went over to Bill, sitting despondently at the reception desk.

'Mr Bill,' he said, 'your people behaved very badly; very badly indeed. They are in serious trouble. They are even being accused of spying!'

It was like a living nightmare. Bill could not believe what he was hearing.

'But Karim, it's… ' he exclaimed, trying to hold himself together, keep the fear out of his voice. 'That's ridiculous – we were working in a joint operation with the CID! Sergeant Mohammed's got my company video camera, for God's sake, to record the whole thing!'

Bill was beginning to hyperventilate: his mind raced; he did not think straight; he was indignant, offended, angry – and shit scared – all at the same time.

'Karim, can't you get on to Sergeant Mohammed? He was in charge, knows all about it. He will be able to tell them the truth!'

'Mr Bill,' said Karim accusingly, 'I called the Head of CID, Colonel Faisal. He says that Sergeant Mohammed has been suspended from duty.'

'What!' screamed Bill. 'This is fucking ridiculous! I'm going to phone General Mohammed din Al Dawley.'

Furiously, he dialled the General's number. He had known him since his first visit to Dubai eight years ago. Then the General had been Head of Special Branch. He wanted a state-of-the-art interrogation centre designed and built.

When it was finished, the facility was a work of art. All the latest technical wizardry of the time had been included. The General had been particularly delighted that he could see and hear what happened in any cell at the click of a switch. Hear his enemies incriminate themselves as interrogators tied them up in knots. Hear them begging for mercy. He could see his rivals becoming ever more disorientated as they were softened up for interrogation. He could see them standing for hours against the wall, arms akimbo, legs spread-eagled, hooded like members of the Ku Klux Klan, watch the guards viciously kicking their feet even further from the wall, see them shaking and quivering as their muscles went into spasm, see them sobbing behind their hoods, could visualise the fear and pain on their faces. No need to use electrodes on the testicles or penis or to pull out any fingernails when these simple procedures were so effective at disorientating and softening up the victims before the skilled interrogators got to work on them. More chance of getting the truth this way, rather than inflicting so much pain that the luckless victim coughed – said wherever it was his torturers wanted to know, always assuming that the victim could actually work out what it was they wanted to know, if he was guiltless, as most were.

Despite the success of the finished product, the General had been embarrassed by the financial shenanigans of the contractor chosen to do the work. Bill had a mixed reception from the General on renewing his acquaintance on his return to Dubai.

He had been welcomed with extreme Arab courtesy and apparent friendliness.

'Sala'am, Mr Bill, it is good to see you again. What brings you back to our Arabian pearl?' he had said. Behind the smiles and pleasantries, Bill had detected reticence and speculation.

'That shit company you brought in – Technical Solutions – they tried to screw me. I lost my name with Sheikh Abdul!' he had said back then.

Now Bill was about to find out whether the General was a friend or a foe. With the immediacy of Dubai, the General answered his mobile. Bill explained the situation.

'Let me see what's happening,' said the General.

He called back on Bill's mobile two minutes later.

'I have spoken with the Prosecutor General. Your people have made statements admitting their guilt!' said the General, his voice heavy with accusation and irony. There was nothing further to be said.

None of this had escaped Karim's notice standing beside Bill. At once, he sensed that Bill would find no salvation from that quarter.

'I'll see if my friend can let you meet your people. They are all being interrogated at present. It looks bad. But it may be possible to get them released on bail.'

Karim shuffled off. Bill paced up and down. He struggled to hold his nerve; to keep himself together. The General's words were still reverberating in his brain when Karim reappeared.

'You can see them now. They're just finishing off formalities. They should be outside soon.'

Karim led Bill through into the section at the back of the police station. They went along a corridor. There were small offices on either side. Halfway along on the left side, peering in, Bill saw his colleagues.

'You can go and talk to them. I'm going back outside. I'll be at the front desk.'

Bill went into the waiting room. He could see that everyone waiting to be interrogated was very shocked. As well they might be, he thought guiltily. This was not the time for friendly banter. Everyone looked anxious and frightened. He kept the conversations to the point – these were his people. He was responsible for them. But he could not afford to talk about the situation; could not afford to talk about anything that they had been doing; could not afford to discuss anything which the police could seize upon to make the case against them worse. However, the atmosphere in the interrogation rooms appeared relaxed, and everyone in them seemed convinced that there was nothing that they had done that would justify any police action against them. Perhaps it was, after all, a genuine mistake, thought Bill.

He went back outside and met up with Karim, thanking him for his help, allowing a feeling of relief to well up inside and take hold.

His mobile rang. It was Rory.

'They're taking us down. They're charging us – putting chains around our necks and ankles!' The phone went dead.

Bill rushed back inside, towards the rear of the building where he had last seen them all. Two policemen barred the way. He caught a glimpse of Rory and the others, heads bowed, arms behind their backs, wrists handcuffed, chains around their feet and up their front to link with the ones around their necks. He was engulfed by a feeling of fear and helplessness. He shouted, the policeman manhandled him into the corridor and dragged him outside, handing him over to Karim. Karim escorted him to his car.

'Go and get a good night's sleep,' he said. It was now after 11 pm. Bill realised that he was completely shattered, exhausted by the mental strain of the past twelve hours.

'There's nothing you can do now. Meet me back here at 8 am. I'll speak to my colleagues. See what can be done.'

Bill drove back through the narrow streets; the last few shopkeepers were closing shop and putting up the shutters, but there was still a considerable amount of activity, even at this late hour. He drove along the Creek. On either side, the lights sparkled like some fairy playground, dancing off the ruffled waters. Last-minute shoppers were returning to their hotels and apartments, crossing the Creek in the abras, plying their way across the water like a flotilla of prehistoric gondolas.

But Bill was blind to all this. He saw it, but did not notice, did not feel. His stomach was knotted with anxiety, his brain whirled with contradictory ideas as to what to do, but was simultaneously numb and paralysed with fear. At times, he seemed like a remote observer of his own fate: knowing what to do, seeing what was wrong, what he should do, but powerless to do it, to intervene to help himself. It was as if he was in a waking nightmare, the only release from which was sleep. Driving unconsciously, he turned automatically away from the Creek into Trade Centre Road, turning left at the Bur Juman Centre and to his apartment behind it. He threw himself onto the bed, not bothering to undress or eat. He slept fitfully and dreamlessly for several hours. At about 5 am, he awoke with the muezzin's first prayer call of the day. He did not get back to sleep

Karim was already there when Bill arrived at the police station. Bill himself had arrived much earlier than the agreed time of 8 am. Unable to contain his anxiety any further, he needed to be up doing something, anything. He had gone for a short run along the Creek. It all looked so peaceful, almost translucent, at this early hour, with the first abras beginning to ferry their passengers across to Deira, their prows gently ruffling the placid water. The clear sky, now light blue, and the strengthening but pleasantly warm sun betokened a version of earthly paradise. But Bill knew that still waters run deep, that he was plumbing their depths and could not touch bottom. He saw the scene but could not appreciate it, the knot in his stomach still there. Surely, he thought, the few people that he passed at this early hour could notice the lump in his throat. Back at the apartment he paced up and down the balcony, unable to relax, the tension unbearable.

It was uncanny how Karim always seemed to appear on cue. It was as if he knew Bill's every movement.

Straight away, as soon as Bill entered the police station foyer, Karim was standing beside him. He showed Bill into an office on the first floor. The station commander, Major Ibrahim Albanna, sat behind his desk, his khaki uniform pressed immaculately, with the blue lanyard on his right shoulder and his hat on the table. He was a large man with the obligatory close-cropped facial hair and moustache. He wore black horn-rimmed glasses.

Karim spoke briefly to Albanna in Arabic. Albanna nodded, looking at Bill. Karim switched to English.

'Mr Bill. I have explained the situation to Major Albanna. He has decided to release your people.'

For several seconds, Bill barely registered the words. Then he was overwhelmed with a feeling of enormous relief, welling up from within him.

'But that's marvellous. It's so far from what I thought would happen, but it's wonderful. Thank you, thank you very much, Major Albanna. And thank you too, Karim,' said Bill.

He could hardly take it all in. Last night, all had seemed so black and threatening. Now, all appeared to have been resolved. It was as if a dreadful error had taken place, and now the slate had miraculously been wiped clean. Suddenly, there were handshakes and beams all round.

'Your people will be brought up from the cells in a few minutes, Mr Bill,' said the Major, who obviously spoke immaculate English. 'In the meantime, let us have some coffee – Arabic gahwa!'

He clapped his hands vigorously and, as if by magic, an Indian char-wallah arrived. It was as if they were all chums from way back; as if nothing at all had happened. After a few minutes, Bill was shown into the waiting room where his colleagues, unshaven and dishevelled, were sitting uncomfortably, looking extremely uneasy and apprehensive, on hard-backed chairs placed around the walls.

182

'Come on, guys. Let's go,' said Bill. They followed him out of the office, not daring to think that their ordeal might be over.

In the corridor, Major Albanna and Karim stood, as if taking the Royal salute. Clearly Albanna too seemed bemused by all that had happened. Karim, however, was content to bask in his moment of glory, to wring the maximum advantage from his apparently charitable and disinterested intervention on behalf of these foreign expatriates. To him, all white men looked like Jews. And Karim had no reason to be kind to Jews.

After Bill and his people had left, Karim accompanied Albanna to his office.

'Karim, you son of a goat, may you be dipped in whores' blood. What in the name of Allah is going on?' stormed Albanna.

'Patience, patience, Major; it's all on Sheikh Abdul's orders. You know it is. I am merely his servant, as you are too!'

'Well, perhaps it is all for the best. It would have been fun though, to see the British men facing the full weight of Sharia. But, in truth, it would have been difficult to have made the case against them stick. There was no justification for arresting these people. Sheikh Abdul's company knew they were going to be caught red-handed. So they made up the complaint. They're the ones who should have gone to court!'

'Careful what you say,' said Karim, looking around furtively to make sure they were not in danger of being overheard. Sheikh Abdul had many sets of eyes and ears everywhere.

Albanna suddenly realised that he had gone too far. Karim was in the pay of the Sheikh. He was a man without honour or loyalty, Albanna knew. But, at the moment, the Sheikh paid the highest price.

'Yes, yes, you are right, Karim. The Sheikh knows what he is doing. For sure all true Muslims should support him. He is our future. He will protect us from the domination of these apostate foreigners.'

Karim left the police station. He called Major Issa. 'Major, all is well, Alhamdulillah. The Englishmen have been released. They have no idea why. But they will be grateful and relieved. They won't tell their people in the Embassy. No need to do so and the attention would be unwelcome. Now we know who we're looking for. We will put this man, Sloan, under pressure. Next time, we'll be able to get them under better conditions, Major, conditions where we are in control and not the police!'

'Good, Karim. You have done well. Contact General Ali. He will give you instructions for the next phase. Collect your money from him as well.'

'Major, Shokran, Ma'a sala'am.'

Karim moved surprisingly swiftly, belieing his obesity, cutting down the street a few blocks. He knew that Bill and his compatriots would be in the Capri Hotel. It was the only one in that part of Bur Dubai which sold alcohol. It was a place where the white men came in the evening to fornicate with the current in-crop of prostitutes. At the moment the Somali girls were the flavour of the month. Not so long ago, at night, the place had been crawling with Russian girls. But they had been moved on by the police, their visas peremptorily cancelled, so that they had had to leave Dubai. Unless they chose to remain illegally, as many did. And soon the Somalis would be forced to leave, to be followed by whom, Karim wondered? Perhaps it was the turn of the Chinese? It did not matter which; whoever it was, Karim had great pleasure in removing them at Sheikh Abdul's command. It was the only way Karim ever got to have any kind of relationship with a woman, watching vicariously as the girls were bundled into the Black Maria vans and taken to the police station to be systematically and brutally examined, showered and cleaned by disapproving policewomen. No-one saw him on these occasions. But he saw them from his vantage point in the control room, where he monitored the CCTV cameras. He was never sure whether he preferred the creamy white skin of the North European Scandinavian or Russian, or the charcoal black of the Somalis, or any of the others in between. All were available in increasing numbers in this small fiefdom, supposedly run in strict observance of the tenets of Sharia. But with his ever-increasing library of pornographic DVDs, passed to him by a chum in the police who was responsible for ensuring that no material unsuitable for Islamic eyes was allowed into the Emirate, he had plenty of time at home in which to make his decision. Sometimes the anticipation in the privacy of his own room was more satisfying than the actual act consummated in some fleapit of a hotel in the souk.

Bill and the others were at the bar, as Karim had expected. They were talking excitedly, the pressure of imprisonment, so unexpectedly imposed and now so unexpectedly released. They all felt euphoric. Bill was the same. His nerves had been stretched to breaking-point. Now, everything was suddenly alright, just as quickly as it had been all wrong.

'Karim, what was all that about?' Bill asked, as Karim sidled up and insinuated himself into the group. They were all keen to thank Karim for his apparent intervention on their behalf. He looked like the cat that got the cream, purring superciliously.

'Thank you for your help, Karim; I don't know where we would have been without you.' Bill raised his glass: 'Here's to Karim; let's drink to Karim.'

They all raised their glasses. Now, Karim appeared embarrassed and did not know how to respond: 'Shokran, Mr Bill, shokran wa'Allah.' It was clear that he felt uncomfortable in the spotlight. Whether it was because he was in a Western-style public house, surrounded by young Englishmen, or whether there was some more sinister reason for his reticence after what should have been a triumph, Bill was unable to determine. However, standing back and observing the scene dispassionately, he was left with the inescapable feeling that Karim's motives could not be divined. Was he being genuinely helpful to a bunch of luckless foreigners whom he had befriended? Was he simply a fair-weather friend, or was he indeed an enemy? The party began to break up.

As they left, Bill said, 'We'll debrief everything at the office first thing tomorrow morning. See where we went wrong and what we do next.'

Karim drew Bill aside. 'Mr Bill, you must be careful. You have been lucky this time. My friends have been able to help you. But in future you must trust me. You must tell me what you are doing. Only that way can you be safe. Otherwise you will be chopped off at the knees!' he said, drawing the side of his palm across his throat in a confusing, but vividly clear gesture.

It was several days since Bill and Andy's last meeting. Malik had been pummelling any and all of his contacts that might get him into the Rub Al Khali Commercial Bank. But, so far, without success. It was late on the Thursday evening, the start of the weekend, but Bill was oblivious to this, closeted in his apartment with a large batch of tapes to go through.

And like someone re-reading the same passage time after time in bed, Bill found his concentration wandering, his eyes closing. Time after time, he would have to wind back the tape and find the last place where he had made notes and then replay it all again. He had already done this several times and was on the point of stopping for the night. He would have to try to get up early and work through it in the morning so that he would have some time left to have something of a weekend.

He could not pick up the significance of the conversation at first, and had to replay it several times. But a sixth sense told him that it was important. The office manager in Fountain Trading had a lengthy conversation with a fellow Iranian, who it seemed to Bill, was in Iran. He had no idea to whom Sajjad Shirazi was speaking. The conversation was in Farsi. He noted the beginning of the call in the record schedule and then the endpoint, measuring the place on the tape against the manual count on the cassettes.

As soon as the call had ended, Sajjad Shirazi immediately dialled another number. The number showed Bill the numbers which had been dialled – 4 56328. This was a Dubai number.

'Sala'am alaikum,' said a voice at the other end, a pleasant Indian or Pakistani girl's voice, Bill thought instinctively. 'How may I help you please?'

'Put me through to the boss,' said Sajjad Shirazi peremptorily. The receptionist clearly knew who was speaking. She did not need to ask.

'Hello Sajjad, my friend, Sala'ams, what can I do for you?' said a guarded voice.

This time, Bill had less difficulty in following the conversation. The two men spoke mainly in English.

'My people across the water have come good! The money's being paid into our account today – two cheques from Isfahan National Trading. Now that we've got these we can put you in funds, and you can supply the stuff to the Guards! How long will it take to get this stuff to Bandar Abbas?'

'Insha'Allah, I can confirm the order at once. I can have the goods, both the processors and the software, there within forty-eight hours of receiving the money.' The speakers switched to Farsi for several minutes, then back to English.

'There'll be a tidy profit for Al Turk and the rest of us, too.'

'Do not worry, my friend. I'll make sure that you get your cut. Just let me know where and when you want it paid.'

'Excellent, but remember Doctor, this bit of the deal is just between you and me. The Sheikh will break my balls if he gets wind of this. If we get this one right, there's more, much more, to come! Our friends in the Guards over there are hell bent on getting these computers working before the Israelis or Amerikis can stop them.'

'Well then, it will be my pleasure to help them do so, Allah Akbar.'

Bill tried to make sense of it all. It would be a hell of a lot clearer to Andy, as he spoke some Farsi. What was it that Sajjad was selling to someone in Iran, making a side deal that would get his bollocks chopped off by one of the sheikhs? It had to be Sheikh Abdul, his boss.

After he had left Andy at the Crown Plaza the other day, Bill had looked at the typed note concealed within the copy of the *Kaleej Times* which he had picked up from Andy. The information was sparse: Rub Al Khali Commercial Bank, Trade Centre Road, Account number 28890672. This was difficult for Malik.

'My source has access to the trading accounts, Boss, but not the details of the accounts without a name.' Andy did not know the name of the company. Now, Bill quickly called Malik.

'Hullo, Boss! I'm just off to church, what is it?'

'Malik, those Commercial Bank transactions you're looking for. We have the name of the account into which funds are going to be paid!'

'That should make life easier. What's it called?'

'It's our old friend Fountain Trading.'

'See what I can do, Boss.'

56

'This is Byzantine, like this whole place. Let's go through it all again to make sure we've got it straight.'

Andy and Bill were at the Sheraton Hotel at a table overlooking the waterfront. It was the brief dusk of Arabia. The nightly onshore breeze flapped the palm leaves, sounding like someone's back being given the wet towel treatment. Increasingly quickly, it seemed, the sun was slipping down over the horizon to their right towards the mouth of the Creek and the open sea.

'Right,' Andy continued, 'first of all we had Isfahan Trading depositing money in Fountain Trading's account.'

'And, now that we know the company name, I've been able to get details of the account. So with luck we'll be able to look at their other transactions – see who else they're dealing with.'

'How much are we talking about?' interjected Andy.

'There were two payments. One due now for $1 million US, and then another for $9 million. That's got to be a deposit and the balance on delivery.'

'That's a fucking large amount! What are they expecting to get for that?'

'It's got to be something to do with WMD!'

'How'd you get to that?' Andy sounded sceptical.

'Sajjad calls a number which turns out to be a company dealing in computers – Octagon – and tells him the deal's on.'

'What deal?' queried Andy.

'We checked the company ownership details of Octagon Computers. The principal director, the largest shareholder… ' he paused for effect, '… is Sheikh Abdul!'

'Yes, OK, but he owns a lot of companies here, although I don't see him as a computer buff?'

'We're not talking about computers here. It's all a front. Do you remember I told you last week that Sajjad in Fountain Trading had spoken to a Doctor somebody? You should have the tape with this on it.'

'Yes,' said Andy pensively.

'Well, another of the directors is the Doctor.' 'My God! I don't believe it. The Father of Pakistan's bomb? What the fuck's he doing here?'

'Making some money, now that Musharrif's rehabilitated him. I'm pretty sure that Sajjad was speaking to the Doctor himself. Almost certainly the same voice as before. This guy's a national hero who's given his country the nuclear bomb. He's not going to be sitting here just flogging computers. All their talk's in veiled speech. Computers are just a cover. He's got to be proliferating. And where better to do that than from Dubai, with its proximity and links to one of the countries which is most desperate to get the bomb?'

Andy said thoughtfully, 'Sheikh Abdul's fishing in troubled waters. It's a lethal mix of overarching ambition, tribal loyalty and personal motives. Shia Iran and Sunni Dubai in bed together! Sheikh Abdul's helping to provide a potential enemy with WMD.'

'As you said, Byzantine is definitely the word.'

'Exactly. You'd think the last thing Sheikh Abdul would want if he takes over here is a bunch of power-crazed Mad Mullahs on his doorstep – just over there – with their fingers on a nuclear button!'

'So,' Bill picked up the analysis, 'they must be getting something from Iran that they can't get elsewhere?'

He glanced towards the mouth of the Creek: along its brightly-lit length dhows lay alongside, piles of Western electronic goods stacked high on their decks. Only nine hours' sailing and they would be unloading in Bandar Abbas.

'Sajjad's taking one hell of a risk asking for a backhander from Octagon Computers. Not content with biting off the hand that's feeding him, he's set about biting off the whole fucking arm. If Sheikh Abdul finds out, he'll definitely break his balls,' Andy observed. 'You need to check out Octagon Computers next.'

'Yes, I know. I'm working on it. We're looking for a transfer from Fountain Trading.'

Tariq had arrived with Andy but he left with Bill.

'Coming out now!' he said quietly into his radio as Bill had settled up for the two coffees and left the café. The 3-series BMW is commonplace in Dubai. In a parking bay directly opposite the café entrance the occupants had a perfect view of Bill as he came out. The click of the camera shutter behind the radiator grille was masked by the noise of passing traffic. The tinted glass of the BMW would have obstructed Bill's view had he been looking, which he was not. Tariq's team had no difficulty in housing Bill a few minutes later, when he went back to his apartment in Sunnyside 18.

Earlier, as they staked out the café after yet again following Andy to it in what was obviously a bit of an early morning routine, they had had every opportunity to take a good look at all those who had been in there at the time and all who subsequently arrived.

'Ibrahim! Do your usual in there. See if you recognise anyone. Be sure to get some good shots of everyone there.'

'Yes, Sahib.' A few minutes later Tariq had seen Ibrahim heading into the café, his briefcase at the ready, just like any other Dubai businessman eager to strike it rich. After about five minutes Tariq called him. The line was distorted and hollow-sounding, like Ibrahim was speaking down a long pipe.

'3 – no-one else here I recognise. Subject's on his own.'

'OK 3 – you're coming over all garbled. What's the problem with your set?'

'I'm in the toilets.'

'Right, stay there and get shots of anyone who comes in.'

'What, in the toilet?'

'Very funny, Ibrahim, get your donkey's ass back into the café!'

Several minutes later, the watchers saw another customer heading into the café. He had obviously parked round to the rear having come along the road behind, which ran parallel to the main Sheikh Zayed Highway. The team all had mugshots of all the possibles who might be Andy's contact. It was 4 round the back who had seen Bill first. He had made the call to alert the others – and then looked at the photos.

'4 – it's almost certainly Yankee 3!' He described what Bill was wearing to make sure that everyone picked him up. A few seconds later, Tariq and the others at the front saw their suspect too. Inside the café, Ibrahim acknowledged that he, too, had heard and was ready to do his business. They were definitely onto something this time, Tariq thought exultantly. Their patience was paying off.

Moments later, he too saw Bill. He went into the café. Tariq pressed the transmission button on his phone so vigorously that he nearly dropped it. This was their man. '2 – over to you now!'

In the café Ibrahim was well prepared. He was at a table with a good view of Andy, who was at another nearby and was facing towards the door. He saw a blurred shape through the swing doors. He immediately pressed the button underneath the handle of his briefcase. Bill entered. It was obvious he was looking for someone that he was due to meet. No-one else in the café heard the whirring of the camera as it dutifully collected its invaluable confirmation that Bill Sloan was their man, as he and Andy greeted each other warmly. Bill sat down at the table with Andy. Immediately they were deep in conversation. It was obvious to Ibrahim that this was no social meeting.

Back at the office later, they debriefed the episode. They now had conclusive proof of a relationship between Bill and Andy.

'Stringer is running Mahmoud Al Abdullah through this Kaffir, Bill Sloan – no doubt about it. I'll tell the Colonel when we finish here. But he'll certainly say that we should put Sloan under full-time surveillance, so we'll start right now. What about codenames?'

The young female clerk, only a small pale brown oval of her face visible, the rest of her shrouded in the voluminous black cloak, consulted her file.

'Good thing she's wearing the abaya!' thought Tariq. He had seen her without it on occasions – a ravishing, raven-haired beauty with high cheekbones and a majestic nose – wouldn't do to have her bared in the manner of the infidel and have all the team lusting over her and distracted from the serious business in hand.

'Banjo!' she said. 'It's the next on the list.'

'Original, I don't think,' Tariq said sarcastically. 'Which son of a whore makes these names up?'

The female members of the team looked primly offended by his language. The men sniggered complicitly.

Tariq spoke out: 'This man Sloan. He is also the one who was arrested last week when he investigated Sheikh Abdul's company. It must be the same man. There's a report from Karim in the file.'

As soon as everyone had been released, Bill had set up a debriefing session. They needed to see if they could work out why the arrests had taken place. Was it simply because Universal Trading had panicked and made false accusations? Just to get Bill's people off their backs? They had certainly done that very effectively. Or was it something more sinister? Bill was frustrated, knowing that Al Abdullah was still out of Dubai. He would not be able to help.

'What the fuck's that creep Karim doing in all this?' Jim had said. 'He always seems to turn up when there's trouble and the job's going wrong. How does he always know what we're doing?'

'Yes!' echoed several of the others, 'the bastard always appears to know where we are.'

'Who is he actually working for?' demanded Jim.

Had he been able to hear what they were saying, Karim might not have been so bombastic when he reported to General Ali in the Diwan.

'They think that I am their friend, General. They won't do anything in future without discussing it with me first,' he concluded.

Sceptical as ever, the General thanked Karim and curtly dismissed him. 'If I cashed in and went to Kentucky I wouldn't have to deal with such scum,' he thought. Quickly he scanned the report on his desk that Colonel Tamimi had passed him yesterday. The common denominator of Karim's and Tamimi's reports was Bill Sloan. His blood quickened as his quarry was magnified in his sights. Sheikh Abdul would be very pleased.

Next morning Bill was up early. He had a busy day ahead and wanted to clear the backlog of the tapes. It was a few days after Bill had had the encounter with the police at the Al Khobar Building. Eventually, he had managed to persuade the manageress that it had all been a big mistake and that Asif had misinterpreted Bill's instructions. Realising that he had gone too far, the policeman decided to extricate himself from an embarrassing position. Causing an international incident would not help his career. Bill was released without charge, provided he did not lodge a complaint.

Since then his life had revolved around this new office. Collecting the tapes from there and those from Al Fadl's house, and reviewing them all, was virtually a full-time job.

The date would be forever imprinted on his mind. It was 28 August. It had started as a normal session for Bill. Yesterday evening he had collected the five tapes from the office at about 5 pm. As usual, he had replaced the tapes with five new ones.

In the evening he drove to Nad Al Sheba and played nine holes on the illuminated course within the racetrack. It was an ethereal scene. Several jockeys were cantering up and down the track, the Irish brogue ringing out behind them as they went past the players. Alongside the track, a dishdasha-clad Emirati trainer relayed his instructions to the jockeys. The lights of the racecourse were brilliant, often blinding the golfers. By contrast, the long shadows cast by the overpowering illumination of the racetrack plunged parts of the course into gloom. The golfers frequently struggled to find their balls on the fairway. Even late in the evening, the heat was intense. The constant dripping sweat and the shimmering light reflecting off the numerous water hazards made the whole experience surreal.

After a quick meal, Bill drove back to town via the house near Choitrams and changed the tape again. It was all uneventful and by now had become a routine. He would transcribe as much as possible that evening, often falling asleep over the recording machine. He ran two machines in tandem. When he came across something interesting he would stop, make some notes, probably listen to it several times, then record the position on the tape and play this section again, this time using the second player to record the extract. This way, he compiled a tape with useful material which cut out all the often interminable dross. He then passed the compilation tape on to Andy.

He had been listening for about a quarter of an hour. Suddenly there was a new voice on the line. An authoritative, deep voice, speaking in Arabic and English. Bill's antennae responded and he became instantly alert. He stopped the tape and rewound to the beginning of this new conversation.

'Good day Sanjay, how are things?'

'Very good Sheikh, very good indeed. I will have those things we talked about next week... the Angels and flowers.'

'How many?'

'Ten of them, the Angels – I got them from Massoud. Then there will be some more training to be done.'

'And the flowers?' demanded Sheikh Abdul.

'Our friends in the Guards have already supplied that to the Emir. It's thanks to the Doctor that they were able to process it. They're happy to let it be used by you.'

'Yes, we're friends at the moment. When will you be ready?'

'In about ten days.'

'Good! I have heard from our friend in the Hindu Kush. His strike against the Towers of Mammon will be in fourteen days time.'

There was further discussion but now in Arabic, and then: 'I will be ready, Sheikh... ' Some of the recording was patchy; perhaps Sanjay was calling from his private jet? 'Have faith. Insha'Allah, all will be well, Sheikh, Ma'a sala'am.'

Bill had replayed the tape innumerable times. There was no doubt about it. The other speaker was definitely Sheikh Abdul.

Quickly, he finished going through the other tapes. Just ordinary chat. Immediately he sent a text to Andy on the prescribed number, requesting an emergency meeting. Two minutes later, Andy phoned back on another number. They agreed to meet first thing next morning.

193

They were at the Crown Hotel by 8 am. Bill put his Spinney's shopping bag on the ground alongside the one which Andy already had beside his chair. The latest tapes were inside.

'It's Sheikh Abdul on the line to this guy called Sanjay. He's the Bollywood man… '

'Yes, yes, I remember – I checked him out when his name came up before. He was in the jihad in Afghanistan during the Soviet occupation. He and Osama bin Laden operated together. Bin Laden provided the funds and the rhetoric, Sanjay did the fighting. He's nothing more than an Indian Mafiosi in reality. I'm not sure that religion features very highly on his agenda. By which I mean that he's very much into religiosity! Outwardly very observant. But with him it's only the money – and the power.'

'My God, and now he's teamed up with Sheikh Abdul – there's more than enough money there!'

'And introduced him to bin Laden, by the sound of it!' said Andy. 'What an unholy alliance that would be.'

'What's their game... wait a minute, on the tape you'll hear Sheikh Abdul say something like "I will avenge the past. The sins of the house of… " something or other, I couldn't catch the name at the time "… will be visited upon the sons. Now my time has come!"'

Bill continued: 'That call that we talked about last time was between Sajjad in Fountain Trading and someone I didn't recognise. You remember, where the other guy was probably in Iran? They were speaking in Farsi. Your guys might make something of it?'

'Go on! What else?' said Andy, impatiently.

'It seems like an attack or something is planned for fifteen days' time.'

'My God! That's the 9th,' said Andy, 'where the hell are we talking about? What's the target? Any idea?'

'Well, they go on to talk about the Towers of Mammon. Very cryptic. Sandy mentioned something about this when he briefed me before I went to Saudi. Seemed to think that it was a figure of speech, a polemical rallying cry, symbolic, or something like that? What if it's actually code for a target?'

Andy picked up Bill's train of thought. 'What's the most significant thing in Dubai, the best target for a terrorist?'

'The DWTC?'

'Exactly, the Dubai World Trade Centre!'

'Something that's anathema to the fundamentalists? That represents the apostate West.'

'Bloody hell! I need to get moving. Must get these straight back to Cheltenham!' said Andy.

He picked up the bag which Bill had brought and rose to his feet. Obviously Bill was going to have to pay for their drinks.

'They'll analyse them there. Send a copy to the NSA too, for them to pass on to the CIA. Once they've made sense of it. But I'll get onto the CIA before that and warn them.'

'Hang on a minute!' said Bill, 'I almost forgot with all that's been going on. That bank transaction you asked me to look into… it was paid into Octagon Computers' account in the Commercial Bank. That's confirmation of A.Q. Khan's involvement.'

'So,' said Andy, half sitting down again, 'A.Q. Khan is selling to Isfahan National Trading, as we thought. It's a front for the Iranian Revolutionary Guards – that's tantamount to selling it to the Iranian government!'

'And the deal's being arranged by Fountain Trading. I wonder if Mahmoud knows about this?'

Andy picked up on the theme. 'Hard to imagine that he does. Probably this is the account that Mahmoud Al Abdullah's not supposed to know about!'

'Sheikh Abdul's involvement means it's the worst-case scenario. A.Q. Khan has to be doing all this with the connivance of the Pakistani government.'

'More likely at the behest of someone in the ISI,' concluded Andy grimly. 'Setting Sheikh Abdul up in the UAE and doing a deal with the Taliban would give Pakistan a secure flank.'

'Yes, it would provide them with friends to counter the threat from India. This is what drives their paranoia.'

'You'd better see Al Abdullah at once.'

61

During one of his earlier operations for Mahmoud Al Abdullah, bugging the telephone of one of Al Abdullah's colleagues and rivals in the Department,

Bill had had no difficulty in also wiring Al Abdullah's private offices. Bill's company was responsible, too, for the regular sweeps of his department that Al Abdullah had requested. He was particularly afraid that General Mohammed din Al Dawley would have the CID bug his offices.

So when he met with Mahmoud the day after he had briefed Andy on the most recent and alarming report, Bill knew that everything they would say would be recorded and would eventually end up in the hands of the CIA and MI6, via Cheltenham and the NSA. That is, unless Bill chose to subvert the whole process, which he could easily have done. In this case, he chose not to do so.

The blood drained instantaneously from Mahmoud's face. Bill could discern this, despite the Arab's swarthy brown complexion.

'You must let me hear the tape immediately! Have you brought it with you?' he demanded urgently.

'You know the procedure, Mahmoud,' said Bill evenly.

'It's only someone like me who can really work out what it all means. Your analysts at Cheltenham wouldn't have the first idea!'

'OK, I'll speak to Andy after this,' said Bill, without conviction.

'It's probably all symbolic!' said Mahmoud, more in hope than expectation, thought Bill. 'That's the way we Arabs think – particularly the extremists and conservative fundamentalists. Their jargon's just like that of a bible-belt minister. All fire and brimstone, you know.' The exasperation in Mahmoud's voice was clear. But Bill was certain there was another emotion overlaying it all.

What would the voice analysts make of their current conversation, wondered Bill. They would undoubtedly detect stress. But would it be good stress or bad stress? Would it show that Mahmoud was excited to be in all this, at the centre of events; able to respond to events with foreknowledge; shape events to his personal advantage? Or was he worried? Was he trying to play both sides off against the middle? Double agents were a fact of life in the intelligence world.

Bill got up to leave. Al Abdullah signalled him to stay. He paused, his boyish face now serious and calculating. It was clear to Bill that Al Abdullah knew something.

'What is it, Mahmoud?' Bill asked.

'Sheikh... Sheikh Abdul!' It was as if he could not bring himself to mention the name. 'Not much happens in Dubai that I don't know about. I think that he is planning something.'

'What sort of thing?'

'He's always wanted to take over from the Ruler,' Al Abdullah continued. 'This must be what they were talking about.'

'A coup?' said Bill.

Al Abdullah nodded imperceptibly.

As Bill left his office, Al Abdullah's mind was racing, trying to assess all the implications of this turn of events.

Should he speak to the State Security people? Tell them what he had heard? That would let them know that he had been consorting with the British. And if he did not tell them and they found out, it would be all over for him. His life would not be worth living.

But what if the information was wrong? He would be risking everything unnecessarily, if he disclosed his hand to either side prematurely.

'Right, Mahmoud, I need you to do whatever you can to confirm this stuff,' Bill had said before leaving. 'Get on to all your sources and contacts. Shake all the trees! It's vital we know the truth before it's too late.'

If he did nothing, the Brits would be after him. They wouldn't hesitate to blow his cover to Sheikh Abdul. But if he did do something, anything, he risked alerting State Security. General Mohammed Ali Makbool would show him no mercy either.

At the same time as Al Abdullah and Bill were meeting in the former's office, General Ali held a small meeting in his office in the Diwan on the other side of the Creek. There were only two other people present. Tariq had been instructed to accompany Colonel Tamimi because he was so close to all the action. Tamimi had commended Tariq for using his initiative to place Bill under full-time surveillance. At the same time, Tamimi's nose had been put out of joint: overly zealous and efficient subordinates can often be a threat, he knew; particularly as Tariq was now face-to-face with the General. It took the General only a few minutes to decide what to do once he had heard Tariq's account of recent activity.

'Arrest Al Abdullah. Pick him up tomorrow. Make sure he has no plans to travel in the meantime. Pick him up on the way to his office in the morning.

Do it somewhere, anywhere, where no-one is likely to see what happens. Get him in your car by pretext or force, whatever. Tell him I need to see him straight away.

'Put him in solitary in the special cell block. Soften him up. Let's see, it's Tuesday today – let him sweat it out until after the weekend. I'll see him on Saturday morning – early.'

'But he can't just disappear like that. Someone's going to miss him and raise the alarm,' interjected Tamimi.

'I'll get someone to phone his wife and his PA,' volunteered Tariq, 'and tell them he's got to get over to the UK on government business immediately; tell them His Highnesses have ordered him to go across to join them. They won't be suspicious of that – it happens all the time. We'll say he's in a meeting at the Diwan and tell his PA to book a seat on the late morning Emirates flight to London.'

'Yup – do that,' said the General approvingly. 'Colonel, make sure that someone sensible monitors his mobile. Some calls may need an immediate response, to avoid suspicion.'

'Wa'Allah, General. I'll send someone to collect the ticket from the check-in desk at the airport.'

'I'll get Sheikh Abdul to make sure that the airport and Emirates make it look as if he has actually travelled – that his name appears on the manifest. Just in case someone gets suspicious and decides to check. The Sheikh's brother will fix that,' said the General.

'Yes, General,' said Tamimi with obvious relish, 'we'll give him the usual softening-up treatment. Lights on all the time, not allowed to sleep; little food, some water and rice only; full hands, waist and foot manacles!'

'That's right. But don't interrogate him. Just do the normal "induction" interview. Don't give him any idea what we know. Don't mention the British or anything like that. And make sure that the cameras and the microphones are on all the time, just in case he mumbles anything in the cell, something that might give him away… And take his mobile away immediately; don't give him a chance to use it.' The General dismissed the other two with a nod of his head.

It was two o'clock on the following Saturday morning when General Ali arrived at the State Security detention facility. Colonel Tamimi was there to meet him. He had made sure that Tariq was not.

'Sala'am alaikum, General, Kayf al-hal?'

'Alaikum sala'am, wayn shokran, Colonel, how is everything going?'

The two had spoken on several occasions since their meeting in the Diwan. In the meantime, life had been turned upside down for Mahmoud Al Abdullah. The shock of his arrest had been overwhelming. To those who had been observing him, his guilt seemed palpable. But they had not questioned him, other than to do the initial holding interview. Al Abdullah had been given no reason for his arrest, despite his beseeching entreaties. So far, all had gone according to plan.

'Have you everything set up, Colonel?' demanded General Ali.

'Yes, Insha'Allah. Here's the remote: all you need do is to start the show by pressing the red button. You'll be impressed with the show, Sir!'

The show was indeed impressive, and left little room for doubt. Andy was seen boarding the plane in Dubai, then booking into the Holiday Inn in London. There was some excellent coverage of Andy Stringer and Mahmoud Al Abdullah having dinner; and some accompanying voice transcripts, in which Andy was heard, indistinctly, to say something like '... at the office ... get you signed on ... procedures'. The video showed Al Abdullah looking very uncomfortable at this point.

Next was a full frontal of Andy and Al Abdullah coming out of Century House. A further shot showed them getting off the train in Portsmouth a few days later, which was followed by scenic views of the south coast with the two of them seen walking along a cliff-top path near a Napoleonic fort well-known to General Ali. They were accompanied by two other Brits, one of whom State Security subsequently identified as the man once known only by the moniker 'C'.

The evidence might not have stood up in a court of law, even in the Emirates, but in the courts of the intelligence world, it was a slam dunk. Wriggle though he might, Al Abdullah would not be able to escape the damning conclusions of the graphic report. In the event, realising that the game was up, he had decided not to resist. His pride dissolved and he threw himself upon the General's mercy. His normally haughty and confident face crumpled; he shook uncontrollably and seemed to shrink in size. The tears welled up in his eyes.

Once the floodgates had opened, it all spilled out in a torrent of words. Al Abdullah seemed relieved to get everything off his chest. Three days alone with his demons, under constant surveillance, had wrought havoc with the hitherto urbane and superbly confident, indeed, arrogant, apple of the Ruler's eyes.

For General Ali, the boil had been quickly lanced. A blow-by-blow account of the traitor's relationship with the foreign intelligence service had been documented verbatim, and the witness statement signed by Al Abdullah. There could be no turning back now. His fate was inextricably bound up with that of General Ali.

Other than confirming Al Abdullah's guilt, there had seemed to his State Security interrogators to be little of consequence in his confession. It spoke more of future intentions than of past intelligence coups for the British. But, for General Ali, one item stood out like a flashing neon sign. This was a reference to Al Abdullah's recent meeting with Bill when he had been briefed by him on the Towers of Mammon report. To General Ali's colleagues, the information represented an item which might merit further investigation. A possible unidentified threat, which might be significant. One which might turn out on further examination to be a red herring, which diverted them from more important tasks. But the General's perspective was completely different. He suddenly found himself with a handful of sticks of dynamite with a short fuse, spluttering and sparking. He would have to move fast in order to prevent them blowing up in his hands.

The General was not a merciful man, but he was a pragmatist. Al Abdullah convicted in the State Security court would have been a personal and very public triumph for General Ali. But it would be a disaster for Sheikh Abdul's plans. And, therefore, for him too. Al Abdullah had to remain in place, had to appear to be continuing to work as normal for British intelligence. But now he would be working for new masters. The intelligence pearl had changed hands.

In Langley, Senior Research Officer Major Carl Jacobsen listened to the British Defence Attaché. The two were chalk and cheese. Jacobsen was a hard-bitten ex-Marine. He had been in Lebanon in 1987 when the Marines' barracks had been blown up by Hezbollah. He did not like Arabs. Tall at 6' 2" and barrel-chested, he had a lived-in face with a jutting jaw and crew-cut hair. Sitting in his office was Lieutenant Commander Ben Bradshaw, a submariner and the seasoned veteran of many underwater tours in HMS *Astute*. He looked by comparison soft, almost effete. He was a couple of inches shorter than Jacobsen and slight of build. His wavy blond hair, although short, was not cut to the bone like Jacobsen's. Bradshaw was new to this post. The two had not met before.

Jacobsen had heard the British officer out. But it was clear that he was sceptical. 'Commander, I don't go for this Towers bullshit. I think you guys are putting two and two together and getting five! These Arabs,' he continued, emphasising the 'A' so that it came across as two words, 'they're all a bunch of ragheads. They couldn't organise a gang-bang in a convent!'

'Well, please yourself Major, but I have to say that a number of our people have analysed all this. They reckon it represents a serious threat against US assets,' said Bradshaw primly.

'Well, don't worry Commander, it's sure in our system – along with one million other similar reports. If we reacted to every one of them, we would be permanently on the highest state of alert. Not even Uncle Sam has the resources to respond to everything. You wouldn't believe how far-fetched these guys' schemes are. Only last week there was a report that the Mossad was planning to carry out a Hiroshima-style attack on Manhattan, made to look as if it had been done by Al Qaeda!'

It was Karim. He poked his head around the door, as if checking to see what was happening, to see if he would be welcomed. He had only been to the office once before, always staying in the shadows and preferring nondescript meeting places. He had never come to the office uninvited before. What did he want?

'Sala'am alaikum, Karim, what brings you here?' asked Bill.

'Alaikum sala'am, Kayf al-hal,' responded Karim, with his trademark midnight shadow and dirty unpressed dishdasha, the ankle-length garment, usually with long sleeves and similar to a robe, worn most often by men in the Arabian Peninsula. In Karim's case, its purity and simple elegance were distorted by stains and a beer belly. For all the world, he was the archetypal scruffy version Arab of Hollywood allusion, not the imperious hook-nosed Sheikh of Lawrence of Arabia! Now he had adopted his most obsequious and grovelling attitude. Looking for money somewhere, thought Bill uncharitably, but not without good reason.

'Insha'Allah, I am asking you when it was that you are in Dubai first time. Please, you tell me?'

'But Karim,' said Bill, surprised at the question, 'you know exactly when I came, I've told you several times and I've never made any secret of it; it was June 1995, on a business trip from Saudi. Is this for your political masters? If they want to know, please tell them. I really hope you're telling them that I'm on their side. Most of what I've done has been for them. I'm trying to help Dubai secure its reputation as a good place to do business. Somewhere that's a level playing field for all those transnational corporations that you're trying to seduce into doing business here.'

'Alhamdulillah!'

'Indeed so; our friend Mahmoud is in the *Gulf Times* almost every day with some novel initiative to attract the mighty dollar. Doesn't sound very Islamic to me. I guess that's one reason why Mahmoud's so unpopular, not to mention that there's a lot of jealousy. If you ask me, I'd say that Mahmoud must be flying too close to the sun! He's breathtakingly photogenic and his picture's in the papers more frequently than Sheikh Abdul's.' Karim maintained his inscrutable mask; or was there a flash of vitriol at the mention of Mahmoud, wondered Bill? Still waters run deep; it was always difficult to determine what Karim's motives were, where his loyalties lay. Indeed whether he had any loyalties, other than to his stomach and the paymaster of the moment.

Karim wrung his hands and shuffled out of the door, closing it behind him. Bizarre, thought Bill, turning his attention back to the red folder on his desk. Without warning, the door burst open and the whole of the office was inundated by a group of stern and self-important-looking young Arabs. About ten men in dishdashas and a bevy of women. It was difficult to tell if the women were beautiful – they were all in the abaya. Only their eyes were visible, and they were giving nothing away.

The leader shouted: 'Stay where you are!'

Instinctively Bill reached for the phone, but who should he call?

'Do not use your phone! Put your phones down; give me your phones! Sit down – men here, women there,' he ordered peremptorily. His minions, without so much as a word, hurried to do his bidding, segregating men and women into different rooms of the office.

No attempt was made to say who they were or who they represented; no explanation was given as to what they were doing; no warrant had been shown. There were no civil rights here.

'Who's in charge here?'

'I am,' said Bill. 'What are you doing; who are you?'

'That's none of your business, Infidel!' said the Arab, pistol-whipping Bill violently across his face and forcing him down onto a nearby chair. Immediately two burly Arabs grabbed Bill's arms and forced them behind his back. He felt the cold steel of the handcuffs as they were forced roughly onto his wrists. And he felt the hot blood from the wounds caused by the barrel of the Arab's pistol trickling down his face and under his shirt collar.

The leader scanned around the office, looking haphazardly at papers lying on the desks. There were several files lying on Bill's desk. The Arab picked them up, riffled through them briefly and threw them down. Changing his mind, he picked up the red folder to which Bill had been referring as a consequence of Malik's earlier call. He skimmed through it, his eyes registering his suspicion. He held on to it.

Quickly his men unpacked the trunk. This was the evidence which they needed. Colonel Tamimi gloated. Now the Emirati traitor was in his hands. Like a spider caught in its own web. The General would be well pleased.

Some time later, the doors of the prison cells clanged shut behind them all. Each was in a frightening world of solitary confinement; each manacled and chained to the wall of the small cubicle which was now their home. Dubai is a land of the flat earth – and they had fallen over the edge.

Six months after he had left the UK, Shahid was returning. He left Kabul airport on a Pakistani Airways flight bound for London having lived, it seemed to him, several lives in the intervening period.

On that first evening, he had had to wait nearly an hour before being collected from his roadside position having, as it were, been abandoned to his fate by his reluctant chauffeur. Some form of initiation, he surmised. Eventually another Russian UAZ69 arrived coming down from the mountain.

There were two men in the front, both dressed in traditional Afghani robes with large coiled black turbans and hair hiding most of their faces. The passenger held a Soviet RPK machine gun at the high port. Several ammunition bandoliers were draped around his upper body. The vehicle slowed to a halt.

'Get in!' the driver said peremptorily after Islamic greetings had been exchanged. After about three hours the Jeep, at times reduced to a crawl in first gear, arrived at a clutch of mud buildings surrounded by tents. A couple of obviously new corrugated buildings lay off on the right-hand side. The only brick building was a mosque. By now it was well into the night but the ambient light allowed Shahid to get a good idea of the layout. The moon was nearly full and the sky clear and full of stars, more than he had ever seen before, with a translucent and vibrant Milky Way. The moonlight cast an eerie glow over the scene. Shahid noticed that there were hardly any lights visible, just a few chinks here and there from several of the tents. Then he remembered that the driver had turned off the Jeep's headlights some moments before they arrived. He heard the sound of many people talking in Arabic. The speakers sounded didactic and self-important, and spoke in an outmoded manner, though he could not hear exactly what was being said. He also heard from several tents, and one of the buildings, voices reciting the Koran rhythmically and monotonously. He heard no sound of laughter.

As the vehicle drew up by the buildings, the muezzin began the evening prayer call. Immediately, all lights were extinguished, tent flaps and doors opened. Shahid realised that there were several hundred people altogether. They made for the mosque, where again there were no lights. His companions told Shahid to go with them to the prayers. When everyone was finally settled and kneeling, the doors were shut and some dim lights came on in the mosque. It had been set up to serve as a lecture room as well as a place of worship. Several large video screens on either side of the mosque came on and a series of clips was shown. They were all similar. A NATO military vehicle was seen moving along a road or track. When it reached the middle of the screen a bright flash of light was emitted followed by a fireball and billowing smoke, accompanied by bits of body and vehicle falling back to earth. Each film clip had a sound track of a Koranic recitation. At the end of each attack a group of Mujahedeen brandishing weapons and wearing bandannas yelled their bloodcurdling cry, 'Allah Akbar! Allah Akbar!' at the camera. The cry was taken up by the congregation. At first, Shahid was taken aback by the barbarity he had witnessed and the bloodthirsty faces around him but, almost involuntarily, he found himself joining in, timidly at first and then with full and passionate voice. When the screens went dead and the sounds drained away, Shahid felt as if he had come to after an anaesthetic, his voice was hoarse and his head and hands shook.

Next morning Shahid was introduced into a small group. They were most recently arrived. There were nine of them altogether, mainly Gulf and Saudi Arabs. As well as Shahid, there was an Egyptian and an Algerian and a villainous-looking individual from Chechnya. All but two of them, Saudis, had already been involved in operations but, like Shahid, only in support roles. Jassim, a Houthi tribesman from northern Yemen had been involved in the attack on the USS *Cole* in Aden harbour last year which had killed seventeen US personnel. The Chechnyan had supported the siege of the school in Beslan and had been arrested and tortured by Beria's and the KGB's successors, the Russian FBS. The group had assembled over the last few days, and were now ready to start training.

An Egyptian known as a redoubtable Jihadist came into the room where they were all assembled.

'I am Abu Al Walid,' he said. 'From now on you do as I say. Your course will last six weeks. After that you will be equipped to attack the infidel across the entire world – Allah's world, peace be upon Him.'

'Allah Akbar,' the others responded. Shahid joined in with the familiar battle cry of the Mujahedeen.

'Welcome to Airport Camp, Shahid,' said Abu Al Walid.

Shahid was introduced to the group, all of whom had been in the camp for several days and already assumed their new names. Shahid was given the Arabic name Saleem Al Farsi. But he quickly became known as 'الإنكليزي, the Englishman'. The others all spoke some Arabic, but their different dialects were in some cases barely discernible to each other. Although Shahid had started learning Arabic, he could not have coped had the training been in that language. It was agreed that it would be principally in Urdu, but it was English which was the lingua franca that, ironically, linked them all together. Shahid was exhorted to continue his Arabic studies. He remembered back to his recitation of the Koran all those years ago. He had learned it parrot fashion and had not really understood what he was saying. Now his early experience helped him to advance rapidly in his studies.

Abu Al Walid immediately introduced the new apprentices to the life on which they had now embarked by quoting Osama bin Laden:

'The pieces of the bodies of infidels were flying like dust particles/If you would have seen it with your own eyes, you would have been very pleased/And your heart would have been filled with joy.'

The recitation was accompanied by the video of an explosion – 'Destruction of the Destroyer *Cole*' followed by news footage of the damaged ship. The 100-minute film also featured footage of bin Laden firing the AK-47, and a clip of him exhorting Muslims to further attacks. 'With small means and great faith, we can defeat the mightiest military power of modern times,' he said. 'America is much weaker than it seems. You will not die needlessly,' he counselled them. 'Your lives are in the hands of God.'

The next six months passed in a flash, with a plethora of new experiences for most of the recruits. They learned how to handle all sorts of weapons: Kalashnikovs, Armalites, Glochs, RPG 7 and others. The Mujahedeen relied for many of their weapons on theft and enemy battle casualties to increase the stocks in their armouries. They handled many types of explosives too, from Czechoslovakian Semtex to PETN. They made their own home-made brand from concoctions of fertilisers and sugar. Much of the information for this had to be drawn from the internet to test their ingenuity and resourcefulness. But they also had some lectures and demonstrations from the renowned bomb-maker, Abu Khabab al-Masri. They studied ways of killing people with their bare hands, and each day's training included sessions of unarmed combat. In this they were forced to fight their opponent for real, any sign of weakness likely to brand them as unsuitable. In the first few weeks several aspirants departed in shame. Of the others that had survived, few had escaped without injury from their comrades.

One day Jamil, who had been brought up in Germany, contradicted Abu Al Walid. Shahid and the others were forced to watch as the instructors, accusing him of being a spy, tortured him viciously, beating him with electric cables and tearing out several of his fingernails.

Each day, immediately after the Fajr prayer call at dawn and before the evening Maghrib prayer call just after sunset, there were periods of religious studies which became more and more political. Shahid, like all the others, was familiar at the outset with the aspirations and teachings of Political Islam and its global quest. But here the philosophy had been honed to a white-hot intensity. Gradually, all their thoughts merged so that their every waking moment was focused on killing the apostate and attaining martyrdom for themselves in order to achieve the global dominium of Islam.

Over the weeks they all became more and more physically fit with body-building and gym work and races over an assault course, the obstacles of which were increased regularly in difficulty. The final obstacle was a 50-metre stretch of barbed-wire entanglement 60 cm above the ground, underneath which they had to crawl in full combat gear as quickly as possible, all the time being harried and berated by sadistic instructors. As novices they started by crawling slowly on their bellies; at the end of that time they were required to run horizontally with only toes, knees and elbows touching the ground and carrying rifles and machine guns, all the time screaming 'Allah Akbar'.

Individual lessons gave way to tactical exercises, laying ambushes, attacking police posts, long night marches, setting up IEDs, harassing but evading advancing regular military forces. Many of these manoeuvres were carried out under fire from opponents whose weapons were fixed to fire overhead on a fixed line. On a final exercise they were required to take out an army observation post. They had to mount an assault, having first negotiated the barbed-wire entanglements. Shahid was one of the first into the wire; suddenly an array of weapons opened up from close by. At first they were all disorientated by this, but their training took over and carried them on. Then they realised that machine guns were firing on fixed lines just above the top of the wire, only centimetres above their heads. Shahid could discern the crack and thump of the rounds being detonated and then hitting the rocks several hundred metres on the other side of the entanglement. It was like listening to stereophonic earphones. He was exhilarated by this. It was as if all his senses were being brought to an overwhelming climax – to an orgasmic experience which could only be satisfied by actual action. At this point the trainers knew they had done their job. Another batch of kids had been transformed into Allah's soldiers. They were ready to slaughter, maim and destroy indiscriminately in his name.

During the following months, Shahid took part in many operations with his fellow Jihadis. These were the final parts of his training. They remained at the camp. Shahid subsequently discovered where he was, now that he was a trusted fighter. The camp was at Al Farouq near Kandahar Airport. All kinds of operations were mounted from the camp. Sometimes they would be pasting up posters in the nearby villages warning inhabitants that they would be killed if they fraternised with the foreign troops. On other occasions they took this intimidation a stage further by burning the shops and houses of those deemed collaborators. Ultimately some offending individuals were assassinated. Shahid and all the others accepted this as a perfectly normal consequence of failure to obey: they never questioned the authority by which this was done; they felt privileged to be able to serve Allah by administering his justice in this way. Shahid soon discovered that the Taliban were operating a shadow government in the area. Here the government writ was barely apparent. All women were being forced to wear the full burka, and schools were closed. But the Taliban did make a point of taking up people's grievances as a way of imposing their control. Shahid was involved in several cases where land disputes were settled unequivocally and arbitrarily by the Taliban. The instructions were always to make judgement in favour of the party most likely to support, or be coerced by, the insurgents. On one occasion Shahid and several of his fellow fighters from his course were ordered to go to a village headman's house in Nad-e-Ali and kill him because he had invited an American Delta Force patrol into his house to eat with him. Within minutes of the Special Forces patrol leaving the village, the Taliban had been told by a village rival. Shahid had been put in charge.

Shahid and his group arrived at the small house in the early hours of the following morning, just before the prayer call. He rushed to the house. He shot the flimsy door off its hinges with a burst of fire from his Kalashnikov and led his group into the dingy low-ceilinged house. There was pandemonium. Several of the women and children began screaming. Shahid was now cold and composed, the adrenaline rush fuelling his brain. His nerves had been settled by the burst of fire and the feeling of power it gave him. He seemed possessed by sensual self-righteous lust. Like a man taking possession of a woman.

A small child, virtually naked, appeared clutching a rag doll in one hand and a bar of chocolate in the other. Shahid saw at once that it was an American Hershey chocolate bar. Instinctively he fired a burst at the child. He saw the bullets impacting the frail and emaciated body as if it were all in slow motion. The child was thrown up in the air and somersaulted backwards; collapsing into a crumpled heap like the rag doll it had been carrying a moment earlier. Arterial blood started pumping and fountaining out of the several grievous wounds in the limp and lifeless body. Blood oozed from the child's mouth and nose. The choking gurgling noise penetrated the stillness which had followed the ear-shattering noise of Shahid's gunfire. A woman, the girl's mother, prostrated herself over the broken body keening pitifully. The other women shook and shivered, riveted to the spot in fear. Meanwhile Shahid's companions had ransacked the property looking for the man of the house. Eventually they found him cowering in a loft in an outbuilding at the back. Two Jihadis dragged him into the main room by his hair; others bludgeoned him into submission. Shahid took a written document out of his pocket. He read aloud the judgement and sentence of the Taliban. The man was blindfolded and propped against the back wall. At a shouted command from Shahid, each of his compatriots fired a burst shouting, 'Allah Akbar, Allah Akbar!' as they did so. The body slumped to the floor, twitching and convulsing briefly. The women now cried uncontrollably, and the wondering children ran to them in awe. Checking their weapons, Shahid and the group left and got into the vehicle. Brandishing their weapons and chattering excitedly like schoolboys returning victorious from a football match, they returned to camp.

Next day at the general assembly following morning prayers, Shahid and his group's exploits were recounted by the council leader, Mullah Hisham. Shahid was singled out for special praise.

Focusing on each new operation to fulfil Allah's commands, Shahid never cast an eye backwards. He did not see the lifeless children or the grieving mothers. He had no reason to doubt that what he had done was right. He was faithfully carrying out Allah's commands.

As a consequence of his successful initiation into a fully-fledged Jihadist, Shahid was sent to Al Sadik camp near Tora Bora. He and his fellow students had started as a group of eleven but only four of them had survived the tough regime. When he arrived there it was evident to Shahid that he was there because he was well-regarded. The camp was smaller than Al Farouq where he had come from.

'Welcome, Brother Shahid, to Al Sadik camp. I am in charge here, Alhamdulillah, and I'm glad that you have been chosen to join me. We do not train as many people here as at Al Farouq – I think Al Qaeda has trained as many as 6,000 people there altogether. Here we concentrate on operations and on the specific training required for particular operations. So you see, my friend, we have something special in mind for you!' The speaker identified himself as a core member of Al Qaeda, Abu Amman; someone whose name had been glorified to Shahid and his companions from the start of their indoctrination as one of Osama bin Laden's right-hand men. Another Egyptian, he had been with bin Laden since the earlier days against the Soviets. He was renowned for leaping from rocks above Soviet tanks and pushing flaming Molotov cocktails down the turrets. 'Here we are working with our Pakistani brethren,' he continued. Shahid's eyes betrayed his thoughts.

'Surprising, yes?' said Abu Amman. He stood up and went over to a wall covered by a large Herat tribal rug. He was a large man, barrel-chested, with thick black wavy hair and bushy eyebrows. Shahid noticed a jagged scar on his neck just visible below the shirt. Perhaps one day he would find out what caused it.

'Yes, we work very closely with the Pakistanis. They provide us with the weapons and some of the money. And, most importantly, with information. It is because of some particularly interesting information that I need you here,' Abu said enigmatically, with a distant penetrating look in his coal-dark eyes.

During the next couple of weeks, Shahid did not see Abu Amman again. He was formed into an operational unit with six others; he knew only one other who had been with him at Al Farouq camp, the Jordanian, Nasser Al Shoaib. Nasser was a disaffected former officer in the Royal Jordanian Army. Attached to the group was a reserved but capable man, Imran Majid. Thin and wiry, his hair receding at the temples and with an aquiline nose, it was soon clear that he was an experienced operator. Some ten days after they had been there, working together, they had bonded into a close knit team. It was clear that they now needed action.

Abu Amman called them together after prayers on the eleventh day.

'Brothers in Allah, peace be upon Him, you have a special calling. Many of our brothers are in jail here in our own country, imprisoned by our own people – by those among us who are Kafir. But we shall free them in Allah's name, Allah Akbar! Allah Akbar!' Quickly the group took up the rallying cry. Briefly, Abu Amman outlined an audacious plan to free Taliban prisoners from Sarposa prison. There were hundreds of Taliban prisoners held there, Abu told them.

'Upwards of 1,000. Some 200 are on hunger strike to protest against their detention. They have been held for over two years. Some have stitched their mouths closed to protest against their conditions!'

Shahid's group was to be supported by a team of thirty insurgents on motorcycles with AK-47s and rocket-launchers. At 9 pm, when it would be completely dark, a suicide bomber in a large petrol tanker was to drive up to the main gate and attempt to drive through it. He was to detonate his vehicle wherever it was stopped. This would kill or neutralise all the police and soldiers in the vicinity of the gate. Then, in the ensuing confusion, another suicide bomber would attack the rear gates. Shahid was to lead an assault party through these. Their task was to free the prisoners. Meanwhile, the motorcycle group would attack the fort on all other sides, firing rockets and rifles to keep the defenders occupied.

There had then followed ten days where all the participants got together and practised the attack. Imran Majid produced detailed plans and aerial photographs of the prison. It was clear that this information had come from official sources. Shahid remembered back to what Abu Amman had told them on arrival about the Pakistanis helping the Taliban. It became clear that Imran Majid was a Pakistani officer and member of the notorious ISI, the Inter-Services Intelligence Agency.

The attack went without a hitch. All the 1,200 prisoners escaped; of those released some were criminals of the worst type who now regained their freedom. But among them were 381 hardened Taliban or Al Qaeda leaders and activists. On the day they were all keyed up and expectant. Shahid's nerves jangled and his mouth was parched making swallowing difficult. A clear sky but with no moonlight had facilitated their approach to the prison. Numerous times during the hard-fought battle Shahid had held off fierce counter-attacks from the police reserves trying to stop the fleeing prisoners. On their victorious arrival back at Al Sadik camp they were feted by their comrades as they watched footage of the aftermath of their strike on Al Jazeera and CNN. Both President Clinton and President Musharraf were forced to make public statements denying that the attack was significant and claiming that it would not have any impact on their resolve to resist the encroachment of the Taliban.

Later that evening, a posse of Land Cruisers arrived at the camp. Like wildfire, the word got around the camp that it was Osama bin Laden and his entourage come to congratulate the team. They were all introduced to the imperious and calm figure that was so soon to dominate world headlines. By his side stood al-Zawahiri basking in the reflected glory of such a successful attack.

Shahid won further commendations for his actions and bravery. Shortly before they left, al-Zawahiri singled him out. 'Sala'am alaikum, my Brother, may Allah be with you. You will get your reward in heaven. How long have you been in our service here in Afghanistan?' he queried.

'For six months altogether. I was at... '

'I know, Brother, and I had good reports from there about you too. It's time for you to fulfil your destiny! Go back now to your home in England.

211

You will shortly be contacted with instructions for your greatest moment. Your name will strike terror into the heart of all Kafir, ma'a sala'am.'

'Welcome back, Mr. Wahab, I don't think!' said the operator to no-one in particular, as she flagged up the report from Immigration at Heathrow. 'The Englishman has returned!'

It was the following day when the supervisor in Thames House reviewed her report. It referred to earlier suspicions that the Englishman had been involved in the attack on Mike's Bar in Israel. He gave instructions to place Shahid under Priority One surveillance.

66

Ahmed had received the message by the usual channels. He knew that it emanated from al-Zawahiri at Tora Bora where Ahmed had met him nine months earlier.

'Sala'am alaikum, you have done well Brother, very well. Your Englishman is indeed a gem, a peach. He has already sown fear in the heart of the infidels' lackeys here in our own country. Treat him well. The Emir has approved him for the task we spoke about. You have done well, my friend, to select such a good man,' he read. 'Instruct him to start training at once. I will inform our friend in Germany. Allah Akbar, God is great.'

Immediately Ahmed texted Shahid: 'Meet me at the mosque tonight.'

They met in the small office at the back of the mosque which the Imam let Ahmed use. Shahid knew that it was used for Hizb business, and that Ahmed was a member. The Imam asked no questions. Now, Shahid too was a member.

They had attended prayers together and were now sitting on either side of the crude wooden table.

'You put in that form applying for pilot training?' asked Ahmed, getting down to business immediately.

'Yes,' said Shahid. 'I haven't heard a thing. But that's not surprising. I've been away ever since.'

'Well, you must go and see this Kafir who's in charge. You must do the training at once. You must apply to go to America.' Ahmed spat derisively on the floor. 'There's a training course there we want you to apply for. There's a course starting in a couple of months. Apply for a visa as well, of course; it takes a long time.'

'What's all this about?' Shahid said anxiously. 'I only got back a few days ago!'

'You have been chosen by our Emir to take part in a very major operation. One which will put the names of Al Qaeda and Osama bin Laden on the screens of televisions all over the world and strike fear into the hearts of the Kafir. You will be immortalised, Shahid.'

Shahid was swept away in the emotion of the event and with Ahmed's enthusiasm. But then reality set in.

'But why should the OTC pay for me to do this? And I can't ask my parents – they couldn't afford it anyway.'

'Your task is to get on the course. I'll worry about the money. It's at Pensacola Naval Air Station in Florida. Tell your parents it's a place that trains many pilots – many foreigners. That you looked it up online. Go to the OTC and ask them to try to book you a slot on the course which starts in early June. As it's the OTC, an application should be received favourably. Tell him that you have the money – you can say that it's from your family. They won't know. Allah will provide. Muhammad will arrange it, peace be upon Him.'

It had all been surprisingly easy. The OTC boss had been delighted to welcome Shahid back.

'I thought you had lost interest?' he said.

'No,' said Shahid unthinkingly. 'I had to go to visit my family – my grandparents live in Pakistan.'

They talked for a bit and the Air Commodore explained more about what the OTC did. He told Shahid about the other members. 'There are twenty-two – that's twenty-three with you – members; girls too!' He winked lasciviously at Shahid, as he had done before.

'Look,' said Shahid, 'I really want to learn to fly. I've been thinking a lot about my future. I want to become a fighter pilot. I'd like to go to America to do a course. I have some friends over there. And I've got the money too!'

Seeing another potential recruit for the RAF, Air Commodore Stokes became as helpful as he could. A telephone call to the Defence Attaché at the US Embassy at Wingfield House elicited the information that, 'Yes, Pensacola Naval Air Base actually did have a reciprocal training arrangement with the RAF. While it would not be possible for a member of the University

OTC to go there on the system, none the less a place could be available if the individual funded it himself. And yes, perhaps a discount could be arranged in this case.'

From there on, it was plain sailing. A place was reserved for Shahid on an earlier course in mid-April. Ahmed produced the money from somewhere. Shahid applied for a visa which was speedily granted. Had MI5 and the FBI co-ordinated their activities satisfactorily, it would have emerged that Shahid was under full-time surveillance and on the inter-government watch list. But they did not. The flight was booked. Again, Ahmed mysteriously produced the money.

Shahid did have some trouble explaining his new-found enthusiasm for joining the RAF to his parents. But when Shahid assured them that all been arranged between the British and American governments and that the former had even paid for it, their concerns evaporated. How proud they would be to have their son's photograph on the mantelpiece wearing an RAF pilot's flying suit and helmet, standing beside a Tornado.

Ten days before his departure, Shahid reported to the military hospital at Milbank on the Thames embankment. He knew he was fit. It would be a formality. And so it proved to be. Until the eye test, that is.

'Did you know you're colour-blind?' said the examining doctor in long-sleeved white coat, stethoscope around his neck.

'I'm afraid that's the end of your flying career!'

The key turned in the heavy metal door. Bill had been lying on the thin paliasse. He was too tired to notice its filthy state. He had slept only fitfully, his mind constantly returning to the same dead-end. No matter what he said, it wouldn't check out. He could not say that he did not know Andy. He had to assume that he had been under surveillance; that they had been seen meeting. He would have to claim that Andy was merely a friend. But how could he explain the frequent meetings – always in different places – during the working day? What if they had been monitoring his telephone as well? Did they pick up the call made on the phone and the responding acknowledgement on another number? Every time he thought that he had worked out what to say, immediately a voice in his head said: 'Yes… but what if they ask this? …. Or that?' Instantly, the whole story would unravel. A chill ran through his body and his stomach churned.

He had lost all sense of time. There were no windows in the interrogation block. The lights were permanently on. The guards were on a constant patrol, looking through the hatches into the cells. Whenever a prisoner was seen to be sleeping, they banged the door and shouted in guttural Arabic. Throughout the interminable hours, Bill heard the other cell doors being opened and his colleagues being taken away for interrogation. Three times he had been hauled out himself and frogmarched, despite the trailing manacles, to an interrogation room. So far, the questioning had been routine and innocuous. Each question and its accompanying response had been transmitted backwards and forwards through an interpreter, between interrogator and interrogated. Then it was laboriously transcribed onto a printed form. On each occasion, Bill had been forced to sign the resulting statement. It was, however, written in Arabic.

It was clear to Bill that even the secret police had to observe some legal niceties. Perhaps it was all part of a typical Soviet-style police state. The authorities themselves were the state; they also made the regulations and drafted the laws. So, as long as they complied with the procedures and observed the regulations, anything they did was, by definition, legitimate. Once you had your hands on the levers of power – the army, communications, the media, and had disenfranchised the population – you could do anything you wanted. Anything to protect your self-interest; it was automatically self-legitimising.

But, during the interminably dragging minutes and hours and days in the cell, Bill had known that the real questioning would begin eventually. Would it be this time? Sooner or later, the red folder would be thrown onto the desk between them by the interrogator. 'What is Boxfile? Who is Barry White?'

Bill knew that the two guards were both large and powerfully built, even though their physiques were concealed beneath their dishdashas. Their unshaven faces were not the deliberate macho designer stubble favoured by so many young Emiratis. They just did not bother overmuch about their appearance. Hauling Bill to his feet, they blindfolded him. Bill tried hard to visualise the route along which he was taken; to work out the geography of his prison. They went along what he thought was a corridor and made several turns. He heard a door opening. One of the guards asked permission of a colonel for him to be taken in. Bill felt that he recognised the clipped, guttural, authoritative voice, but it was from a time that to him now seemed an age ago.

'Put him in the chair… no, not that one. This one! Take off the blindfold.'

The blindfold was removed. He was forced to balance on a three-legged chair. Bill recognised the interrogator as the leader of the party which had arrested him at the office – how long ago was it now? In his immaculate dishdasha, Colonel Tamimi sat at the desk, idly playing with his worry beads, his aquiline features and hooked nose betraying nothing. Bill had to struggle to keep his balance.

The Colonel began: 'I am sorry about the chair. It's to help you stay awake and answer my questions. The sooner we can get it all done with the better, that way we can both go and get some sleep.' Tamimi spoke in a solicitous, almost apologetic, voice.

'Would you like a cigarette?' He proffered a packet of Marlboro.

'No, thank you,' said Bill, 'I don't smoke.' He tried to keep his inner angst out of his voice; to be calm and polite, but non-committal. 'Anyway,' he thought involuntarily, 'the chances are the Marlboro is fake! Perhaps it's from the container Rory and I failed to seize those several weeks ago.'

'Well then, have one of these.' Tamimi thrust a can of what looked like a soft lemon drink into his hands.

'Yeah, have one,' he said. 'Have some of this – it's ProEndorphin. We use it to keep us going in the middle of the night and so on. It's very refreshing.'

Suspicious, Bill declined the fizzing, citrus-flavoured, effervescent cocktail. He tried to keep his mind clear. Bill wondered why his interrogator would offer him something which would make him alert and therefore better able to resist the techniques of interrogation. It did not make sense. However, it was very evident that Tamimi had a game plan. At the moment he appeared to be very friendly. But it had not started in earnest yet.

'So, what are you doing here, Mr Bill?'

'Just exactly what I told all your colleagues when they asked me this before.' He tried to keep his voice even, to achieve some degree of control over the proceedings.

He did not see the guard's scything leg as it smashed into his chair. He collapsed in a heap on the floor. Unable to use his manacled hands to break his fall, his chin hit the table. His head hit the rough-hewn stone floor with a sickening thud, his face scraping across it as the chair twisted.

'Answer the Colonel's question, Kafir!' shouted the guard. Tamimi let fly a string of invective at the guards and ordered them to put Bill back on the chair. He could feel the blood running down his forehead into his eyes. Tamimi ordered the second guard to clean Bill's face, which he did with obvious disgust. All part of the softening-up process, thought Bill; the good cop, bad cop routine. Straight out of the MOD Manual of Interrogation.

'I'm very sorry about all that,' said Tamimi. 'Ziad is very difficult to control. It won't happen again,' he said. Both knew that it would.

'Tell me again, then!' commanded Tamimi. Bill recounted his stock line: he was simply a businessman undertaking a normal commercial activity. He had been asked by Tamimi's own government, in effect, to assist in the investigation of a government entity, RAKA. He had been assigned to work with Mahmoud Al Abdullah, nothing more, nothing less.

'But we find all this equipment in your office: wire, crocodile clips, recording devices. Whose phones are you bugging? Don't you know that it's against the law to bug someone's telephone here? Just like it is in your own country. We're not the savages you think we are!'

'But the instructions came from Mahmoud Al Abdullah. He works for His Excellency, he's part of the government!' exclaimed Bill.

'Which government?' said Tamimi archly. 'And all these documents?' He waved a large sheaf of papers in front of Bill's nose. It was evident that they were printouts from the files on Bill's computer. 'All this information! Who are you passing this to? The British government? The Israelis?'

Tamimi's voice rose in intensity, his dark eyes staring malevolently at Bill. He managed to retain his composure, but he had lost his professional calm. Bill sensed it was all becoming very personal. Tamimi paused, then rose abruptly jabbing a finger at Bill.

His backhanded swipe caught Bill across his right cheek. Trying to avoid it, Bill overbalanced and again crashed to the floor. One of the guards, the one who had hit him first, decided it was time for some practice for the World Cup starting in a few weeks' time in May.

Leaving Bill on the floor, Tamimi and the guards went out of the room. Bill picked himself up and took stock. His right eye was half closed already and swelling quickly from multiple contact with the toecaps of the guard's boot. His body felt like it had just been through ten rounds with Mike Tyson. He did not sit down; trying to balance on the inhospitable stool was exhausting. He tried to focus; to maintain contact. He looked around the room. He saw the pile of files behind Tamimi's seat on a small table. They were all from his office. Was the red folder there? Instinctively he moved 'towards the pile. Just in time, he caught himself. He could not see the camera, the small aperture recording his every move. But he knew that it was there. He could visualise Tamimi back in the control room, watching intently to see if Bill would betray himself. Had Tamimi already called the Boxfile number for Barry White? Heard the refined voice of one of MI6's girls answering: 'International Trading Services. How may I help you?' And, of course, the Office would have heard long ago from Andy that Bill had been arrested. It was public knowledge, for goodness sake. It had been headline news in the Sunday papers all those months ago. They would be monitoring the situation daily. The damage limitation plan would have been implemented.

But would Tamimi have got to the truth when he peeled off the layers of cover, as the writhing belly dancers in the sheikhs' palaces peeled off their seven veils, to get to the naked reality? As one professional to another, would he have arrived at the true facts; at the reality behind Barry White? Either way, there would be much activity and consternation in the appropriately convoluted, modern Byzantine edifice across Vauxhall Bridge. The door swung open. Tamimi strode in.

'Here, the penalty for spying is death.'

He collected his papers and left. Five minutes later, Bill was back on the straw paliasse in his barren cell.

It was just after five in the afternoon. Now in early September, the Gulf weather was beginning to show signs of moderating from the thermometer-topping heights of recent months. By this time of day the sun had lost some of its heat, and a warm balmy evening, perfect for sitting out with a cool beer, was in prospect. None of this was significant to Bill, however, lying on the thin paliasse on the hard concrete floor.

Suddenly, an enormous cacophony of shouting, clapping and cheering erupted from the area of the State Security offices adjacent to the cell block. The noise was just discernible through the concrete walls. Doors into the cell block opened and the guards took up the exultant chorus.

Bill heard cell doors being opened amid the commotion. His door was opened. He and his fellow prisoners were frogmarched down the corridor, chains clanking, and into a comfortable reception area. The room was full of young Arab men. Bill recognised many of them as being those who had arrested him or interrogated him. The large TV stood in one corner, tuned to Al Jazeera.

Mockingly, the Arabs pointed to the screen. The surreal image of the second plane, slamming into the World Trade Center North building, almost slicing completely through it and coming out the other side, was being played continuously, over and over again in a repetitive loop. The TV anchorman's banal words, repeated like the film clip, were in sharp contrast to the enormity of the event.

'Oh my goodness, there's another one... Oh my goodness. There's another one!... This has to have been on purpose. It can't be an accident.'

In the immediate aftermath, there were rumours of American and British flags being burned, along with effigies of Bush and Blair, in various parts of the Gulf. Tensions everywhere were running high.

Bill was largely oblivious to the swirling fact, fiction, innuendo and rumour incriminating the UAE in involvement in the 9/11 attack. One fact was that the UAE recognised the Taliban government. Another fact was that Saudi Arabia did so too, and that both these countries had poured enormous amounts of money into the funding of Madrassas of the strict Wahhabi School there. Another fact was that US entry visas had been issued to the hijackers in Saudi and the UAE, and that a majority of them were citizens of these countries.

Pakistan was the only other country to recognise the Taliban government. The rumours suggested that these three countries did not support the Taliban out of altruism; indeed, that they had ulterior motives.

In October, Operation Enduring Freedom launched Bush's War on Terror. At a stroke, Bill found himself in even greater peril than before. He was now incarcerated on a charge of spying in the cells of a country which was a key ally of one which had just been invaded by his own. Sensationalist theories of a war of civilisations had come home to roost for an infidel held captive by revanchist Muslims.

Sheikh Abdul and General Ali had been closeted together at the Sheikh's palace for much of the day. A scented incense pervaded the atmosphere.

Innumerable pots of coffee and tea had been brought. Usually the servant was told just to leave the pot, not to serve. On a number of occasions when he was summoned to produce more, he found the previous pot sitting unused.

'So what do we do now?' said the Sheikh, his saturnine features illuminated by the passion with which he spoke. His eyes were hooded, dark and inscrutable. Like the hawks he flew. Both men had been taken aback by the chain of events since the 9/11 strike. They had supposed that the Americans would want to punish the supporters of the Taliban. They had reasoned that both Pakistan and Saudi were too significant to US interests to be attacked. But not so the UAE. After all, many of the highjackers held UAE passports. An example could be made of them by the neocons. It would send the necessary message. But it would not invoke a response of any consequence. Nothing that they could not live with. They could visualise the neocons, Cheney, Rumsfeld and Bolton, arguing the case in their obdurate and blinkered way:

'We've got to make it clear to that bastard, Mr President. If we don't make an example of someone now, immediately, it will come back and bite us on the arse. Strike while the iron is hot!'

'Yup, that sure is right. All these motherfuckers are either with us or against us. They can't have their cake and eat it. Those mother fuckers in the planes were either Gulf Arabs or Pakistanis. One lot are bankrolling all those goddamn Madrassas everywhere, and those cock-sucking Pakistanis put the Talibs in power. But they've got nuclear weapons! This'll give us the perfect opportunity to sort out the whole region, leave the Israelis in charge, and then take out the Beast in Baghdad!'

General Ali resumed, 'It's only the international pressure that held them back. Blair wouldn't have been able to support any invasion of Saudi or Pakistan. Risks would have been too great. But the neocons were foolish enough to have tried it.'

'But they didn't even have the balls to take on the Emirates!' said the Sheikh, 'so now we have a problem.'

'I have an idea, Your Highness. I think that we can turn this to our advantage.'

'Tell me!'

General Ali moved across the room and pulled back a large tapestry hung on one of the walls. Behind it was a large map of Afghanistan and Pakistan. It was the one which they normally used for planning their hunting trips.

'Sanjay already has enough weapons and men to carry out a major operation. Our activities in the markets have given us a war chest. We've got Osama's support – everything you want is in his interest too. It's all near the border with Pakistan. And Pakistan has one thing that we both need!'

He picked up a diamond-encrusted letter-opener off a nearby antique table. He pointed to several places on the map. It took him only several minutes to outline his plan. Sheikh Abdul listened attentively. Several times he nodded in agreement.

'So,' Sheikh Abdul ruminated, 'if the ISI can take over there, I can do so here?'

'Exactly!'

He picked up his mobile, stabbing the numbers.

'Sala'am alaikum, friend. We need to meet. Urgently! And with our other friend. You'll fix it?'

They were all back at Tora Bora. It was two days since Sanjay had been called by Sheikh Abdul. Events had moved on fast in the meantime. American and British Special Forces were heavily engaged in Afghanistan. It would not be long before bin Laden and his inner sanctum would be killed or forced to flee from all the places known to the Americans. Tarnak Farm and Tora Bora would be obvious targets; obvious places to look for bin Laden. For him, anything that Sheikh Abdul could do to relieve the pressure would be welcome.

'Let them come tomorrow,' he had said when Sanjay called him.

Events were now critical for bin Laden and for Sheikh Abdul. For the latter, the current instability presented the ideal opportunity to stage his coup. The Americans would be too preoccupied to do anything about it, even if they wanted to. In fact they would probably be only too happy to see the Emirates getting their comeuppance.

Bin Laden was like a rugby hooker who had pulled down the scrum on top of himself. Despite the rhetoric, he had been more successful than in his wildest dreams. He wanted to embarrass his far enemy, to tweak the American tail; to rally Muslims globally against a common enemy.

'The jihad is a training course of the utmost importance to prepare Muslim

Mujahedeen to wage their awaited battle against the superpower that now has sole dominance over the globe, namely, the United States,' al-Zawahiri had said. Bin Laden's real objective however was to deal with the near enemy, the House of Saud and local infidels. But 9/11 had so enraged the Americans that George W. Bush was coming to get him 'dead or alive', and at this moment they were not too far away. For Sheikh Abdul, the near enemy was the Ruler of Dubai.

Both men, bin Laden and Sheikh Abdul, needed each other; and they needed to look each other in the eye to be sure that they could trust each other. Now they did so. General Ali's scheme was endorsed by bin Laden. Sanjay was instructed to make the necessary plans. He would have to be ready in four days. Sanjay left at once. The Sheikh and the General stayed overnight, before leaving in the Sheikh's Hercules the next morning. They had plenty of time in which to discuss what they would do after Sheikh Abdul's attack.

It was at these times, lying on the rough paliasse on the cell floor early in the morning, looking backwards with regret, that he saw the sweep of his life. He thought it was morning but it might have been the middle of the night. Deliberate sleep deprivation, being interrogated at any hour of the day or night, and seeing no natural light but with the dim, bare light bulb on all the time, meant that he had soon became disorientated. He told himself he should not look backwards in times of trouble and despair, but how could he stop it? For many years he'd been aimless and erratic, dissipating life through lack of focus, dictated by irrational and impetuous whims.

Emotional depression had been the basis for ordering his life, rather than an unemotional assessment of what was in his own best interests at any particular time. At many times opportunities had arisen to put his life back on an even keel. Did he do the right thing? Was it predestined that he should have done what he did? Looking back, it was very painful to remember what he had done. It seemed so irrational and self-destructive. He had alienated himself from the mainstream, deliberately cutting himself off from the company of kindred spirits, even though that was not what he had wanted to do. He yearned now in the loneliness of the dark void for the scenario of a past life in which he thrived. But anxiety and stress, that unseen but perceptible incubus, had queered the pitch of his life. Where had it got him, he wondered, as he lay there facing perhaps jail and execution as a spy, or bankruptcy, or both? He felt criminalised and sullied by the whole affair.

He could cope with the physical pain, but what repeatedly overwhelmed him was a sense of guilt and despondency at the perception which the outside world would have of him. Particularly at the thought of having let down, even abandoned, Mary. How would she be coping? His stomach knotted at the thought; he felt emasculated and helpless, knowing that his fate was in the hands of others. He was a bystander observing his past life and his future pass him by. And had he enjoyed the intervening time from any perspective? And then he thought how lucky he had been in life in so many ways, knowing such a wonderful woman. He should be thankful for all that he had and relent from this destructive self-punishment and flagellation. He had to hold on to and enjoy what he did have. If he ever got out of here, he vowed to make it right with Mary.

It was all just life. What is important now, he thought, was to move on and face each day as it came without looking backwards. But life was in suspension. It was in limbo. He just wanted to move on and get away from here and start the rest of his life. He knew there were plenty of new things that he could be doing which would excite him, which would get the adrenaline flowing again; and then the inner voice told him that it was all too late. He had ruined his life. He felt criminalised and misunderstood; unappreciated by those he had been trying to help. He felt again the regurgitated bile of past failure and unfulfilled ambition and that overwhelming, dragging negative disposition smothering his powers of action. But he must be positive, he thought, he had achieved a lot. He was being successful. But now it was all at an end; he had no control over his own destiny, his life was curtailed and manacled, just as the chains and metal bands around his wrists and legs incapacitated his body. He felt guilty and dirty, his reputation besmirched. It went to his very core; it was as if he had been raped.

In the present imbroglio, his past caught up with him. As he surveyed the wreckage of his career, he found it hard to live with himself. He had consistently made life difficult for himself and everyone, especially Mary. In trying to sort things out, he had made everything worse. Just like a daddy-long-legs trapped on flypaper, every move it makes to try to free itself only succeeding in adhering it more firmly to where it will ultimately perish. He had been unable to stabilise, a psychologist would say, in or with anything on a long-term basis, and consequently had not found peace of mind. The depression and anxiety which had been a recurring theme were major contributory factors; or was this just a cop-out, a way of shifting the blame for his own inability and failure to some intangible third party?

He was pretty sure that the Prosecutor from the Dubai Courts believed his story. Late on the Friday after their arrest, surprising for the day of prayer, they had been taken to the Courts.

'Tell me exactly,' said Khalid Al Mustafa, 'what it is that you do, please. I want to understand this business that you do.' So Bill had done so. Subsequently, a member of the Embassy staff visiting Bill had informed him that the Prosecutor had fallen out with the Prosecutor General because he refused to lodge charges against the British prisoners. 'It's not these men who should be punished,' said the Prosecutor. 'If anyone should be, then it should be Mahmoud Al Abdullah and the others who instructed them to undertake their investigations.' This did not go down well with the Prosecutor General. He knew that Al Mustafa was pointing a finger at Sheikh Abdul.

Bill felt that he was in limbo, that fate which, for Roman Catholics, meant the place to which those who are not baptised are consigned to await the Final Coming. They cannot go to heaven, having not been baptised. But as they have not sinned, they cannot be sent to purgatory. The concept, thought Bill, illustrated the dilemma faced by all religions in the interpretation of God's word. And it illustrated his present predicament. The Prosecutor might hold that there was no case to answer for Bill and his colleagues. But more sinister forces were at work behind the scenes. With such a high-profile arrest of Bill and his colleagues, news of which had quickly been beamed around the globe on the AP wires and the internet, the local authorities found themselves stymied. Sheikh Abdul and his henchmen needed to keep Bill out of circulation. They didn't know exactly how much he did know. He knew too much, that they knew. The endless interrogation going over and over the same ground was intended to elicit this information. For his part, Bill realised that divulging what he did know, even after the event, whatever that was, would be death: metaphorical indeed, but possibly literally too.

Dubai depended upon foreign business to maintain its fiction that the

Emirate was a good world citizen; perhaps not a democracy as such, but nevertheless supportive of democracy, good governance, human rights, freedom of speech, liberal thought. Dubai was courting the West: the supernational corporations, the high net worth individuals with money to burn, and the ordinary Western tourist with young children for whom the sun, sea and apparent security of Dubai would encourage them to return to the golden beaches time after time. It was imperative for Sheikh Abdul that the outside world did not realise the truth about Dubai: that it was all a construct, none of it true; that the oil would run out in less than five years. At least not until the plan had been executed and Dubai had taken over the region. And that he, Sheikh Abdul, had taken over Dubai.

The fundamentalism of all religions, reflected Bill, is a device used by men to exert control over 'their flock'. The Bible and the Koran, 'the record of God', are merely interpretations by men of what they conceive to be God's will. Or, more cynically, something which some individuals use to enslave others to their cause. Hinduism is the least demanding, doctrinaire and arrogant religion. In medieval times it was Christendom which was the most extreme and demanding in its strictures. It was a regime which spawned the Crusades: the sacking of Jerusalem, the rape of Muslim women, the pillage and subjugation of Islamic lands. The knights of the Lionheart forgot their chivalric code when they left the shores of Europe behind them, but were given a lesson in chivalry from Saladin, the nemesis of the Crusaders, on more than one occasion.

In today's world, the tide had turned, Bill mused. The increasingly secular Western democracies were ever less inclined to defend their principles. Indeed, they perhaps hardly knew what those principles were, other than the pursuit of happiness, by which people meant the accumulation of goods and chattels at the expense of spiritual wellbeing and charity.

Now the roles had been reversed. It was Islamic fundamentalism which was on the warpath. It was Huntingdon's *Clash of Civilisations*, but with only one contestant aware that the struggle was joined. The Crusaders shrouded their true objectives of territorial acquisition and world domination under the cloak of piety and religiosity. So too today. The threat was not from the religion of Islam per se, but from extremists with a political objective: the desire to extend the Umma; to impose Sharia law on all lands; to recreate the city of Cordoba, once the heart of the ancient Islamic kingdom of al-Andalus. In short, it was a grab for power, but temporal not spiritual.

Then, behind the curtains of his own predicament as he reviewed his past, he had a sense of solidarity with the downtrodden peoples that had been a large part of his life. What hope had the Catholics of Northern Ireland before the advent of civil rights? Was it only at the dawn of a new millennium that they had been given any prospect of equality with the other inhabitants of that small piece of land, who had hitherto been placed over them solely by an accident of birth?

And here in the heart of Islam, how could one contemplate the predicament of Muslims in general and the Palestinians in particular with any equanimity or without a sense of guilt and shame as a subject of the former colonial power? There could be little doubt that his present incarceration was in some tenuous way a consequence of the sordid history of the region. Otherwise, what he knew would be a reason for congratulation by those who were now instead his tormentors.

Could terrorism ever be acceptable? Always, one man's terrorist was another's freedom fighter. But he knew in his heart of hearts that as an Irishman, had he been born on the Falls Road he would have fallen in alongside the IRA, no matter how repugnant their actions seemed to him, because he could sense the overwhelming fear and the persecution, such as he himself was now experiencing, which anyone assuredly feels when their life is in the hands of others.

Just the same thing applied, he reasoned, in the present circumstances. Muslims had a sense of persecution, of inferiority, of loss of freedom, which had been festering inside the national psyche for generations, almost from the time of Saladin. Surely, had he been in their shoes, he would have joined the Holy Jihad and the Mujahedeen?

And so another day passed, and another night, as day and night merged into each other. Each day was dominated by anxiety. He wasn't sure which days were the worst: the ones when he knew he might hear the cell door being opened at any time and the call to go for interrogation ringing out; or the days of the weekend, on Friday prayer day and on Saturday, when he knew that none of his accusers would be working and he was spared the fear of interrogation and the humiliation that it implied. But then if there was no interrogation, there would be no release either. Release could only come through further interrogation and an attempt to prove to his torturers that he had not done anything which was against their interests. But would they believe him?

This time it sounded as if they really would be freed. The Consul had worked tirelessly on behalf of Bill and his fellow prisoners. On several occasions it seemed that it would all be over soon: that shortly the door would open, his passport would be given back to him, and State Security would apologise to him, 'It's alright, Mr Bill, you're free to go. We made a mistake. We are sorry.'

But each time all seemed to fail at the final hurdle, and then their predicament became worse. It was like a game of virtual snakes and ladders played by the gods, in which Bill was a luckless pawn. But not this time, surely! It had been a personal message from the Brigadier, the Ruler's PA, to the Consul: 'Yes, they will be taken to see the Prosecutor and, yes, they should get their passports back and be free to go at once.'

After the previous disappointments, Bill tried not to get his hopes up too much. But his mind was racing ahead. How about that first beer of freedom? And would he have a steak that first night – this evening – a delicious, thick, succulent rib-eye with mushrooms, cooked in shallots and red wine, accompanied by chips and sauce bois boudran, all washed down with a sonorous claret! Suddenly the bolts on his door rattled. He heard the sounds of the doors of the other cells being opened. The manacles were taken off by his gaolers. Outside in the corridor he saw his fellow prisoners, many for the first time since their incarceration. How long ago was that now?

Together, Bill and the others trooped through the detention block. They were ushered into a waiting minibus. It was only a short drive and then they were at the Law Courts, beside the Creek. The bus stopped by the Prosecutor's office. It was where they had first been formally interviewed. All those months ago.

They were taken to the third floor where the Prosecutor General had his office. Their lawyer was already there. Fawzi came from Sharjah. Bill hoped this gave him some impartiality; some independence. Perhaps he would also have a sense of justice. He seemed to have done as much as he could to assist them. But there was not much he could have done; Bill knew that most lawyers in Dubai considered him and his associates as spies, enemies of the state. None could be trusted to act in the prisoners' interest.

They were led into the Prosecutor General's office. A senior prosecutor read from a script. Bill looked at Fawzi. His pirate-like face with its prominent hook nose was now inscrutable. Did he know what was going on? Was he, too, complicit in their fate? Then Bill saw Fawzi's face cloud over. They were all ushered out of the office and without being allowed to speak or to ask any questions, they were taken back to the bus and retraced their steps. The detention centre, the manacles and their cells awaited them.

'You are charged with spying,' said Fawzi, noncommittally. 'You need to sign the paper confirming that you have been informed. Your case will now be transferred to the Supreme Court in Abu Dhabi.'

Less than a quarter of an hour ago, Bill had expected his passport to be given back; that his ordeal would finally be over. Now he was back down, down at the bottom of a deep narrow shaft. The light at the top was barely discernible. The likely verdict of the court on a charge of spying was death; he could expect no mercy. The current anti-Western fervour would demand it. The Emiratis had long since realised that they could treat British citizens with impunity. The Royal Navy was no longer able to deploy gunboats to enforce HMG's will.

In his elegant residence in Abu Dhabi, the British Ambassador smiled to himself when he received the news from his Consul in Dubai. His failure to help Bill had achieved its objective. But it was good that his Consul did not know the true objectives of HMG. To the outside world the Consul's efforts on behalf of Bill gave the impression that the British government really was doing all it could to have him released. But the Foreign Minister had been explicit to the Ambassador. He had called him back to London to make it very clear:

'The last thing we want is to have Sloan back here at this stage! The negotiations with Sinn Fein are at a critical stage. We can't afford to have the Good Friday agreement scuppered by Sloan telling the Bloody Sunday tribunal what he knows about MacGuiggan! I'm relying on you to make sure that he can't!'

Back in Abu Dhabi, the Ambassador had been assiduous in working to carry out the Minister's remit. An austere, acerbic and arrogant man, Brian Wilson did not deign to sully his hands dealing with intelligence matters. And he despised all those who were involved in them.

But back in London things were very different. There was uproar in Parliament when Bill's MP asked the Prime Minister to account for the Government's lack of action:

'Could the Right Honourable member explain to the House exactly how a clearly innocent British citizen, one who has served his country honourably and been of considerable assistance to the government of Dubai, supposedly an ally of ours, now finds himself indicted for spying by that same government?

'What has our Ambassador been doing – or, more to the point, what has he not been doing – that he should have done to get Mr Sloan released? Has the Government been asleep on the job? Is the Foreign Office not fit for purpose?'

A baying chorus from the Opposition benches indicated that the questioner had hit the right spot. The Prime Minister's response only added to the fury.

'I have to inform the Right Honourable gentleman and this House that the Government has done all it can to secure Mr Sloan's release,' he answered. 'He will appreciate that we are not able to tell another country how to handle its judicial procedures!'

It was about ten o'clock the next morning when Mary heard the first knock at her door. In her dressing-gown and with face not made up she did not feel at her best. Unthinkingly, however, she opened the door. Several bright flashes caused her to recoil. She slammed the door shut, but she had seen them. All standing there expectantly with notebooks, cameras and recorders at the ready. Perhaps twenty of them already. Instantly she was afraid. If the press could track her down so easily, so too could anybody else. Perhaps her brother, or even worse, some of his vicious associates. She poured herself a strong coffee from last night's grounds; searching around, she managed to find a cigarette. She had been trying to give them up. She lit it. Her hands trembled. She caught sight of herself in the mirror. Was that really her? She looked much older than her thirty-five years, with gaunt, hollow cheeks. Her once vivacious complexion was dull; her hair, once with a lustrous blonde sheen, looked lank and lifeless. She turned on the television. The *Morning Show* was reviewing the papers. There it was, in all its stark reality:

'One of our spies? FO abandons British man to his fate.'

Mary called her only real friend in the village. Anne knew little of Mary's background. She was flabbergasted when she heard the news. But she was a true friend and very active in the life of the village. She immediately went to Mary's house, pushing past waiting newsmen, upbraiding them forcibly for trespass and harassment. Nevertheless, she made them all tea and appealed to them to go easy on Mary. She galvanised the village to help and they did, rallying round Mary as if she were one of their own. None the less, it was subsequently reported, picked up probably from one of the villagers, that… 'Oh yes, she only came here recently. Last year it was. Getting away from something, we all thought, from a failed relationship or something. We heard that she came across from Ireland.'

Then Mary's phone rang. Anne answered, prepared to give the caller short shrift.

'My God!' she said. 'Hang on, I'll get her, she's just here… '

Passing the phone across to Mary, she said, 'He said his name was Bill!'

She heard the voice, that voice she knew so well. The voice she had once loved; the voice she could never forget.

'It's me, Mary! Have you heard the news?'

'Heard the news?' she laughed hollowly, 'I'm surrounded by it here! There are about thirty pressmen sitting the house! What have you done?'

'Look, listen carefully. I haven't got the phone for long… '

'How did you get it?' interrupted Mary, wondering what was going on.

'Never mind, I'll tell you later,' he said, the strain evident in his voice, no time for niceties. He knew that Colonel Tamimi would not allow him to have it for long. Why had he let him have it anyway – compassion? That was not a shortcoming that Tamimi suffered from. He must be monitoring all the calls, Bill realised, his alarm heightening. But he had to tell Mary. His predicament could not be made worse by anything he did now.

'Here's what I need you to do. Tell the MP all about it – PIRA and Bloody Sunday, MacGuiggan, the whole nine yards. Tell him to raise it in Parliament; that my evidence must be heard. Look, I've got a real favour to ask. It's Royal Ascot next week. Sheikh Abdul always attends. I'd like you to be there when he arrives and to accost him – he'll be joining the Queen in the Royal Stand! Would you do that for me? Warn off the press to be ready to report it all. That should put pressure on the Government to pull their fingers out. I'm sure the bloody Ambassador here's been scheming to get me kept in prison. I've got to stop now. I've probably said too much already. Goodbye and look, I'm really sorry to have got you into this horrific mess. Thank you for believing in me.'

Back again in his cell, Bill was plunged even deeper into the depths of despair, down into the deep abyss. Like a fly trying to escape from a jar of honey, every time Bill made a move he seemed to become more and more enmeshed in the morass in which he was trapped.

73

Within a few weeks of his medical failure, Shahid was back in Afghanistan. Initially dismayed by his failure, he was quickly reassured by Ahmed.

'Worry not, Brother, our friends will know what to do. It is Allah's will, Insha'Allah.'

Ahmed had immediately contacted al-Zawahiri. 'A pity perhaps,' said al-Zawahiri when he heard the news. 'But we can use this man here. I need someone like him to lead Sheikh Abdul's operation. Get him out here at once.'

Ahmed told Shahid that he had been transferred to another, equally important operation.

'What's more,' said Ahmed, 'the first meant certain death and the opportunity to enjoy the seventy-two virgins in paradise. But this may allow you the chance to live longer. Perhaps to enjoy even more virgins here on earth, immortalised as a Jihadist hero!'

Again Shahid had wondered at Ahmed's lack of orthodoxy, his apparent love of those things of the flesh which Shahid had presumed were off limits for those, like Ahmed and himself, who claimed to aspire to a life of complete obedience to Sharia and the diktats of the Prophet Muhammad. Shahid challenged Ahmed: 'How can you say that? You're always preaching that the highest attainment in a person's life is to sacrifice that life to the greater glory of Allah, peace be upon Him!'

Like a father, Ahmed had put his arm around Shahid's shoulders. 'You're a bright guy, Shahid. In the land of the blind, the one-eyed man is king! You're not cannon fodder like so many others. It's a case of don't do as I do, do as I say!'

It was a few weeks after 9/11. Shahid knew that he would have been one of those hijackers on the planes. He was at first ecstatic about the success of the attack. But then he was overcome by a feeling of immense loss at having not been part of this, the greatest victory of Islam since the fall of Jerusalem to Saladin, all those years ago. He felt survivor's guilt. And then he gradually became glad that he was not, after all, dead. He wondered at his own commitment, just as he wondered about Ahmed's motives.

He was passed through a chain of contacts, cut-outs, each person not knowing where the other came from or where they went to. Eventually he arrived at Tarnak Farm. Training for the intended coup in Dubai had been interrupted by the events of 9/11 because it had not led to the expected occupation of Dubai by US forces. As they cheered the event, all the participants wondered what their fate would be now. Under al-Zawahiri's direction, Jihadists were never allowed to remain idle. He knew that this would have led to boredom, lack of commitment, to the fighters drifting off in search of more excitement elsewhere. The insurgency in Chechnya was in full swing, gaining even more traction as the Russians licked their wounds and rethought their strategy. Good news overall for the Jihadis that there were other battles to be waged, al-Zawahiri knew.

Sanjay was at the camp when Shahid arrived. Immediately he incorporated Shahid into the team. During the next couple of weeks, Shahid and Sanjay became close. One afternoon, after they had spent all day doing live firing training, Sanjay took Shahid aside.

'I want you to become my second-in-command. We have to keep the team at white-hot intensity. In a few days there will be a meeting here. It's to decide what we do next. The Sheikh from Dubai will be here. I want you to attend with me.'

Shahid was both surprised and flattered. During the next couple of days, however, his beliefs were shaken to their core.

He and his group were sent to supply some provisions to a local school run by the Taliban. It turned out to be a brainwashing centre – for the 200 to 300 children living in the compound. The parents sent them there believing that they were getting an education, he thought, and, more importantly, free food. The militants were saying to them: 'Life's a waste here but if you do a good thing you will go to heaven; immediately to heaven.'

Part of the compound consisted of four rooms, each wall adorned with brightly-coloured paintings in clear contrast to the barren and harsh landscape surrounding it. Shahid had never seen such elaborate paintings of so-called heaven. The children were told this was what awaited them in heaven. Each of the images had a river flowing through it. Some had people playing in the water. In others, women lined the banks. Shahid heard one of the teachers, pointing at the picture while talking to his class.

'These are rivers of milk and honey; the women are the virgins that await you in heaven. Here, you will live in the company of the Holy Prophet and be served feasts,' he said. Shahid realised that they were being cynically indoctrinated to believe that their life in this world was worthless, that life only started in the hereafter. The Taliban was offering them a fast-track option to paradise, a longed-for escape from their daily reality surrounded by violence and squalor.

Shahid was sickened by the whole concept. It offended all his sensibilities. He realised there and then that he could not accept that the end justified the means. He saw that the oppression of the Taliban was no better, in fact was much worse than, the corrupt society it sought to replace. The Ummah of Osama bin Laden and al-Zawahiri, of Ahmed and Sanjay, was the same as that of Hitler, Stalin or Mao Tse-tung. The Sharia these men looked for was the Sharia of men, of themselves, not of Allah. The barbarity of Genghis Khan had surely been more honest than that of these oppressors?

He thought back to the inconsistencies in Ahmed's behaviour. In a blinding flash, this Damascene moment changed Shahid's destiny.

Feeling as he did, Shahid realised none the less that he must behave as if nothing had happened. Throughout that night, sleep failed to come to him as he tossed and turned, going over all the innumerable options as to what he should do. By the morning he had made up his mind. He could not just leave; resign his membership as if it were a gentlemen's club on Piccadilly. Perhaps had he been back at home he could have done that, but not here, not knowing what he had seen and what was planned. But he knew too, that even if he could just walk away, that would not be enough. He couldn't just go back home as if nothing had happened and resume his old way of life. He could not be neutral; sit on the fence and look the other way. No! He had to do something to root out this false credo; this pernicious distortion of Allah's teachings. This evil, which had so recently seduced him.

Later that day he spoke to his sister back in the UK on a Skype link. Fadwa was overjoyed to hear from him.

'Where are you, what are you doing?' Questions tumbled over each other seeking answers. Shahid was cheered to hear her bubbly voice, so full of the love of life.

'I can't say too much! You know? But I'm worried.'

'Worried, what about?'

'All of this, everything that's going on, it's wrong! We're being led up the garden path.'

Down in Cheltenham the familiar voice was immediately picked up by another equally bubbly girl of Fadwa's age. Flagging it for special attention, she signalled to her nearby supervisor, 'It's our friend, the Englishman. Sounds like he's not at all happy with something or other!'

74

Closing the Skype connection, she logged off the computer. She had never heard her young brother sounding so bereft, so unsure of himself, so lonely. She looked around the room at all the memories of childhood that she and Shahid had shared. Their parents had had other children before them but they were a lot older. Then she and Shahid had come along, after a gap, and it had always been just the two of them. It was a small room; all the rooms were small. But they were warm and comfortable, and it was home. From Shahid's Snoopy duvet cover to her Fisher-Price dolls' house, the chintz coverings on the settee and chairs, in the two-up two-down configuration of so many of the houses where the Pakistani diaspora lived in the ghettos of the UK, it was home.

And what of Shahid? Where exactly was he? And what was he doing? What had he seen that had wrought such a change? Innumerable questions flashed through Fadwa's mind as she pondered the situation. Instantly, she made up her mind. She must get hold of Ahmed. He would know what to do. They had been lovers almost since the evening that Shahid had introduced them. On the second occasion that they went out, they spent the night together at Ahmed's flat. He had a spacious, well-appointed apartment in a newly-developed area at Shadwell. Had Fadwa not been so besotted, she might have stopped to wonder why an Islamic extremist preaching such an austere creed would be living in such an upmarket apartment.

She sent a text to Ahmed telling him she needed to see him. He was at the mosque. She could go straight there. She could hear the note of expectation in his voice, but another night of passion was far from her own mind at this moment. She took the Northern line. Three stops to Aldgate East. Between Stepney Green and Whitechapel she suddenly realised the danger of talking to Ahmed. She could not tell him that Shahid was thinking of quitting. Only Shahid could do that. Several weeks ago, inspired by Shahid's fervour and Ahmed's manipulation, she too had joined the Hizb. The train arrived at Aldgate East. At the mosque she saw Ahmed waiting for her, welcoming and expectant.

'Sala'am alaikum, Sister, why the hurry?' His tone was complicit; his eyes suggestive. He had always made a point of not letting any of the others know that he and Fadwa had any agenda other than Hizb business.

'I want to go and serve Allah, but not here. Insha'Allah, I want to join Shahid, to do jihad with him. I spoke to him just now. He's... ' she paused, searching for words '... so fulfilled, so committed.' She stopped suddenly, wondering if she had overplayed it. But Ahmed nodded thoughtfully. Quickly he assessed the situation. He did not want to forego the carnal pleasures of Fadwa's luscious body. But the Hizb needed as many female bodies as possible. He shuddered at the thought of that body being blown to smithereens in the blast of a suicide vest. But there are many other pebbles on the beach, he reflected. Then again, perhaps he would be able to arrange things so that he could go with her? To have his cake and eat it, at least for a time.

'Leave it to me. I'll see what I can do,' he said. 'What are you doing tonight?'

Sex was the last thing on her mind. The thought of Ahmed's sensuous hands caressing her body, recently so seductive, now suddenly seemed like an outrage in the face of Shahid's predicament.

'No, sorry,' she said, hesitatingly, 'I have to go with my mum this evening to visit my aunt and uncle.'

Over in Tarnak Farm, Ahmed's recommendation carried weight. Another Black Widow supplicant was always welcome; an English one, doubly so.

'Just think how this will speak to our people in the United Kingdom,' said al-Zawahiri, 'and what resonance it will have on CNN and Al Jazeera, and around the world! Yes, let her come – at once!'

James Logan had been in the British Consulate in Islamabad for a couple of years; five altogether, if you counted his earlier stint as a second officer. The first time, all had been plain sailing. The Soviets had just increased their occupation force to 120,000 men to cope with the resurgent Mujahedeen. The CIA were in the driving seat, with virtually unlimited funds to throw at any Afghani who gave even the slightest hint that he didn't really have a lot of time for the Russians. AK-47s, Stinger missiles, Claymore mines, radios – they had them all. And they wanted to dish them all out – no questions asked – as if they were hot cakes.

James and his team had been more than happy to pile into this bonanza like it was Christmas. They grabbed as much as they could handle to pass on in turn to any likely new Mujahedeen candidates. But that was yesterday. James was now that much older and wiser, now in charge and with the unenviable task of trying to cope with the unforgiving law of unforeseen consequences.

Today he was sitting with Chuck Klondyke, himself a veteran of that earlier period of excess generosity. Klondyke was a smart operator, James knew. Big and barrel-chested with his broad, open face and crew-cut, sandy-coloured hair, he looked like Mr US Everyman, like Bart Simpson's father, thought James. He looked just like what he was, and made no pretence of appearing otherwise. He was chewing on a fat Cuban cigar; eating his way through it, thought James, as any light had long since been extinguished.

'What a motherfucking mess those bastards at Langley have gotten us into!' exclaimed Klondike, in his lazy Texan drawl. Despite the vocabulary, it was evident that whatever it was that was exercising Klondyke, he was hugely enjoying the whole affair. 'Those goddamn bastards want me to pay 2,000 bucks a throw to buy back each motherfucking Stinger from the Mujahedeen. What a load of crap. We threw them around like confetti. Now we have to grovel around on the ground and pick up each and every piece.' Sounding apoplectic, he still seemed to consider it all a big joke.

A product of Eton and Balliol College Oxford, James, at 6' 3" tall and slim with dark wavy hair, glasses and a serious mien, looked like the straightforward civil servant which he claimed to be, but was not.

'But surely that's not a problem?' queried James. 'Why can't you just go to the chieftains – the tribal leaders – and get them to collect them for you from their people and hand them back, now that they don't need them? You must have the inventory of who got what. So it should be easy to account...'

'You fucking limeys, with all your proper shit and holier than thou attitude, really make me laugh,' Klondyke interrupted genially. 'There are no fucking records. That's just the point. As I said, we threw them around the place like so much shit. And anyway, the time to collect them up was after the Russians had buggered off. But we took our eye off the sodding ball and headed off to screw Saddam Hussein.'

'And now those nice Mujahedeen lads have become the naughty boys and we've become the new liberators,' said James, somewhat primly. 'Definitely a case of unforeseen...'

'Don't give me that dandified crap about unforeseen consequences!'

Klondyke interrupted forcefully. 'It's fucking blowback, James. The whole thing's one great cock sucking blowback.'

'And those same Kalashnikovs and RPGs are shooting your lads from Idaho, and ours from Wotton Bassett,' continued James.

'And those motherfucking Stingers are shooting down your Hercules and our Chinooks.' Klondyke paused, then continued, 'And I'll tell you another thing, James – just between you and me. Not long ago, I flew up to the Panjshir Valley to beard the goddamn Lion of the Panjshir in his lair. It was several months ago, just before the bastards got him... '

'In other words, a few days before 9/11?' queried James.

'You've got it. Thought I'd take a Chinook. So there'd be plenty of room for all those Stingers we sent him – the ones on that non-fucking existent inventory!'

'How many do you reckon you sent to him altogether?' interrupted James.

'As far as I can be sure, it's about 2,000. And the cocksucker claimed he only received eight. Can you fucking believe that?'

'That's a bit of a discrepancy, Walter,' said James, his feeble attempt at humour bypassing Klondyke.

'You bet your sweet ass it is, James,' said Klondyke, 'and you know, it's just possible that he's telling the truth!'

'How come?'

'All the stuff, money and weapons, nearly everything for Massoud was channelled through one of his brothers. The cock-sucking bastard's lying low. Massoud claimed that even he couldn't find him. Sod it, I'm actually prepared to believe him. You can't trust any of these bastards. I'd make an exception for Massoud, though. He was one of the best: what you saw was what you got, and when he said he'd do something, he did.

'Anyway, beefing about this is not why I stopped by to see you, James.' He continued, 'I saw Ziad Al Hazim at the ISI HQ this morning. Started off as just a routine liaison meeting, but then the General drew me aside. Offered me a coffee. Asked me to pass you a message.'

'Why on earth didn't he just call me then? We see each often enough; he knows I'll come running if he offers me anything interesting.'

'I think he was a bit embarrassed. Didn't want to lose face. He had contact from a Brit – a second-generation Brit. The son of a bitch claims to be a Jihadist, but he lives in London. Seems he walks into the ISI office in Kabul the other day and says he has some hot intel. Wants to change sides. Won't tell the Pakis what he knows. Wants to work with you bastards because he'd be crapping on his own people from Hizb ut Tahrir in London. Wants protection. Doesn't trust the Pakistanis, if you ask me. Who does? All these guys have the same problem. Identity crisis. They don't know if they're British or Pakistani. Back home in the UK they're just regular guys – black, what the hell these days. But when they come here, their heritage grabs them, the romanticism deceives them and they have an identity crisis. I've seen it all the time – you must have done so as well, James?'

James nodded, thoughtfully. 'Yes, I saw it a lot in Ireland. There it was American dollars bankrolling the hardened killers of the Provos!'

Hard-bitten and combative though he was, Klondyke nodded imperceptibly. Quickly moving back to the matter in hand, he said: 'Al Hazim has given you an introduction to one of his bright young officers who debriefed this guy. You're to get in touch with him. Here's the details.' James took the crumpled piece of paper proffered by Klondyke.

It was the next day before James Logan was able to contact Captain Hussein Jafari at the ISI headquarters in Kabul.

'Yes, good day, Alhamdulillah, Mr James,' said Captain Jafari, 'please to come to my office at ten o'clock if this would be acceptable to you? You know the location?' said the Captain, in precise English. James responded that, yes, he had been there before.

In fact, he had already been there on several occasions over the three months since he had been posted here again. Not to mention the numerous occasions on his previous incarnation. Now in the Captain's office, the ritual of meeting and greeting had been observed. Many pleasantries had been exchanged and coffee drunk. The exchanges had been conducted with extreme cordiality and politeness, but had been stiff and formal. James sensed a reticence on the part of his opposite number. Newly-arrived on the scene again, despite his seniority and previous experience, James was definitely the new kid on the block. So far, despite increasingly desperate entreaties back to London, he had not been provided with any worthwhile information with which to trade. For all his bonhomie and apparent openness, Chuck Klondyke had hitherto kept his cards close to his chest. In the relationship with the Pakistanis, the CIA held all the cards, or should that be all the money, James thought to himself. This meeting with Captain Jafari might be the breakthrough he needed. He had better make sure he did not screw it up.

It was only after the second cup of coffee that things began to develop. Captain Jafari was a well-set, angular man with a thin moustache, the epitome of the British Raj army officer. But, as was evident to James, he was also a consummate professional.

'Mr James,' he began, 'two days ago we had a walk-in to our office in Kandahar. We have one man there for just that sort of thing, to make it easy for Jihadis to come across if they want to. This young man is an English Pakistani; he lives in London. He claimed that he has been on the jihad. He joined the Hizb, he would tell you, at the Greater London mosque, less than a year ago. But in the short time since he joined, he claims that he has made contact right up to the top of Al Qaeda. He says he now wants to turn back from the path of jihad, because he has seen that the Islamists are not true Muslims but, in his words, "only people who seek to acquire power for themselves and to cloak the world in darkness".' He paused reflectively.

'This is all very normal to us. Al Qaeda is a very flat organisation; not hierarchical like our armies and police and so on here, in England or in Pakistan. We have come across a lot of young aspirant Jihadis who have been introduced to senior commanders such as Osama bin Laden and al-Zawahiri at a very early stage of their Jihadist career. It gives them inspiration.'

'So what's different about this case, Captain?' queried James. 'Your boss did not ask the Americans to contact me just because it's a normal case.'

'Exactly, Mr James, you are right. This man – he says his name is Harb Inklizi – claims that he has been selected to carry out a major suicide attack. He described it as another 9/11. He would not give us any more details. He said that he doesn't know them all himself. Heard that it has something to do with nuclear facilities. He wants to have someone from the British security services who will meet him, so that he can tell them all about it.'

'That seems rather strange. If he was prepared even to admit to his involvement, why did he not tell you more about it?'

'Wa'Allah! Perhaps he believes some of the rumours that everyone knows about? That we torture our prisoners!' said Jafari, smiling complicitly at James, his eyebrows raised.

Or perhaps, thought James, it was because they didn't want to act on the information themselves. That would likely have damaged the byzantine relationship which the ISI had with the Taliban. But supporting the Taliban in Afghanistan and resistance groups in Kashmir was one thing. On the face of it, if it involved an attack against the UK and they buried the information, this would be a major threat to Pakistan itself. The British would never trust them again, nor the US either.

239

'Right,' said James, positively. 'What happens next?'

'We took a photograph while he was waiting in reception,' said Jafari, handing James a manilla-coloured envelope. '"Harb Inklizi" means "Brave Englishman". It's his fighting name, not his proper name.'

It had taken Shahid much soul-searching and a lot of courage to do what he had finally done. He remembered the farewell suicide ceremony with Omar and Bakri back in London – was it only a year ago? It seemed like a lifetime. He remembered how Ahmed had psyched up the would-be self-killers of Islam's new holy war. Not murderers, but selfless martyrs, in the language of Hizb ut Tahrir. Now he practised the same techniques on himself, keeping his newly-focused rage against his former comrades-in-arms and his self-loathing at white-hot intensity.

When, finally, the opportunity had arisen, it had all been very easy. After a detailed night-long planning session with al-Zawahiri and the other team members, each group had been ordered to visit one of the many areas along their route to the eventual target and to familiarise themselves with everything about it. They were to take photographs, if possible; otherwise to draw pictures from memory. Subsequently, each group would brief the complete team on their area of responsibility. This way all would gain a thorough knowledge of the whole route. The route that would lead some of them to martyrdom, at the instigation of others who would be far away from the scene. Shahid observed how the main instigators cajoled and exhorted, and even threatened eternal damnation to all the others. However, they were careful never to choose roles for themselves which involved any risk of death or injury. The one exception was Sanjay, whose record in the jihad was well-known and attested. He was clearly someone who led from the front. He was to be the principal operation commander for the spectacular which was planned. In talking to them after they had been selected, bin Laden had said: 'Acquiring weapons for the defence of Muslims is a religious duty. If I have indeed acquired these weapons, then I thank God for enabling me to do so. And if I seek to acquire these weapons, I am carrying out a duty. It would be a sin for Muslims not to try to possess the weapons that would prevent the infidels from inflicting harm on Muslims.'

Together with two others, both Yemeni Jihadists who had taken part in the operation against the USS *Cole* in Aden harbour in 2000, Shahid was to carry out the reconnaissance of Islamabad. Sanjay had briefed them all.

'This is where we will stay the night and collect some supplies for the next stage of the journey. Here are the details of our contact there.' He passed one of the Yemenis a small piece of paper. 'Memorise it, all of you, and be sure that you destroy it before you leave tomorrow morning. You'll enter the town this way, and then you'll leave after the first prayer call the next morning on this route.' His finger traced the path on the map. 'We'll need sufficient places to stay, but no more than two people together. Otherwise you'll attract attention to yourselves. You must also get sufficient food for the next twenty-four hours for everyone. So make sure you know the route inside out, and also the rest houses, and then get in touch with our contact.'

He paused, and then continued, 'There are many Kafirs in the city and many apostates, too – make sure that you don't attract their attention. But see here,' he jabbed a finger at the map spread on the sandy floor, 'I've marked the position of the Crusader Embassies... and these here are the Afghan police and army places. The Pakistanis have a place here, too.' Again, he jabbed his finger at the map. 'There are intelligence people: many of them are friends, but you must not make any contact with them. There are American and British agents with them, looking out for anything unusual.'

When younger, Shahid had done some orienteering with a youth club in London; they had been taken by the club leaders to Wales. He had loved the freedom of walking alone with only compass and map; of climbing up Pen Y Fan in the Brecon Beacons; of bivouacking overnight in the few fern-covered places that afforded a degree of shelter. Now his mind automatically recorded all the details of the briefing and stored them away.

They left early the following morning and had an uneventful journey to their objective. On the second day in Islamabad, Shahid managed to persuade the other two that they should separate and work independently, pooling their knowledge later. This way, he argued, each would be forced to learn his part of the brief thoroughly, rather than relying on the others. Thus, together, they would be much stronger as a team.

Moving fast, Shahid was able to complete his work with time to spare before they were due to meet up again. He knew exactly where to go, but went with great care to ensure that he did not attract any unwelcome attention. He had timed it so that dusk was falling, providing good cover in the quickly fading light. The souk was very busy as Shahid cut through it. The stalls selling nuts, raisins and spices were doing good trade. Shahid ignored the insistent pleas of the stall-holders to purchase their special prunes and bread, or their nutmeg and raisins. He barely noticed the alluring scents mingling in the balmy evening air.

The ISI offices were in a smart area of town, with many smart buildings. The ISI offices in Rawalpindi are behind a high wall and protected by watch towers, with nervous armed guards ready to shoot off at the slightest alarm. But Shahid knew that there was an office here too. This one was unobtrusive. Only a few people knew of its existence. Shahid had been briefed on its location by al Zawahin. The area was much cleaner than most of the rest of the city, even the air was fresher. Shahid knew that if the sanitary workers stopped working for a week the area would turn into a garbage dump. But ironically, right in the middle of two of the most prestigious Sectors he came across some of the worst slums. 'It was squalid and unhygienic. Rats ran everywhere through the mounds of untreated garbage. Shahid retched involuntarily as the awful stench hit him. This was where the Christians lived. They were the lowest-paid City employees. But they kept the city clean and running.

He felt nervous and apprehensive, his mouth dry and his palms sweating profusely. But he forced himself to approach the ISI offices, his shemagh covering much of his face, in a friendly and confident manner. He was inside the office before the guard reacted. He asked to see the duty officer. The guard eyed him suspiciously and pushed him down on a seat in the waiting room. There were half a dozen other people there too. But no-one looked anyone else in the eye. It was as if there was a tacit agreement that they all wanted to remain anonymous; that they really didn't want to be there, but had no option. After what seemed an interminable wait, Shahid was directed to a small interview room.

Quickly, he told his story and made his request.

"'They're planning an attack in London!" He amazed himself by his ability to lie so fluently. I have information that will prove to them what I say is true. But I have not time now to explain it all. If you don't do as I say and detain me, then you will lose the chance to catch all these people. The operation will be called off.' The words came tumbling out of his mouth. He pleaded with the Pakistani officer: 'Quick, in the name of Allah! If I can't get back soon to meet the others, they'll become suspicious.'

Quickly, the Pakistani made up his mind. He was a young but experienced operator. He might have been Shahid's brother. He had interviewed many genuine, not-so-genuine, and downright bogus Jihadis over the past year since being posted here from training. 'Why would he be telling me all this if it were not true?' Shahid had risked arrest, and worse, by disclosing what he had already done. Shahid would know that the ISI could simply arrest him and beat the information out of him. From there he would just disappear. Added to which, if this man was to be believed, it was the British who were the targets, who would have to verify his authenticity, not him. He could, of course, just say nothing – kick Shahid out back onto the streets. But what if an event that Shahid said would be another 9/11 were actually to take place, what would happen to him? Any investigation after the event, when Shahid would have been identified as the bomber, would reveal that Shahid had been here and that he had interviewed him. He could not expunge Shahid's name from the register at reception, or his memory from the guards who had admitted Shahid and had called him to see this visitor or his image from the CCV tapes.

He made his decision: 'Wait a minute.' He left the office. In three minutes he was back with a mobile phone.

'Here, take this,' he said authoritatively. 'It has one number programmed into it. If you need to contact me in an emergency – if your plan changes – use it. But only if you need to, remember.' He paused. 'Otherwise wait, someone will send you a text, make sure the phone is on silent all the time. So no-one else can hear the notification signal. Follow the instructions in the text. Go quickly now, and may Allah be with you.'

He ushered Shahid quickly out of the office. There was a rear entrance, leading to a quiet alleyway near the souk. He push Shahid though the door.

It was late; an hour later than they had agreed to meet. Hurriedly he went to the meeting place. The others were there, looking very agitated.

'Wa'Allah! Where have you been, brother?' queried Jassim, worriedly. He was the one with whom Shahid got on best.

'I went the wrong way in the souk! By the time I realised it, I'd gone a long way in the wrong direction. All the way to Sectors F-6 and F-7. I couldn't believe the squalor that people in the slums there live in. It's a shanty town. They're surrounded by high buildings, as if the City fathers were trying to hide them from view.'

As he said the words, they sounded lame and unconvincing. He saw Haroun looking at him with narrowed eyes. They'd never got on. Haroun was jealous of Shahid; angry that Shahid and not he had been selected for the star role. 'How could he get lost?' thought Haroun. 'There's no way he could get lost in the souk. Quickly, they told each other how they had got on.

243

Each one said that they had completed their task. It was now night-time. Overhead, the sky had gone quickly from light to dark, in that brief transition that is the eastern dusk; from translucent blue it quickly became black. But not the dense, all-enveloping black of England by night. Here the night was balmy, welcoming after the earlier heat of the day, relieved by a cooling breeze which ebbed and flowed, carrying the exotic scents of oleander and hibiscus mixed with the delicate smell of a myriad of spices from the souk. Overhead, the crescent moon of the Arabian sky lay on its back, cradling the stars... It was a beautiful night to be looking for a beautiful girl and the pleasures of love, thought Shahid regretfully, contrasting it with the reality of his present situation, planning mayhem and murder.

Agreed on their arrangements for the next morning, the three conspirators went their separate ways.

As he moved through the narrow twisting alleyways, Shahid had an uneasy feeling. He was nearly at the house, in a particularly dark section. There was a sudden rush. Shahid felt himself being almost lifted bodily off the ground. He was flung against the rough basalt rocks of the wall.

'Right, Brother, now tell me what you were really doing.' He recognised Haroun's voice. Saw the flash of moonlight reflected on the knife blade. It disappeared as the blade went under his chin and was pressed firmly against his windpipe.

'Come on, tell me! You're a traitor to our cause. I've been watching you, I know what you think,' screamed Haroun.

Shahid's wildly swinging left hand caught Haroun a glancing blow on his temple. It was enough to distract him. Shahid managed to get his other hand free and grab the wrist that held the knife. Haroun was strong, but Shahid was given the extra strength of fear. Locked together, they rolled along the wall, Haroun being forced backwards. Suddenly he trod on a large loose stone and stumbled backwards. Together they fell, both still holding the knife. Shahid fell heavily on top of Haroun. There was a hiss of breath, like a deflating child's rubber ring. A strangulated, gurgling scream escaped from Haroun; Shahid felt the knife catch on flimsy shirt material, felt the blade briefly impeded by the elasticity of the diaphragm and then plunge, as if through butter, into the deeper recesses of Haroun's stomach, slicing through the soft membranes of gut and tissue, up under the ribcage, to lodge in Haroun's heart. Haroun twitched several times, blood bubbled up and spilled from his mouth. Finally, he lay still. Shahid scrambled to his feet, horrified and shaking.

James had immediately been summoned back to London by the office. He arrived back in the evening as the light was fading. Driving up the M4 in the car sent to meet him, he saw that late autumn was having its effect on the leaves, now beginning to fall fast, spiralling downwards in the strong wind, onto the wet road. Back in Kabul, there was already snow low down on the mountains and the night temperatures were bitter.

Next morning, he left the club in St James's Square and went across Battersea Bridge to the office. His boss and several colleagues were there. They exchanged news and jokes over a cup of coffee. They were joined shortly by a large, elderly man with a bucolic mien and the heavily pock-marked and veined, red nose of a man who knew a good malt when he saw one – and wasn't adverse to sampling the contents. And then by a smart-suited and serious younger man. James was introduced to Sandy and to Douglas Jardine. He had not met Sandy before; but his name was well-known to all members of James's service. His war-time exploits were legendary. He wore the kilt, with an ash Shepherd's Crook in his hand and a blue Tam-o-Shanter balanced precariously on his head. Nothing less like a senior intelligence officer could be imagined, thought James irreverently; and yet, thinking back through the history of his service, perhaps Sandy was typical of the eccentrics that most of those who were involved were in his era. Douglas Jardine had travelled only the short distance along the road and across the river from his office in Century House. He was there to represent MI5. By comparison, he resembled a caricature of a *'Yes, Minister'* civil servant.

James's boss briefed everyone succinctly. 'In conclusion, it's been decided by C and the Director General that we should send Bill Sloan,' he paused, as everyone assessed the implications, 'to meet with and run "the Englishman", as we will all call him from now on. And, just to confirm, this information is classified top secret!'

Douglas Jardine interjected, 'But that's ridiculous! This man is a British citizen, who is reporting on a British domestic situation. They're planning an operation here in London! We should take control.'

'Yes, Douglas, I know, but it's been agreed by the JIC – SIS is to run him!' And, as if to placate Jardine, James's boss continued, 'The reason for the decision is your own intelligence. You are already onto the Englishman. You remember that your people did the initial research and, to cut a long story short, they discovered that our man Sloan's father had been at primary school with the Englishman's father. And that they had become close friends, albeit at a tender age. It's a no-brainer that we should use Sloan, therefore, to run this guy.'

'But I thought that Sloan was banged up in a Dubai jail!' interjected James.

'Yes, James, indeed he is. That's our little problem. How to get him out! But, as they say, we have the exit plan. We're working on it. Even if it wasn't logical to use him, with all the political flak flying around, HMG is pulling out all the stops to get him out. A major face-saving exercise. They're between a rock and a hard place. If they get him out, they risk scuppering the Good Friday agreement. If they don't and are seen to abandon him to his fate – which might literally be a death sentence – the government is likely to lose any vote of confidence and fall.

'Right, I've dragged Sandy away from his beloved malts because he knows Bill Sloan like a father. Sandy, please tell everyone how you've been getting on with the conundrum.'

Sandy lurched unsteadily to his feet. He went to the top of the table. An aide pressed a few keys on a small laptop computer on the table. A map of the Near East was displayed on the large projector screen.

'You all know,' he began, 'about Bill's girlfriend Mary Duffy. She's a very brave woman. She and Bill broke up when he left Ireland, but they've kept in touch over the years. She still holds a candle for him, would be my guess.

'I met her a couple of days ago and told her everything!' There was a sharp intake of breath from Jardine, who obviously considered this a breach of security.

'She's had more experience in the field than some of us!' said Sandy pointedly, looking at Jardine. 'She's fully demonstrated her loyalty to the Crown. And now we need her again. So the least we can do is to level with her!' He paused, and took a sip of neat water. Clearly age was beginning to tell.

'Anyway, in summary, she is now over in Dubai being looked after by one of our people there. Our people are riding shotgun to make sure she's not under surveillance – from the press particularly. She met with Bill yesterday. She is confident that she got the message across to Bill. The guards were not very attentive. He's agreed to work with the Englishman. And, as you've heard, we have the exit plan to spring him. I won't go into all the details now. But our man in Dubai, Andy Stringer, has all that in hand. The escape is planned for tomorrow night. In short, after Bill's release he'll travel across Iran and meet up with the Englishman. We've organised an Iranian companion to drive with him. Someone we've used before. He has a mobile contact for the Englishman to activate in order to make the arrangements for meeting. After that, we wait to hear more about this major attack the Englishman claims to know about.'

The meeting broke up. James and Sandy went to the in-house bar. This time, Sandy dispensed with the water. They discussed the arrangements for Bill's support once in Afghanistan, and the link-up with James. After a sandwich, James was on his way back to Heathrow and Kabul.

Back in London, MI6 was indeed running a slide rule over all the options. The Operations Officer put through a call to Andy in Dubai. Automatically switching to secure mode, he began:

'Andy, look. The secret police are nosing around you all. It's probable that they've sussed out the link with the Rower.' Andy's involuntary intake of breath was followed by a vivid expletive. 'That's how they got on to you and Bill.

'And that bastard Tamimi. He's been probing the Barry White cover. It's not that deep as you know; only set up to deal with a cursory check. Not to withstand scrutiny by a professional HIS – particularly one trained by us!' he ended cynically.

'Certainly the local hostile intelligence service may not be the Sovs. But they're no mean slouches,' Andy responded, his concern evident in his voice.

'But I've been thinking,' said the Operations Officer. 'Do you remember Reindeer? I've had Research on the job. They've discovered that he's a Secret Police guard working in that place where Bill's being held. I need you to get to him and make him an offer he can't refuse!'

'What's that, then?' said Andy, both intrigued and apprehensive.

'That he gets Bill out of jail free or goes back to face the music in Gaza.

He knows that if Hamas gets hold of him, they'll string him up alive by the balls. As soon as he realises that we're serious, that we'll drop details of his new identity with Hamas, he'll be on board.' He paused, then continued: 'There's another reason as well for needing to get Bill out urgently, other than for his own health. I'll brief you on that later. In the meantime get working on Reindeer. Give me a call as soon as you've tracked him down and made the proposition. Then we'll work out the fine print of where we go from there.' His colleague rang off, leaving Andy with much to contemplate.

Early the following morning, Andy was in the Central Registry, behind the time-locked metal grille in the Embassy basement. The one terminal which was authorised to access the Agents Control Database was here. Checking his Special Designation e-mail account, Andy saw that there was one message from Control – a set of hieroglyphics. Andy had known that Operations would have arranged for this to be passed to him immediately. This gave him access to the ACD files.

Quickly, he called up the Reindeer data. He knew that his first problem would be to identify Reindeer. Then he had to track him down. And then make contact with him without anyone else becoming aware. Easier said than done. It wasn't always so, but fortunately in this case, the contact information he needed was fairly detailed – and recent as well, Andy noted hopefully. There was a very good recent photograph. And why not, thought Andy: Reindeer's face had been plastered over the world's media not that long ago, when he had 'retired' and come in from the cold. Given a new identity, he had been directed to get a job with the police here in Dubai. A sleeper, who could be reactivated at the drop of a hat. Against such an eventuality as had just occurred. But how would he react to being contacted and given the Office's ultimatum? But there again, thought Andy, Reindeer knew the rules of the game; knew that if he failed to co-operate, he would sign his own death warrant.

The photograph showed an intelligent, classical Arabic face, with alert blue eyes, unusual for an Arab, and also the palest complexion. The file confirmed what London had told him, that he worked as a guard in the State Security detention centre. The facility that now housed Bill. This information was relatively recent; last October, within the last year, when he had contacted Andy's predecessor to report on his current situation. Hopefully nothing had changed. Helpfully, there was a record of agreed contact details. 'Thank God for that!' thought Andy; not many former agents were so willing to keep in touch. Signing out of the Registry, Andy went back to his office and at once texted the number that was in the file with the enigmatic message: 'Dine with Jew but seek shelter from a Christian.' Andy did not expect an answer, but both men knew what would happen next.

It was a normal morning, just like any other. The prisoners had been allowed to shave, but only two at any one time. This had been one of the few occasions when they got a chance to talk to each other. But now that they had been put in the normal court procedure, having been formally charged and were awaiting transfer to Abu Dhabi and trial, Dubai's State Security had lost interest in them. They had done their work. The evidence was clear, incontrovertible, and precise. There could be no doubt about the outcome. The guards had become bored. They had relaxed the previously strict regime. At times, doors were left open. Prisoners were able to wander around, or sit in the corridor and chat with each other and the guards. Their guards became more friendly, more human. Cigarettes were offered to the prisoners. A bantering relationship developed. Perhaps, Bill had reflected, it was symptomatic of the Stockholm syndrome. One guard, Mansour Al Din, had always from the beginning seemed to be more sympathetic, compassionate.

On this day, Mansour was on shift. He gave the prisoners their breakfast. Bill heard the noise of the other cell doors being opened and closed, and the rattle of spoons on metal dishes. His own door rattled. The viewing window was opened. The keys rattled in the door. It swung open and Mansour passed in the plate, rattling like the others, to Bill. The door shut. The rattling process continued down the corridor.

Resignedly, Bill looked at the offering. Who in their right mind would want chicken biryani at this time of the morning? Particularly as he knew it would also be served at lunchtime and then again at supper time. But he was hungry. It was the third spoonful of rice. He bit into something hard but pliable – perhaps a piece of gristle? He spat out the offending thing. He poked it. It was a bit of paper wrapped up in a tight wad. He cleaned it off and opened it up. It was a note. He recognised the writing. It was Andy's: 'Mansour is working for us. You can trust him. He will get you out of there.'

Andy had outlined the plan. It was very simple. 'Get rid of this. Eat it. Enjoy your breakfast!' the note finished. It didn't taste very good but to Bill, his heart racing excitedly, it was like manna from heaven. A few minutes later Mansour came to collect the dish. There could be no mistaking the look he gave Bill. No doubt about the inference of the 'Insha'Allah, Alhamdulillah!' as he left the cell. Mansour's shift was finished now. But he would be back on duty at 7 pm for the night shift. That was when it would happen. Bill paced the small cell restlessly. Back in the control room Mansour checked the CCTV footage. Well versed in such matters from his training with the Mossad, it was not difficult for him to ensure that the pictures of Bill discovering the note were corrupted. An unnecessary precaution, perhaps, as none of the supervisors bothered to check them out any more.

The day passed interminably slowly. Bill's nerves were taught, jangling, stretched to breaking point. But he tried to appear relaxed. Even if no-one was monitoring the tapes now, they sure as hell would be scrutinising them later if he'd managed to get out. He and Mansour would have to do a really good piece of acting.

At the same time, outside, Andy was making the final arrangements. He met with Mansour immediately after he came off shift. Mansour confirmed that he was sure Bill had digested the note, literally and metaphorically.

'Make sure you make it all look authentic!' he said, shaking hands with Mansour.

'Don't worry! I know what serious torture's like. I don't want that again, but that's what'll happen to me if it doesn't work out! A few bruises will be nothing by comparison.' With that, Mansour headed off.

It had been easy to identify Mansour at the Dome Café. Andy had been inside the far corner from the Trade Centre Road. He was early, to make sure Mansour did not have a tail. Mansour sat down and ordered a citron pressé. Andy went over to join him. It was a perfunctory meeting; each man sizing up the other. Mansour had suffered a lot for his beliefs. It didn't seem to Andy that he had been broken by it. The price of his decision was obscurity and a menial job. Perhaps he would welcome a taste of action again?

It did not take long to decide how to arrange Bill's escape. Now it was time for Andy to do his bit. He called Eskandir.

'It's on! Tonight! I'll meet you in the car park opposite the Intercon at 12:30 this evening.' Eskandir Salmani acknowledged. Eskandir was an Iranian Émigré, from a highborn Anglophile family forced to flee Tehran around the time of the Shah's overthrow. He had maintained contact with the British since those days. He was always ready to help. Now his help was to be invaluable.

Bill lay sleeplessly on his lumpy paliasse. Would this indeed be the last night? If the plan went wrong, he would not get the paliasse next time. He would be in the notorious Abu Dhabi prison at Al Wathba, chained, kneeling, to the wall. He looked at his watch. Was it still only 10:30? Three hours to go.

'I need to go to the toilet!' Bill mouthed into the intercom, the blue light indicating that the message was being transmitted.

After three or four minutes there was still no response. Usually the guards did not bother to call back on the intercom; they just arrived at the door of the cell. Normally it took only a couple of minutes before the prisoner would hear that they were on the way. But not this time! Bill felt his heart beat quicker. Had Mansour lost his nerve? Was he going to betray Bill? He pressed again, repeating his message, this time with even more emphasis.

This time the call produced a reaction, and after a couple of minutes, Bill heard the cell block door creaking as it was opened laboriously. Was it Mansour alone – or was he accompanied by State Security? Perhaps Colonel Tamimi was even now in the corridor, exulting in another chance to humiliate Bill.

He heard the key being inserted into the door's lock. It turned slowly and the door was pushed back. Bill stood to one side as Mansour entered the cell. Bill thrust Mansour aside violently, nearly pushing him over. He ran down the corridor. Mansour recovered and gave chase. Bill reached the cell block door. It was closed but not locked. As he began to open the door, Mansour cannoned into him and began to pummel him, shouting loudly in guttural Arabic as he did so, sounding the alarm.

But Mansour had done his homework. He knew that there was no-one else on duty in the cell block. The nearest people were in the adjacent building. His shift partner was asleep in the room beside the control room. Mansour knew that he would not hear the commotion. He knew too that the area where they were fighting was not covered by CCTV. Mansour presented his face to Bill. He winced, his eyes watering, as several blows landed on it. Not enough to knock him out, but still it hurt like hell. The resulting bruising would certainly look realistic. Bill ripped the keys and handcuffs off Mansour's flimsy webbing, which shredded in the process. With a compliant Mansour, it took only seconds to handcuff him to a thick air-conditioning pipe.

Quickly Bill took the keys. Mansour had marked the ones he would need with coloured stickers, as Andy had explained in his note. This facilitated Bill's rapid exit through three doors into the main compound. Bill was careful to remove and pocket the stickers before throwing the keys into a nearby rubbish bin. Mansour did not have access to the main gate keys, and opening that would have attracted attention. But he had left a coil of rope below the stretch of wall to the rear of the detention centre. Bill ran over to that point and quickly discovered the rope. He threw it over the wall, whistling as he did so. He was answered by a comforting tug on the rope. On the other side Eskandir pulled hard as Bill scrabbled up and over the wall. He jumped from the top; a height of about 6 feet. He fell awkwardly on his ankle. Eskandir hoisted him up and they sprinted to the latter's car parked behind the small building. Bill barely noticed the pain in his ankle as he jumped into the Land Cruiser's passenger seat. Eskandir gunned the engine and a couple of moments later they were on the main road heading for Sharjah. They bypassed Sharjah, heading past the airport and the university towards Ajman and Ras Al Khaimah. After about two hours driving fast, having passed only a couple of vehicles, Eskandir pulled into the side of the road. Being fired up, then the wind-down of the adrenaline flow during the action, the ease with which it had all gone and the monotony of the drive, had quickly lulled Bill into a fitful doze. He woke up with a start, now feeling cold.

'Afwan, Bill, I am sorry but I need to disturb you. We are close to the border now. It's very lax here normally. But we must not take any chances. The alarm may have been raised. You see that hill on the right?' He pointed out the window. Bill nodded.

'I would like you to go up there. There's a track which runs around the side of the hill. I'll go out with you to make sure you get on it. Follow it; it will take you over the border – there's no fence or marking of any kind – then, after about half a mile, it swings round to the left and joins up again with the main road. I'll be waiting for you there.'

Again, all went according to plan. Now, just as dawn was breaking, Bill and Eskandir were standing beside the vehicle staring towards the sea. They could hear a rhythmic beating noise. Bill sensed that it was being made by something mechanical. Now the sky was brightening perceptibly. Suddenly Eskandir pointed, 'Look – over there! There they are.'

Out to sea, Bill was now able to discern the shapes of an armada of little boats rapidly approaching the shore. He could hear the increasing crescendo of the outboard motors powering each craft. There were small assault craft, such as he had seen the Royal Navy use for amphibious operations. There were twenty to thirty of these craft. The rapid approach now more evident,

Bill saw that some were carrying a few people, but all had small animals, probably goats, on board.

Quickly Eskandir explained. 'These guys are out every night. They take cigarettes, electronic stuff and so on across to Iran – to Bandar Abbas. It's only just over 10 kilometres away. Then they come back like now with animals, goats, whatever, in exchange. And sometimes people!' He pointed to one of the boats, 'People who might not otherwise get out of Iran alive!'

'You mean they're smugglers?' asked Bill.

'Exactly! Most of the cigarettes are counterfeit. The electronic gear has hefty import duties into Iran.'

That explains a lot, thought Bill. He often wondered how the UAE could absorb so many cigarettes.

'What happens now?' he said.

'This is where we part company. The next leg of your mystery tour will be with Mirza Abbas.' He pointed to one of the boats just being made fast by its skipper.

The journey across to Bandar Abbas had been straightforward – exhilarating, in fact, with the small craft rearing and bucking into each wave like an untamed bronco. There was a heavy sea running and they had been heading into it for most of the crossing. When they reached Kish Island, just off the Iranian shore, they were in the lee and the water was like a millpond for the final stage. Bill remembered when he had first heard about Kish Island, listening to that tape. It seemed like a lifetime away. The light was fading fast, with a crescent moon rising over the horizon to the right as they approached the shore.

'Insha'Allah, Mr Bill, we will be there in five minutes.' They had spoken little on the crossing. Bill was absorbed in thoughts of his recent experience. In the event, it had all gone smoothly, but Bill shuddered at the thought of what might been happening to him at this moment had it all fouled-up. The reputation of Al Wathba prison was well-known. Stories of its sadistic killers were rife in the Emirates.

Now, with Mirza's warning, Bill shifted his focus.

'Do the guards patrol the coast? Are they likely to be looking for us?' he asked Mirza, apprehensive now as reality beckoned again. He must not allow himself to relax, to fall into a false sense of security. From now on he would be in alien territory – behind enemy lines. State Security was certain to have got on to their opposite numbers in VEVAK once they realised that Bill had gone. There were not that many places he could have gone to. The alternative to the sea crossing was the endless swelling and shifting soft sands of the massive dunes of the Empty Quarter – the feared Rub Al Khali.

'I do this journey several times every week. I am always going to the same place – where we go to now. The local police are friends of mine,' he said with heavy emphasis. 'You could say that we are in business together!' He smiled knowingly at Bill. Obviously the police got their cut from Mirza's operations. But would he be a worthwhile commission for Mirza's friends? Perhaps State Security in Dubai would have raised the bidding?

He looked at Mirza, now staring intently ahead into the pitch-black night. Mirza had a devil-may-care attitude, and joked and laughed continually. He was so relaxed that it irritated Bill, constantly on the qui vive, looking over his shoulder and then focused landward the next moment, wondering fearfully whether the police would have a reception party waiting for him.

Mirza was in his mid-50s with a creased, thin face and a ready smile never far away. He had a short greying, stubbly beard joining up with sideburns and a dark moustache. He wore a hodgepodge of Western-style clothes, topped off by the typical Baluchi beehive woolly hat. So far, Bill had not seen him without a thin cheroot with drooping ash held between his tobacco-stained front teeth.

Mirza muttered something; it was almost a grunt of satisfaction. Looking landward, Bill's eye was attracted to a small but intense red light. He realised that this was what Mirza had been looking for. In a few minutes they had landed in a small sandy cove. It was evident that this was a well-practised procedure. Within minutes one of the reception party, 'my cousin', Mirza explained later, had taken charge of Mirza's boat. Then Mirza was at the wheel of a battered Land Cruiser. Bill was in the passenger seat.

They drove fast. Mirza seemed to know the way like the back of his hand. After several hours, Mirza pulled into the side of the road. He stretched his legs, relighting an old cheroot. Then he fished out some chapattis and dates. Handing some of each to Bill, he motioned him to eat. Before eating his own, he took out a prayer rug and went off a little way to pray. He faced more or less back the way they had come, in a south-westerly direction. Mecca lay well behind where Bill now found himself. Coming back to join Bill, Mirza started eating.

'Soon we are at Jirift and then Bam. Kandahar take all day, all night. Hard – bad road. Many thieves.' He grinned, 'My friends!' His grin widened, that of a little boy enjoying himself mischievously. Bill's alarm subsided. It was clear that these mountainous areas held no fear for Mirza. He was among his own.

'You drive?' asked Mirza.

Bill nodded. 'Yes, I do.'

Mirza held out the keys and made for the passenger seat. Soon, he was snoring intermittently beside Bill. Great wracking, tumbling noises from the depths of his belly. Once he got going and was concentrating on the driving, Bill was able to relax. He felt free, master of his own destiny.

Occasionally he had to nudge Mirza when the route was unclear but most of the time it was straightforward – there were no other roads. They saw only a handful of other vehicles. And so it continued through the next day and the following morning. Stopping only to change over driving, to eat some of Mirza's seemingly limitless supply of chapattis and for Mirza to pray, they made good time. Bill was driving at first light the next morning. As the sun rose up over the mountains in front, he saw the stark beauty of his surroundings. There were occasional buildings. Farmsteads, some with a green oasis of cultivated land. The air was fresh and scented with the perfume from occasional clumps of wild flowers where they stopped.

Approaching evening, Mirza was driving. Bill had been dozing beside him. When he opened his eyes, Bill saw in the distance a large and sprawling town. 'Kandahar!' Mirza confirmed.

So this was the fabled Kandahar known to all English prep school boys. It occupied a significant position astride an ancient trade route; a route travelled by Alexander the Great after whom it is thought to have been named. Now, after the rise of the Taliban, it had become a household word throughout the world. The heart of the revanchist Pashtu struggle, it was centre-stage in the latest episode of the Great Game. As one great power, Russia, had exited stage left, now the only remaining superpower found itself centre-stage, enmeshed in the shifting sands of local power struggles and the global clash of Christianity and Islam.

Bill was shaken out of his reverie by the ubiquitous but oddly out of place sound of a police siren. He might have been in the Old Kent Road or in downtown Manhattan. A policeman in leathers astride a Harley-Davidson motorcycle with blue flashing lights pulled alongside, motioning them to stop. Bill's heart raced. They must have traced the vehicle; known that Bill was in it. He braced himself to make a run for it. But Mirza remained calm, the smile not leaving his face. He stopped the vehicle. He reached for some documents under the dashboard. Bill saw a 100-Afghanis note being inserted inside what he took to be Mirza's driving licence. The policeman had parked his bike and was now standing by the door. Mirza wound down the window. A torrent of apparent abuse descended on Mirza's head. The smile remained in place. He passed the documents to the policeman, who flipped quickly through them, deftly removing the note, inspecting it and pocketing it all in one swift, well-practised move, unnoticed by the small crowd of onlookers that had gathered. The policeman smiled and handed back the documents, saluted and went back to his bike. 'My brother!' said Mirza. The policeman drove off. Bill's pulse rate dropped.

'Wake up, Boss, for fuck's sake!' The rasping, nasal Glaswegian accent was accentuated by Corporal Tony McMullen's vain attempt to whisper in the bitterly cold night air. Bill came to with a guilty start; despite the jaw-numbing temperature, he had dropped off. The continuous exertion of the last seventy-two hours had strained every sinew in his body. Now it had all caught up with him.

'Shit, sorry Tony,' Bill whispered, feeling like a small boy caught in the act of peeing his trousers. He heard the Corporal chuckle, but he knew that he'd not be allowed to forget this; at least not until he coughed up for a round of beers when they got back to camp at the Monte Casino base.

'OK. There's some movement!'

He knew Corporal McMullen well. One of the veterans of the days when Bill had been in Ireland, McMullen was a Royal Marine. As hard as nails the Marines had been then, and were still now, the backbone of that other nondescript and unnamed unit from the West Country. Unerringly he had navigated the patrol to which Bill had attached himself, the senior person present but not in charge – not at this stage, at any rate. His time would come when contact was made. They had arrived at the RV in good time. In time to stake it out for several hours before Shahid was due to sneak out of the camp and meet up with them. It would not do to ignore the fact that Shahid might be under suspicion and might be being trailed – or to assume that Shahid would not double-cross them. So much for the SAS's oft-quoted jibe about the Marines, that they could not read a map. Tony had been spot-on. It was a moonless night. Once they made distance from the ambient light of Kandahar, it became pitch black. At times the patrol had had to hold on to the rucksack of the man in front to keep in contact. They had exited the chopper some ten clicks south of Kandahar airport. Close enough to the ground for the team to jump out. The Chinook had not touched the ground. It moved slowly forward throughout. It took less than half a minute for all eight passengers to disembark. On any watching radar screen it would appear as a routine approach to the airport. Pakistani air traffic controllers were co-ordinated by the ISI. They had instructions to alert headquarters to any suspected ISAF or US air activity. Despite Pakistani obfuscation, their support for Mullah Omar was well documented. As, in turn, was Mullah Omar's for bin Laden. Bill had been briefed that, back in 1998, the CIA had developed a plan to snatch bin Laden from the Tarnak Farm complex. At the last moment it had to be called off. A well-placed source in Pakistan reported that the plan had been compromised and bin Laden alerted. He had immediately gone into hiding.

It had taken them three and a half hours to get to the farm, moving ever more cautiously as they approached the target.

Major Fred Matthews' briefing had been both detailed and succinct. He finished off: 'Your job is to get our friend here' – he gestured to Bill standing beside him – 'to this spot... ' The pointer hovered over the ridge 400 metres from the Tarnak Farm complex on the large-scale computer-generated map which dominated the base's ops room. Several ranks of captains and majors, sergeants and sergeant-majors sat at the desks ranked in rows along one wall of the building. The eyes of each occupant were focused on the screens of their individual laptops; headsets covered their ears. There was a continuous murmur of instructions being given and received in terse, jargon-laded military-speak. They appeared oblivious to the briefing going on in front of them, but Bill sensed that it was all being taken in; that these men and women knew that they had a vital part to play in supporting his operation.

'... to protect him,' Bill's attention swung back to the briefing, 'and to get him back here without a hair on his head being touched! Any questions?' he said, challenging anyone to suggest that he had not covered every single aspect of the operation in meticulous and unambiguous detail.

Shahid was growing increasingly nervous. It was now over three weeks since he had made contact with the ISI. And still nothing. Now the attack which he needed to tell the Brits about was imminent. He could not stop it on his own. Had the Pakistanis decided to ignore his information? Worse still, instead of telling the British, had they told the Taliban?

But the die was cast. He could do nothing but wait. What would he do if the attack started and there was still no contact? He closed his mind to this possibility. Every day confirmed him in his conviction that what he was doing was the right thing.

Only the other day a young couple who had eloped to Kunar Province in eastern Afghanistan had been stoned to death. Family members persuaded them to return to their village, promising to allow them to marry. When they got back they were seized by the Taliban, who convened local mullahs from surrounding villages for a religious court. After the Taliban proclaimed the sentence the adulterers, Siddiqa, dressed in the head-to-toe Afghan burka, and Khayyam, who had a wife and two young children, were encircled by the male-only crowd in the bazaar. Taliban activists began stoning them first; then villagers joined in until they killed first Siddiqa and then Khayyam. Both bodies were reduced to heaps of mangled, bloody flesh. They were left where they fell. The Taliban decreed that they must lie there for their remains to be devoured by the pie-dogs and vultures. Shahid reckoned that about 200 villagers participated in the executions, including Khayyam's father and brother, and Siddiqa's brother, as well as other relatives.

A spokesman for the Taliban, Zabiullah Mujahid, had praised the action. 'We have heard about this report,' he said, interviewed via cell phone. 'But let me tell you that according to Shariah law, if someone commits a crime like that, we have our courts and we deal with such crimes based on Islamic law.' Shahid had nearly been physically sick watching; and, hearing the Taliban's justification, was suddenly appalled by the depravity of it all.

Several days later he was at a lecture given by Mullah Awlaki, who sat behind a desk with a sheathed dagger in his belt. 'Well, not so much a lecture as a harangue,' Shahid thought, as the Mullah's voice rose another octave as he vented his spleen against the infidel. He urged his fellow Jihadists to kill 'without hesitation'.

'Do not consult anyone in killing Americans. Killing the Devil does not need any fatwa.' Through the internet and YouTube he sent a chilling message to all Americans: 'It's either you or us.'

Suddenly Shahid's phone bleeped. Too late, he realised he had failed to put it on silent. Now all eyes looked at him as the Mullah paused, even he being distracted from his tirade. Sheepishly, Shahid took the phone out of his pocket and turned it off. He murmured an apology, 'Afwan, afwan... one of my sisters, Alhamdulillah.'

It was much later before he was able to read the text message. Ever since Haroun had disappeared, his closest friend Jassim had been suspicious of Shahid. The disappearance had remained a mystery; unexplained, unsettling to all. But there had been no chance to investigate; to do so would have imperilled the mission. Al Zawahin had forbidden it. Now, Shahid knew, this suspicion would have increased. Jassim would be watching him like a hawk. He read the message in the toilets: 'Be at the crossroads in Mandi Sar at 02:30 on Tuesday 3rd,' it said. 'When you are challenged, use the password "Eid". You will get the response "Mubarak". Bill.'

Shocked now, fearful, his pulse racing, he checked the date. That was early tomorrow morning. In only five hours' time! He would need to make sure that he could slip out of the camp without being seen. Fortunately he had already worked out a way of getting out unnoticed. The RV was about 2 kilometres away. He knew the village, with a prominent rock by a well. He came back to the present with a jolt. This was it!

'Eid!' he called quietly.

'Mubarak!' came the response in a coarse Glaswegian growl. Then several figures approached his position.

'Here you are, Sorr, this here's yer mon!' Another Scotsman, thought Shahid, as he saw the shadowy figures. He went with the small group, their weapons at the ready, covering him, to the nearby building. It was a burnt-out school which had fallen foul of the Taliban. Some bits were still habitable; here a safe base had been set up.

Bill scrutinised Shahid by the light of the Tilley lamp suspended from a beam. Both men sized each other up. Bill was in a foreign country, a fugitive from justice, but among his own. Shahid was more vulnerable. He too was in an alien country, despite the proximity to the land of his fathers. These men were not his kith and kin, but they shared the same citizenship. His former co-religionists would now be his sworn enemies. Like Bill, he too was a fugitive. Both were beyond the pale.

Bill wanted to make Shahid as comfortable and relaxed as possible. But

Shahid knew that he did not have much time. If his absence was noticed, then he was as good as dead.

As they talked, they began to empathise. During his briefing, Andy had told Bill that Shahid was the son of his father's Asian friend of all those years ago. Now, as he looked at Shahid, he found it difficult to believe that this was the son of his father's best friend from way back. Bill shared his knowledge with Shahid. Had Shahid's father told Shahid about the encounter – about Bill's father? Shahid reacted with surprise. He peered intently at Bill. He was searching back in the corridors of time. Bill had done his homework.

'Did your father tell you about the time they got attacked by those swans at the Black Loch? Your dad nearly fell into the water!' Suddenly, it was as if they themselves had travelled in the Doctor's Time Machine, back together again all those years ago.

'Yes,' said Shahid animatedly, 'and those bastards who tried to mug them.'

Shahid was somehow exorcised by the chance to speak in the vulgar vernacular of his upbringing; so much more comfortable than the rigid polemical diatribe of extremist Islam. This was where he belonged. But could he do enough now to be allowed to cross back over?

Bill felt uncomfortable at the memory of his father recounting the squalid encounter. Shahid continued: 'Yes, they did my father over alright, busted his nose. Took some explaining to my grandparents! But the one thing he was glad about was that your father managed to get away. My father said that it was all his fault that your father got caught up in it as well!' The years fell away and the bonds of their fathers' childhood friendship also bonded them together.

'Look,' said Shahid, 'I've got to get back before it's too late. All I know at the moment is that a major attack is planned. It's imminent – we'll be moving any day now to another place. There's to be a major attack in Pakistan. Something to do with... '

'Pakistan, did you say? We were told that it was to be in the UK!'

'I only said that so that the ISI guys would put me in touch with you. Otherwise they'd probably have handed me over to the Taliban. They're planning to steal some weapons but I don't know what sort or when, only that it's from somewhere in Pakistan. I'll try to let you have details as soon as I know.'

'Excellent,' Bill said, 'you must keep in touch – same procedure as before. I'll text the password. Text me when you have the details.' He paused, searching in his rucksack. 'Here, take this, hide it somewhere in your clothing. It's a beacon. We'll be following you all the time. If you have a problem – if you think they're on to you – text me with "EXIT PLAN".'

Corporal McMullen took Shahid back to the place where they had met. Soon he was lost in the darkness as he headed back to the camp.

It was a moonless night, but there was enough ambient light for Shahid to make his way comfortably back. Tense and pent-up though he was, Shahid was aware of the beautiful array of stars rimming the mountains on the horizon. He felt exhilarated. Despite his fear, he knew that he was doing what he had to do. He slipped through the fence. Moving stealthily and noiselessly, he was soon back in the tent. All appeared calm. In a few moments he was asleep, exhausted by the stress of the last few hours. In the far corner of the tent, Jassim was not asleep. He sat up slowly, meaning to ask Shahid what he had been doing. He had been away for over an hour. Changing his mind, he lay down again; his mind racing, he did not get back to sleep.

After the prayer call next morning, a day of feverish activity ensued. Everyone was keyed-up like the coiled springs of an over-wound clock. All knew that they were now about to fulfil their destiny. Jassim continued to observe Shahid closely, wondering whether to confront him.

At dusk they assembled. There were nearly three dozen of them, all highly-trained, many with the scars to prove that they had already been tested and proven in the white-hot heat of battle. They climbed into a dozen vehicles, a mix of UAZ69s and Land Cruisers.

The unusual activity was observed high above them, and seen also in Monte Casino Camp, and at Langley back in the States.

'Holy shit! Hi, Sarge, come and look at this.' Private First Class Chuck Harborne knew a good target when he saw one. 'Shall I scramble 102 Squadron? Those widow-making motherfuckers would make mincemeat out of that lot!'

'Goddam it, no!' said Sgt Jean Jones. 'We've been told to lay off that lot.

There's one of our assets in there somewhere. Just keep your eyes on them. We need to know where they're headed for.'

It was not only the American watchers who knew about the anticipated move. Bill would have been shocked to learn that his report of his meeting with Shahid had already had such global dissemination. How many people now knew about the Englishman? How many people, how many agencies, were able to monitor the signal from the bleeper carried by Shahid, as his group began its journey eastwards?

Their destination was about 5 kilometres south of Kandahar airport. It was a squat, crudely-built, two-storey building with several single-storey buildings attached to it on the right and some outbuildings. Behind this main complex, there were serried rows of small, low huts, over fifty in all. They were greeted on arrival by al-Zawahiri and Sanjay. There was an air of eager anticipation.

'Sorr, look here!' Corporal McMullen beckoned to Bill as the software zoomed in on the building. 'Looks like they're setting up shop there.' They looked at the computer-generated map on the large screen above to check the location.

On the other side of the world, Sergeant Jones contacted her boss: 'They're at Tarnak Farm, sir. What do you want me to do about it?'

On arrival, they all prayed together. Then al-Zawahiri gave a short, impassioned rant, exhorting them all to do everything for Allah:

'Those who are chosen to be martyrs from among us will be the fortunate ones, Allah Akbar, Allah Akbar.'

Then Sanjay projected a photograph on a large screen. It showed a complex of buildings. He briefly explained the plan and described the buildings. He had marked on the photograph a route from the back of the installation into a large storage area.

'What we want is in there.' He changed the photograph on the screen. 'This is a spent fuel rod. These are what we want. There are fifteen of them. There – we need six, Shahid.' He turned around. 'Shahid, that's your job!' Shahid nodded. He had trained with his group for this task, as the other groups had for other tasks. Up until now, most had not known what the target was. They still did not know where it was. But now they all knew that they were to steal the components of a nuclear bomb. Now they all knew that they were going to Pakistan.

Shahid looked around; he caught Jassim's eye. Jassim immediately looked away. After the meeting broke up, Jassim sought out Sanjay. He told him of his suspicions.

'He was the last one to see Haroun alive. Now he's been going off on his own. He's changed as well. Used to be so strong, so committed. Now he seems to have lost his passion for the cause – for Allah!'

Sanjay passed the information on to al-Zawahiri. 'I think Jassim's imagining things. Just doesn't like Shahid – he's jealous of him because he thought he should lead that team, wa'Allah.

'None the less, you must keep a very close eye on him, Sanjay. You must not let him out of your sight.' Sanjay nodded.

'I'm due to meet with General Abu Khadr tomorrow when I get back to Pakistan,' said al-Zawahiri. 'Sheikh Abdul will be there too. I'll ask Abu Khadr if they've picked up anything at all to suggest that we have a problem.'

'Right, Brothers,' said Sanjay to the four group leaders the following morning. 'We will be here for two days, then we will leave at dawn on Wednesday. Do as much final preparation as you can now. Then, Alhamdulillah, we will meet our other brothers who will provide support for our endeavours. Allah Akbar, Allah Akbar!'

'Where are we going? Where's the target?' asked Shahid.

'Patience, Brother, you will find out all in good time.'

General Abu Khadr was a small, thin man with round, rimless glasses. He was full of eager energy, always on the go. He nodded appreciatively.

'Good, good, I like that indeed. With this plan, we will all be winners! Pakistan will be looking for a new president.' The General was a man of some considerable ambition. Second-in-command of the ISI was, in his opinion, not his ultimate destiny. So far, he had managed to walk the tightrope between Western demands and fundamentalist pressure.

When al-Zawahiri asked about security, a look of concern crossed the General's face. 'Why do you ask?' he said. Al-Zawahiri explained his concerns.

'Well, I know that the Americans are on full alert at the moment. They're definitely expecting something. The other day one of my officers interviewed a young British man. He passed him on to the British – to the MI6 contact. That's the usual protocol, unfortunately. I didn't think much of it at the time. I only heard about it later on – it was in the monthly report. I couldn't have done much about it anyway, not without arousing suspicion.'

'Gentlemen, excuse me. I have to make a call.' Al-Zawahiri went outside. He seldom used a mobile. He knew that the call would be picked up in Langley, in Cheltenham, in New Delhi, and in Islamabad.

In London it was still quite early in the day. Ahmed took the call. 'Jabil here.'

Ahmed recognised the voice at once. It must be serious for al-Zawahiri to call him on an open line. 'Alaikum sala'am,' he responded noncommittally.

'I think your son may be sickening for something. Or perhaps he's just homesick. I think you need to be with him!'

'Ah afwan, afwan, you have been very good to him. I hope he will be alright. I will come immediately.'

To the worldwide audience of analysts the message was not at all clear. But in Cheltenham they at least recognised the number – it was on the MI5 watchlist. It was clear that the phone owner, Ahmed, would be travelling somewhere immediately. A4 were quickly deployed to cover him on a twenty-four-hour basis.

Ahmed called Fadwa: 'Sorry, I can't make it tonight.'

'But you promised,' said Fadwa, petulantly.

'It's urgent – it's Shahid, something's wrong. I have to go and see him.'

'In Afghanistan?'

'Yes, I'm leaving tonight. It'll only be for a few days.'

'I must go with you,' Fadwa demanded, immediately making up her mind.

'You can't do that! I need to go alone.'

It took Fadwa only a couple of minutes to change Ahmed's mind. After all, she was Shahid's sister; if anyone could help, she could. Now too, she was a newly-pledged member of the Hizb. No, Ahmed reasoned, al-Zawahiri would be pleased if he took her. And, of course, it would be good to have her all to himself, away from prying relatives and friends.

The arrangements were quickly made and, before midnight, Ahmed and Fadwa sat side by side, leaving Heathrow on the evening flight to Moscow. In Moscow the following evening they would get the Ariana Afghan Airways overnight flight arriving in Kabul at 06:30 the following morning.

The A4 report raised eyebrows at Vauxhall Cross. It was quickly relayed to the SIS offices in Afghanistan/Pakistan.

On arrival in Moscow, Ahmed was able to get through to al-Zawahiri using a pay-as-you-go phone card.

'Sala'am, Brother, the timing is good. Sanjay should be leaving just about now. He should be in the Korengal sometime this afternoon. Give me your number and he will arrange to meet with you. Head for Jalalabad. He will call when he's near there.'

As darkness fell that evening, Sanjay's cohort had set up their camp at

Korengal. They had met up with Ahmed and Fadwa on the route north from Jalalabad, at Pashshad. Fires had been lit. The dancing flames were reflected in the eyes of those encircling them. The overhead sky was clear and vibrant. The night air was cool. They closed in on the fires. Their Korengali hosts were welcoming. It had been Sheikh Abdul's idea to use the Korengali for support.

'Of all the Afghans, they are the most xenophobic – they even speak their own language,' he said to Sanjay. 'No matter what happens, they'll never submit!'

'But why do we need them?' Sanjay had queried.

'Because they provide a safe haven for us, and also there are many Jihadis there as well. They move in and out of Pakistan through the valley, from Bajour across the border. We can use their safe routes into Pakistan. And we can get extra men from the Caucasus Emirate.' Sheikh Abdul had explained that this was an umbrella group of fighters from the Second Chechen war. 'They can be used as hired guns. They'll take on anything.'

'Good,' said Sanjay, 'we'll use them as the assault force then. Yes, I like that. With them and the Korengali, we'll be able to get into Pakistan easily, and travel safely. There were some Amerikis in the Korengali but they've been withdrawn. Not long ago.'

This discussion had been at their meeting in Tora Bora previously. Now Sanjay was in the Korengal and all was in place. 'The only fly in the ointment is Shahid,' thought Sanjay.

Ahmed and Fadwa had met Sanjay's people at the point where the road from Jalalabad turns sharp left, almost back on itself, before heading up the Korengal Valley. To the right, close by, was the border with the Federally Administered Tribal Areas, a salient of which intruded between Afghanistan and the North-West Frontier Province.

Fadwa had rushed at Shahid immediately on seeing him. Throwing her arms around him, she clutched him in a tearful embrace. She was overjoyed at seeing him safe and well. But she detected some reservation on his part, particularly when Ahmed came to embrace him as well. Nothing outwardly visible, only the sixth sense of a sister's intuition. For the rest of the journey, Shahid and Fadwa were able to travel together. But they knew that Ahmed and Sanjay were watching them closely. Ahmed joined Sanjay. Sanjay explained the reservations about Shahid. 'If it's true, we shall have to kill him,' ended Sanjay. 'But what about Fadwa; what will she do?'

'As God wills, Alhamdulillah!'

In the other vehicle, Shahid was angry with Fadwa. 'What are you doing? Why have you come here?'

'I've joined the Hizb!'

'What! Why did you do that? It is man's work! You'll get hurt. It's all because of Ahmed. You're infatuated with him!'

Fadwa slapped him hard across across the face. The vehicle swerved wildly as Shahid instinctively took his hands off the wheel to feel his face. The vehicle lurched towards the precipitous edge of the road, as Shahid fought to regain control.

'I'm sorry,' he said. 'It's just that I'm worried about you.'

'What's wrong?' asked Fadwa. 'Something's changed. I can tell. Before, you'd have been glad that I'd joined the Hizb.' But Shahid had remained noncommittal.

Back in Monte Casino Camp, Bill and Corporal McMullen were trying to make sense of the readings.

'What the fuck are they doing there, Boss?'

'Beats me! Now that the Yanks have pulled out, there won't be any targets. Perhaps they're trying to draw them back in?'

'Aye, Sorr, but that would'na be a big deal. Not the "big 'un" they've been threatening.'

'Time to have another word with our friend, eh?'

'Have a good look at the satellite cover, will you. See if you can find a good place for a meet. Then I'll send him a text.'

In the Korengali, Sanjay had finally got everything prepared. He had had to meld his disparate group into one team. For two days, they had all prayed and trained together. Time after time, they had practised the final actions at each location.

Now it was time to tell his people what they were going to do. There were gasps of amazement. Everyone nodded with enthusiasm, their eyes lit up.

'You are the chosen ones!'

A few started clapping, some began crying, the intense emotion too much.

'Allah Akbar, death to the infidel!' The cry was taken up by the others; the building rocked with the stamping of feet and the full-blooded chanting of some forty or fifty men. Holding up his hand for silence, an exuberant Sanjay said, 'Brothers, your time has come to write history; to assert the rights of Islam; to establish the Kingdom of Allah, peace be upon Him. We leave tomorrow, at last light. It will take us about four hours to get to Kahuta.'

The group broke up excitedly. Most went to the mosque to pray.

'What are you going to do about Shahid?' said Ahmed to Sanjay after everyone else had left.

'I want you to be responsible for him, just in case he is double-crossing us. You must watch every move he makes. Get a couple of Korengali fighters and some of the Caucasus Emirate fighters. Some of them are very good trackers. If he leaves, follow him. See if you can find out who he's in contact with. If he is up to something, it'll probably be making contact with a Kafir intelligence agent. If he's just making a phone call, follow him back here. Don't show your hand. If he meets someone, kill them both!'

Earlier that day, Shahid had received the text from Bill. He had identified the small shepherds' hut to which Bill was referring. He could tell him about Kahuta, the spent fuel rods, and assembling a dirty bomb. But would that be enough? Sanjay had been very careful. Shahid still did not know where the final attack would take place.

He slipped out of the tent as if to go and urinate. All seemed quiet behind him. It was just after 2.15 am. By this time there was a bright, three-quarter moon, high in the sky. It was possible to see quite well. A brief flash of light caught his eye – a shooting star crossed the heavens in its last, orgasmic gasp. Occasionally clouds obscured the moon, plunging all back into darkness. Shahid negotiated the fence. It was not much of an obstacle – just a demarcation mark really. Looking back he saw no signs of movement.

Crouched beside the tent, Ahmed and Jassim could see Shahid quite clearly as he went through the fence. Jassim had quickly alerted Ahmed. With two the Korengalis leading and Ahmed behind they moved silently, like spectres in the pale greyish light. Now that he was clear of the camp, Shahid was moving quite fast but quietly. His attention was focused to his front to ensure that he did not miss the little goat track that led off to the left, towards the hut. Now he could see the track, and then the hut.

The beacon carried by Shahid recorded his every move, alerting Duty Officers in Ops Room around the globe; one of which re-transmitted the signal back to Bill and his back-up team.

'Eid!' Even though he was expecting it, Shahid was startled.

'Mubarak!' His voice sounded strangulated, the words coming out louder than he had intended. Some 30 metres behind him the lead Korengali scout heard it too. He dropped his hand below his knee in a positive, deliberate movement; the signal was passed down the line. All sank seamlessly to the ground. Ahmed went forward a little with the scout. They could see the hut.

There was a brief flash of light and a scraping noise, as the door opened. They did not know that the colonial-style house was surrounded by highly-trained British Special Forces troops with heavy fire-power pointing in their direction. But, as yet, the SAS had not detected them.

Calling up the rest of the group, Ahmed led them around to the left and up a small re-entrant which curved up to a point just below the house.

'Allah Akbar, Allah Akbar!' Ahmed jumped to his feet and, with the whole group following, rushed towards the hut all firing wildly as they did so, spraying bullets randomly. Surprise was on their side. They were upon and through the protective screen before the SAS troopers could react effectively. When they turned around, Bill and the others debriefing Shahid were in their line of fire. They fixed bayonets, closing in on the attacking force as several of the Jihadists managed to get inside the hut. Unrestrained and indiscriminate in using their weapons, the attackers had a brief advantage.

Ahmed and two of the Arab fighters forced their way into the shed at the same time, guns blazing. Two Tilley lamps illuminated Bill and Shahid, who had been sitting at the small table. Several more Korengali joined them in the hut. Ahmed fired again, this time with aimed shots. Shahid had already been hit. He was lying on the floor. Ahmed saw the line of bullets entering his body, each accompanied by a spray of blood, the bullets seeming to dance across his torso. Having also been hit, Bill too had fallen to the floor and was lying trapped underneath Shahid. Ahmed forced his way out of the hut, calling on the others to pull out. Now the intensity of firing increased as the SAS were able to fire without restraint. For several of the Jihadists, this was their chance to attain paradise. They stayed, fought, killed and were themselves killed or captured. This provided a brief respite for those who chose to flee. They went in all directions, like a starburst. Some were hunted down and killed or captured. Ahmed eventually got back to the camp, just as Sanjay was moving out. Somehow he had remained unscathed. Dawn was breaking as the last straggler found his way back to the group. Seven Jihadists did not return.

Powerless to affect the outcome of the battle, when he heard the shooting Sanjay had quickly taken control back in the camp. He got everyone to grab as much material and food as possible. They moved into the cover of a deep ravine close by. Minutes after they had abandoned the camp, a pair of A-10 Tankbusters attacked with bombs and cannon-fire. Within seconds the area was a mass of flaming material. Sanjay despatched several of the escorts to act as guides for any stragglers.

'Are you sure you killed him?' he challenged Ahmed, as soon as calm had been restored.

'Yes, Brother, Alhamdulillah!' Several of the party confirmed that Shahid could not have survived his grievous wounds.

'We cannot be sure that he didn't manage to tell them the plans. Praise be to Allah that he did not know about the final stage of the plan.'

'What are we going to do now?' said Ahmed, relieved that he had killed the person who had betrayed him, and put his position within the organisation at risk.

'Move as planned. If we wait, they'll hunt us down and slaughter us like helpless lambs. God is great, Allah Akbar!'

Initially, Fadwa was distraught, inconsolable. Then she heard that Ahmed had killed Shahid. She knew immediately what she must do.

Awakened by the commotion when the party returned, the first person she saw was Jassim.

'What's going on?' she demanded.

Even in the dim light in the tent, Jassim's reaction was palpable. He was exultant. With a malevolent stare at Fadwa he said: 'We have killed a traitor! God's will has been done, Alhamdulillah! Ahmed killed the traitor, Allah Akbar, Allah Akbar!'

Now she was with Ahmed. But she did not disclose what Jassim had told her. With her decision had come a steely determination to avenge her brother. All emotion was extinguished. She was instantly cold and focused. She listened dispassionately to Ahmed's account.

'One of the locals, it was; lives just outside the camp. He came and told us that there was a party of foreigners – British – soldiers over there. We took them completely by surprise, God was with us. Shahid will be in paradise now. We must carry on to avenge your brother, killed by the British state! Allah Akbar, Allah Akbar!'

Fatwa listened impassively. Then she rose, imperiously, determinedly.

'I will avenge my brother!' she cried. 'Tell Ayman that I'm prepared to lay down my life. I want to be a Black Widow!'

They had buried Shahid and the other Mujahedeen where they fell. The graves were shallow, scraped out of the thin soil. Earlier, Bill had gazed sadly at the already stiffening body of Shahid as rigor mortis set in. How diverse, yet intertwined, their paths in life had been. Now it seemed to Bill that Shahid had protected him from lethal danger, just as Shahid's father had done for his father all those years ago. Ahmed's burst had danced through Shahid's body from top to bottom, opening him up as if under the surgeon's knife for some total body surgery. Brain matter and guts had spilled out onto the dusty, sandy tent floor, the blood quickly soaking away. Now the body had disappeared from sight under the thin covering of stony soil. When the firing had started, Bill had instantly grabbed Shahid and pushed him under the table. Getting up momentarily, Shahid had then fallen on top of Bill. It was only a flimsy rustic table. The high-velocity AK47 bullets sliced through it, splintering the wood. Several had struck Shahid. Death had been instantaneous. Reacting more quickly, Bill had managed to avoid Ahmed's burst, but two rounds had hit him in his left leg. They were only flesh wounds, quickly dealt with by one of the highly-trained SAS medics.

'We're a bit fucked now, Boss!' Corporal McMullen said fingering the beacon recovered from Shahid's body.

'Well, at least we know that they're planning to leave tomorrow sometime, unless tonight's party has changed all that. And we know they're planning to cross the border.'

'That means telling those bastards in the ISI?'

'Yes, but when exactly? We know next to bugger-all about their target. Except that it has got something to do with WMD. That's what the Englishman told me right at the beginning.'

81

They left as quickly as they could. The sun was dropping below the rim of the mountains behind them. A translucent purple glow transfused the sky. Al-Zawahiri joined them for a final prayer and blessed them all. Shaking hands with Sanjay, he said, 'The Doctor's man is expecting you at eleven o'clock. He'll be waiting just outside Kahuta – I showed you the photograph?'

'Yes, Ayman, I have all that. And I've got his mobile number if necessary.'

The three heavily-laden tracks lumbered off, the passengers balancing precariously on banal items of everyday living, stacked higgledy-piggledy atop the torn canopy and covering the more lethal cargo below. To the east, ahead of them, the thick, black clouds of the monsoon were building up. After about an hour and a half they reached the Khyber Pass and crossed the border and headed for Peshawar. Refugees from Afghanistan were a frequent sight for the border guards. The beautiful young wife with this group provided a welcome distraction for the guards from their usual monotony. Fatwa smiled provocatively at the guards, then lowered her eyes demurely. Underneath the canopies, the Jihadis fingered their guns nervously. The remainder of the journey passed uneventfully, if uncomfortably. They were at the RV in good time. A tall, bearded man wearing dishdasha and shemagh with bandoliers slung over his shoulder and with an AK-47 stepped into the glare of the truck's headlights as they drew to a halt.

'Sala'am alaikum, alaikum sala'am.' The exchanges were perfunctory and businesslike. The Doctor's man was the key to the last component of Sheikh Abdul's plans. The Sheikh himself had financed the project. The Korengali provided the protection, and Sanjay the fire-power. Although no friends of Al Qaeda, it had suited the Iranian Guards to supply the necessary weapons-grade plutonium to bin Laden.

'Anyone who is an enemy of our enemy is our friend,' they had said.

Now all that was required to complete the puzzle was inside the Kahuta Ordnance Depot. And the doctor's man had all the necessary codes.

'Let us hope that Ayman's meeting with the ISI will prove fruitful!' said Sanjay to Ahmed as they prepared to move on. 'Otherwise we'll have to fight our way in.'

'We are well prepared for that, Brother!'

'Alhamdulillah!'

In the event, it all proved remarkably easy. The guards at the facility had been well briefed. 'Resistance would be futile,' they had been told, 'so throw down your arms and live to fight for Allah another day.'

General Abu Khadr had remained silent and unresponsive after al-Zawahiri had made his proposal. But inside, his mind was computing all the possible permutations. He too was a devout Muslim of the Wahhabi school. He despised the President with his weak and snivelling civilian government, always cosying up to the Americans. He was also a vain and ambitious man with one eye on the main chance. Al-Zawahiri's plan would cause chaos and instability. Exactly the right conditions for a coup d'état. And he was the man to lead it. In al-Zawahiri's presence, he picked up the phone. The conversation was short. Putting down the receiver, he turned to al-Zawahiri:

271

'Right, Insha'Allah, it is arranged. They will put up only a token resistance. Lots of firing into the air! You must ensure that your men do the same. I'll make sure that the right press release is put out to Al Jazeera.'

Sanjay's men had quickly loaded the spent fuel rods under the guidance of the Doctor's man. Now they were back on the road they had come by. They went as far as Rawalpindi, where they turned south onto route M-2. They had about four hours' driving ahead of them. It was just after 1 am.

The phone rang. It was Moira, the doyen of the Garden Room girls.

'The White House is on the line, Prime Minister,' she said matter-of-factly.

'Right, thanks. Put them through please.'

There was a click on the line, a pause... 'G'day Prime Minister, how you all doing?' A straightforward, no bullshit salutation, none of the 'Yo Blair!' stuff of that embarrassing previous meeting at the G8; the PM cringed at the recollection. 'Yes, Mr President, good day to you. We're well here and I'm glad to have this chance of talking with you.'

'Good, Tony, good! Now look here – what do you make of this latest piece of intel your folks have dug up? How's your team rate it?'

'Well, Mr President – George – it's couched in all the usual intelligence jargon, of course. All those caveats which sometimes cancel each other out! However, we had a JIC meeting this morning... '

'Yes, I know! Ambassador Jones told me you were having it. I wanted to get the assessment from you personally.'

'OK, yes – we had a very good... very detailed review – a preliminary assessment only, as there's a lot we need to check out. Much of it needs to be done with your fellows at Langley. But we rate this report pretty highly. There's a lot of collateral pointing to something like this. We all know it's an obvious thing for Al Qaeda to try to do. The Taliban are on a surge in the border regions and ever more able to operate with impunity on the Pakistani side too, so the likelihood of their doing so has increased markedly.'

'But, Goddamit, there's a world of difference between aspiration on the one hand and capability and intent on the other, Tony!'

'Indeed so, George, but look at it this way. There can be little doubt about capability. The country's stuffed with weapons – anyone can buy an AK-47 for the price of a few cups of coffee. They've got balls – the Taliban in Kabul showed the way for an operation like this when that group of forty or so got into the Afghan Interior Ministry and took our IT specialist and his guards hostage. Not only were they dressed authentically as soldiers but they also had access – it was an inside job. What's to stop OBL and his cronies from emulating something like this in Pakistan? The authorities are riddled with sympathisers – someone in the ISI's got to be complicit in this, hoping to ride the tiger that would be unleashed. That ghastly attack on your CIA operatives at Kandahar last year demonstrates capability and intent in spades!'

'That all sounds pretty grim, Tony! What's the upside?'

'Well, the source of this information – you'll see him referred to as "Sentinel" in our Intelligence reports – is a recent walk-in, so we haven't... '

'Hang on, Tony, this is beginning to sound a lot like that Jordanian guy who blew himself up at Kandahar. You can't trust any of these bastards. Once they're infected, it's with them for the rest of their lives, like a birthmark.'

'I understand your concerns, Mr President, but we can't afford to ignore this one. We're damned if we do and damned if we don't!'

'Yes, I guess we are. If it's a trap and we take the bait there'll be a lot of dead bodies, some of them your guys, and a lot of egg on both our faces. If we ignore it and it's true, then it'll be a catastrophe... '

'Agreed, Mr President – George – the implications don't bear thinking about!'

'You're damn right they don't!'

'But, if we work on the assumption that he's the real McCoy – at the same time taking every precaution in case he's not – then we are in a good position.'

'This is what I want to hear.'

'We've had this source under surveillance for some time, so he's not unknown. He was part of the group that carried out the attack in Israel some time ago... '

'Remind me, would you?'

'It was at a place called Mike's Bar in Tel Aviv in 2003. The first serious incident involving home-grown British Islamists. One suicide bomber blew himself up. Killed three people, and more than fifty were wounded. The other bomber didn't go through with it. He fled the scene and seems to have drowned himself. His body washed up on the beach ten days later. Our man

273

was part of the back-up team. We decided to let him run – to keep him under observation. We've had some very good material from this. Contacts and that sort of thing. We had indications some time ago that he was becoming disillusioned with the whole jihad thing. When he finally walked in – went to our Embassy in Kabul – and we told him all we knew about him, how he'd been set up by his Jihadi mentor, this really convinced him to come across. That's why we rate him highly.'

'Sounds like your guys have done some really good work over there.'

'We hope so.' This was praise indeed, given the Americans' previous criticism, when a senior US general said that 'he was particularly dismayed by the British effort'.

'But why don't we take them out with a drone strike, Tony? Have your guys told you about our latest developments? Reckon we've taken out about 650 extremists in the FATA alone in the last two years. Got Al Qaeda's third-in-command in North Waziristan back in May and his successor Sheikh Fateh al-Misri only four months later. We could use our new Predator, the MQ-9 Reaper. My guys in Langley can do it all sitting on their asses at their desks there!'

'Our men are right in there. No way you could do it without killing them as well. We have a good man as the source's Op O, in there with them. But there's plenty of top-notch surveillance and back-up in place. So we feel that we can control this one. Our main concern is to stop the Pakistanis picking up on it.'

'Well, I guess you've got it all covered?'

'Yes, but we need your support, Mr President. We could do with one of your Langley fellows here with the JIC.'

'You've got it, Prime Minister. I'll get that fixed straight away.'

After a brief discussion on other key issues, they rang off.

83

Exasperated, Bill paced up and down in the Ops room. Still nothing. No trace. Now the cloud cover over North-West Pakistan was 10/10ths as the storm raced through. Outside, his men sat at instant readiness in the Chinook.

'Alpha Charlie One, incident at Kahuta – 33.614, 73.292. Get Sunray on the secure means for my Super Sunray immediately, over!' The ISAF commander wanted to speak to Bill.

It was as if a bolt of lightning had struck the building and discharged into everyone. The tension was palpable. The General emerged from the secure communications facility.

'Gentlemen, we have a little problem on our hands. It seems that our friends have attacked the A.Q. Khan Research Facility at Kahuta. They've got away with several spent fuel rods!'

The collective intake of breath was palpable.

'We need to know where they're headed. What the target is. They're not just going to go away and hide them. They are going to blow something up, or threaten to do so. We've got to stop them. Get the AWACS up there now.'

'But General, the weather... '

'Get the fucker up there now, Major!'

'They're in two Jingle trucks and a ZIL-157. All fully loaded but with canopies, so it's hard to know what's underneath, according to an eye-witness report,' said the General's accompanying staff officer.

Within minutes the ungainly and cumbersome machine, so beautiful and effective in flight, was lumbering up the runway. Inside the aircraft the team of analysts, both American and British, men and women, peered intently at their radar screens and computers and listened to their Amplivox headsets for the slightest indication of the presence of their target. The navigator had set course for overhead Kahuta. From there a wide-area search would be undertaken. The latest weather forecast beamed to them indicated improving conditions.

It was nearly an hour before SAC 'Taffy' Gwyn Griffiths made his dispassionate announcement.

'Got them! Just north of Khan. Heading south on route M-2. You can see the trucks in detail. They've taken the covers off the two Jingle trucks. I can see the weapons and other equipment. Must be about forty ragheads. The ZIL's still got its canopy on. That must be where the spent fuel rods are!'

'Scramble YF40!'

The call came through loud and clear in Bill's headset. He grabbed Corporal McMullen. The pilots got the call too. They all arrived at the chopper at the same time. Within two minutes of the alarm, they were airborne.

84

General Walt Bonetti was in the tradition of Generals Patton and Stormin' Norman Schwarzkopf. He took no prisoners.

'What the fuck's going on there, General?'

His opposite number at Pakistan Army HQ outside Islamabad was also a stern disciplinarian. But, unlike many of his predecessors, he was a democrat and determined to keep the army out of politics.

Ignoring the profanity and the implied insult, General Bashir Dilawar responded.

'They managed to escape completely. I've got people heading there now to find out exactly what went wrong. Somehow, they managed to penetrate the security without activating any alarms. As you know, many, many of our brave soldiers have died in our joint fight against fundamentalism. But I still haven't eradicated it in sections of the army, particularly the ISI. I suspect they're behind it. I'll find out. In the meantime we are searching for them high and low. Everyone is on full alert. Do you have any information?'

General Bonetti glanced at the large, constantly changing map display and the associated graphics on the wall in front of him.

'Yeah, looks like we may just have found them. We're getting assets on the ground to deal with them now.'

'Where are they?'

'On the road south of Faisalabad – just past Khan.'

'Aaaah, Sargodha!' exclaimed the Pakistani. 'Sargodha – it's our nuclear stockpile! It's near there. They've stolen some spent fuel rods from Kahuta. They must be planning to use them to explode a dirty bomb at Sargodha!'

'That'll create a massive amount of radioactive fallout. God knows what area of the subcontinent it'll affect. Particularly with the monsoon winds! Holy shit, General, I need to get going on this!'

As they drove along the martyr group, in the middle vehicle, was being fitted out with suicide vests. They had all practised this before leaving the Korengal. As she clipped the last buckle of the webbing harness in place, Fatwa knew that her destiny was upon her. There were five of them. Led by Sanjay, the Korengali and the Arab fighters would clear the way into the facility. This time they knew it would be no walkover. The ISI had no penetration into Sargodha. The Pakistani troops guarding it were hard, experienced and loyal. They had seen too many of their comrades killed by Al Qaeda and fanatical Islamists. The truck with the spent fuel rods would smash through the gates, followed by Fatwa's truck. The suicide martyrs would fan out and, at a shout from their leader, detonate themselves.

At about the same time as the General's message reached them, the watchers in the sky saw the three trucks, one after the other, turn off the main road towards Bhalwal.

'That route will take them directly to Sargodha – it's less than 50 clicks away!' said the shift leader. 'Get the General on the line!'

Now there was no doubt. They were headed for Sargodha. The trucks were making good speed, going as fast as the conditions would allow. They had planned to arrive before dawn, less than an hour away now. To attack at first light; the traditional hour of attackers. Twenty-five minutes to the target, Sanjay calculated, readying his men.

Up in the air, the same calculation made in the AWACS was passed to Bill.

'Bhalwal to Sargodha is 33.3 clicks,' the operative told Bill. 'They're doing on average 65 kph, so less than half an hour!'

'We won't have time to set up a fixed-piece ambush,' he radioed to Corporal McMullen in the other chopper. 'We've still got twenty-five minutes flying time to target! We'll fly around to the south, and then approach directly from behind them. That way, they won't be able to hear us until we're more or less on top of them.'

'OK, Boss.' The Corporal radioed his men. Both pilots had heard Bill's instructions both immediately altered course accordingly, now that they had a fixed destination to aim for. They lost altitude, until finally they were screaming along less than 100 feet above the road at top speed, 196 miles per hour. By now they were still 50 miles from Sargodha. It would be touch and go.

For all concerned, it was a nail-biting quarter of an hour. It was like watching a slow-motion movie. Constant reports updated the maps in Ops rooms across the globe. Four Star officers and private soldiers alike bit their fingernails and held their breath.

Then Bill's voice came over the radio again. 'You land behind the target – as close as you can damn well get. Fan out and encircle them. I'm going in from the front. We don't want anyone to get away!'

'Don't worry, Boss – they won't!'

'Look, there it is,' said Sanjay, climbing out of the cab of the front truck which had slowed down. The other two trucks closed up. Sanjay's message was clear.

'Go now, and Allah be with you, Allah Akbar, Allah Akbar!' he screamed. All the other fighters took up the chant.

The drivers pushed the accelerator pedals of the lumbering trucks to the floor, straining their engines to breaking point, the radiators already steaming from the stiff climb towards the facility.

Bill saw it too. Now, for the first time, he could see the trucks. They were closing rapidly. They were less than a kilometer away. He could see people running around inside. The gates were being shut.

But he was going to be too late! The Jihadists would be inside before he and his men could get there. He would not be able to stop them. Then he saw the two Jingle trucks slow down and stop. The ZIL seemed to be carrying on.

The flash temporarily blinded Bill and Corporal McMullen, and the two pilots. The choppers slewed dangerously as the pilots struggled to regain control. Ahead, a dark cloud of smoke billowed where the trucks had been a split second before. The watchers saw chunks of metal and debris being tossed about and falling back to earth. The middle truck virtually disintegrated as Fatwa detonated herself. The front truck ran off the road and rolled over several times as it careened down the side of the road into a culvert, now a twisted wreck. The third vehicle cannoned into the middle one and burst into flames.

By the time Bill and his men debouched from the choppers and closed warily to investigate the site, it was clear that virtually no-one had survived unscathed. Quickly they secured the site. Two of the less seriously wounded Jihadists started firing their weapons. They were quickly killed. The others were so seriously injured and disorientated by the blast that they offered no resistance. No-one else had survived.

Bill radioed back to HQ. Many people in Islamabad and Washington and around the world heaved a collective sigh of relief. Particularly one American and one Pakistani general, whose careers were now assured.